RABBIT STEW RANCH

MISTY MALONE

Published by Blushing Books
An Imprint of
ABCD Graphics and Design, Inc.
A Virginia Corporation
977 Seminole Trail #233
Charlottesville, VA 22901

Misty Malone
Rabbit Stew Ranch

Print ISBN: 978-1-63954-238-3
v1

Cover Art by ABCD Graphics & Design
This book contains fantasy themes appropriate for mature readers only. Nothing in this book should be interpreted as Blushing Books' or the author's advocating any non-consensual sexual activity.

CHAPTER 1

NEBRASKA, 1890

"You're awfully quiet this evening, Lizzie. You've hardly spoken during supper. Anything wrong?"

"No, Papa. I guess I'm a bit tired, but that's all."

"Daughter, I'd appreciate it if you'd look at me when you're speaking to me. I can always tell when you're hiding something if I can see your eyes." He waited until her head rose and she was looking at him, and then smiled before going on. "Thank you. Now, you're sure you're not feeling poorly?"

"I'm fine, Papa, honest. Like I said, I'm just a little tired."

He narrowed his eyes, not particularly believing her entirely, but satisfied for the time being. He'd watch her the next couple of days and see if he could pick up on any clues that might help him determine what was on her mind. "Maybe if you're finished eating you should call it an early evening and go upstairs a little early tonight."

"I think I will, as soon as I help Ella with the dishes," Lizzie responded, standing and gathering dishes from the table.

"I'll help Ella tonight, my dear. You can go on upstairs if you want. You look a bit peaked to me. If you say you're just tired, that might be it, but I'd feel better if you'd get a good night's sleep. If you're not yourself in the morning, we'll see if we need to call Doc Avery."

"Papa, you don't need to call the doctor. I'm fine, just a little tired. I can help Ella, though. Then I'll go upstairs."

"I'm perfectly capable of drying dishes," Benjamin Morgan said with a bit of a huff. "I helped your mother nearly every night years ago, when you were just a baby. "Besides, I have something I'd like to talk to her about, and I found out years ago that she's much more likely to talk while she's working."

Lizzie looked over at her father with a look of concern. "What do you want to talk to Ella about?"

"Nothing you need to be concerned about, my dear." When he saw the concern on her face intensify, he relented. "Okay, okay, I'll tell you. It really isn't anything you need to be concerned about, but I can see by your face you won't be satisfied until I tell you. I got a letter today from my brother, Ralph. He and his wife and their daughter are going to come for a visit. I want to talk to Ella to see if she would get a couple of extra rooms ready for them."

Lizzie's eyes lit up. "Oh, how wonderful. I haven't seen Aunt Jane or Cousin Eloise in years. When are they going to get here? Will they be able to stay long?"

Ben was happy to see Lizzie smiling and excited again. Lately she'd seemed rather subdued, which was why he was concerned. Maybe a nice visit would bring her back around. "They'll be here Tuesday of next week. I'm not real sure how long they'll be staying."

"I hope they can stay more than just a few days. I'd love to be able to show Eloise around the ranch. It would be a good way for us to get to know each other again."

Ben's foreman, Coy Clemson, took his meals with Ben and Lizzie. The first part of the meal usually included conversation between Ben and Coy relating to the ranch. Coy had been listening to Ben's news of the upcoming visit, and smiled at Lizzie's excitement. "Is your cousin about the same age as you?" he asked.

Lizzie momentarily froze and her face paled. Ben noticed her reaction to his question, and watched the two of them closely. She turned to face Coy and Ben could tell she was choosing her words carefully. "Yes, Eloise is about the same age as me, and we get along very well. We'll more than likely be together everywhere we go while she's visiting."

Coy caught her eyes momentarily, but Ben couldn't quite make out the meaning behind the look on his face. He would have to ask Lizzie about it sometime when they were alone. He had no idea why, but his daughter had never cared much for his foreman. It seemed no matter how hard Coy tried to befriend her, she wanted nothing to do with him. It bothered Ben, since they were both important people to him, but he never could figure out why Lizzie seemed opposed to any sort of friendship between them.

Maybe he needed to have a talk with her and ask her directly. He'd asked her general questions about all the hands he had working for him, and although she'd never mentioned a specific complaint about Coy, it was quite obvious to him there was something about him she didn't care for. He'd hoped if he gave her a little more time to get to know him she'd come around, but if anything, she seemed to be trying to avoid him more. It was about time he found out what it was she had against him.

Ben was true to his word, and encouraged Lizzie to go on

upstairs to her room. He knew she enjoyed reading before retiring for the night, and suggested she might want to do that this evening. She thanked her father and stood. She turned to head for the stairs, when Coy said, "Sleep well, Miss Lizzie."

She stopped, but didn't turn back around to look at him. Instead, she simply said, "I hope to," and went up the stairs.

Ben questioned the strained relationship between her and Coy again, but didn't say anything. He took a handful of dishes into the kitchen once he watched her climbing the stairs. Coy took his cue and gathered his own dishes and took them to the kitchen, as well, before taking his hat off the hat pegs by the door and leaving for the evening, to return to the foreman's cabin.

Ella seemed surprised to see Ben carrying dirty dishes, and tried to take them from his hands. "Is something wrong with Lizzie this evening?" she asked out of genuine concern. Ben knew Ella loved Lizzie like her own daughter, and in a way, she was. Claudine, Lizzie's mother, died during an outbreak of influenza when their daughter was only six. Ben had done his best to raise the little girl from then on, but he would be the first to admit he wouldn't have been able to do it without all the help he had gotten from Ella.

When Claudine first got sick he and the wife of one of his ranch hands tried running the house and taking care of little Lizzie, while trying to nurse Claudine back to health. When it became apparent she wasn't getting better and may be fighting this illness for some time, he hired Ella. She had recently lost her husband and needed a place to stay and a way to support herself, but she was also exactly what Ben needed. She had been a godsend, both at the time and since his wife's death. She helped care for Claudine while she was bedridden, and took over the household chores. When Claudine succumbed to the illness several months later, Ella agreed to stay on. She had been like a mother to Lizzie, teaching her all the things a mother would normally teach her daughter. Ben would always be grateful to her for that.

"She said she's tired this evening, so I told her to go on upstairs to rest. I told her I'll help you with the dishes tonight."

"You don't have to do that, Ben. You've worked hard all day. I'm perfectly capable of cleaning up the kitchen myself. I've told Lizzie that numerous times, but she's such a sweet girl, she always insists on helping."

"Thank you for the kind words about my daughter, Ella. I appreciate hearing things like that, but I want to help you tonight. There's something I'd like to talk to you about, and I thought maybe we could do that while we get the dishes washed up."

"You don't have to help me with the dishes for us to be able to talk, but if you insist, let me grab the rest of the dishes from the other room, then I'll wash and you can dry."

He chuckled as he followed her into the dining room. They came out moments later with the rest of the dishes. He told her about his expected guests as they washed and cleaned up the kitchen. She asked about any favorite dishes they might have, or any type of food they might not like, and assured Ben the guest rooms would be clean and aired out by Tuesday.

With that subject sufficiently addressed, Ella changed topics. "I've been a little concerned about Lizzie lately. She doesn't quite seem to be herself. It seems like something may be on her mind. Have you noticed anything?"

"Yes, I have, and I've been concerned, too. I was hoping you'd have some insight into what may be troubling her."

"I haven't been able to think of a thing. I've tried to talk to her about it, but she insists she's fine."

"She tells me the same thing," Ben said. "Maybe I'll try one more time to talk to her, and as I always say, there's no time like the present."

He turned to leave, but Ella stopped him with a hand on his arm. "Ben, your baby is a grown woman now. You may not have noticed it yet, but she's become a very pretty young lady. What used to be cute brown hair is now a beautiful chestnut color with streaks of lighter brown, almost a dark blond through it, and those streaks highlight her bright sapphire eyes that sparkle. That's why the young men at church are paying so much attention to her and talking to her after services. She's become a young woman on the inside, as well. Before you barge into her room, knock and ask if she's still dressed. If she has her nightgown on, your talk can wait until morning. A young lady her age needs some privacy, even from her father."

Ben felt his face blush, but nodded after a rather lengthy pause. "Thank you, Ella. You're right; as much as I still think of her as my little girl, she is a grown woman. I would have knocked, then gone on in, and that would have been wrong."

"I wish you luck with your talk, but if she's not ready to talk yet, don't try to force her. She may have something she's still trying to sort out in her head. Give her time to do that before trying to make her talk to you. She's eighteen now, and I'm sure she's starting to see some things differently. That can be confusing. There are some things and feelings she may have that she needs to sort out for herself. It's fine to remind her that you and I are both willing to talk anytime she wants to, but don't force her to until she's ready."

"Ella, I don't know what I'd do – no, what Lizzie and I would do without you. I'm looking at this through only my eyes as her father, and I want to help her with anything she needs help with. Once again, though, I think you're right, much like when you talked to me about my reaction when the Robinson boy asked to court her. You were right; I can tell her the young men I feel she should stay clear of, but I can see now that it would be a lot better if she came to that conclusion on her own."

"As her father, you should keep a watchful eye on her and the young men she talks with after church and make sure she's safe. But it is better if she decides for herself the ones that are more interested in your money than in her." After a few moments she asked, "Do you think that's what this is about; a boy?"

"I honestly don't know. Hopefully I'll find out soon, though."

"Good luck. Let me know if I can do anything to help," she said as he was headed for the stairs.

Ben stood outside her bedroom door for a couple of minutes, collecting his thoughts, before knocking. "Lizzie, are you still dressed?"

She opened the door moments later, fully clothed, and holding a book. "What is it, Papa?"

"May I come in for a moment so we can talk?"

"Yes, of course," she said, stepping aside so he could enter. He sat down on the bed and she sat down next to him. "Is something wrong?"

"That's what I wanted to ask you," he said. "I just talked to Ella, and she's been concerned about you. You said you're tired, but not ill. Is something on your mind?"

"I'm fine, Papa," she tried to assure him.

"Honey, if there's something bothering you, I hope you know you can talk to me or Ella. We both love you and will listen and try to help you with whatever has you bothered."

She started to assure him again that she was fine, but when she saw the concern in his eyes, she stopped. "You're right, Papa, there is something bothering me, but I'm not sure you want to hear what it is."

"Nonsense, daughter. Of course I want to know what it is so I can try to fix it for you. What has you so upset?"

"Please don't be upset with me, but it's Coy. I simply don't like him."

"Coy?" Ben's shock was evident. "What don't you like about Coy, and why does it have you so upset? If you don't especially like him, you don't have to spend much time around him." He stopped then, and picked up her hand. "Except that you do, at meals. Is that what the problem is? I know you've been awfully quiet at meals the last few days. Does he bother you that much, that you aren't able to enjoy your meals with him at the table?"

"I don't want to be around him at all, Papa. I know you two discuss ranch business over meals, and it wouldn't be fair for me to ask you to stop, but that's why I haven't been very talkative. Would you mind terribly if I took my supper with Ella, at least once in a while?"

"Nonsense," Ben said quickly. "You're my daughter, and if anyone leaves the table it will be Coy. But let me just say, you're usually very good dealing with people. I've never seen you quick to judge people, and even if you don't care for someone, you generally hide that fact well. May I ask what Coy has done that has you so upset you're not able to enjoy our meals with him at the table?"

"Papa, I don't like the way he looks at me. He's always trying to get me alone with him, and I don't trust him."

Ben's eyes were instantly as big as saucers. "Surely, Lizzie, you're not suggesting you think he would take advantage of you?"

Lizzie dropped her head, but Ben watched as she soon squared her shoulders and willed herself to lift her head and look at him again. "I'm sorry, Papa, but that is what I'm saying. You've never seen the looks he gives me when you're not there with me."

Ben sighed and thought a few moments before responding. Finally, he took her hands in his. "Lizzie, I'm not sure if this is the right thing to do, but I feel I need to explain something to you. Coy came to me a couple of weeks ago and asked for permission to court you. We talked for several minutes, and I can tell he's very smitten."

Lizzie looked horrified. "You didn't tell him he could, did you?"

"No, I haven't," Ben said, surprised at how upset his daughter was at that news. "I told him I need time to consider his request. There are a few things I felt I needed to consider. First, he is my foreman. Is he truly interested in you, or does he see this as a path to this ranch some day? Also, one of the hands asked me last year for permission to court you and I turned him down."

"Really? Who, and why did you turn him down?"

"I'm not sure if you remember him. He left shortly after I said no. His name was Harold Buckner."

Lizzie thought several moments. "Wasn't he that old man?"

Ben had to chuckle. "That old man was forty, and although that's not an old man, it's too old for a seventeen-year-old. But the point is, a few of the hands know I turned him down, and he told them it was because he works for me. That's not why I turned him down, but I never corrected him, thinking it might be better to let the men believe that. There have been a few men working for me that, although they seemed okay when I met them, after they worked for me a while I wouldn't have allowed them to court you. I thought it was probably easier to let them all think I wouldn't give any of them permission. If one of them was interested enough in you and they were a good man, they'd come to me and ask, even if they thought I'd say no."

Lizzie smiled at her papa, seeing again how much he

cared about her. Then her mind wandered back to the reason for their talk. "Please don't say yes to Coy. I really don't like being around him."

"Honey, I won't say yes if it bothers you this much." She breathed out a long sigh and smiled, until her father went on. "At least not yet. I would like you to give Coy a chance, though. You said you don't like the way he looks at you, but I think he's looking at you the way he is because he cares for you. You're young, and living on this ranch, you haven't had an opportunity to be around too many young men."

"I've met several at church, besides the ones I went to school with."

"Yes, but you haven't gotten to know any of them well, either. Coy's a good worker, and he's given me no reason to be concerned about him as a man. Now that you know why he's looking at you the way he is, would you please give him a chance? I'm not asking you to have dinner with him in town or anything like that. I know you don't feel comfortable enough with him right now for that. What I am asking is that you not judge him, but keep an open mind about him and give him a fair chance. Talk to him a bit at meals, answer questions he asks with more than a quick yes or no, and allow yourself to get to know him while I'm here, as well. Then if you still don't like him, I'll understand. Could you do that much for me, please; just give him a chance?"

Lizzie was torn. Something about Coy made her uneasy anytime she was around him, but her papa didn't ask much of her, so when he did, she hated to turn him down. She slowly nodded. "I guess I can do that much for you."

"Thank you, honey. Even if you decide you don't want him to court you, I'll understand. It would be nice, though, if you two could at least become friendly enough that we could continue to share meals since he is my foreman."

She forced a small smile. "I'll try to be nicer and give him an honest chance."

THE NEXT MORNING Lizzie was downstairs early, helping Ella with breakfast. "What are your plans for today, Lizzie? Are you going to work with the colts again?"

"No, I don't think so," she answered a bit slowly. Ella noticed her shoulders slumped a bit, as well.

"Do you have something else in mind?"

"Not really. I might just stay inside today. Do you need help with anything?"

Ella stopped cutting out biscuits and turned to face the younger lady. "Lizzie, you know I always enjoy your help and company, but what's wrong? I know how much you enjoy working with the horses, so why aren't you going out there with them?"

"Maybe I need something different today."

"Or someone different?"

Lizzie whirled around to stare at Ella, eyes wide open. "Why would you say that?"

The older lady, who had been like a mother to Lizzie, laid her hand gently on her arm. "Your father told me you're not as impressed with Coy as he seems to be. Does he have something to do with your decision to stay inside today?"

Ella watched as Lizzie raised her head high and started to say something. When Ella caught her eyes, however, her shoulders slumped again. "Yes."

"Honey, talk to me about Coy. This isn't like you. I can't think of anyone else you've felt this strongly about. This isn't just a personality clash, is it? Why don't you want to be around him?"

"What do you mean?"

"There's a reason you're so skittish toward him." She moved closer and lowered her voice. "Did something happen your father or I should know about?"

There was a long moment of silence, during which Ella was growing very concerned. Finally, Lizzie shook her head. "No, not really." She looked up at her second mother with a helpless, scared look in her eyes. "I don't like the way he looks at me at all. He scares me. He's always trying to get me alone with him."

"Did you tell your father this?"

"I did, but he said he thinks it's because Coy asked him a couple of weeks ago if he could court me. Papa thinks he likes me, and I just haven't been around enough young men to know that that's how they look at you when they have feelings for you."

Ella thought a few moments. "Do you think he could be right?"

Lizzie slowly shook her head. "Not really. There were a couple of boys that I'm pretty sure liked me our last year or two in school, and they looked at me different, but it wasn't scary. They weren't always trying to get me alone with them, either."

"How does he try to get you alone?"

"One time I saw a little cut on my horse, Shadow. I was going to get some balm to put on it, but he started back to the tack room, too, saying he'd show me where it was. I told him I knew where it was and didn't need any help, but he said he didn't mind showing me. I didn't know what to do, but thankfully Papa called him then and he cursed under his breath, but turned around."

"I'm glad your father called for him."

"I was, too. Another time he came into the barn as I was putting the saddle on Shadow. He headed straight for me, so I asked him if he needed something. He spoke real soft and said he just needed a few minutes alone with me. The look on his face scared me, so I spoke real loud when I called out for Clem, one of the hands that I knew was at the other end of the barn, checking on a new foal. I asked how the baby was doing. When he answered, Coy again cursed and said he didn't know anyone else was around."

"You didn't tell you father about those times?"

"No. He seems to really like Coy, and he thinks I'm just not giving him a fair chance. I thought maybe if I stayed out of the barn for a while, maybe in time he'll quit."

"But you love being out there, helping. You've helped your dad since you were a little girl, and we both know you'd much rather be out there than in here. He especially counts on you for helping him run the part of the ranch involving the horses. He himself says Coy knows cattle, but you're better with the horses."

"I know, but when I try to work with the horses, sometimes Coy shows up. For the time being, anyway, I don't want to take that chance. Maybe when Uncle Ralph and Aunt Jane come to visit, Eloise and I can spend our time together. With two of us surely he wouldn't dare try anything. If he looks at me in a scary way maybe she'll see it and can tell Papa she saw it, too."

"Two of you will definitely be safer, so maybe you can start going back out to the barn then. Let's hope Eloise likes to be around colts."

"The last time she was here she loved petting the animals, especially the smaller ones. I'm hoping she still does. At least if she sees the look he gives me and it looks creepy to her, too, I'll know it's not just my imagination."

"And if that happens, you let me or your father know. Maybe he can talk to Eloise and she can convince him it's not a proper way to look at you."

She nodded. "Thank you, Ella, for understanding and believing me."

"Of course I believe you. I don't think it's a matter of your father not believing you, but if he hasn't seen any reason to doubt his foreman, he's probably thinking you're simply misinterpreting his looks."

"Maybe, but I don't know why he should have any reason to doubt his own daughter, either, but he does."

Ella went to Lizzie and wrapped her arms around her. "Let's hope he sees it that way soon, as well."

CHAPTER 2

Over the next few days Lizzie stayed in the house so she could avoid Coy. During meals she tried to be a bit more social toward him, but it was difficult. When he asked her a question she answered more fully, but she found she just couldn't look him in the eye. Every time she tried to a shiver went through her. Her father noticed it one time and looked confused. "Are you cold, Lizzie?"

"No, not cold, but I just felt a bit of a chill."

"That's rather odd, it's a warm day today."

"I'm not sure what caused it, but I'm sure it's nothing to worry about."

Her father nodded after looking at her again. She looked up once a minute or two later, but looked back down quickly when she saw Coy's attention focused on her. The look on his face caused her to shiver again, and she was glad her father hadn't noticed it this time. The rest of the meal she was quiet. When Coy asked a question she tried to answer without looking at him.

She continued the same way, trying to make it through each meal, one at a time. Finally Tuesday arrived and she and her father went to Gully Ridge to meet the stagecoach and bring Uncle Ralph and his family home for their visit. She was afraid her father would want to talk to her on the way in about Coy, but he didn't. She kept him busy talking about her memories of the fun she'd had the last time they came to visit, which was about four years earlier.

They were standing at the train platform to wait, since the stagecoach stopped in roughly the same area as the train depot, and it arrived right on time. Lizzie saw them depart and was bouncing on her heels. Ben laughed as Eloise turned toward them, saw Lizzie, and the girls ran into each other's arms. "They seem happy to see each other," Ben said, giving Jane a kiss on her cheek and his brother a hug.

"They certainly do," Ralph said. "The whole time we've been on this last part of our trip here, on the stagecoach she's been talking about everything the two of them did together the last time we visited. She's hoping you have some colts or other young animals she and Lizzie can spend time with while they visit."

"She'll be happy then," Ben assured him, "because Lizzie works with the colts all the time. She has a natural way with them and does a wonderful job."

"They'll be happy then," Jane said with a smile.

The girls came back to join their parents, smiling and giggling. "Mama, Lizzie says we can spend lots of time with their colts, and they have several," Eloise enthused. "They also have some new kittens and some sheep that have little lambs. I've never even touched a lamb!"

Jane laughed, along with the men. "Well, it sounds like you two young ladies will certainly enjoy our stay," she said.

Ralph and Ben gathered their bags and loaded them into the wagon. "The buggy would have been a little more comfortable for the ride back home," Ben apologized, "but I wasn't sure if you'd bring trunks or a couple of valises for each of you, and I wasn't sure it would all fit. The wagon has two benches, though, so we should be okay. Although it's not enclosed like the buggy would have been, it's nice out today, so I hope you won't mind too much."

"The wagon's fine with me," Jane said. "I personally am glad we'll be able to ride outside in the fresh air. The train and stagecoach were a bit stifling, so being outside sounds nice."

"I agree," Ralph said. "You chose well, brother. I don't think the girls will even notice what we're riding in, as long as they can keep chatting and laughing."

Ben looked over at Lizzie and Eloise, still chatting away, and agreed. "I see what you mean. Well, let's go to Ruby's restaurant and have some lunch before we head for home," Ben suggested. "Ella's planning something special for us for supper tonight, but since I brought the wagon I planned to stop at the mercantile before we head for home to pick up a few supplies Ella needs, unless you'd rather I didn't take the time."

"No, that's fine. We're in no hurry," Ralph said.

"I agree," Jane said. "In fact, I'd like to see if they have any readymade dresses that might fit Eloise. She had a bout of influenza that she struggled with for a month. She's healthy again now, but she lost some weight while she fought it. Her every day dresses are all too big on her, so the ones she brought won't be the best for spending a lot of time in the barn with animals. Maybe we can find her one or two that would fit her."

"We can look and see what all they have, but if they don't have any you like, she looks to be about the same size as Lizzie. She and Ella are pretty good at sewing, so I think they can probably get something fixed up to fit her. I'm glad she's feeling okay again."

"Me, too," Jane said. "We were getting concerned for a

while there. The doctor said this trip would probably be good for her now that she's feeling better, to be out in the fresh air and sunshine. He thought it might help her get her strength back and gain back some of the weight she lost."

"Let's hope it helps," Ben said. "We can leave the horses and wagon here and walk over to Ruby's, if you're all ready for something to eat."

"That sounds good to me," Ralph said. "The food on our trip was sufficient, but nothing special. I would sure welcome a good meal."

"Ruby's a great cook, and I think you'll like her meals."

Later they were headed home, after eating at Ruby's and a trip to the mercantile. They bought one new dress for Eloise, but they didn't have many ready made in her size. Lizzy assured her she was sure they could alter a couple of hers easily and they would fit her fine.

When they got back to the ranch Coy assured Ben he would help unload the wagon, then take care of it and the horses. Ella came out of the house to greet them. Jane had her in a hug as soon as Ralph helped her down from the wagon, and the two ladies went in the house talking easily. Lizzy and Eloise walked hand in hand into the house, where both planned on changing into Lizzie's barn dresses so they could go to the barn and see the colts and lambs.

"Let me know if you need help with any alterations," Ella managed to say before they ran up the steps.

"We'll be fine," Lizzy assured her as they hurried to her bedroom.

The ladies, who were pouring lemonade into glasses, laughed. "Eloise has been looking forward to this day ever since we first talked about coming to visit," Jane said.

"Lizzie has been just as excited," Ella said. They had two glasses of lemonade for themselves, two for Lizzie and Eloise, and two for the men as well, who were emptying the wagon before coming into the kitchen. They were putting out a plate of cookies as the girls came barreling down the steps, through the kitchen and toward the door. Ella stepped in front of the door with her hand up. "Whoa, girls. How about some lemonade or cookies first?"

"Thanks," Lizzie said, grabbing a cookie and glass of lemonade. Eloise did the same, and they again headed toward the door.

Ella shook her head and warned, "Be careful with the glasses and don't forget to bring them back in." Both girls nodded as they walked a little slower out the door, not wanting to spill their drinks.

Jane looked at Ella a bit surprised, but smiling. Ella sighed. "I probably shouldn't let her take a glass out to the barn, but she works out there with the colts a lot, and she's always been very careful not to set the glass anywhere that it might fall and break. She's also very good about bringing it back with her. I know how much she's been looking forward to Eloise coming to visit, and I just couldn't say no."

Jane laughed, but agreed. "I understand completely. Since Eloise was so sick a couple of months ago I've had trouble saying no to her for anything. I have to get over that, though, before she becomes spoiled."

"I doubt if that will happen, but I understand your concern. Lizzie has been a great help to her father. The truth is she's a good cook and is a big help to me, as well, but she would rather be at the barn working than in here. She seems to have a natural way with the animals, especially the colts, so we tend to let her spend most of her time there. Ben sees nothing wrong with it and appreciates her help, but I worry sometimes if we're doing what's best for her. When she meets a young man that captures her attention she may wish she would have spent more time learning how to take care of a house."

Lizzie and Eloise were leaving the kitchen door holding glasses and headed toward the barn as Ben and Ralph were heading toward the kitchen with some of their luggage. "You look to be in a hurry, daughter," Ben chuckled.

"We are, Papa. Ella has lemonade and cookies for you in the kitchen."

"Okay. You two have fun, but be careful. Remember Eloise isn't used to being around animals."

"We'll be careful," Lizzie promised.

When they went in the barn Lizzie took them straight to the colts. She showed Eloise where they could set their glasses of lemonade on a shelf on the wall across from the pens before she introduced her cousin to the colts. She stopped to pet each one and tell Eloise its name. Eloise was in no bigger hurry than Lizzie, and stopped to pet each one and repeat its name as it was introduced to her.

Before long they were talking and laughing, catching up on their lives as they worked with the colts. Lizzie showed Eloise what she'd been doing, getting the colts used to having a harness on and being led around the pen. She praised them when they cooperated and gave them a carrot and lots of rubbing their neck, which they all enjoyed. Eloise caught on quickly and soon they were leading two at once around the pen, and out into the corral.

Lizzie kept her eyes open for Coy while they were in the barn and corral. She considered warning Eloise about him, but decided against it. She wanted to see if Coy did come around, and if he did, she wanted to let Eloise get a true first impression of him, without any preconceived ideas from her. She wouldn't allow the two of them to be alone at all, but she wouldn't warn her about him, either.

She didn't have long to wait, which didn't surprise her much. They had just taken two colts out to the corral and were beginning to lead them in a figure eight pattern when

Coy walked up to the fence. He watched a couple of minutes before climbing over the fence and heading toward Eloise. "Lizzie, aren't you going to introduce me to your guest?"

She headed her colt toward Eloise, as well, and waited until she got to her before making the introductions. "Eloise, this is Coy Clemson, the ranch foreman. Coy, this is my cousin, Eloise Morgan. She and her parents are here visiting from Virginia."

"Nice to meet you, Eloise. You enjoy horses, I see, like Lizzie?"

"I don't get much chance to be around them at home, but I love being around them when we visit. I can tell Lizzie is good with them, and I'm glad she's willing to show me what to do and let me help."

"Lizzie is real good with horses. In fact, why don't we let hers go in the corral and if you'll stay here to keep an eye on them, I'll go help her get a few more to bring out. Come on, Lizzie."

"No," Lizzie said quickly. "We're working with two at a time because they haven't been led much yet. I want us to keep control of them while we're here, and we can't do that if we have more than two in here."

Coy looked at her, but Lizzie quickly diverted her eyes, not wanting to look into his. He shrugged and suggested, "Then I'll help you with these two."

"We're doing fine ourselves," she said. "I'm sure with Papa inside visiting with Uncle Ralph and Aunt Jane there are other things you should be handling, so go ahead. Eloise and I are fine."

He didn't make any move to leave, and when he looked at both of them again, Eloise turned to Lizzie. "You know, we probably should go back in soon. We haven't really sat down and visited any since we got here, and I'm sure they're wondering where we've been."

Lizzie was a little surprised by Eloise's words since they all knew they were going to the barn to see the colts, but when she looked up and saw her eyes, she immediately knew what the problem was. "I was thinking the same thing. Let's take them back to the pen and go inside before they come out here looking for us." Without waiting for a response from Eloise or Coy she turned and started leading her colt back to the barn. She went slow enough that Eloise could catch up with her and they walked side by side back into the barn.

She didn't want to give Coy the satisfaction of turning back to face him, so she talked with Eloise next to her and never looked back. Luckily, when they got to the pen for the colts she opened the latch and turned to let Eloise take her colt in first, and was glad to see Coy had apparently left. She didn't see him in the barn or in the corral. She moved closer to her cousin so she could talk quietly while she took the harnesses off the colts. "We'll talk once we're in my room." Eloise nodded and they gave each of the colts a final bit of attention before grabbing their glasses and headed toward the house.

Neither of them said much until they got close to the house, and Eloise spoke, still whispering. "I'm sorry if you weren't ready to come in yet, but thank you for backing me up."

"After we talk I may be thanking you," she whispered back, which earned her an inquisitive look. "First, though, we better spend a little time visiting with the family before we escape to my room."

"You're probably right." They set their empty glasses in the sink on their way through the kitchen to the living room, where the rest were gathered.

"I'm surprised to see you two inside already," Ralph said.

The girls looked at each other, and when Eloise looked a

bit wide-eyed, Lizzie responded. "We had to go say hi to the colts, but we didn't want to be rude, so we came in to visit. We'll have lots more opportunities to spend time with them in the next several days."

"And I'm sure the colts will love every minute of the attention you give them," Ben said with a little chuckle. "So, Eloise, I understand you had quite a battle with the flu and lost more weight than you should have. How are you feeling now?"

The conversation continued easily, catching everyone up. When Ella got up to finish supper, Jane followed. Lizzie and Eloise offered to help, as well, but Ella waved them off. "Jane and I can handle it easily while we visit more. I'm sure you two have lots to talk about, so go ahead."

"Thank you, Ella. We'll be in my room if you need us."

The girls hurried up the stairs to Lizzie's room, where she closed the door and they sat down on the bed, eager to talk. "So, was it just me, or is that foreman kind of --"

"Creepy?" Lizzie offered.

"Yes. I didn't like him, even though I know I shouldn't say that. I mean, I just met him, but he made the hairs on the back of my neck stand up. Did you see the way he looked at you?"

"I did, and to be honest, he scares me. I hardly ever go out to the barn anymore because I'm afraid he'll get me alone."

Eloise gasped. "It's that bad? I thought maybe it was just me, and some sort of odd reaction I had to him."

"No, it's not. He's always trying to get me alone, and that thought scares me. He's tried several times, but I've always managed to get away, but I hardly go out there anymore because of him."

"What do you think he'll do?"

"I don't trust him. The way he looks at me is scary. I'm glad you're here so we can go out there more, but I think it's important that we make sure we stay together. No matter what he suggests, we can't let him split us up."

"Okay, we'll be careful. What does your father say about him? He doesn't stop him?"

"He doesn't believe me," Lizzie said sadly. "I've told him I don't like him and don't trust him, but he said he's never done anything to make him question him, so he thinks I'm imagining it. He asked Papa if he could court me, so Papa thinks if I think he's looking at me funny it's just because he's fond of me."

"No, that was not what that look was," Eloise stated with certainty.

"I don't think so, either, but Papa thinks it is. Would you do me a favor? Will you watch him while you're here, and if he does anything else, looks at me like that again or says something untoward, would you please go with me to talk to Papa again? Maybe he'll believe me more if you're agreeing with me."

After a brief hesitation, she agreed. "Of course. In the meantime, we'll be careful when we're out at the barn."

"Thank you. I'm so glad you came to visit." They spent the rest of the afternoon catching up as Eloise tried on a few more of Lizzie's dresses and they took a couple of them in so they would fit her better and she could wear them while they were visiting.

Lizzie was looking forward to meals again, since Papa had agreed that he and Coy would talk about the ranch in the morning and evening privately rather than during meals while Ralph and his family were visiting, so they could enjoy their meals with just family. It would be so much nicer and more relaxing without Coy at the table.

Later that evening while she was indeed enjoying supper with family and not Coy Ben asked, "Lizzie, do you girls have plans for tomorrow?"

"Not specific plans, Papa. We want to spend a lot of time with the colts, and we haven't even gone to see the sheep yet, but we have time for both of those, since they get to stay two weeks. Did you have something you wanted me to help with?"

"No, but Ralph said he'd like to see the ranch, so I thought we'd take horses out tomorrow and we'd look at some of my favorite places on the ranch. I thought if you two don't have other plans you might like to join us."

Lizzie always loved riding with her father and enjoyed seeing different parts of the ranch that were further from the house, but she didn't want to accept his offer if Eloise didn't like the idea, as well. She looked at her cousin and was happy to see the excited expression on her face. "We'd love to," she answered for both of them. When Eloise squealed, she knew her cousin was just as eager to go as she was.

Ben and Ralph smiled at each other, a knowing look passing between them. "I thought they might like that idea," Ben said. "We'll go right after breakfast. Jane, are you sure you don't want to join us?"

"I'm sure I'd enjoy myself much more staying here to visit with Ella while you're gone. She says there are some raspberry patches around, and if I help her pick some she'll show me how to make them into jam. That's something I never did learn how to do, but always wanted to try. I love raspberry jam."

"So do I," Ben said, "and Ella makes the best raspberry jam I've ever tasted. If you're going to learn how to do it, you couldn't have picked a better teacher."

"I'm eager to learn, although I don't know where I'll find raspberry patches in the city when we go back home," she said with a chuckle.

The rest of the meal was filled with talk of other things they wanted to do or learn while they were visiting. As they finished their meal, Lizzie turned to her father. "Papa, Eloise hasn't had a chance to see the sheep yet, so is it all right if we do that now?"

"As long as you don't stay out too late, of course it's okay. Just remember, you'll be walking past the colts on the way back and you know how jealous they get if you give all your time to something other than them, so don't spend too long out there. You'll have plenty of time while they're here to see the sheep again."

Lizzie giggled, but agreed. "They do seem to get jealous if I spend too much time with the sheep," she told her cousin. "Papa says I have them spoiled, and he may be right."

"I know I'm right," Ben said, "but I also know you have a way with the colts and horses that I've never seen with anyone else, so I'm not going to object. You're a big help with them."

He turned to Ralph and explained, "This ranch is known for some of the best behaved horses around, and that credit goes to Lizzie. She's the one in charge of the horses, from the time they're first born. She's out there with them, letting them get to know her within a day of their birth, and starts training them before they're a month old. Their mothers have known her and trusted her from the time they were born, so they know they can trust her with their foals."

"I'm glad you approve, Papa, because I'd miss them terribly if you didn't allow me to work with them."

"And they would miss you just as much," he said with a smile. "That job is yours as long as you're willing to do it."

Jane watched the interaction between father and daughter and thought back to her earlier conversation with Ella about Lizzie. She was right, she did seem to enjoy her time at the barn, but it was also evident to her that she loved her father and the time she spent with him. They had a very close father, daughter relationship.

CHAPTER 3

Lizzie and Eloise were downstairs early the next morning. "Good morning, Ella," Lizzie said as she gave her a quick kiss on her cheek. "What can we do to help with breakfast?"

"My, you two are up awfully early. That wouldn't have anything to do with your ride to see the ranch today, would it?" she asked with a sly smile.

"We're so excited about it," Eloise confirmed. "I don't get to ride much at home, so I always look forward to it when I do, but this is going to be even better, getting to see the ranch. I remember the last time we were here Lizzie showed me some places that were so beautiful, I'm looking forward to seeing them all again. And if we go with Dad and Uncle Ben we won't have to worry about running into the foreman." As soon as she said that last part she turned pale and covered her mouth with her hand. "I'm sorry, I didn't mean to say that."

Ella put down the bacon she was ready to fry and turned to face Eloise. "No, I'm glad you did. While no one else is around, would you please tell me why you said that? Did something happen I should know about?"

"No, not really," she said quickly.

Eloise turned to look at Lizzie, obviously unsure what she should do. "It's okay," Lizzie said, "I've talked to Ella and she knows I don't feel comfortable around him. I'm actually kind of glad you did say something."

"So I take it it's not just something Lizzie is imagining," Ella said. "Eloise, I care a great deal about Lizzie and want to make sure she's safe. Please tell me what exactly happened that made you say that. If this keeps up and her father doesn't see it, I'm going to talk with him about it myself, so I want to know what happened that made you say that."

"Okay," Eloise said slowly, "but I'm not sure I can explain it very well. He came over to us yesterday while we were out with the colts. He just made me feel very uneasy, the way he was looking at her."

"Did he say anything upsetting?" Ella asked.

"I guess not exactly, but he was trying to split us up, and I didn't want him to be alone with her after the way I saw him look at her."

"How did he look at her?"

"I can't explain it. It was just creepy."

Lizzie jumped in, trying to help. "Ella, I hadn't said anything to her about Coy because I wanted her real thoughts. I know Papa thinks he's a nice man and I'm worried about nothing, so I wanted her honest opinion of him."

"She hadn't warned me at all. After he left is the first time we talked about him, but I felt the same way she does about him. He scares me."

Ella nodded her head. "Thank you for sharing that with me, Eloise. I think I need to talk to Ben."

"Ella, I appreciate you trying to help," Lizzie said, "but could you wait a little while?"

"Why? If he's a threat, your father needs to give the situation more thought."

"I know, but I don't want to ruin their trip here. Eloise has agreed to stay with me while she's here, no matter what he tries to do to separate us. If anything specific happens she said she would talk to Papa with me to tell him about it. Maybe then he'll believe me. If nothing else happens, we can talk to him shortly before they leave. That way he can hear her opinion, too, but it won't ruin all of their trip."

Ella looked from one of them to the other, while she contemplated what Lizzie had said. Finally, she seemed to reach a decision. "That plan does have some merit to it. It may be more convincing to him that way. Will you both promise me you'll stay together anytime you're outside of the house?"

"We will," Eloise assured her as Lizzie was nodding. "After the look I saw on his face when he looked at her, I would never leave her alone with him. And if he does or says something that causes me to worry more, I promise I'll go with her to talk to Uncle Ben."

"Okay," Ella said, "but be careful, both of you."

"We will," Lizzie assured her. "Now, what can we do to help with breakfast?"

"You don't need to help, but if you're sure you want to, why don't you set the table and get out the milk and butter? Oh, and put out some jam for the biscuits."

"Did I hear jam for biscuits? Yum," Jane said as she walked through the door. "My, you're all up early today. I thought I was getting up early to help Ella, and here I'm the last one."

"Good morning, Jane," Ella said. "The girls are a bit eager for their ride today across the ranch. I think that has a lot to do with why they're down here so early today."

"She's right," Eloise said as she reached up to give her mother a peck on her cheek. "I can't wait."

"Ah, I should have known," Jane said. "What can I do to help?"

"I think we're ready to take the food up as soon as the men come in," Ella assured her. Just then the door opened and Ben and Ralph walked in, causing the ladies to chuckle. "Jane, if you want to pour coffee, the girls and I can get the food on the table while they wash up."

Fifteen minutes later while they were enjoying breakfast Lizzie turned to her father. "Papa, where were you planning on going today on our ride?"

"Is there someplace in particular you'd like to go?"

"Well, not especially, but I thought Uncle Ralph and Eloise might like the view of the ranch from the plateau."

"We think a great deal alike, my daughter," Ben said with a laugh. "I thought we would take a lunch with us and eat it up there. From up there if you look down in the valley you can see a good portion of the ranch."

"That sounds like a place I would very much like to see," Ralph said. "It'll give me a good idea of the layout of the ranch."

"How about you, Eloise?" Ben asked. "Is there any particular place or thing you would like to see?"

"Not that I can think of, but thank you for asking, Uncle Ben. Oh, maybe seeing some sheep in a pasture would be nice. We saw the sheep in the barn last night, but it would be nice to see them in a pasture."

"We can arrange that," Ben said. Looking around the table, and seeing all empty plates, he pushed his chair back. "Is anyone ready to go riding?"

Both ladies jumped up and headed for the door, but Lizzie paused and turned back toward the table. "Let me help Ella with the dishes, then I'll be ready."

"Oh, nonsense," Ella said quickly. "You all go ahead. I have lunch ready for you to take. I can do the dishes."

"I'm going to help her with the dishes," Jane spoke up. "Then we're going to go pick some berries. Hopefully we'll have some raspberry jam for you to try with supper this evening. You go on now."

"Thanks, Aunt Jane," Lizzie said as she and Eloise skipped out the door and down to the barn, followed by Ben and Ralph, who were chuckling as they gathered the lunch Ella had packed for them.

Once the horses were saddled and they got started, Lizzie and Eloise followed behind Ben and Ralph. Lizzie pointed out different things as they passed, and Eloise asked if they could stop a few times when she saw something really pretty. She and Ralph were both impressed when they got to the plateau. Ben pointed out different pastures, and ponds, while Lizzie pointed out areas she often saw wildlife.

Working together they got the blanket and spread it out in an area where they would have a good view of the valley below while they ate. As they ate they took turns pointing out different things that caught their eye. "Look, Papa," Lizzie said as she pointed toward an empty pasture, "some of the men must be checking the fences."

"I see that. I told Coy to have the men check the fences so we can move cattle over there next week. I'm glad to see he's doing that." He paused before adding, "He's been a good foreman, making sure everything gets done in good time."

Lizzie and Eloise exchanged a look, but neither said anything. Ralph pointed out four or five deer gathered at a creek, and their attention turned to them. Fifteen minutes later Eloise pointed out that one of the men that were working on the fences was leaving.

"That's Coy," Ben said. "I'm not sure where he's going. He's headed back toward the barn, so maybe they need something they don't have and he's going back to get it." As they watched him ride away, he continued toward the barn until he went over a hill. Once he was beyond the hill he veered off to the side.

"He must not be going to the barn," Lizzie said. "I don't know where he's going, though. There isn't much over that way."

"No, there isn't," Ben agreed. He sat up a little straighter to watch. All eyes were on him as he rode to a large shade tree in an empty pasture. "What is he doing in that pasture?" He gasped as they watched him go to the tree, climb down from his horse and tie him loosely to one of the branches, and sit down, leaning against the trunk. He repositioned his hat so it covered his eyes as he crossed his legs."

Ralph chuckled. "Well, I'll be. It looks like your foreman has no idea you could be watching him and has decided he's ready for a nap."

Ben's eyes were big as he watched his foreman. "I'd say you're right," Ben agreed reluctantly. "I have to say that surprises me. He's always been such a good worker."

"At least when you're around," Ralph said with another chuckle. Looking around more, he sat up straighter to look further down, and pointed. "Is that a flock of sheep coming over that hill?"

Ben turned his attention away from Coy and in the direction Ralph was looking. "Yes, it is. They were over that hill and we couldn't see them, but they're coming over this way now."

"It looks like a pretty good number of them," Ralph said. "How many are there in that pasture?"

"They pretty much stay together, so since they've started coming this way I'm sure you'll get to see the whole flock. There are right around two hundred of them there."

Ralph and Eloise were mesmerized with the sheep and

were watching them, as more and more of them appeared over the hill. Lizzie kept glancing back at her father, and wasn't a bit surprised to see him more often looking in the direction of his foreman. She knew he was surprised to see him literally sleeping on the job, and hoped it would help her convince him Coy isn't the man he believes him to be.

They finished their meal and cleaned up, putting everything back in their saddlebags. "Do you want to go check on your foreman?" Ralph asked.

"No, I don't think so. I want to wait and see if he mentions anything. Frankly, I'm surprised, and not real happy with what I'm seeing. He's still sleeping. We came up from that direction, so let's go back down the other way. There are a couple of areas over there I think you and Eloise might enjoy seeing."

"So we'll be going by our fishing hole?" Lizzie asked.

Ben smiled and patted his daughter's arm. "I did plan on going past there. I brought some line with us, so we can all make a fishing pole and try our luck if everyone wants to."

Eloise was instantly excited. "We can try fishing?"

"We can indeed," Ben said. "Lizzie and I have caught many a fish from our fishing hole. We make our own pole, and on occasion we've even caught one or two with our hands. I won't guarantee we'll catch any, but if the fish are biting we'll be able to catch a few and take them home. We'll clean them and if we ask, I'm sure Ella will cook them for us."

With that, they set off, taking their time and stopping occasionally to watch some wildlife or let Ben or Lizzie point out something of interest. When they got to their fishing hole they tied string to sticks they found lying around the area and tied small hooks onto them. They collected worms and insects from the area and were soon fishing. Two hours later they were headed for home, with eight nice sized brook trout.

When they got back to the house Ella and Jane were just finishing a batch of raspberry jam. When she saw the fish she clapped her hands together. "Wonderful. We haven't had fish for a while, and it sounds good. I made some stew for supper, but that will easily keep until tomorrow. I'll put it in the spring house overnight and we can finish cooking it tomorrow. Ben, while you and Ralph clean those fish we'll get the rest of supper ready and the skillets hot. It won't take long to cook the fish."

"Fresh fish does sound good," Jane agreed. "Fresh fish, fresh biscuits and fresh raspberry jam sounds heavenly."

Supper that evening was a bit like a holiday. There was lots of relating happy moments from the day, and when combined with the special food, smiles and laughter were plentiful.

LIZZIE AND ELOISE spent much of their time at the barn with the horses and sheep over the next week and a half. They talked and laughed, sharing their innermost secret thoughts with each other after looking around carefully to be sure they were alone. Coy showed up several times, and suggested things that would split the girls up, but they wouldn't budge, and stayed together.

The girls wanted to go out riding on the ranch again before Eloise and her family left, but they were afraid Coy would find them. One evening over supper Ralph asked Eloise if she'd been able to do everything she'd hoped to do while they were visiting. Lizzie saw an opportunity and answered for her, while kicking her foot under the table, hoping she would catch on.

"Actually, I wanted to talk to you and Papa about that," Lizzie said. "We've talked about going riding on the ranch again, but I wanted to ask if you two would be interested in going along." When her father looked at her with a question in his eyes, she tried to explain. "Papa, I know I go out riding alone all the time, but I know what to watch and listen for, and I know how to handle my horse if a wild animal is around. I can take my rifle along, but I'm a little worried about being able to keep both of us safe if something were to happen. She'd not used to riding or being out there."

Ben nodded in understanding. "I hadn't thought of that, Lizzie, but you're right. It would be safer if we accompanied you. I know you can handle a horse and your rifle, but we've spent a lot of time together out there, and you're right, Eloise hasn't had that opportunity. Ralph, what do you think; are you up for another ride?"

"Actually, I think that sounds wonderful. I miss seeing the wild countryside, and I'd like to see Eloise have the chance to experience more of it while we're here."

"How about tomorrow then?" Ben asked. "It looks like we should have good weather tomorrow. Does after breakfast tomorrow suit everyone?" It wasn't hard for the adults to see how excited the girls were about their upcoming adventure, and they talked about it some after the girls went back to the barn to check on the horses one more time.

"I'm glad Lizzie said something. I'm used to her going out riding whenever she wants to, but I hadn't thought of her being hesitant for the two of them to go alone. She used to go out riding just about every day," Ben said, appearing to be rather deep in thought, "but she hasn't been going too much lately."

"No, she hasn't," Ella agreed. "It's one of the ways she's changed." She looked right at Ben, hoping he would pick up the message she was trying to send.

He met her eyes, and she was pretty sure he understood

she was referring to Coy. Maybe she would talk to him again in a few days, after their company left.

THEIR RIDE the next day proved to be a lot of fun for all of them. At one point their horses all became a bit agitated, and Ben slowed up to help Eloise with her horse while they stopped and looked around. Lizzie was the first to see the mountain lion watching them from the woods. They pointed it out, and although it made Eloise a little nervous, she was happy to have seen one. Ralph used the rifle he had with him to scare if off, and the horses settled down and they went on. When they got back to the house Eloise was eager to tell her mother what they'd seen. She declared it one of the highlights of their trip.

The day before they left they were in the barn talking. They hated to have to say good-bye the next day, but they were talking, reminiscing about some of the fun they'd had over the last couple of weeks. While they were laughing, Coy approached them. "Good afternoon, ladies. You seem to be mighty happy."

"We have to leave tomorrow, and we were talking about some of the things we've done the last couple of weeks," Eloise said.

"You seem to enjoy the foals."

"I do, very much," she agreed.

"Well, why don't you stay with them a few minutes, and Lizzie, could I get you to help me?"

"Help you do what?"

"I need a little help outside. It won't take long."

"I'll come help, too," Eloise offered.

"No. No, it's a two person job. You stay here with the

foals, since you won't get to see them after you leave. Come on, Lizzie."

"What is it you need help with?" Lizzie asked, looking around, hoping to find someone, anyone.

"It's not hard and it won't take long. Just come along and I'll show you."

Lizzie started to panic when she saw the look in his eyes as he headed toward her, and knew she had to do something quickly. There was no way she was going to allow him to pull her out alone. She grabbed hold of the gate and held on. "No, I'm not leaving Eloise. If the foals get upset, she won't know what to do."

"Nonsense. You know as well as I do that they're familiar with her now and won't get upset when you leave. Now come on."

He was close enough to reach out for her when she saw some movement in the shadow on the other side of the barn. "Clem, is that you?" she yelled. "Do you have a minute?"

"Yes, it is, Lizzie," Clem said as he stuck his head in the door, "and I always have a minute for you. What do you need?"

"I don't really need anything, but Coy does. He wants me to help him do something, but Eloise and her family are leaving tomorrow and we wanted to spend our last day together."

"And you should spend your time together," Clem said. "What do you need help with, Coy? I'll be happy to help."

The look Coy gave Lizzie made her shudder. "That's all right, Clem, I'll do it later. What are you doing back here? I thought you were helping them move the cattle into the back pasture."

"I was, but we had a problem with a pack of wolves. We run 'em off, but we're all lower on ammunition than we like to be now, so I come back here to grab some more just in case we have any other problems out there."

"Well, go get it then and get back out there," Coy said rather abruptly.

Lizzie didn't like the way he was looking at her at all, and turned to Eloise. "Well, we best be going in to help Ella and Aunt Jane. We told them we'd be in soon, and I don't want them worrying and coming out looking for us."

"You're right," Eloise answered quickly. "Let's go back in there." Without another word the two of them hurried out of the barn, while Clem was still in the barn collecting more bullets.

As they approached the house, Lizzie said, "Thanks for going along with me."

"I'm glad you thought of a way to get us out of there. I sure didn't like the way he was looking at you."

"I didn't, either," Lizzie admitted.

"What are you going to do once I leave?"

"I'll just have to stop going to the barn again. I can stay inside with Ella."

"But that's not right. I think you need to try talking to your father again."

"Will you go with me? We can tell him about this afternoon. If you agree with me maybe he'll listen."

Eloise stopped and looked down at the ground. "I don't normally like talking about other people," she said rather slowly, "but in this case, yes, I will. He scares me and I think your father needs to know about it."

"Thank you," Lizzie said. "I understand your hesitancy, but I appreciate it. Let's talk to him tonight after supper."

"Who are you going to talk to after supper tonight?" Lizzie and Eloise both jumped as they turned to see Ralph coming up behind them. "I'm sorry, I didn't mean to scare you, but I heard you say you plan to talk to someone after supper, and you both look a little peaked. Is everything okay?"

Eloise caught Lizzie's eyes momentarily before turning back to her father. "Not really, Papa. I think we need to talk to Uncle Ben."

"This sounds serious. Ben's in his office now looking for a bill he wanted to pay tomorrow in town. Let's go see if he has a few minutes. Do you want to talk to him alone?"

The girls looked at each other, and Lizzie shrugged her shoulders. "You're welcome to listen, too. You may be able to offer some advice."

Ralph's eyebrows raised. "Advice? Whatever it is you want to talk to him about, I'll help if I can."

CHAPTER 4

Ralph accompanied Eloise and Lizzie into the house, where he knocked on Ben's office door, which was already open. "Ben, the girls have something on their mind they'd like to talk to you about. Is this a good time, or are you busy?"

"No, this is a fine time. Come on in and sit down, all of you." He watched as they came in, and could tell the girls were looking pretty sullen. When Lizzie closed the door behind her his eyebrows raised. "What would you like to talk about?"

"Papa, I know you want me to try to be nicer to Coy, and you think I'm confused about the way he looks at me, but I want to tell you about what just happened."

"Something just happened now?" he asked. "I thought Coy was going to take the men out and move the cattle to a new pasture."

"That's partly why it bothers me," Lizzie said. She explained what had happened, and that luckily Clem had come back for more ammunition. "Papa, he never would tell me what he wanted help with, and when Clem said he'd help, he turned it down, said he'd do it later. He seemed upset that Clem was around, thinking he'd be with the rest of them. I think he was once again trying to get me alone with him, and the look he gave me made me shudder."

"What do you mean it made you shudder?"

"I don't know how to explain it, but Eloise saw the look, too."

Ben looked to Eloise, who nodded. "The first time I met Coy he didn't seem right. He tried to split us up and get her to go with him, and the look in his eyes was just scary. I didn't trust him. After we left I asked Lizzie about it and found out she's scared of him, too."

Ralph looked from the girls to Ben, who seemed uneasy. Trying to help, or at least understand it himself, he asked Eloise, "What do you mean the look in his eyes was scary?"

"It's not the normal way people look at someone, and it's not like boys look at me if they're going to ask me to dance with them or something like that. This is a scary look."

Ralph looked back to Ben, who still looked upset. "Ben, is this something new you're hearing about?"

"No, not exactly," he admitted. "Coy is my foreman and he's asked if he can court Lizzie. I haven't answered him yet because Lizzie doesn't care for him and says he looks at her funny. He's never given me a reason to question him, so I think he looks at her with longing, but she's not used to that."

"No, Uncle Ben, that's not how he's looking at her," Eloise said. Everyone turned toward her, and she shrugged her shoulders. "I'm sorry, but I've seen young men look at me a different way, and they talk to me and I can tell they like me. That's not at all the same look. This look is scary."

"Ben, you say he's never done anything to cause you to question him, but I have to ask, is he the one we saw riding off and taking a nap under the tree?"

"He is, and I admit that's bothered me some, as well. It's

not like him, but I'm glad you brought it to my attention. I honestly can't say right now what I'm going to do about it, but I will be giving it some serious consideration."

"Thank you, Papa," Lizzie said as she stood. He stood, as well, and gave her a little hug before she and Eloise left.

After they left Ralph closed the door again. "Ben?"

"I honestly don't know what's happening, but I will be finding out. After you leave and things settle back into normal, I'm going to have a talk with him and see if I can find out what's going on."

"Are you still considering letting him court Lizzie?"

"No, not if she's actually scared of him. But I want to find out what he's doing that has her feeling this way. If she's legitimately scared of him, not only will he not court her; I don't want him on my ranch."

~

BEN AND LIZZIE TOOK RALPH, Jane and Eloise to Gully Ridge the next day to catch the stagecoach. Lizzie had tears in her eyes as she hugged each of them good-bye, but she and Eloise promised to write each other often.

Ben took the opportunity to talk to his daughter on the way back to the ranch. After answering a few more questions she was relieved to hear he wasn't going to allow Coy to court her. He hadn't completely decided yet about meals, since the foreman eating meals with them had been the custom, and it was convenient. She assured him as long as she knew she wasn't going to have to allow him to court her, she could be civil and try to get along during meals.

Ben didn't tell Lizzie, but he planned on watching Coy carefully during meals to see if he could pick up on anything. If he was indeed up to no good, it was time to fire his foreman and start looking for a replacement.

Lizzie tried her best to be friendly to him at supper that night, but it was difficult. She tried not to make eye contact with him, but a couple of times when her father was looking down at his food she caught Coy looking at her, and it was an uncomfortable feeling. He asked her a few questions about her visit with Eloise, and she tried to answer them politely, but with short answers.

He did get her full attention when he mentioned their neighbors, the Hamiltons, were to arrive back home the next day. Clyde and Alva Hamilton and their four sons, Joseph, Bryce, Grant and Wyatt, owned and operated the ranch next to theirs, and had since before Lizzie was born. Their sons were all older than she was, but she and Wyatt, the youngest, had become friends. Hearing Coy say they were returning brought back memories of when she and Wyatt were young.

When Lizzie was born the Hamilton boys were ten, nine, seven and three. The three older ones had considered themselves too old to play with a little girl as she was growing up, but since Wyatt was only three years older than her, they always played together when the families got together.

They lived quite a ways from the closest school, and when she was old enough to start attending, her father wasn't comfortable with her walking alone that far. The Hamiltons agreed it was too far for a little girl to walk alone.

The four Hamilton boys generally cut across the back of their ranch and the Morgan ranch to get to school, which was a much shorter walk. However, it involved them going through a woods that was full of briers and known to have wildlife you had to be careful to avoid. There was also a creek they had to cross. They were all pretty tall, with long legs that allowed them to jump across the creek. They wore long pants so the briers weren't a problem, and they carried shotguns with them. With all four of them together and watching for bears, wolves or coyotes, Clyde felt the four of them would be safe.

It wasn't possible for Lizzie to go with them, though. Even if the boys watched out for her as far as keeping her safe from animals, Lizzie had always been small and wouldn't be able to jump across the creek. The briers would be a problem, also, catching on her long skirts. Knowing her going with the boys was out of the question, Clyde and Alva turned to their youngest son to assist. Even though they had grown up together and were friends, Wyatt hadn't been thrilled when his parents asked him to go to the Morgan ranch and walk with Lizzie to school along the road.

By the time he was old enough to go to school he'd matured enough that his older brothers were finally accepting him more, rather than thinking of him as a little kid. He'd learned how to shoot and went hunting with them and his father. Hunting was something he enjoyed, and the four of them always watched for game on their way home from school, all eager to be the one to present their mother with the next day's supper.

Now instead of being able to participate in that he had to walk Lizzie to school. It was a much longer walk taking the road and he had to leave earlier than his brothers. He and Lizzie may have grown up as friends, but now he was beginning to see her more as a bit of a pest.

As it turned out, that didn't last long. Having been raised by her father, she'd spent most of her time with him outside. She'd followed him everywhere and wanted to learn to do everything he did. At her request he'd taught her how to shoot a gun before she was quite five, once she'd proven she was quite capable of riding a horse on her own.

As she and Wyatt began making the long walk to school and home every day they found themselves talking about things they enjoyed most, which were much the same things.

They pointed out wildlife along the way, and she soon had the idea they should ride their horses to school instead of walking.

Wyatt liked the idea, as well, but wasn't sure if her father would allow her to ride her horse that far, without being with her himself. After they walked home the day they talked about it, he stopped at the barn and talked to her papa. Ben had been impressed with Wyatt for talking to him about it, making him even more impressed with him and proving once again that Wyatt was very mature for being nine.

After thinking about it for a day, he knew Lizzie was a good rider and good with a gun and hunting. He also knew Wyatt was very good with both a horse and a gun, and most importantly, he knew Wyatt would watch out for Lizzie. He always had, which is something Ben had noticed and appreciated. He talked to them the next day after they got home from school, and after asking a few questions about procedure and how they would handle certain situations, he agreed. From the next day on they rode their horses to school and back home, often bringing home meat for one family or the other.

That time they spent riding their horses and hunting strengthened their friendship. Before long they considered each other their best friend, and often shared private thoughts with each other on their way to and from school. That close friendship had continued from the time Lizzie started school when she was six. They had shared a lot of thoughts and experiences over the years.

Lizzie was totally lost in her thoughts of Wyatt and herself in their younger years, but when she heard Coy mention they were expected home by supper time the next day, it quickly brought her mind back to the present. "Would it be okay if I make them a pot of stew and a pie?" she asked. "If they're not home yet when I take it to them I'll just leave it on the stove for them. Then she won't have to worry about cooking as soon as they get back."

"That would be nice of you, Lizzie," Ben said. "I'm sure they'll be tired from their trip and a nice meal would be appreciated."

"I'll help you deliver it to their house," Coy offered.

Lizzie froze, and Ben saw her reaction. "Thank you for the offer, Coy, but I'll go with her. I'd like to talk to Clyde and see how their trip was."

"I wish we had some rabbits," Lizzie said. "I love rabbit stew, and so does Wyatt."

"We haven't had a chance to go hunting much lately," Ben said. "Why don't we take a couple of hours right after breakfast and see if we can't scare us up enough rabbits for a big pot of stew for both families. We can take out enough for us and take the rest down for them."

"You would take off work long enough for us to do that?" Lizzie asked, excitement filling her eyes.

"I like your idea of surprising them with a nice meal. If we have four rabbits by ten o'clock will that give us enough time for you ladies to have rabbit stew ready for supper?"

"It should, I think," Lizzie said, turning to Ella for confirmation.

"We can cook it a little faster than normal and it should be fine," Ella agreed. "We'll want it done a little earlier than we normally eat so you have time to get it down there before she cooks something else, but I'll wash and cut up the potatoes, carrots and onions while you're getting the rabbits. Then as soon as you bring the rabbits in we can start cleaning them and we'll be ready to go. We can make some pies for us and them while the stew cooks."

"Lizzie and I can clean the rabbits and as soon as we have one done you can start cutting it up. We'll bring them in as they're done so you can get them on to cook," Ben suggested.

"Thank you, Papa," Lizzie said, bouncing in her seat. "I'll be ready and we can go as soon as we have the kitchen cleaned up after breakfast."

"No, I'll clean up the kitchen, you two get out there as soon as you're done eating," Ella corrected. "The sooner we can get the stew on the better it will be. I'd hate to have you show up with stew for them after she's already got something else on to cook."

Ben and Lizzie agreed, and their plan was set.

THE MEN WERE in for breakfast a little earlier than usual the next day, and Lizzie and Ella had it ready so they could all sit down and eat. As soon as they were finished, Ben and Lizzie hurried to the barn, where Clem had their horses saddled and ready for them to go. Ben thanked him and he and his daughter set out.

Both of them had missed hunting together, and they promised each other to make time more often and not let so much time pass between hunts in the future. Luck was with them and they were back just over an hour later with seven rabbits. Ben stopped in to talk to Leo, the bunkhouse cook. "Leo, Lizzie and I have some rabbits. If you don't mind helping me clean three of them up for us, you can have the other four."

"I heard you were hoping to get two or three to make stew for you and the Hamiltons. Mighty nice gesture. You say you got seven? I'll be happy to help you clean them, and I'm sure the men will appreciate some good rabbit stew tonight. Thank you."

With the extra help cleaning the rabbits, Ella and Lizzie had the stew on almost two hours earlier than they planned, and once they had it on they made the pies. By midafternoon the stew was almost ready and the pies were cooled. They also had a big batch of biscuits done and wrapped in clean towels to stay warm. Lizzie went out to the barn, hoping her father had come in early since they had the meal ready, but she froze when she walked inside and saw Coy. Seeing her he walked toward her, a lecherous smirk on his face.

She looked around quickly, but didn't see anyone else. Not wanting to be alone with him, she thought quickly. "I have a message for Leo. If Papa gets here before I get back tell him where I am." She turned quickly and headed toward the bunkhouse kitchen, but Coy stopped her with a hand to her arm. "No one's here right now but us, and I've been waiting for this. I don't expect your papa back until closer to supper, so we're going to the tack room for a little while."

"I'm not going anywhere with you," Lizzie said, struggling to get her arm loose from his hold.

"That's where you're wrong," he said, tightening his hold on her and pulling her toward the back of the barn and the tack room.

"What's she wrong about?" came a booming voice from the back of the barn.

They both turned to find Ben walking through the door, and Coy immediately cursed under his breath, but dropped his hold on her. "I was telling her I'd like us to be friends, even if she doesn't want to court me right now. I suggested once she gets to know me better she may feel differently."

Ben looked at the two of them, and seeing the look on her face, he wasn't sure he believed that, but felt this was not the time nor place to discuss it. "Is the stew ready, Lizzie? I came in early so we can get it down to the Hamiltons' ranch early."

"It's ready, Papa. That's why I came out, to see if you were ready to take it down to them."

"I certainly am. I asked Leo if he'd get the horse and buggy ready for us and I see it's ready, so let's go get supper and head down the road." He'd reached her by then and they headed back to the front and out the door before Coy had a chance to say anything else. Once they had the buggy loaded and were headed out the lane, he took her hand in his. "Are you okay, Lizzie? You seemed pretty shaken in the barn."

"I'm fine now, Papa. I'm glad you got to the barn when you did. Coy was taking me to the tack room, and I didn't want to be in there alone with him."

"I don't like that idea, either. If he wanted to talk to you he could have done that in the open barn. I may have to have a talk with him." He changed the subject then and they talked about the Hamiltons and the trip they'd taken back east to see their sons, Joseph and Grant, who were now married and both lived in the Boston area.

When they pulled into their lane they were surprised to see their wagon up at the house and Clyde, Bryce and Wyatt unloading it and setting trunks and valises in the yard. They all stopped working and turned to welcome their neighbors. Ben shook Clyde's hand, then Bryce's, while Wyatt went straight to Lizzie. He picked her up and swung her around before putting her back down. She was giggling and he was smiling big. "It sure is good to see you, Wyatt," she said.

"It's good to be home again," he said, studying her face. "Everything okay?" When she didn't answer immediately he took her elbow in his hand and turned her away toward the side of the house. "Lizzie, what is it?"

"I would like to talk to you sometime when you have a chance," she said quietly, "but this isn't the right time." He nodded and they turned back toward the rest. "How was your trip, and how are Joseph, Grant, and their families?"

"Let me take a couple of trunks in and I'll tell you all about them while we go to the barn. I'm anxious to see the horses again."

"I'll get the trunks, Wyatt," Clyde said, "if you'll check on the horses and feed them. I know how eager you've been to see the horses again, and how much Lizzie likes seeing them, as well. Maybe the two of you can feed them while you're out there?"

"Sure thing, Pa," Wyatt said with a grin. "Thanks." He held out his arm with a big grin, Lizzie eagerly slipped her arm through it, and off they went toward the barn.

Ben chuckled as he watched them. "I swear those two like their animals more than any two people I know."

"That they do," Clyde agreed. "They're both good with them, too.

Bryce came out of the house after taking the last of their luggage inside. "Pa, if you don't need me for a spell I'm going to go see my girl."

"You go ahead, son. Tell Mary Lou's pa I said hello."

As Ben watched him hurry down the lane he asked, "Do he and Mary Lou have a date set yet for their wedding?"

"They do. Bryce wanted to go along with us to see his brothers, and I thought that was a good call. Once he gets married they're going to live in the foreman's cabin at her father's ranch. They're going to work together for a few years, and then her dad wants to move back east. He's from Boston, but he met and fell in love with his wife while she was going to school out there. Her family had a ranch out here, and when her father died of pneumonia they moved out here to help her mother. Once she passed on the ranch was theirs. He liked ranching, but when he lost his wife a few years back the ranch wasn't as appealing to him. It had too many memories for him, so he wants to go back to Boston and his family's business.

"They never had any children other than Mary Lou, so she and Grant will take over the ranch. Once they get married he'll be busy learning how that ranch works and getting to know the hands working there and earning their respect. He won't have time to visit his brothers in Boston for a spell, so they put off their wedding until after we got back. They're planning on getting married within a couple of months or so now. I'm sure they'll be sending you an invite for it."

"We'll be at the wedding. I think they did good waiting so he could go with you for a good visit."

Clyde nodded and pointed toward the barn. "I'm a little surprised those two haven't been seeing each other yet. I figured Wyatt was waiting for her to come of age, but now that she's eighteen I kind of figured they'd be courting and planning a wedding."

Ben's eyebrows raised a bit, but after a few moments he nodded his head. "I'm still having a hard time thinking of my little girl as a woman, but you make a good point. I kind of thought, too, they'd be together some day. They've been so close growing up, maybe they still see each other as friends, a little like brother and sister."

"Maybe," Clyde agreed. "One of these days they'll realize they're young adults now, and we'll see what happens."

"I guess we will. Wyatt would make a fine husband for Lizzie, that's for sure. She hasn't really shown much interest in courting anyone yet. How about Wyatt?"

"Not really. I always figured he was just waiting for Lizzie, but you might be right. They might see each other more as a sibling."

CHAPTER 5

Ben and Clyde carried the meal into the house and visited with Alva, who was very appreciative to see supper. "Oh, my goodness, that looks and smells delicious," she said. "I was just trying to think of something I could pull together for a quick meal. This will be so much better. I can see there's plenty of it here. Will you stay and eat with us?"

"Thank you for the invitation, Alva, but we've got a pot of it at home waiting for us, too. Lizzie and Ella made a pot for each of us. They thought you might appreciate having a meal ready when you got home tonight. Lizzie wanted to fix rabbit stew, so she and I went out this morning for the rabbits, a couple of the men helped clean them, and the ladies hurried to get it together so it would be ready in time."

"Well, I'll have to thank all of them. Did Lizzie come with you?"

"She and Wyatt are at the barn tending the horses. When they get back in we'll go home to eat and let you all eat and get settled back in. You'll have to stop up someday soon so you can tell Ella and Lizzie about your trip. I'm sure they'll want to hear all about it."

"I'll do that for sure," Alva said.

While they were in the house talking, Wyatt led Lizzie to the barn. As soon as they were inside he turned her to face him. "Now, what's going on? I can tell something's on your mind. You look worried about something."

"I am." She told him about Coy, the looks he gave her, and that he kept trying to get her alone with him. She also told him she'd told her father, and the conversation they'd had. "I don't trust him at all. Papa said he's not going to let him court me, but I still worry about him."

Wyatt listened carefully, and picked her hand up to hold in his. "I don't like this," he said. "Let me think about this overnight, and see if I can come up with any ideas. In the meantime, maybe you should stay in the house."

"I've been doing that a lot, but you know me; I like being outside or at the barn. It's not fair."

"No, it's not, but you have to be safe. I'll try to get away tomorrow or the next day and I'll come over and we'll go riding. We can talk again then."

"Thank you, Wyatt. I knew I'd feel better if I talked to you about it."

"I'll do what I can, but be careful until we come up with a plan. If I can't think of anything else, I can at least go talk to your father. We've always gotten along well. Maybe if I tell him you were concerned enough to talk to me about it, he'll do something about it. I'm surprised he hasn't taken you more seriously."

"I think Coy has him fooled. Papa thinks he's a good foreman and hasn't given him any reason not to trust him."

"I'll make it over tomorrow or the next day and we'll talk again. Let's finish feeding the horses so we can go inside. Are you and your father going to stay for supper?"

"No, we brought supper over for you, but we have our own at home."

"You brought supper over for us?"

"Yes." She grinned as she said, "Papa and I went hunting this morning and got some rabbits so Ella and I could make some rabbit stew."

"My favorite," he said, licking his lips. "Thank you. What a welcome home."

"You're welcome. We also brought a cherry pie and some biscuits."

He saw the cute grin on her face and pulled her in for a hug. "You know all my favorites. I'm lucky to have such a good friend."

"I'm the lucky one to have you as a friend. Thank you for giving my problem some thought." They worked together to check each of the horses and get them fed. "It looks like your foreman and the hands did a good job with the horses while you were gone. They all look good," she said as they headed for the house.

After Ben and Lizzie left the Hamiltons enjoyed their rabbit stew. "We're lucky to have such good neighbors," Alva said. "That was so thoughtful, and it's delicious."

Wyatt agreed completely, and found himself thinking once again about the young lady that had grown up as his best friend. He wasn't sure when or how it had happened, but lately he'd been thinking of her more often, and not just as his best friend. He loved the little lady, but wasn't sure what exactly to do about it, or how.

He considered talking to her honestly, as they'd done so often in the past, and telling her how he felt about her, that he wanted her as more than just his best friend. He wanted to go through life with her as his wife. If she didn't feel the same way, though, he could ruin the friendship they had now, and he certainly didn't want to chance that happening. She was three years younger than him, so perhaps she wasn't to that point in her life yet.

For now he felt his best course of action was to bide his time and see if he could pick up on any clues that might tell him how she felt. He also planned on spending more time with her. Maybe they could go on a picnic or two. That should give them a chance to relax and talk. Maybe that would help her start thinking of him as more than a friend. He knew what he wanted. Now he just had to find a way to make it happen.

~

WYATT DIDN'T SHOW up the next day, but Lizzie wasn't really surprised. They'd just gotten home and she knew he would have a lot of work to do. During breakfast the following morning her father and Coy were talking about what their plans for the day were. While they talked her mind was wandering, hoping Wyatt had a chance to visit later, when she picked up on something her dad was saying that got her attention.

"Coy, I want you to take Frank and Bill and go over to the Dravenstott ranch to pick up the rest of the horses I bought. I picked them out and paid for them last week and I brought two home with me, but there are six more to get yet. If three of you go over, you can each bring two home with you."

"Two of them should be able to bring them home. They can either tie them together and each bring three, or they could take a wagon and tie them on the back. Either should work okay."

"I'd rather have three men. You never know when one or more of them is going to get spooked. If that happens, two men may not be able to handle them. Take Frank and Bill, and the three of you should be okay."

"Okay, we'll go right after we finish up the morning chores then," he said. "We shouldn't have any trouble making it back before dark then."

Lizzie wanted to jump for joy. Since Coy would be busy and away from the ranch all day that meant she could work with the horses without having to worry about him, and even go for a ride. She loved taking her horse out for a good ride, but hadn't been able to do that for the last several months, for fear of running into Coy. As soon as breakfast was over she started helping Ella with the breakfast dishes.

"My, you seem to be in a hurry this morning, Lizzie. Do you have plans?"

"Yes, I do," she said, looking around to be sure no one was around. "Coy's going to be gone all day, and --"

"So this gives you an opportunity to work with your horses," Ella finished.

"Not only that, but I can finally take a ride again. I haven't gone riding alone in a few months, and I miss it."

"While you have this opportunity, you go get your riding skirt on and get out there. I can finish this up. You go while you have the chance."

"Thanks, Ella," Lizzie said as she rushed upstairs to her bedroom to change. Once she was at the barn she worked with the horses all morning. She was still working with them when her father came up to the corral and leaned against the fence. "Good to see you out here again, Lizzie. Are you ready for lunch?"

She looked up at the sun and nodded. "Yes, let me put this one up and I'll be ready. I guess I got carried away and didn't realize it was about noon already."

"I'll walk with you," he said, falling into step beside her as she led the young horse back to her pen. After brushing her out a bit she checked the latch on the pen, and the two of them went to the house. Over lunch they talked about the horses and how she was coming along with them.

When they went back outside, he went to check on a herd of cattle, and she worked with another foal a little bit, then saddled Shadow, her horse. She told Leo she was going out for a ride, and set out. It felt great to be out riding again, with the wind blowing in her face. One of her favorite places to ride was over next to the Hamilton ranch, and she headed in that direction.

She was riding along a creek close to the border between their ranch and the Hamilton ranch, enjoying her ride. As she approached some woods, a man shot out on a horse, heading right at her. It scared her, and when Shadow reared up, she was thrown. She landed hard on her side, but Shadow took off. She always had a rifle with her, but it was still tied onto Shadow. Before she could even turn around to see who the man was or what he was doing, she heard his voice, and cringed. It was Coy.

"Finally," he said with a snarl, "nobody's around to save their precious little Lizzie. Your father told me I won't be courting you, and I know it's because you told him you didn't want to. That was a mistake. You should have allowed it. We could have courted a little, then we would have been married and you would have been able to stay on your precious ranch. I would have owned it and been running it, of course, but you could have at least stayed there. But you thought you were better than me and wouldn't allow it. Now you're going to get what you deserve."

"No," she yelled. "Get away from me, Coy."

"Yell all you want, bitch, but no one's out here to save you this time. I made sure of it."

"How did you know I'd be here?"

"I figured once you thought I wouldn't be around all day you'd go riding. All I had to do was make sure you thought I went with Frank and Bill, then I doubled back and watched you. As soon as you went out on your horse I knew I'd get my chance. You like riding over here, so I hung back until you were far enough away, then hurried ahead and waited in the woods. I thought you'd never get here. But now you are, and here we are."

He grabbed hold of her and pulled her up next to him. "And you're mine to do with as I please."

He leaned down and kissed her, and she pushed back against his chest. "No! Get away from me. You're disgusting. Help!"

"Scream all you want, bitch. Like I said, no one's around to hear you. Besides, I kinda like hearing you scream and beg." He leaned down and kissed her again, and she struggled. When she was able to pull back from him, she spit in his face. "You no good little whore," he said, and slapped her in the face.

Instead of being quiet and begging, like he thought she would, she yelled again, and again. "Help, anyone! Please, please, help!"

WYATT WAS out checking on their horses, going to each pasture and doing a thorough visual check to be sure they seemed safe and healthy, no injuries. As he finished with one pasture and started toward the next he thought he heard something. He paused and listened, but didn't hear it again, so he started on his way again. A couple of minutes later he heard it again, and this time he was sure he heard something. Again he stopped, listening closely. He soon heard it again, but this time he knew what it was. It was Lizzie, and she was yelling for help.

He immediately got his horse turned around and headed

toward the area he thought her scream came from. He was running the horse at a full gallop, hoping he was heading in the right direction, when he heard another scream. It about killed him to hear Lizzie scream, but it pointed out the direction he needed to head. The more he heard her scream, the more he knew which direction to head, but the more determined he was to not only save the lady who had become so important to him, but to make whatever or whoever it was causing her to scream to pay for their acts.

Without pausing to consider his safety, he urged his horse to jump a creek with a steep bank, as well as an old stone fence separating their land from the Morgan ranch. As he topped a knoll his heart sank. Up ahead he saw Coy, the very man she'd been worried about, standing over Lizzie, who was laying on the ground, and not moving. He was about to yell, when he thought better of it. If he yelled, Coy would more than likely jump on his horse and ride off. Wyatt would stop to help Lizzie, allowing Coy to escape. That was unacceptable to him. Whatever he'd done to Lizzie, he wanted Coy to pay for it.

His primary focus was still on Lizzie as he made his way closer. Coy must be extremely focused on Lizzie, otherwise he should be able to pick up on Wyatt's horse coming in at a full gallop. That worried him and urged him on. He expected he would certainly hear the hoof beats as he got closer, and Wyatt didn't want him to have a chance to jump on his horse and escape.

An idea started to form in his mind. He and his brothers had all learned how to use a lasso. Occasionally as they were working with horses they'd bought that hadn't been trained, they'd needed to lasso them to get them under control. His brothers and father always said he was better with a lasso than the rest of them, so he was often called on to catch an uncooperative horse. Maybe that skill would be useful now.

With that in mind, he pulled the lasso free from where he kept it fastened to the back of his horse, and started swinging it as he slowed a bit and approached Coy.

Coy apparently finally heard Wyatt approach. He stood up straight and turned toward him. Seeing him, he took a few steps to reach his horse and mounted in just a few seconds and took off. He was fleeing, and further away than Wyatt had hoped, but Wyatt swung his lasso one last time and gave it a hefty toss. He heaved a sigh of relief when it settled over Coy and tightened, pulling him off his horse, which kept going.

Wyatt wasn't sure which he should attend to first, but seeing Coy already trying to get his hands free, he went to him first. He may have had a knife, or even a small derringer in his pocket. He pulled the rope tight around him and quickly slid off his horse and ran to Coy, who was trying to stand. Wyatt kicked his feet back out from under him, causing Coy to fall again. "Hey, come on, let me up," Coy pleaded. "Let me go and I'll give you a turn with her after I'm done."

"That was your second big mistake today," Wyatt said as his fist contacted Coy's face. He was livid, and he pummeled Coy. He was getting carried away, when he heard a grown from Lizzie. He gave Coy one final punch, which knocked him out, and ran to Lizzie.

He knelt down beside her and took her hand gently in his. "Lizzie?" She started trying to fight him, to pull his hand away, but he held onto it. "Lizzie, it's okay, it's me, Wyatt. You're okay. Nobody's going to hurt you."

"Wyatt?" she whispered.

"Yes, I'm here, and you're going to be okay."

"Coy --"

"Shh, I know, I know, but he can't hurt you anymore."

"He tried to --"

"I know, sweetheart, but I won't let him hurt you anymore."

"Is he gone?"

"No, but he won't hurt you. I punched him and knocked him out. I'm going to go over there and tie him up to make sure he can't get away. We'll take him into the sheriff's office and let them deal with him."

"He's still here?" She started trying to move again.

"Shh, quiet down. He's over there but he's unconscious. I'll tie him up so when he wakes up he won't be able to move."

"Do that now, please," she said in barely a whisper.

She was obviously petrified of this man, so Wyatt patted her hand. "Okay, you stay right here while I do that, then I'll be back. Will you be okay while I do that?"

"Yes. Don't let him hurt us."

Wyatt grabbed some rope he had tied onto his horse and went to Coy. He quickly tied his legs together, then tied his hands together. He tightened the lasso around his body but left it in place, then used more rope to tie the lasso to his hands, and one to tie it to his feet, insuring he couldn't move a bit.

He hurried back to Lizzie and spoke softly as he took her hand in his again. "Okay, he's tied up and won't be able to move a bit when he wakes up. Now that we don't have to worry about him, let me look at you. Are you okay? What hurts the most?" He cringed as he took a better look at her. She had bruises on her face and hands, and her dress was torn in several places. As he looked her over a bit closer he saw one boot was missing, and there was a bruise on her lower leg.

"I hurt all over," she whimpered, as she tried to sit up.

"I'll help you sit up in a minute," he said, holding her

down, "but first let me check for broken bones. Is there any place that's especially sore that I should check first?"

"I don't think so," she said, not objecting when he started running his hands down her arms and legs, feeling for any possible breaks in her bones. She winced a couple of times, but when he pulled her sleeve or dress up enough to check an area he saw a nasty bruise, it didn't feel like a break. He checked her back and ribs next, and found one rib he was concerned about. She asked if he would please help her sit up, and he did, suggesting she hold the one rib area he was concerned about as he did. Once she was sitting up, leaning against his chest and breathing okay, he suggested she sit still a few minutes and make sure she felt okay before they try getting her on her feet.

While she was catching her breath, he came up with a plan to get her back to her house. He took her hand in his again and asked, "Do you think you'd be able to sit in front of me and ride back to your house?"

"What about him?" she asked, shivering as she glanced over at Coy. He was still unconscious, which was fine with both of them.

"I'm thinking we have a couple of options. If you don't think you can sit in front of me I'll fire off a rifle shot, wait a minute or two and fire another. That's our signal for help, and if Bryce or my Pa hear that they'll come to check on us. We can have them get a wagon so you can lay down on the way back."

"No, I think laying down would be harder. I'd probably feel every bump even more than sitting on a horse, but I'm not sure I can ride back myself."

"If you want to go back on a horse you'll ride in front of me. I'll keep my arm around you to be sure you're safe, and you won't have to worry about controlling the horse."

"I think I could do that. Thank you. But again, what about

him?"

"I considered leaving him here while I take you home. He can't move, so he's not going anywhere. We don't have to worry about him running off. Once we get back to your house we can have someone bring a wagon out to pick him up and take him to the sheriff."

"What if a cougar or bear find him?"

Wyatt shrugged a shoulder. "As far as I'm concerned it wouldn't be anything he doesn't have coming to him." He paused and took a deep breath. "However, another part of me wants him to have to answer to your father. He obviously had him convinced he was such a great guy; let him explain this. As long as he's unconscious I should be able to drape him over his horse or one of ours and tie him on so he doesn't fall off."

"What if he wakes up on the way back?"

"Part of me hopes he does," Wyatt said with no remorse. "Riding draped over a horse won't hurt him any, but it might give him a start if he wakes up during the trip."

Wyatt was looking at her and saw the small smile his comment brought to her face. That smile, no matter how small, was so good to see. He cared about her very deeply, and knowing what Coy was trying to do, or possibly may have already done, was tearing him apart. He truly hoped he'd gotten to her in time, before Coy had a chance. He had to get her back to her home, where she could feel safe. He was sure Ella could talk to her and help her through it. He would be there for her, as well, no matter what had happened, but he hoped for her sake he'd gotten there in time to keep her virtue intact.

"I think I'd rather we take him back on a horse, but can you get him up on one? Coy's not a small man, and I don't think I'll be able to help much."

"I'll get him up there," he assured her. "It doesn't look like his horse is coming back, so we'll have to use my horse and yours. Shadow is a smoother ride, with less head shaking, so why don't we ride her. I'll drape him over mine and tie his lead to Shadow's saddle so he follows us in."

She watched Wyatt untie his rifle from his horse and tie it onto Shadow. Then he led his horse closer to Coy, and double checked the bindings he'd put on his hands and feet. He undid the strings between the lasso, hands and feet which kept him in a fetal position, and stretched him out. He tied the lasso closed so his body was bound, as well as his hands and feet. Satisfied he was safely secured, he bent down, got his hands underneath the man, and stood up with him. He carried him to his horse and talked softly to the horse to keep it still while he draped Coy over the saddle. He made quick work of tying him to the saddle and harness in several places so he wouldn't fall off, or be able to move if he woke up.

As Lizzie watched him she couldn't help but notice how strong Wyatt was. She'd thought of him as her best friend for so long, she hadn't noticed how big and strong he'd become. He was definitely a young man now, and a nice looking one at that. She'd always loved his hair that was so dark brown it was almost black, and had just enough curl in it to lay nice. His eyes were a deep brown, as well, and always seemed to be able to make her feel safe. Whenever she was scared or frightened of something, looking into those dark brown eyes while he told her they'd be okay always made her believe him. And he had always been right. He'd always kept her safe when they were together.

She was sure she would always think of him as her best friend, but right now she was also seeing him in a different light. Now he was a young man, a very nice looking young man, and the man that saved her from something awful. She would be forever grateful.

CHAPTER 6

Wyatt checked the ties holding Coy to the horse one last time before going back to where Lizzie was sitting up. "Okay, he's secure. Are you ready for me to lift you onto Shadow?"

"I can get up on her," she said.

"That may be true, but it would be a lot easier on your ribs and other bruises if you don't strain those sore areas. Let me help you stand first, and we'll see how that goes. If you have any sore areas, tell me so I can be careful of them going to the house."

Lizzie had a little smile as he lifted her. He was being so gentle with her. That didn't surprise her at all, since he'd always watched out for her. From the time they were little he was her protector. Whether he was accompanying her to school or back, or they were out riding for fun, hunting together, or any of the many things they've done together over the years, he always made sure she was safe. She'd noticed over the years that he was naturally protective, but especially of her.

In this case, he had his arm around her waist and lifted

her. He kept his arm around her until they were sure she was okay, not dizzy or lightheaded. They moved over to Shadow, and he simply said, "Okay, here we go," and without giving her time to argue, he picked her up around her waist and set her in the saddle. Once he was sure she was okay, he climbed up behind her and immediately wrapped one arm around her waist while he took the reins in his other. "Ready to go?" He waited until she nodded. "Now, if you get sore and need a break, let me know. We don't have to be in any hurry."

"Thank you."

He leaned down and kissed the top of her head, which surprised her a bit, but she liked it. She was sure finding her like this had to be hard on him, as well, since they were good friends. She thought about that as Wyatt started moving them slowly to the house. She was sore and was glad he was going slow to avoid bumps and jars, but that was very much Wyatt, protecting her all he could.

THEY SLOWLY MADE their way back toward the house. Wyatt turned around to check on Coy from time to time to be sure he hadn't moved or slid any, and kept his arm around her waist. As they topped a knoll they saw two riders heading in their general direction, but a little off to the east. Wyatt stopped while they looked at the riders, trying to identify who they are and what they were doing. They apparently saw them, as well, and turned their horses toward them. As they got a little closer Lizzie recognized them. "That's Bill and Frank, hands of ours," she told Wyatt.

"Good guys?"

"Yes, I trust them," she said in answer to the question she knew he was asking.

"Good," he said as he waved at them. "Frank, Bill," he

yelled loud enough for them to hear, "I'm Wyatt Hamilton and I have Lizzie. We could use a little help."

They spurred their horses on and got to them quickly, but paused when they saw Lizzie's bruised face, torn clothes, and Coy tied onto the horse behind them. "What in the world happened? Are you okay, Miss Lizzie?"

When she didn't respond right away, Wyatt spoke up. "I heard screaming and when I ran to check it out I came across Coy trying to have his way with Lizzie."

"I never did trust that man," Bill said. "I didn't like the looks he had on his face when you were around. I'm sorry this happened. I thought he was supposed to be gone all day."

"So did I," Lizzie said softly. "That's why I thought it would be safe to go for a ride. I'm so glad Wyatt was close enough to hear me."

"So are we, and I'm sure you papa will be, too," Frank said. "Wyatt, what can we do to help?"

"I'm going in slow so I don't bounce Lizzie around. She's already sore enough. Would you mind taking Coy in? Keep him tied, but the main thing you can do is tell her father and Ella. I'd like them to be ready for us, and could someone ride into town and get Doc Avery? I'd like him to check out a couple of her cuts and bruises, and I guess he might want to look at Coy, too. I knocked him out."

"Good for you, Wyatt," Bill said as he took the lead for the horse Coy was on. "We'll take him back and let her father and Miss Ella know you're coming in. They'll be ready and waiting for you."

"Thank you," Wyatt said, handing over the rope for his horse. That's my horse, Chestnut. Coy's horse ran off."

"His horse came back to the barn without him. That's why we're out, looking for Coy. I'm glad you found him first. Thank you for your help, Wyatt, especially with Lizzie."

"I'm just glad I heard her and found her before he did any worse."

The two men turned around and headed toward the house and barn at a faster pace. Bill kept the lead for Chestnut, while Frank pushed on ahead. After they were out of sight Wyatt sighed. "I'm glad they came along and could take Coy. Now I can concentrate on trying to keep you as comfortable as possible. How are you holding up, Lizzie?"

"I'm okay. Thank you for talking for me back there. I just couldn't seem to find the words to tell them what happened."

"Lizzie, I'll do anything I can to help you. I hope you know that."

"I do."

"Good. Not just right now, either. Over the next few days I'm sure it's going to be rough for you. I'm not a lady so I'm not going to pretend to know how you feel or are going to feel, and I don't know what he did to you before I got there, but I want you to know that I care about you a great deal. I always have and I always will. If he did anything he shouldn't have, it won't change the way I feel about you at all. I'll always be here for you. If talking about it will help, I'll listen, and anything you say will stay between us."

She was quiet a few moments before putting her hand over his arm that was holding her around her waist. "Thank you, Wyatt. I know you, so I know you mean that, and I can't tell you how much that means to me." She took a deep breath and exhaled slowly before continuing. "He didn't do anything to me other than slap me, mostly trying to get me to stop fighting him, but he was going to."

He heard a couple of sobs and knew she was fighting back tears. "You don't have to tell me anything if you don't want to, Lizzie."

"I know, and thank you, but you deserve to know. I want you to know. He told me all the awful things he planned on doing to me." Wyatt cringed and tightened his hold on her a little. "I fought all I could, but I couldn't get away from him. The only thing I could do was scream, but I didn't think anyone would hear me. Then he hit me one more time and knocked me to the ground. That's the last thing I remember until I heard your voice. I was so relieved. I knew then I'd be okay."

Her words came as a surprise to Wyatt, but he relished them. He was glad to hear his voice soothed her. That meant she trusted him, and he considered her trust a precious gift he would honor and protect. "I'm glad I got there in time," he said, and gave her another little kiss on her temple. "Feel free to lean back against me and rest the rest of the way in. I'm going to take it slow so we don't jar any of your sores or bruises.

"Thank you," she said as she did just that and leaned against his chest. He loved having her lean against him like that, but he hated what had happened. By the time they were nearing the house he'd decided once she was healing from this event he was going to tell her his feelings for her had changed from just good friends. He wanted her as part of his life from now on, and he hoped she had similar feelings.

As they approached the house things started moving quickly. Ella and Ben were at the house waiting for them, and several of the hands were at the barn watching them approach. They called out greetings, telling Lizzie they were glad she'll be okay, and thanking Wyatt. It was obvious to him just how much the hands on their ranch thought of her.

He stopped at the house and Ben helped her down from her horse, with Wyatt helping. Once she was down he slid down, as well, and Frank was there assuring them all he'd take Shadow to the barn and take care of her. He also told Wyatt Chestnut was in the barn being brushed down and they were giving him some grain. Wyatt thanked him as Ella pulled Lizzie into a hug. "Let's get you inside and cleaned up," she said, heading her toward the door. She turned back to Wyatt and Ben to say, "I'm going to take her to her room to get her cleaned up and check her injuries. I'll be out to talk to you when I'm done. If Doc gets here send him up."

Wyatt nodded. "Are you okay to walk up the stairs, Lizzie? I can carry you up if you're too sore."

"Thank you for your concern and offer, but I'll be okay," she said as she looked back at him. Their eyes locked for a moment, and Wyatt's heart about stopped. He nodded and she turned back toward the stairs.

"Thank you, Ella," Ben said. "Come on in, Wyatt. Ella made us some coffee. I'd like to hear what happened." Wyatt nodded and followed him into the kitchen, but his eyes stayed on Lizzie as Ella helped her upstairs.

Ben poured them each a cup of coffee and motioned to a plate of cookies Ella had put on the table for them. "Son, I think there are a couple of things we need to talk about, and I believe now would be a good time to do it."

"Yes, sir."

"The first of which is I believe you have feelings for my daughter that go beyond the friendship you two have shared since you were small."

"Yes, sir, I do. I've felt that way for a little while now, but I realize Lizzie is younger than me. I wasn't sure if she had similar feelings for me or if she still thought of me just as a friend, so I gave her some time. While we were on our trip out east I had decided when I get back I was going to talk to you and ask if I could court her. I'd like to tell her my feelings for her have changed, or maybe intensified is a better word, and see if she's interested in courting. I had planned on coming over this evening after supper to talk to you."

"Well, you are the fourth young man to ask me about courting my Lizzie. I turned the first three down because either I felt she wasn't ready yet, or she wasn't interested in courting the man. However, I would be very happy if you would court her. I don't have any hesitation about it, or I don't feel I need to ask her first because I know she's very fond of you. I honestly can't say if she thinks of you as more than a good friend, although from the look you two shared before she went upstairs just now I'd say she does. But be that as it may, you have my blessing to court her."

"Thank you, sir. I care a great deal about Lizzie and will keep her safe when she's with me."

"I know you will, Wyatt, and I appreciate that. You were a good boy and I felt good about you two being friends as you were growing up, and you've grown into a fine young man. If it goes well for you I'd be proud to have you as a son-in-law. I know you'd protect my daughter."

"Thank you."

"Now, as much as I hate to hear this, I need to hear what happened out there. Frank said Coy tried to attack her, but luckily you heard her scream and found her."

"Yes, sir."

Ben was shaking his head and looking down. "This was my fault and I feel awful. Lizzie told me she didn't trust Coy, but I didn't think he would hurt her. He asked if he could court her, and I thought he truly cared about her."

"Mr. Morgan, this isn't your fault. Coy attacked her, not you, and I'm sure he did and said all the right things to make you trust him. He was your foreman, and I know he did a good job or you wouldn't have kept him in that position."

Ben sighed. "Even that's not true. Just last week I saw him get some men busy fixing a fence, then riding off and taking a nap. Instead of talking to him about that like I should have, I assumed he hadn't slept well the night before. What a fool."

"Mr. Morgan, I know you and you're not a fool. You're a very kind and fair man, so it's not surprising that you would trust an employee and give him the benefit of the doubt. In this case he didn't deserve that trust, that's all."

"Thank you, Wyatt, for your kind words, though I'm still not sure I deserve them. But now I have to ask, what did happen out there today?"

Wyatt spent the next twenty minutes explaining what happened from the time he came upon them. Ben nodded in understanding several times, asked a few questions here and there, and when he had finished his explanation, he could tell there was one more thing on Ben's mind, and he was pretty sure what it was. "Mr. Morgan, I honestly can't tell you if her virtue was compromised, but I don't believe it was. I pray it wasn't."

"What makes you think it wasn't?"

"She told me he told her some of the things he planned to do to her, but I got there before he did any of it. She did say he hit her then and she passed out. Now, I realize he could have done harm to her while she was unconscious, but I don't believe he did because when I got there he was standing over her, and both of them were fully dressed. Her dress was ripped, but still on her and she was completely covered."

"Oh, thank God," Ben said. "I agree, that would seem to indicate you were able to stop him before he had a chance to do any of the awful things he'd planned. I can't thank you enough, Wyatt."

"You never have to thank me for helping her. I just hope she's okay, and I'm glad Ella is here for her. I'm sure she'll want to talk to a lady."

Ella helped Lizzie up the stairs and into her bedroom. "Let's get this dress off of you so I can see what all injuries you have and how bad they are."

"Ella, I know someone went to get Doc Avery, but please don't have him look at me. I'm not hurt bad, thanks to Wyatt, and I don't want him looking at my body like this. He'll want to look at Coy, but I don't need him to check me."

"I understand, honey, and that's why I want to look at them first. If they're not that bad I'll assure him I can treat them. I'm thinking the worst ones may be on your face, and he can look at those, but unless there are any that concern me, I'll tell him I can and will treat the rest."

"Thank you."

"Let's get your dress off and see what injuries you have." After a thorough check of her body, Ella spoke to her honestly. "Lizzie, there are three areas I have some concern about. I'd like him to look at them to be sure they're okay and to tell me how I should treat them. The rest just need cleaned up and bandaged, and I'll watch them to be sure they heal okay."

"What three areas do you want him to look at?" Lizzie asked nervously.

"Relax, honey. I want him to look at a couple of places on your face, and your ankle." She anticipated Lizzie's objection to her ankle, and held her still. "Listen to me, Lizzie. It's just your ankle, nothing above it, so I'll tell him he can keep your skirt in place and just look at the ankle. What happened to it?"

"He kept telling me what he was going to do and how much he was going to enjoy it, and I couldn't let that happen. I kept screaming, but he said he kind of liked watching me try to get away and screaming, and suggested I beg. Instead when he reached down to pull my dress up I kicked him. I'm pretty sure it hit him in the arm and it hurt, because he cursed at me. Then he grabbed my ankle and jerked it. It hurt, so I kicked him with my other foot and he dropped my ankle. But then he got really mad and pulled me up and hit me in the face. I must have blacked out then because I don't remember anything else until I heard Wyatt's voice. I opened my eyes, expecting to see that awful man over me yet, but he wasn't. Wyatt had him tied up and I was safe."

"I'm so glad Wyatt was close enough to hear you and help."

"Me, too. He saved me from him, and he might have saved my life."

"I don't even want to think about what could have happened," Ella said, giving Lizzie a hug. "I'm sorry, but I have to ask, if you blacked out some, is there a chance he could have done something horrible to you? Should we have the doctor check you?"

"No," she insisted quickly. "No, please don't. I'm sure he didn't do anything because I'm sore in a lot of places, but my private parts is not one of them. Besides, when I came to, Wyatt had him tied up and all of his clothes were on. Wyatt said when Coy saw him he got on his horse and tried to escape."

"How did Wyatt catch him?"

"With his lasso," Lizzie said with a little giggle. "I knew he was good with one, but wouldn't you have loved to watch that? He got the lasso around him and pulled him off his horse. He tried to fight Wyatt to get away, but Wyatt's getting to be pretty big and strong. I never noticed how broad his shoulders are, but --"

"Wyatt's grown into a formidable young man," Ella said with a grin, "and if my hunch is right, he cares a great deal about you. I'd say that gave him a little extra reason to make sure he didn't get away."

Lizzie looked at Ella, like a deer caught in the headlights.

"Do you mean he likes me like the good friends we've been since we were little?"

"I think he likes you as more than that."

"Why would you say that?"

"He's always been very protective of you, but lately he seems to be even more so. I've also seen the way he's looked at you a couple of times. He's a nice young man, but I've never seen him with a young lady at barn dances or church socials, other than you. If he wanted to court another young lady, I don't know of any father around here that wouldn't welcome that. Nor do I know of any young lady around who would turn him down. That tells me he's been waiting for you."

"So what do I do now?"

"Would you welcome him courting you?"

"Yes, very much," she said rather quietly as she felt her face blush. "When Papa said Coy wanted to court me I said no. I wanted to tell him I've been hoping Wyatt asks, but I didn't. I was afraid he still just thought of me as a friend and if he didn't want anything more, I didn't want to lose that friendship."

"Then my suggestion is just keep being his friend. If he's been waiting for you, you'll know it soon enough. For now, when the doctor gets here I'll tell him I'm comfortable treating everything, except I'd like him to look at your face and your ankle. Is that okay?"

"Thank you."

"Of course. Now, there are two men downstairs who are very worried about you. Would you rather get in bed and wait for the doctor or --"?

"No, I'm not sick, I don't need to get in bed. I want to assure Papa I'm okay, and I want to thank Wyatt again."

"Okay, let's go downstairs then so you can ease their worries. Let me help you down the steps so you're not putting too much weight on your ankle until the doctor looks at it."

"If it was broken I don't think I would be able to put weight on it, so I think it's just sore, but it makes sense to take it easy until he looks at it." Ella nodded and helped her hobble to the stairs, where they made their way down slowly and carefully.

They'd made it about halfway down the stairs when they saw Ben and Wyatt's heads turn toward them. Wyatt was instantly on his feet and up the steps. In one easy move he swooped Lizzie up into his arms and carried her downstairs and into the kitchen. Ben smiled and pulled a kitchen chair out. Wyatt set her carefully in the chair and sat down in the chair next to her. His eyes darted between Lizzie and Ella before settling on Lizzie. "Are you okay?"

"I'm fine, or I will be. I'm a little sore, but I'll be fine."

"From the looks of your face I'd say you're more than a little sore, my sweet daughter. I'm so sorry I didn't listen to you when you tried to tell me about that no-good man."

"Where is he now?" Ella asked.

"The men are keeping an eye on him at the barn. I'm sure they won't let him get away. We'll take him into the sheriff after the doc comes and checks on you."

"We may want to have him check on Coy, too," Wyatt said. "When I saw him standing over Lizzie sneering I was livid. I got my lasso out and once it was around him I pulled him off his horse pretty hard. Then when he tried fighting me to get loose I hit him hard enough that I'll admit my fist is a little sore."

"Good for you, son," Ben said.

Wyatt smiled at him, but was concerned when he saw Lizzie's face. "Are you okay? You look pale, Lizzie. Maybe you should lay down and rest until Doc Avery gets here. Would you like me to take you to the couch?"

"No, I'm okay," she said, looking at him. "It's just --" She paused and looked at her father. "Papa, do you really have to take him to the sheriff?"

"Of course I do. You don't want him getting away with this, do you? He needs to spend time in prison."

"But Papa, then everyone would know what he did. I would even have to testify in court, wouldn't I? That would be so embarrassing."

Ben, Wyatt and Ella exchanged looks with each other before looking at Lizzie.

CHAPTER 7

Ben reached over and patted Lizzie's arm, while Wyatt took her hand in his. "I hadn't thought of that," Ben admitted. "To be honest, I'm torn. I certainly don't want to embarrass you, but he needs to spend some time in prison. We can't just let him go. He won't work another day on my ranch, but I can't just let him walk away." He turned to look at all three of them. "Can I?"

"I don't want everyone to know what happened," Lizzie said. "Everyone would talk about me, and I wouldn't be able to hold my head up in town or at church, or anywhere I go."

"You have nothing to be ashamed of, Lizzie," Wyatt told her, squeezing her hand. "What happened was in no way your fault."

"It doesn't matter. You know how people talk," she said, looking down.

"Unfortunately, there is some truth in her words, and we all know it," Ella said. "We know it wasn't in any way her fault, and most people would probably realize that, too. But it won't keep them from talking."

"So what should I do?" Ben asked, looking at all of them.

"Lizzie, I certainly understand what you're saying, and I don't want to put you through anything else. But letting him walk away free is letting him get away with it, and he's free to go to another town or ranch and do the same thing."

"I'd hate to think of him hurting someone else," Wyatt said.

"Someone else might not be as lucky as me," Lizzie said, looking over at Wyatt.

They were quiet, each pondering the problem, when they heard a buggy coming up the lane. "That's probably Doc Avery," Ben said. "Maybe we can ask him about this situation. He may have some ideas about it."

"It certainly won't hurt to talk to him about it," Wyatt agreed. He went outside to meet Dr. Avery and take care of his horse for him, but Clem was already waiting for him, and ushered him into the house.

"Thank you for coming, Doctor," Wyatt said, as he met him on the porch. He opened the door for him, and the doctor hurried inside.

"I was told I was needed here, but I didn't hear why. Is someone hurt or sick?" As soon as he was inside he looked around, and his eyes stopped on Lizzie. "Good heavens, Miss Lizzie, what happened to you?"

"Coy Clemson, my foreman, did this, Doc," Ben said. "He'll no longer be working on this ranch, but he attacked her out in an open field. Luckily, Wyatt here heard her scream and got to him before he did any of the terrible things he planned on doing, but he did manage to cause some bruises."

"I'd say he did. Miss Lizzie, why don't we go somewhere private so I can check on you. I need you to be honest with me as to what all he's done so I can check you."

Ella spoke up, as she stood, and Lizzie's face blushed. She helped Lizzie stand, and they started toward the stairs. "Dr.

Avery, let's go to her bedroom. I'm sure she'll be more comfortable for you to check her there. When she came in her dress was pretty torn, so I helped her get undressed and checked her injuries. I can tell you I feel comfortable treating all of them with the exception of three that I would like you to look at."

Wyatt saw her limping and quickly went to her and swept her up into his arms. He carried her up the stairs and to the room they pointed at. Once he set her on her bed he took her hand in his and brought it to his mouth for a quick kiss. "When you're done, let me know and I'll take you back downstairs, unless you want to stay up here and rest a bit."

"Thank you, Wyatt, but I'm sure I'll be okay."

He nodded, then turned to Ella. "Let me know if you want my help."

"Thank you, Wyatt," she said with a smile. She closed the door behind him and turned back to Ella to help her lay back.

"Now, I'm sorry, but I have to ask some questions you may find embarrassing," Dr. Avery said, "but it's important you're honest with me."

"Doctor, I've talked to her in detail about what happened, and luckily, Wyatt got to her in time. Her virtue has not been compromised."

He turned to Lizzie. "Is that true?"

"Yes, sir. I was very lucky Wyatt heard me and was able to get to me quickly."

"And where is Coy now? I have a feeling if Wyatt caught him harming you, with an obvious intent of doing terrible things, Wyatt either chased him off, or did some damage of his own."

"He's out at the barn," Ella said. "Wyatt caught him and brought him back unconscious. The men are standing guard, making sure he can't do any more damage."

"Good for Wyatt," Doc said, rather surprising both ladies. "I suppose I should look in on him before I leave to be sure he's okay. Are they going to haul him into the sheriff?"

The ladies looked at each other before answering. "I'm trying to talk Papa out of it," Lizzie admitted.

"Talk him out of it?" Dr. Avery's eyebrows shot up, but after a moment, he nodded his head. "You don't want it getting around town and have people talking," he said more than asked.

"Exactly," Lizzie said.

"Ben's not too fond of that idea, but he doesn't want to put his daughter through anymore. We've been hoping you may have a little insight for us."

"I'll talk to Ben when I go downstairs, but I understand what you're saying. Right now, let me check these injuries. I assume these bruises on her face are some you want looked at, Miss Ella?"

"They are. There are a couple of bruises that look awfully sore on her face and one cut above her eyes. I got the bleeding stopped there, so I think it's okay, but you might want to check it to be sure you agree. I believe when he knocked her down it may have bruised a rib or two, but I don't believe they're broken. They'll be sore for a while, but I don't know of much that can be done for them. Then her ankle is pretty swollen. I'd like you to check that. I assume it's sprained, but not broken, since she can put weight on it, albeit it with pain. The rest are smaller and I'm sure I can watch those."

"Okay, let's have a look." Fifteen minutes later the doctor agreed with Ella's assessment of Lizzie's injuries. "Cool cloths on your bruises on your face this evening may help with the pain and keep them from bruising quite as bad. Your ribs will just take some time to heal. Ella has done a good job of getting a cloth wrapped around them, and that helps support them a little so it's not quite as sore when you move. Your ankle is going to be sore for a while. Stay off of it for a couple of weeks, then take it easy for another couple of or three weeks. Rest it as much as you can to let the swelling go down."

"Thank you, Doctor," Lizzie said as he was closing his doctor's bag. "I appreciate you coming out."

"Oh, you're certainly welcome. I hate to see you in pain like this. You take good care. If you decide not to go to the sheriff, you may want to stay home from town and church for a while so people don't see your bruises and ask questions. If you do that, tell them you're not feeling well or whatever you decide to say, rest assured I'll back up your story."

"Thank you, Doctor."

"Of course. I'm going to talk to Ben about this before I go see Coy. If you'd like to be there, as well, how about if I tell Wyatt he can come help you downstairs, and I'll wait until you two are there for us to discuss it."

"That sounds like a good idea, Doctor," Ella said. "While Wyatt comes up to get Lizzie, why don't I go down and get you some lunch. I know you don't always have time for meals, and I have some good rabbit stew that won't take but a minute to heat up."

"Ella, you know, I can never turn down your rabbit stew. Rabbit stew and biscuits is about the best meal I know of, and you and Miss Lizzie make the best I've tasted."

"Well, we made this stew together, and Lizzie made the biscuits. I'll heat some of them up for you, too."

"Thank you. I didn't get lunch today and I am a bit hungry." He turned back to Lizzie. "Let that young man help you around while he's here, Miss Lizzie, and I'll wait until you two are down there before talking to your father. I have a feeling Wyatt will want to take part in the discussion about what to do with Coy."

"I'm sure he will, too," Lizzie said with a shy smile. "Thank you again."

The doctor and Ella left, and Lizzie waited for Wyatt. Dr. Avery seemed to understand that Wyatt was more than a friend, too. She wondered how he and Ella seemed to know that, but she didn't. Oh, well, she hoped they were right, and he wanted to be more than good friends.

She didn't have long to wait until the man in her thoughts came bounding into the room. "Doc says you're going to be okay, which is wonderful. I understand you're to stay off your feet for a couple of weeks or so, though, so allow me to help you downstairs," he said with a smile. To her surprise, he leaned down and kissed her forehead before picking her up. She put her arms around his neck and as he turned them toward the door he said, "Before I leave I want to talk to you."

"Okay," she said hesitantly. "Is anything wrong?"

"No. In fact, as far as I'm concerned, something is very good. I hope you feel the same way."

Seeing the big smile on his face made her hopeful. Maybe Ella was right, and he had feelings for her. She hoped that's what had him in a good mood, although it could just be because Dr. Avery assured him she was okay. She would soon find out.

Wyatt carried her into the kitchen, where Dr. Avery was just digging into a bowl of rabbit stew and biscuits. He looked up at her as Wyatt carried her past him and set her down on a chair at the other end of the table. "Miss Lizzie, this is the best meal I've had in quite some time. If Miss Ella is the one who taught you how to cook, she did a fine job. Whatever young man is fortunate enough take you as his wife will be a lucky man." He looked over at Wyatt and smiled. She was happy to see him smiling back, and it made her more hopeful.

They made pleasant small talk while the doctor ate his fill of stew and biscuits. When he was finished he thanked the ladies for the fine meal, and looked to Ben. "I understand you're not sure what you want to do about Coy, and I understand why."

"I hate to see him walk away with no prison time, but I understand my daughter wanting to keep this quiet. Do you have any suggestions?"

"Well, first let me ask, how loyal are your men? The absolute worst thing that could happen would be for you to decide not to take him to the sheriff for your daughter's sake, then have one of the men talk about what happened and why Coy's not working on the ranch anymore. Sometimes men go into town on Saturday night, get a little drunk, and talk more than they should."

"I hadn't thought of that," Ben said, looking at the others. After a few thoughtful moments on his part he continued. "Frank came in a little bit ago to make sure Lizzie is okay. The men all care a great deal about her and were worried. I told them I would let them know, but she insists she's going to be fine, and thank goodness Wyatt got to her before he could do too much damage. I think they can all be trusted to keep it quiet if we tell them why we want it kept quiet."

"That's good. Let me share my thoughts on this subject, and you can do with it what you want. There aren't many trials in Gully Ridge, so when there is one a lot of people attend. That can't be stopped since all trials are public. So, with a trial, people will know and talk. Unfortunately, there aren't a lot of options. I have heard of a couple of times where the family told the attacker he was going to report it to the sheriff the next day. So if he didn't want to be arrested he best leave now and get out of the area and never come back. That usually gets him away, never to return for fear of being arrested. The bad part is it does let him get away with it."

"Hmm," Ben said. "As much as I hate the thought of letting him go without paying any kind of penalty, that does make sense. It would get him away from here, and if the sheriff knows about it, if he returns the sheriff could arrest him. Lizzie might still have to testify in court, but it would be talking about something that happened in the past. She would be older, quite possibly married then, and people wouldn't be as apt to talk about it because she wouldn't be a young, unmarried woman who could have lost her virtue."

"Exactly," Doc agreed. "But give it a little thought to be sure you can trust your men not to talk, because I'd hate to see you let him go, and then have one of the men open his mouth while he's drunk and say something. Then Coy got away with it for nothing, as Lizzie would still have to deal with the gossip. I wouldn't want that to happen."

"Nor would I," Ben agreed.

"I just want him far away from here," Lizzie said.

"I think we all do," Wyatt agreed. "If we do chase him off instead of taking him to the sheriff, I'm glad I at least knocked him out."

Ben grinned, but agreed. "I was thinking if he was knocked out, we don't really know for sure how he is, if he never actually got up and walked away. If we're lucky, maybe he got hurt when he was pulled from his horse. Now, that would be getting what he deserved."

"It would be indeed," Dr. Avery said. "I guess I better go out and check him now. Thank you again for a mighty good meal, and you all take good care of Miss Lizzie the next couple of weeks. I'll be back in a couple of weeks to make sure it's healed enough to put weight on it again. If you have any problems or questions, let me know and I'll come back sooner." When he got to the door he turned back to Ben. "When I check on him, I'll let you know if there's anything that would prevent him from riding out if that's what you decide to do."

"Thanks, Doc," Ben said.

After the doctor left, Ben looked around the table. "I think I know what Lizzie wants. You want me to send him on his way with a warning never to return; am I right?"

"Yes, Papa."

"And Ella, you agree with her?"

"For her sake, yes, I do."

"And Wyatt?"

"You're asking my opinion? I'm not family."

"You're the young man that saved her life, and I'll be forever thankful for that. And yes, I very much want to know what your opinion is."

Wyatt sighed, but took Lizzie's hand in his. "I don't want to see her go through any of what might happen if you turn him over to the sheriff, so for that reason that would be my desire, too. At the same time, I don't mind saying I hope he'll be sore for at least several days."

Lizzie chuckled and put her hand over his. "I rather like that possibility, too."

"I think we'd all like to see that," Ben said. "Well, I guess after Doc looks at him, as long as he's okay to ride out I'll tell him all the things I'd like to do to him, and assure him my men that he's been working with would be more than willing to help. Then I can tell him I won't hesitate to do any of it if I see him back in these parts again, and I'll make sure the sheriff knows what he did so he can arrest him on sight if he returns, then let him go yet tonight. I don't want to have to worry about him overnight, or ask my men to take turns watching him."

"I don't blame you for that. Do you think he'll go, or are you worried he'll double back and cause trouble?"

"Do you think maybe I should have a couple of men hang back, but follow him and make sure he leaves?"

"My only concern with that is if he should happen to see them, if it upset him he may be more inclined to turn around and return once the men quit following."

"Good point. We don't want that. I guess I'll just tell all the men to watch for him the next week or two, and let me know if anyone sees evidence of someone camping out anywhere. They can listen for any word around town of someone seeing him. I have to think, though, he's smart enough to take the opportunity to leave the area and not risk going to prison."

"I have to think he's a pretty smart man, or he wouldn't have been your foreman for this long," Wyatt said. "A smart man would leave while he can."

"I hope he is smart enough to leave and not come back," Lizzie said.

"Me, too," Wyatt said, turning to face Lizzie. "How are you feeling? Are you tired or sore and want to lay down, or do you feel up to a talk?"

"No, I'm okay. What do you want to talk about?"

"You two feel free to go to the living room to talk, or wherever you'd like to go," Ben said. "I'm going to go see what Doc says about Coy, and have a talk with him."

"I've got to get some supper on. Wyatt, why don't you stay and join us for supper?"

"Thank you for asking, Miss Ella, but I need to go home pretty soon. They're going to wonder where I am. I don't want them worrying about me."

"I understand. Please feel free to come back and join us after talking to them. You're always welcome at our table."

"Thank you for that, and I'll remember it. If you'll excuse

us, I think I'll take Lizzie in and get her comfortable on the couch, then we'll talk a little."

"Go ahead," Ella said. "Why don't I bring in a pitcher of lemonade and some glasses. You might like some while you talk. It's been a long day for both of you, I'm sure."

"That would be wonderful, Ella. Thank you." He carefully picked Lizzie up and carried her to the living room. He'd barely gotten her settled on the couch before Ella came in with the lemonade. "If you need anything else, just ask," she said as she left.

Once they were alone, Wyatt sat down on the couch next to Lizzie, and took her hand in his. He started rubbing his thumb over the back of her hand as he started the conversation. "Lizzie, I can't tell you how glad I am that you're okay. I also can't tell you how scared I was when I heard a scream, and I knew it was you. Or when I saw you laying on the ground hurt, with Coy standing over you. You see, Lizzie, over the last year my feelings for you have gradually been changing. Don't get me wrong, I still think of you as my best friend, but now I see you as more than that. I've been trying to wait, to give you a little more time since you're a few years younger than me, but after seeing you today, laying there hurt, I'm not sure I can wait any longer. I talked to your father while Dr. Avery was with you upstairs, and I asked him for permission to court you. He's given his blessing, if it's something you want."

"It is something I want," she said, meeting his eyes, "and not just because of what you did for me today. I missed you while your family was gone. I knew when you left I would miss you, but I didn't realize how much. When I talked with Papa about Coy and he didn't believe he was the threat I saw him as, it bothered me."

"Your father feels bad about that."

"I know, but he doesn't need to. I understand why he

didn't readily believe me. Coy has been his foreman and has done a good job for him. That's the part of Coy Papa always saw. That's not the side I saw, and Coy kept the side of him I saw hidden from Papa. But to get back to us, as soon as I talked to Papa and could see we didn't see things the same way, I knew I had to talk to you. I'm not sure why exactly, but in my heart I knew I had to talk to you about it, and I would feel better."

"Hearing that makes me feel honored."

"Well, it was true, and when I did talk to you, even though we didn't have much chance to actually talk about it, knowing you knew I had a problem and wanted your help, I felt better. I knew we would find a chance to talk. Instead, I truly believe you saved my life. But the point is, while I was waiting for you to get home so I could talk to you, I knew then that my feelings for you had grown to more than just my best friend. I've spent time thinking about that and wondering what to do about it."

"You have, really? I've thought about us a lot, especially while we were on our trip. I wanted more than just friendship from you, but I was afraid if I push you and you didn't feel the same way, I would lose the friendship we have, and that thought terrified me."

"It did me, too," she said with a bit of a smile. "Apparently we were having similar thoughts. I wanted more from our relationship, but I wasn't sure I was willing to risk losing what I have to get it."

"That was exactly my thinking." He paused several moments. "So, does this mean you're willing to allow me to court you?"

"I would like it a great deal."

"May I kiss you?"

"I think I would like that a great deal, as well," she said with a mischievous little grin.

He grinned back as he pulled her in against his chest for a quick hug, and his lips gently found hers. They lingered just a few seconds, but he was determined to be a gentleman, and reluctantly pulled back, even though he would have loved to extend the kiss much longer. She'd just been through a traumatic event, though, and he wasn't about to upset or worry her with a longer kiss than was acceptable for a first kiss, which he reminded himself this was. Even though they had been friends, very good friends for a long time, she had just agreed to court him, and they were already experiencing their first kiss. He would do well to give her time to absorb all that had happened, and everything they'd told each other, exposing their hearts to each other. They would have plenty of time for more kisses. In fact, he was hopeful they would have a whole lifetime.

CHAPTER 8

Ben left the house knowing Wyatt planned to talk to Lizzie about courting. He felt good about that. He'd known the Hamiltons and knew they were good people. More specifically, he'd known Wyatt since he was born and had watched him and Lizzie grow up together. There were several times he'd been glad the two of them had become such good friends. Since Lizzie was an only child, she didn't have any siblings to play with growing up. Wyatt filled that empty slot in her life nicely.

As they'd gotten older Ben had watched Wyatt become protective of his family, watching out for them. He was just as protective of Lizzie, which Ben was happy to see. It allowed him to feel comfortable with them being together as they got older and walked to school together or went riding. He knew Wyatt would watch out for his little girl.

He was extremely glad that Wyatt was in the area and able to watch out and protect her today. With that thought, his mind went back to the reason he was heading to the barn. He had to deal with Coy. He still couldn't believe he'd been so wrong about his foreman. He felt bad about it, but looking back wouldn't do him any good. He needed to send Coy on his way, and make sure he knew better than to return.

He reached the barn just as Dr. Avery was leaving. "How is he, Doc?"

"He's sore and he's not at all happy, but he'll be okay."

"If he's not happy now he won't want to hear the chewing out I'm about to give him, right before I boot him off my ranch." Dr. Avery chuckled and wished him luck before climbing into his buggy to leave.

Ben walked into the barn and heard what sounded to be all his men. He stayed where he was, in the shadows and out of sight while he listened. He had to smile as he heard the men, who all technically still worked under him, telling Coy exactly what they thought of him treating Miss Lizzie that way. They couldn't understand how he could do something so disgusting to a young lady who was nothing but kind to people and animals.

He came out of the shadows and walked on into the barn and saw Coy. His arms were tied behind his back and his legs were tied to the chair he was sitting on. He was surrounded by his men. When the men looked up and saw him, they acknowledged him and moved to the side so Ben could see Coy, but they didn't leave the area. It was obvious he wasn't going anywhere and they weren't going to leave him alone with Ben. They were staying to be sure he didn't hurt anyone else.

Before he addressed his foreman, Frank asked, "Ben, we've all been worried something terrible about Miss Lizzie. Doc told us she'll be okay, but he wouldn't say any more than that. He said anything more than that would have to come from her or you. Is she okay, really okay?"

"She will be, yes," Ben said. "She has some bruises on her face, some cracked ribs, and an injury to her ankle. She has to stay off her ankle for a couple of weeks or so, but yes, she should heal okay. It will take some time and she's sore, but --"

Ben was shocked when Clem, who was probably the quietest of the hands working for him, muttered, "You son of a bitch," and his fist slammed into Coy's face.

His hand came back to hit him again, but when Ben yelled, "Clem, no," several of the others grabbed him and held him.

"Clem, there ain't a one of us here that wouldn't like to do the same thing to him for what he done to our Lizzie, but wait and hear Ben out first," Frank said. "We don't want anyone getting into trouble but him when we drag his sorry ass into the sheriff."

"Well said, Frank," Ben said. "I'd like to do a hell of a lot more than that, but you're right, he's not worth any of us getting in trouble." He turned then to look at Coy, who was looking at the floor. "Coy, I can't begin to tell you how disappointed I am. I just can't believe you did that. But you did, so now I have to deal with it. You deserve to spend a long time in prison, and there's nothing I'd like to see more. However, I'm not taking you in to see the sheriff, unless you give me no other choice."

It got extremely quiet in the barn and everyone turned to stare at him. "You aren't?" Frank asked, speaking the question on all their minds.

"No, I'm not. This was a tough decision for me to make, but Lizzie asked me not to. She doesn't want the whole town talking about it, and after thinking about it, she's right. This was not in any way her fault, but she's suffering enough. She shouldn't have to worry about everyone talking about her and the awful thing that happened. You know how gossip spreads. She doesn't need that."

"No, she doesn't," Bill agreed, "and I want us to do everything we can to help and support her. But what about this no good piece of scum? You aren't going to just let him go, are you, scot free?"

"Here's what I plan on doing, and Coy, you listen up good. We're going to let you go, and I want you to get the hell out of here. You leave the area and don't ever come back. I'm going to tell the sheriff what happened, let him see Lizzie and get a statement. He'll make out a report and share it with all the sheriffs in the surrounding towns. If you ever show up in Gully Ridge or anywhere around these parts again you'll be arrested on sight."

Coy had a leery look on his face. "So I'm free to go?"

"As long as you go, and go far away. All the sheriffs around here will have a report and description of you, and if you ever come back you'll be arrested. If you have any sense at all you'll take this opportunity to stay out of prison."

"Let me saddle up my horse and an extra pack horse, grab some supplies, and I'll be off first thing in the morning," he said.

"You'll saddle your horse and only your horse and get out now," Ben said, raising his voice. "You're not taking any of my horses or our supplies, and if you're not gone in twenty minutes I'll change my mind and haul you in to see the sheriff."

"But it's dark out now. How am I going to see any predators out there, and what am I going to eat?"

"You'll eat whatever you catch or kill. You have a rifle. I don't care what you eat or how you stay safe, and I don't much care. But if you want to go, you do it now, and you don't stop until you're out of Nebraska. Go ahead and untie him, boys, and let him go. I want him off my land."

A couple of the men cut the rope holding him to the chair and he hurried toward the stall holding his horse. After he was out of hearing range Ben looked at Frank and spoke softly. "I'd like a couple of you men to follow him to make sure he leaves. Wait until after he leaves to saddle up, and stay back so he can't see you, but make sure he leaves. If he goes to Gully Ridge make sure he goes on through. I don't want him hanging around for a day or two and causing trouble."

"We'll do that," Frank assured him. "How long do you want us to follow him?"

"You don't have to follow him far, just enough to make sure he's leaving, and not just going a little ways and stopping. If he goes toward Gully Ridge, make sure he goes beyond it. Then come on back. Make sure he doesn't see you. I just want to make sure he's gone."

"Will do," Frank said. "Clem, you're the best tracker I know, and you know how to make sure he doesn't see or hear us. You want to go with me?"

"I'll be happy to, and Ben, I think that's a good call. We'll make sure he's out of the area, then come back."

"Thank you," Ben said, taking one more look at Coy, who was managing to get his horse saddled, even though he was obviously sore. He shook his head and left the barn.

As he left he saw Wyatt on his horse, turning toward the lane. Wyatt saw him and walked Chestnut over to him. "I'm going home to let my family know I'm okay and where I've been."

"Good idea. Thank you again for all you've done, Wyatt. Did you talk to Lizzie about what we talked about earlier?"

"I did," he said with a big smile, "and she's amenable to courting. If it's okay with you I'd like to stop in at least for a few minutes daily while she's healing."

"Of course it's okay with me. Son, please feel free to stop in anytime you want. You're welcome to eat supper with us any day you're free. I'm a little afraid when this all hits her she's going to have a rough time with it. I'm sure she'd appreciate seeing you. She often confides in you, and she may have some feelings or fears she'd be willing to share with you."

"I'm willing to listen to her anytime, and I'll encourage it, especially if I feel she's keeping something inside her."

"I appreciate that. She does keep things buried inside her at times. If you know of anything Ella or I can do to help her, please let us know."

"I will, and thank you for the invitation. Maybe I will have supper here some night."

"Ella always makes more than we ever need, so feel free to eat with us every night for a while. She's got some healing to do, whether she likes it or not."

"Yes, she does, and I'm betting she won't like it," Wyatt said with a chuckle. "Have a good evening."

"Same to you," Ben said with a laugh of his own. He was glad Lizzie had agreed to court Wyatt, and hoped that might help keep her spirits up over the next couple of weeks. Staying off her ankle was going to be difficult for her. Hopefully it would help knowing that once her ankle was healed she would again be free to go out to the barn and work with the horses without having to worry about Coy.

~

BEN THOUGHT a great deal that night about talking to the sheriff the next day. He talked to Frank and Clem the next morning, and was told they had followed Coy long enough to see he was indeed heading away from the ranch. He didn't head toward Gully Ridge, but in the general direction of Silver Creek, the next closest town. They assumed he would camp somewhere in that vicinity that night and get supplies from the town the next morning, before moving on.

With that information, Ben decided not to make a trip to town to talk to the sheriff the next day. He knew there were a couple of new young sheriffs around that were eager to prove they could do the job as sheriff. After thinking about it, he was afraid one of them may get the telegram from Sheriff Williams and go out actively hunting for Coy right away. Sending him off in the middle of the night like that, he hadn't had a chance to think before he left. Ben was afraid he might go a little ways off, a couple of, three little towns over, and take a couple of days to think about what he might want to do.

It would be terrible for him to decide to do that, possibly camp out somewhere for a few days while he decided where he wanted to go, and have one of the young, overzealous sheriffs go out searching and come upon him. He'd arrest him and Coy would be returned to Gully Ridge for a trial. Ben certainly didn't want that. As long as he was away from Gully Ridge and his ranch, he didn't care if he took a few days to make plans. He could take a train back east somewhere for all Ben cared.

He decided to give Coy a couple of weeks to get completely out of the area. Then he would talk to the sheriff. If the sheriff wanted someone that could back up his story, he could talk to Lizzie, Wyatt, Ella, any of his men, or Doc Avery. In the meantime, just to be safe, he asked all his men to watch for any signs that he may circle back and show up on the ranch again.

~

THE FIRST SEVERAL days after the horrific incident were not easy for Lizzie, but she tried to stay busy. She and Ella came up with a way she could lean against Ella on one side and use the wall for support on the other to get from the kitchen table to the sofa. Once she was settled Ella gave her things she could do to help. She spent most of her time working on something at the table, and she and Ella talked while Ella did the cooking. Wyatt stopped in daily to check on her recovery and visit. He ate supper with them a couple of days, which pleased everyone.

The next few days were more challenging for everyone. Her ankle was feeling better, and keeping her off of it proved to be difficult. She woke up a little earlier than normal one day, and rather than wait for Ella to get there to help her get dressed, she hobbled around, holding onto furniture as she went, and got herself dressed. She made it to the stairs holding onto the wall and hopping on one foot, then sat down and slid down the steps one at a time.

When she stood and started maneuvering her way to the kitchen Ella heard something and went to see what it was. "My goodness, Lizzie, what on earth are you doing? Here, let me help. Lean on me now, like we usually do." She helped her to the table, and once she sat down she looked down at her. "Why didn't you wait for me to help? We certainly don't want you to hurt your ankle worse. It will be that much longer before you can walk on it again."

"But Ella, it feels much better now. I don't see why I can't put a little weight on it. I'll take it easy, but I don't think putting a little weight on it will hurt a thing."

"Lizzie, I know you're eager to be up and around, especially to get back out to see your colts, but I think you need to listen to the doctor. He said he would be back out in a couple of weeks to check on it, and you can ask him about it then. But until then, you don't want to risk hurting it again and making it that much longer you'll have to stay off of it, do you?"

"But it feels fine, and you don't know how boring it is."

"I know, and I'll try to spend more time with you today. In the meantime, I have to finish breakfast. If I get you the eggs will you please break them in a bowl and scramble them so I can cook them as soon as this bacon's done?"

"Yes, of course," she said, still pouting a little.

Ella had just finished breakfast when Ben came in. He leaned down and kissed his daughter on her forehead. "How are you feeling this morning, Lizzie?"

"I feel fine," she said a bit harsher than she meant, which drew a look from her father.

"You don't sound fine. What's going on?"

She sighed as she said, "Sorry. I'm feeling better this morning."

Ella set the rest of breakfast on the table and sat down to eat with them. She did that occasionally, especially when there was something she wanted to talk to Ben or both of them about. He noticed it, and as soon as he had filled his plate and taken his first bite he looked at her. "I assume something is on your mind, Ella. Does it have anything to do with my daughter's mood this morning?"

"Yes, it does," she said with a smile. She looked at Lizzie almost apologetically before looking back to Ben. "Lizzie came downstairs by herself this morning." When Lizzie looked at her with a frown on her face, she explained, "I'm not saying that to get you in trouble, Lizzie, but to try to explain the situation to your Papa. I understand how you feel, and I'm hoping he may have a solution."

"What situation is that?" Ben asked, looking between the two.

Ella looked over at Lizzie and nodded, encouraging her to talk to her father. She squared her shoulders and did just that. "Papa, I feel much better, and I'm so tired of staying in here and not doing anything. Can't I carefully make my way out to the barn and sit with the small horses? Not only would it give me something to do, but if I'm not out with them for two or three weeks I'll have to start all over with my training because they won't remember me and what they've learned so far. I'll be careful, I promise."

"No," he said firmly.

"That's it; just a flat no?"

He gentled his voice as he patted her hand. "Lizzie, I understand you're eager to get back out there, but even though I'm not a doctor, I know that's a bad idea. If you think about it, you'll admit it, as well. I know how much you like spending time with the foals and colts, and I also know how good you are at working with them. But you have to admit they can be unpredictable. If one of them gets a little antsy you have to be able to step out of the way quickly, or you're apt to get stepped on."

"But I'll be careful to stay out of their way."

"The only way you can do that is if you're standing and able to move quickly, which right now you aren't," he said rather firmly. "Look, I'm glad you're feeling better and I understand you want to get outside again. I know you and your love of outdoors and the animals. I just don't think it's safe for you to be with the horses again. Since you're feeling better why don't you let Ella or me help you outside to the porch swing. I know you enjoy reading, so maybe you would enjoy reading out in the fresh air."

Lizzie's shoulder slumped. "I'll try that, Papa. I really feel I can get up and do a little something, though. I'm not asking to go back to my normal routine, but I really would like to be able to do a few things, like helping Ella out if I can't go out to the barn yet." An idea came to her mind and she looked at him with a hopeful expression. "Or maybe someone could help me out to the barn with a book and I could just watch the foals and colts and talk to them some and read some out there. At least they would be used to seeing me and hearing my voice."

Ben looked almost defeated as he shook his head. "I'm sorry, honey, but not yet. It would be very difficult for you to sit there and see them, talk to them, but not get up and go to them when they came to the aisle. I'm afraid you would be tempted to stand up and hobble over to pet them. But I'm also afraid of what would happen if you didn't."

"What do you mean?"

"You're training them to come to you. It would send a mixed message for them to see you and go to you, without getting the encouragement or treat they're used to getting."

She sank back in her chair as she realized he was right. "So how much longer do I have to wait?"

"Doc said he would be out here to check on you in a couple of weeks, and that's only a few more days. After he looks at your ankle he'll tell us if he thinks you're ready to put any weight on it yet."

"So I have to wait three more days yet?" She sat back, obviously upset.

"I'm sorry, Lizzie, but you heard what Doc said; stay off of it completely for two weeks, and then he would check and see if it was healed enough to start putting a little weight on it. We have to go by what he says."

She nodded and took a bite of scrambled eggs. He knew she wasn't happy, but there wasn't anything else he could do. She would just have to wait.

WYATT ARRIVED that evening to find Lizzie sitting outside on the swing. He slid down from Chestnut and tied her up as he greeted her. "Good evening, my lovely Lizzie."

"Hi, Wyatt."

He finished and looked up at her. "Did something happen, or are you feeling worse today?"

"No, I'm okay. Why?"

"You sound upset. Are you sure you're okay?" He climbed the porch steps two at a time and put his hand to her forehead.

"I'm not sick, really. I'm just tired of sitting and not doing anything."

"Ah, so you're pouting," he said very conversationally.

"I'm not pouting," she insisted.

"Yes, you are," he said casually, "but I'm not too surprised. I know how much you like being up and about, especially at the barn, so I knew it was going to be difficult for you to stay down, especially once you started feeling better. Can I assume by your mood that you are indeed feeling better today?"

"Yes, I am," she said, still pouting, though this time she was more upset by his easy acceptance of the situation, or even expectation of her mood.

"I'm glad," he said as he leaned down and gave her a kiss on her cheek before sitting down in the swing next to her. He picked up her hand and held it. "Lizzie, I know this is hard for you, but I am glad to hear you're feeling better. Doc said he'd come check on you in another three or four days. I hope he says your ankle has healed enough for you to start putting some weight on it."

"I feel sure he will. It feels so much better."

"I'm glad to hear that, but we'll have to wait and hear him out. If he says it's not ready for any weight bearing yet, you'll have to wait a while longer."

"No." His head snapped up to look at her, and she was surprised with the look she saw on his face. She immediately backed off a bit. "I mean, I don't think he will. He better not."

The look she wasn't familiar with was still on his face as

he turned toward her. "I hope he doesn't, either, but the fact still remains, what he says goes."

Lizzie was momentarily speechless. She'd only ever seen that look on his face one other time, and that had been several years ago. In a flash the memory returned and an involuntary shiver made its way up her back. It had been an extremely hot summer, and she had told her father she was going to ride to the swimming hole they occasionally visited on hot days, and cool off. He had told her he didn't have time to go along with her today, and she was not to go there alone, or to any other water that was more than knee deep. She'd insisted she knew how to swim and would be fine, but he told her he was serious, and she was not to go swimming alone.

She saw Wyatt later that morning and complained to him about what her father had said, but he had agreed with her father. He explained why he felt it wasn't safe, and even told her he and his three older brothers were not allowed to swim alone. They had to have at least two of them before they could jump in the water, and he pointed out to her that they were older and had been swimming longer. She pouted and told him she thought they were both a couple of worrywarts.

The next day was even hotter, and her father again said he didn't have time to take her that day, but he would take her on Sunday afternoon if it was still so hot. Upset, later that afternoon she took her pony and went swimming on her own. While she was there, Wyatt and his brother, Grant showed up at her house, planning to take her swimming. Ella told Wyatt she'd taken her pony out for a ride, hoping it would cool her off. They decided to go out looking for her, and found her in swimming, alone.

Turning and see them sitting on their horses watching her shocked her and she froze. Before she could register what was happening she was going underwater, and was so scared when she resurfaced that she wasn't thinking straight and panicked. She started flailing her arms, and before she could grasp what was happening Wyatt dove in the water and was pulling her up to the surface. With his arm around her he told her to relax, that he had her. He pulled both of them to shore, where Grant helped him get her on land. He thanked Grant for his help and assured him he would take care of her and get her back home. Grant nodded and left.

Lizzie was still catching her breath when he helped her up and helped her walk with him over to a fallen log, where he sat down. She started to sit beside him, but he'd stopped her. Instead, she'd found herself face down over his lap. While she struggled to get up he lectured her on not only the danger of swimming alone, but also about ignoring her father, and him. When he finished his lecture he spanked her. She kicked and fought, to no avail. She told him she was going to tell her father what he did, and he said he was okay with that.

He didn't stop the spanking until she'd been crying. When he was finished he pulled her up and sat her on his lap and handed her his handkerchief. He then explained that if she wanted to tell her father what he'd done, he was fine with it. He'd even told her if her father would have done that once in a while as she was growing up instead of spoiling his only little girl, she wouldn't have gone against his orders in the first place. He also asked what she thought her father would say when he found out she'd ignored him and gone swimming alone. They talked then, and in the end she never mentioned it to her father.

Now, as he looked at her, that memory was crystal clear in her mind, and she had to do something to get rid of that look. "Okay, okay, but I still think he'll say it's fine."

With that look still in place, he nodded. "And if he says it's not ready for you to put weight on it?"

"Then I guess I won't," she said quietly.

"That's my girl," he said as a big smile replaced that scary look. She definitely wanted to keep that smile in place. She hoped Dr. Avery gave her the okay to walk again, because even as she told Wyatt that, she had doubts in her mind. Surely she could figure something out.

CHAPTER 9

Wyatt stayed and had supper with them, hoping he could help cheer her up a bit. Instead, he became more concerned about her staying off her ankle. Now that Coy was gone Ben had no foreman. During meals he and Lizzie now talked about the ranch, and what got accomplished that day as well as what needs to get done yet. It was clear to him that once Lizzie was able to be on her feet again the two of them would be running the ranch together until he found a foreman. That made sense since Wyatt knew that although Lizzie may be a female, and not a large one at that, she knew how a ranch should be run and was quite capable of doing what needed to be done.

During their talk it was clear to Wyatt that Ben was struggling, trying to do what he normally did as the owner, as well as acting as foreman, and Lizzie knew it. "Papa, I can help with some of that," she said at one point. "If someone helps me out to the barn there are things I can do without having to move around too much. I'll be fine."

Before Ben could respond, Wyatt beat him to it. "No,

Lizzie, you can't, or at least not safely. We talked about that out on the porch swing just a little bit ago. If you're working with animals you have to be able to move out of their way quickly if they get riled, and you can't do that yet."

Lizzie gave Wyatt an annoyed look and turned to her father. "Papa, my ankle has had over a week to heal and it's feeling fine now. I'll be okay. You need help doing everything that needs to be done, and I can help."

"Ben, how about any of the other men working for you? Would any of them be a good foreman, at least until you find another one to hire?"

"Unfortunately, not really," Ben said. "Clem is older and has made it clear several times he's not interested in being foreman. Frank and Bill are good workers, but they're young, and this is their first experience working on a ranch. They're catching on quickly, but not ready to be foreman. Walter and Leo are the two young brothers, fourteen and sixteen, that lost their parents. They died of influenza within a week of each other, and the boys didn't have anywhere to go. They lived in town in a rather small house. The boys tried getting jobs in town, but there isn't much around. I heard about them and offered to teach them ranching, if they're willing to learn it. In the meantime at least they have a place to stay and three meals a day."

"Definitely not foreman material," Wyatt said. "That was nice of you to hire them on."

"They're good workers. Ranching isn't coming natural to them, but they're sure not afraid to get in there and pull their weight. They're slowly catching onto it. But for now, you're right, they're a long way from being a foreman. In fact, the foreman has to spend a little more time with them teaching them what they need to know."

"Which takes extra time that you don't have right now,"

Wyatt said, thinking out loud. "We're not that busy right now on our ranch. Let me talk to Pa to be sure, but I'm pretty sure he'll say it's okay for me to come over and give you a hand now and then. Let me know if you're going to be doing something you could use an extra hand for, and I'll come help you out, at least until Lizzie is given a clean bill of health from Doc."

"I appreciate that offer, Wyatt. Maybe I'll stop over and talk to your father tomorrow. I could use the help, but I want to be sure it won't cause a problem on your ranch."

"I understand. I'll talk to him tonight so he'll know you're stopping by."

"I appreciate that," Ben said.

They finished their meal, and Lizzie said she wanted to go back to the porch for a bit. When she stood and asked Wyatt to help support her so she could hop out there, he reached down and lifted her up into his arms. "Ben, I apologize if you're not comfortable with this, but I hate seeing her struggle when I know I can make it much easier for her to get out there."

"No apology necessary, son," Ben said with a laugh. "I've considered doing that myself, but I wasn't sure she'd want her dad to carry her. I'd say you're a different story."

"Papa," Lizzie scolded as Wyatt set her down in front of the porch swing. She did notice Wyatt smiling, however, and when he winked at her she felt better. He helped her settle onto the swing, then sat down next to her.

"I'll leave you young ones out here to talk and visit a bit, and I'm going on to bed. I hope to see you tomorrow for supper, Wyatt."

"Thank you, Mr. Morgtan."

"Please feel free to call me Ben."

Wyatt nodded in appreciation. Once Ben was inside Lizzie leaned her head against his shoulder. "That was nice of you to volunteer to help Papa if you can until I'm back out there again."

"I'm glad to help, however long it is until you're back to full health again."

"I should be ready to go back out and start helping in a couple of days. I may have to take it easy for the first few days, but at least I'll be able to help."

Wyatt had been pushing the swing with his foot, but he stopped it and turned to look at her. "Lizzie, do we need to talk about this more? You are going to follow Doc's orders. If he says you're ready to start putting a little weight on your foot, gradually, that's what you'll do. But it will be gradually like he says. And if he says it needs a few more days yet, you'll stay off of it for a few more days."

"But Wyatt --"

Even as it was getting darker in the evening she could see that look on his face again. "I know, I'm going to talk to Dr. Avery and make sure he knows it's feeling fine now."

"No, Lizzie, that's not how it's going to work." His stern voice was new to her and a little scary. He'd always been protective of her, but she couldn't remember him being this intent before. His voice gentled as he took her hand in his. "Lizzie, as you know, honesty is very important to me, so I'm going to be totally honest with you."

"Okay."

"I care a great deal about you, and I have for a while now. I'm very glad you've agreed to courting because that means you have similar feelings for me. But the total truth is that I hope you will soon agree to become my wife. If that happens, you should know that as my wife I will do everything I can to protect you and keep you safe and happy. That means things like listening to what Doc says. If he says you're not ready to go back to working with the horses yet, but I listen to you telling me you are, how would I feel if a horse stepped on your foot and injured it further?"

"But that won't happen," she argued.

"You can't say that. You don't know what's going to happen, or when a horse is going to take a step back. If your ankle isn't completely healed and you can't get out of his way quickly enough, yes, it will step on your foot. And although I know your ankle is the main injury, I also know your foot is bruised, as well. So there will be no arguing with what Doc says. He's the doctor, not you or me, so what he says is what we will do."

"But Wyatt --"

"Lizzie, you may as well know another thing, as well. I know your father never spanked you. I think that was a mistake on his part, but at the same time, I understand it. It would be very difficult for a man to raise a daughter on his own, with a ranch to run. But he did it, and he did a good job. But by never spanking you when you needed it growing up, you never learned to listen, to him or anyone else, like Doc."

"I do listen," she argued.

"If it's convenient, yes, but if one of them says something you don't like, you set out to change their mind. Well, that won't work with me. If Doc says you're not yet ready to get back out there and do what you did before, we'll wait until he does say that. If I tell you not to go swimming alone because it's not safe, I mean that and I expect you to listen. If it takes a spanking or two to make you see I'm serious about that, so be it."

She gasped. "But I'm an adult now, Wyatt."

"And as an adult I'm assuming you can understand why I feel it's so important to listen to people who know what they're talking about and are trying to keep you healthy, like Dr. Avery. If not, I imagine a spanking or two will change your outlook on that."

"But I don't want to be spanked," she said, sounding like a much younger child, even to her own ears, which made her scowl.

"I don't imagine anyone does," he said with a little chuckle. "I didn't when I was younger, but it taught me a lot. One of those things is why you need to listen to people telling you things to keep you safe. It also taught me how much Ma and Pa loved me."

She looked at him with her eyebrows scrunched together and a frown on her face. "You knew they loved you because they beat you?"

"They didn't beat me, Lizzie, they spanked me. Yes, it hurt, but not for long. It was a temporary hurt, while what they were teaching me with the spanking may well have kept me from experiencing a more serious hurt that may not have been temporary. I also learned that Pa loved me enough to correct me."

"But I'm an adult now and I don't want spanked."

"But now you know what to do to avoid it. Just listen to me when I'm trying to protect you." He brought her hand to his lips for a soft kiss. "My precious Lizzie, remember, I wouldn't even consider doing that if I didn't care so much about you and it wasn't so important to me to keep you safe."

His last comment caught her off guard, and she had no argument. How could she be upset about him caring about her and protecting her? That thought sent a tingle through her body, and she had to admit it felt nice knowing he was watching out for her. She would think more about that later, but for right now, she simply nodded and leaned back against his shoulder. It felt good, and even better when she felt his arm go around her shoulder.

They sat in very companionable silence for several minutes. After visiting a little longer, Wyatt sat up straighter.

"I better get home, Lizzie. Promise me you'll stay off your ankle tomorrow, please."

She was about to hedge, saying she knew what they'd talked about, but seeing his stern expression again made her rethink that. "Okay," she whispered.

"Good. That makes me feel better, knowing you'll be safe. Now, why don't I carry you to the outhouse, and then back into the house?" When she nodded he easily picked her up and did just that. Instead of setting her down in the house, though, he found Ella. "Miss Ella, if it's all right with you I thought I'd take her up to her bedroom so you two don't have to struggle to get her up the stairs without putting any weight on her ankle. Would you mind following us up?"

"Of course not," she said easily. "Thank you, Wyatt, that is helpful. The stairs are a challenge."

"I can imagine," he said, turning and starting up the stairs. She hurried ahead of him when they reached the top of the steps so she could open her bedroom door. "If you'll put her down by her bed, I'll help her change."

"Thank you." He gently set her down by the bed, and gave her a quick kiss on her cheek. "Good-night, Lizzie. I'll be by to see you sometime tomorrow."

"Good-night, Wyatt," she said with a smile.

He left, and they heard him going down the stairs, and the door open and close. "Wyatt has turned into a good young man and he cares a lot about you, Lizzie. You're a lucky young lady."

"I certainly am," she agreed.

~

WYATT'S TALK with Lizzie helped, and the next day she stayed off her ankle. She waited for Ella to help her get dressed and down the stairs the next morning, and spent much of her day helping her do things she could do while sitting at the table. Ella took a couple of breaks to sit with her and have tea and cookies, as well. She could tell Lizzie was smitten with Wyatt, and no longer saw him as the good friend he was growing up. She felt good about that, thinking it was time Lizzie found a good man and got married, and she didn't know of any better man for her than Wyatt.

He had supper with them again that evening, and after the meal he carried her out to the porch swing again. "I'm proud of you for staying off your ankle," he said as he squeezed her hand he was holding in his.

"I thought about what you said last night. I know you're just looking out for me, and I appreciate that."

"I'm glad you see that. Doc said unless he's needed elsewhere and can't make it over he'll be by tomorrow and check on it. We're all hoping he says you can start putting some weight on it again."

"I feel confident he'll say it's okay to walk again. It's not sore any more. I sure hope he can make it tomorrow. It'll be awfully hard if I have to wait an extra day."

"I hope that doesn't happen. I'll be over tomorrow to see what he says." He changed the subject and they visited another half an hour before he once again carried her inside, where Ella was ready to go upstairs with them and help her get ready for bed. After setting her down gently, he leaned down to kiss her cheek. "Sleep well, my sweet Lizzie," he said softly before turning, leaving her with

Ella, who was smiling at the two young people.

The next day Lizzie again waited for Ella to help her. She sat at the kitchen table by the window so she would be able to see Dr. Avery when he arrived. It was afternoon and she was beginning to worry he wouldn't make it, when she saw him coming up the lane. Ella greeted him at the door.

"Someone is sure anxious to see you," she said with a grin and a look toward Lizzie.

"That must mean the ankle is feeling better," he said with a grin, looking from Ella to Lizzie.

"It is," Lizzie assured him. "It doesn't hurt at all any longer, and the swelling is down."

"Good to hear that. Let's have a look at it."

"Did you want me to help her upstairs to her bedroom, Doctor?" Ella asked.

"I don't think we'll need to do that. I should be able to check it right here, if that's okay with you, Miss Lizzie?"

"Of course," she assured him.

"I'll go out and get some laundry off the line while you do that, Doctor. It'll give you a little more privacy. If you need me for anything, I'll be right outside the back door. When you're done, I have some chicken and dumplings heating on the stove. Ben is busy checking on some cattle today, but he left money in here to pay you, so I'll do that when I dip you up a good hot meal."

"Miss Ella, you're going to spoil me with your thoughtfulness and good cooking. Thank you."

"Thank you for coming out to check on her again."

She went outside and Dr. Avery knelt down next to Lizzie. He felt all around her ankle, watching her face for any reaction. He saw her wince a couple of times, but she quickly recovered, smiling again. "Does this hurt any?" He pushed on a couple of spots and again saw her wince, but she shook her head.

"No," she said, "it feels fine."

He furrowed his eyes and cocked his head to the side a bit as he met her eyes. "Miss Lizzie, I need an honest answer to my questions."

"It doesn't hurt."

He held his hand up to stop her. "Now, I know that's not

quite the honest truth. You have a bruise there, and it will always hurt some when you push on a bruise. It's very important that I know what does and doesn't hurt, and how much, but I had a sneaking suspicion you're telling me nothing hurts so I'll say you can walk on your ankle again. That's why I pushed on the bruise and asked if it hurt; so I could judge how honest you're being with my questions."

She looked down at her lap and quietly said, "Oh."

"The fact that you have a bruise and a little pain doesn't in and of itself mean you can't put some weight on it, but I do need to know where it hurts and how much."

"Okay, Doctor. I'm sorry."

"It's okay, I understand why you did it. Let's try this again, and this time please tell me what does and doesn't hurt, okay?"

"Okay."

"Good," he said, patting her hand to let her know he wasn't angry.

He pushed on a couple of spots around the ankle and got no response. He pushed a little on a different bruise and she winced again. This time she also said, "That hurt a little."

He felt relieved, knowing she'd admitted it this time. "Okay, thank you for being honest. How about this?" He pressed a few more places, watching her expression each time.

There was one area that still had some swelling in it, and he'd saved that area for last. When he moved his hand to that general region, she winced and said, "Yes, that hurts some, as well."

He was surprised, since he'd barely touched it yet, but was careful not to let his facial expression show that. Instead he said, "Okay, how about here?"

He touched a portion of her ankle that was outside of but near the swollen area, assuming she would be okay there, but she again winced. "That area is sensitive, too, but it's not horrible."

That alarmed him, so he had to check it out more. "Okay, I'm sorry, but I have to press on another area that may be a little sore, and I need you to tell me if it is in fact still sore, and how sore it is, if it's as sore as that spot. I'm sorry, but I have to make sure this last spot is healing all right."

"It's okay, I understand."

He pressed another spot and could easily see her fists clench in her lap. "That hurt a little more, Doctor, but not enough that I feel I need to stay off of it. When this first happened that part was terribly sore."

"That's the part that hit him when you kicked, isn't it?"

"Yes, it is. That part of my ankle hit his arm. At the time it hurt so bad I was afraid I might have broken it, but I could tell within a day or two that it wasn't because it quit hurting near as bad. It's a lot better than it was. Now it doesn't hurt at all unless you press on it. That means it's healing, right?"

"Yes, it does, and I can tell it's healing. The swelling is way down from what it was and the color of the bruising tells me it's healing."

"Good. I'm so glad to hear that," Lizzie said with a smile.

That smile gradually left, though, as he kept talking. "It's healing, but I can tell it was a bad bruise. There's still a little swelling, and it's pretty tender yet. I'm sorry, Miss Lizzie, but I don't think it's healed enough to walk on yet."

"Dr. Avery, please, there's got to be something I can do to start getting around again. Now that Coy's gone, Papa's trying to do what he did and the foreman's job. I have to get out there and help him, or I'm afraid he's going to work himself to an early death."

"Lizzie, I'm sorry. I know how much you want to get out there and help him, but I'm afraid if you try to do things now it's going to injure it more and you'll end up being off your feet even longer."

"How about if I walk slowly and carefully out to the barn. I can get one of the hands to saddle my horse and help me up on it. I can help Papa, then he can help me back off and into the house. Would that be okay?"

"I'm sorry, Lizzie, but no, that wouldn't be okay. It's not just keeping your weight off of it that's important, but keeping it elevated. If you sit your saddle for a couple of hours at a time that ankle will more than likely swell again."

Before Lizzie had a chance to argue her case anymore, they heard a horse coming up the lane fast. Doc looked out the window to see if he recognized the horse. "That's probably someone coming to fetch me, and it's probably not good. People don't ride that hard coming up anyone's lane unless it's an emergency. I'm going to gather my things up in case, and if I have to leave quick tell Ella I'll catch Ben in town sometime for pay, and I appreciate her thoughtfulness heating up that food."

He stood and went to the door. He opened it just as one of the hands from a ranch on the other side of Gully Ridge was ready to knock. "Doc, I'm glad I caught you before you left. Mel's wife is having her baby, and something ain't right. You know my wife has helped deliver any number of babies in the past."

"She does a fine job of it, too," Doc said.

"Well, she's there with her, but she says something ain't right and told me to fetch you as quick as I could."

"Okay, let's get going." He turned quickly back to Lizzie and shook a finger at her. "Now, you heard what I said, Miss Lizzie. Stay off that ankle longer. I'll come back in four or five days and check it again. Until then, stay off of it." He didn't wait for an answer, but ran out the door and was soon on his way down the lane.

Not long after that Ella hurried into the house. "Did Doc leave without his chicken and dumplings?"

Lizzie explained about the emergency, and passed on Doc's thanks. "Oh, what a shame. I hope he gets there in time and everything goes okay. Right now, though, I know how anxious you were for him to get here. How did the visit go and what did he say? Can you put weight on your ankle yet?"

CHAPTER 10

Lizzie had been thinking about the poor lady who needed Doc, and had momentarily forgotten about her own problem. Ella's question caught her off guard. She took a moment to think before she answered. It wasn't like her to lie, but she'd seen her father come in exhausted every night. She had to start helping him. She quickly thought back to what all Doc had said. "He said it's healed a great deal. It still has some bruising, but it's not nearly as bad, and the swelling is way down."

"That all sounds good."

"It is," Lizzie agreed.

"So you can start putting weight on it again?"

Lizzie paused another moment. So far she hadn't lied. Doc had said all of those things. But she had to get out there to help her father run the ranch, so how could she answer Ella's last question? As she thought about the specific question Ella asked, she smiled. She didn't mention Doc; she just asked if she could start putting weight on it again. Technically, yes, she felt sure she could. Doc didn't say she should, but she was sure she could. Without thinking it through any further, she turned to face Ella. "Yes. I need to take it easy at first and rest it if it hurts, but I'm going to be helping Papa again. Isn't that fantastic?"

Ella hugged Lizzie, knowing how much she wanted to get back to working on the ranch. "I'm so happy for you, honey. I'm sure your papa will be, as well."

"Yes. He needs help on the ranch." She accepted the hug from Ella, but was already beginning to worry. She hoped she was right and she would be fine putting weight on her ankle again. And how would she explain why Doc would be back in a few days to check on her again? She started planning ahead in an attempt to cover everything. She would have to somehow arrange to be working close to the barn when Doc returned in four or five days, then convince him it was the first time she'd put weight on it, because she was really needed that day.

Hopefully he would understand and not be too angry. Her papa wouldn't be happy if he found out, but she'd always been able to talk her way out of his anger. Wyatt was the one she was more worried about. He knew her well, probably better than anyone, and there was a good chance he would know if her ankle was hurting. She would have to be extra careful not to say anything about it being sore, or wince. If he saw her do that, he might – well, she didn't want to think about what he might do.

She decided if she was going to pull this off she had to make it believable, so she offered to help finish up supper. "I'll make the biscuits and get them in the oven for supper while you finish the laundry."

"Okay, thank you, if you're sure your ankle feels good enough to stand on it."

"It'll be fine." Ella went back outside and Lizzie slowly and tentatively stood. So far so good, so she took her first step toward the kitchen counter. Her ankle was a little sore, but she was sure it was from not using it, and it would improve. She concentrated on making the biscuits. It felt good to be doing something productive again, and she slid them in the oven as Ella came back in.

"Thank you. You should start putting weight on that ankle again slowly, so why don't you go rest it for a bit now while I put these clean clothes up. When I get back we'll finish supper up. I have a feeling Wyatt will be here, eager to hear what Doc said."

Lizzie nodded with a smile, that soon faded after Ella left the room. She sat down to rest her ankle, and her mind wandered back to her problem and what she could do to about it. She was still lost in her thoughts when Ella walked into the kitchen. "Do you want to set the table? I'll take the roast out of the oven and slice the meat while you do that. Then when Wyatt gets here and your papa comes in the biscuits should be done and we can take up the rest of the meal."

"Sure," she said, standing again. She went to the cupboards and got all the dishes and silverware she would need and took them all at once rather than make several trips from the cupboard to the table, like she normally would do. Ella didn't notice since she had her back to her and was busy with the roast. Once she got it all to the table she found herself shifting all her weight to her good ankle while she reached around the table, doing as much of it as she could before moving.

She realized if Ella or Wyatt saw her acting like this, they would know something was wrong, so she squared her shoulders and walked to the other side of the table to finish setting the table. She finished, and sat down, hoping to rest her ankle a minute or two before the men came in, ready to eat.

Ella finished slicing the meat and after looking around,

sat down across the table from her. "I think we're ready. When the men get here we can take up the potatoes and peas and pour the drinks. How is your ankle doing? Is it feeling sore?"

"It's not bad. I feel it, but I would expect that after having stayed off of it for a week. It'll be fine. I'm sure it will get better every day as it gets used to it and back to normal."

"I suppose. But if it gets sore, rest it."

"I will. I'll rest it in the evenings, too." Ella nodded her approval, and Lizzie squared her shoulders. Before the men arrived, she had to pull herself together and act naturally. No wincing or complaining. She had to look, sound and act like she was glad to be walking again, which she was, and that it didn't hurt. She had to get out there and help her father. They had a ranch to run. She would rest it in the evening, after helping during the day.

Shortly after her pep talk the men arrived. She heard a horse coming up the lane and looked out the window. Recognizing Chestnut, she went outside to meet him. As he approached the house she saw her father coming in from the barn, as well. They arrived at the porch at the same time, both smiling. "You're standing," Wyatt said. "I take it Doc was here?"

"He was," she said with a big smile.

"That's wonderful," her father said, leaning down to give his daughter a kiss on her forehead.

"What did he say?" Wyatt asked. "Is it healed, or do you still need to watch out for it?"

"I'll be taking it a little easier than normal during the day and resting it at night, but it's doing much better. He said the swelling is way down and even the bruising, which will take some time to go away completely," she said with a proud smile. She hoped they left it at that so she wouldn't have to actually lie. She had her fingers crossed behind her back.

"That's certainly good news," Wyatt said as he leaned down and kissed her cheek. "Does it hurt to walk on it at all?"

"I'll admit it doesn't feel quite normal, but I'm not sure I'd say it hurts. I feel it, but I'm sure it will be like that the first few days until it gets used to having weight on it again. I know one thing; it sure feels good to be able to walk and move around again."

Both men laughed, knowing how much she meant that.

During supper she convinced Ben to bring her up to date on the ranch. He hadn't talked about it during meals, knowing it would only upset her to hear what all needed to be done yet. The two of them talked about what was most urgent, and she convinced him she was ready to help again. Among the three of them they decided which of the things that needed done would be easiest for her to oversee. She assured them she would be perfectly fine taking a few of the men and moving a rather small herd of cattle from one pasture to another, since she would be on Shadow. "I can have one of the men open and shut the gates and I won't even have to get off my horse at all."

"And I'm sure the men will be happy to do that and keep you off that ankle as much as possible for the first few days," Ben said. "Okay, if you'll do that in the morning, I'll take the rest of the men and we'll ride the fence in the lower pasture. If we get all the fence in good shape by the time we stop to eat dinner at noon, maybe you can oversee moving the horses into that pasture this afternoon."

"Sure, I can do that," she agreed with a big smile.

"That would be a big help," Ben said. "The herds all need to be rotated to fresh pasture, but I just haven't had the time to do it."

"If you can help some of the men get the fences in shape, I'll help the other men move the herds," she assured him. "In a few days we'll have them all on fresh pasture. Then we'll be able to focus on other things we need to get done, like getting those younger horses used to saddles so we can get them broke."

Wyatt sat back, watching and listening to father and daughter discussing the ranch and what needed done first. They sounded like when he and his brothers used to talk to their father about the same thing while they ate supper. He knew Lizzie had grown up right next to her father on the ranch and was as experienced as most ranch hands, but he hadn't realized until right then just how knowledgeable she was about running the ranch. It was quite obvious to him she hadn't just been helping on the ranch; she'd been helping him run it.

Once Ben had hired Coy about a year ago as the foreman, she had begun focusing much more on the horses, which she was naturally good at. Although Ben still ran the ranch, he and Coy decided what needed done the next day and he let Coy make sure it got done while he concentrated on other things, like getting the bills paid and going to town for supplies when they needed them. He still helped on larger things, like at branding time, but allowed him to make sure the day to day work got done.

During the past year he had also grown his herds. He'd gone numerous places looking at cattle and horses. When he found some he liked he bought them and added them to his stock, introducing new blood lines. Wyatt had seen the new calves and foals they'd been getting and was impressed. He'd done a good job of picking the right cattle and was sure in the next several years it would pay off. He had some nice looking younger stock.

Now that Coy was gone, growing the ranch more had been put on the back burner. He had to go back to running the ranch on a day to day basis, and it was a lot for one man to do, along with the other things he did. Wyatt could see that Lizzie would indeed be a big help for him until he found another foreman to hire.

He sat back and enjoyed watching the two of them. He knew without a doubt there was a lot of love between them. There always had been. But now he was seeing how much respect they had for each other and their knowledge of ranching and their opinions. They didn't argue, but they did discuss things, and the discussions were respectful and helpful.

Watching that made his respect for Lizzie grow just a little more, if that was possible. He hoped some day they would have a ranch of their own and could have discussions exactly like that, while deciding how to run their ranch. He also hoped they would have children some day and could teach them the importance of that kind of respect.

He shook his head a bit, bringing his mind back to the present. He'd been having those thoughts of the future frequently of late, and he had to keep focused on now. There would be plenty of time for the future, but his Lizzie was still young, and it was important that he give her enough time to grow and mature. He wanted her to be sure that was what she wanted, as well, before he put his plan, or wishes and hopes, into action by asking her to become his bride.

When they finished their meal Wyatt suggested they visit on the front porch swing a while. "I'd like that, but let me help Ella clean up the kitchen first," she said.

"No, you go ahead," Ella insisted. "You have something to celebrate tonight, so go on out and visit."

"You can walk out yourself now," Wyatt said with a grin. "I'm glad you can use your ankle again, but now I don't have an excuse to carry you anymore."

Ben laughed, but shook his head. "You're wrong there,

son. I always said you don't need an excuse to take a special lady in your arms, as long as she doesn't complain."

Wyatt laughed, leaned down and in one quick swoop picked her up into his arms. "Unless you're going to complain, we're going to the porch swing."

"You won't hear a complaint from me," she said, matching his smile.

Ben and Ella's eyes met and they smiled as the younger couple of made their way out the door. "We may be planning a wedding before too long," she said, and he nodded. "How would you feel about that?"

"I'd be happy with that. As much as I hate to see my little girl move out, she's not a little girl anymore, and I won't be around forever to take care of her. I want to see her happily married with a family of her own, and I don't know of any better man she could find than Wyatt. He's always protected her and I have no doubt he would continue."

"I agree with you there, Ben," Ella said.

Lizzie was actually happy Wyatt had carried her to the porch swing. As they were talking, Clem walked Chestnut from the barn to the house and tied him to the rail. "I brushed him and gave him some hay and water, Wyatt. I figured you'd be leavin' before too awful long, so I brought him back for you."

"Thank you, Clem. You didn't have to do that, but I sure appreciate it."

"Ah, you're welcome, Wyatt. It wasn't much. It wasn't near what you did for us, rescuing Miss Lizzie. We all appreciate that."

"Trust me, no one is any happier that she's safe than me," he said as he gave Lizzie's hand a squeeze. He loved watching her face blush.

"Well, we men were talking, and it's sure good seeing you

two bein' sweet on each other. You're two good people, and we hope it works out for you."

"Well, I thank you for that, Clem," Wyatt said.

Clem chuckled and said, "Leo and a couple of others said it was about time you two saw each other as bein' as good for each other as we knew you'd be, but Leo says better late than never." He chuckled as he turned and headed back to the barn. "Have a good evening, both of you."

Wyatt laughed out loud, and Lizzie had to laugh, as well. "I'm sure Leo and some of the others that watched us grow up together have said that," he said. "I guess once you're good friends it takes a little while to see each other as anything other than that."

"Yes, I guess so. At least I know it did for me. I'm glad we finally managed, though."

"Me, too," he agreed. "Me, too." After a companionable silence while they both thought back on what Clem had said, he switched the topic to how well she and her father seem to be at running the ranch together. "We kind of grew into it," she said. "We ran it together clear up until he hired Coy. I'm sure we'll be able to do it again until he finds a new foreman."

"I think you'll do just fine. I was in town getting supplies a couple of days ago and I talked to Sheriff Williams a few minutes. He said your father had been in and told him he's looking for a new foreman, so the sheriff's been spreading that news. Hopefully the right person will come along shortly."

"I hope so. I like helping run the ranch, but I prefer just working with the horses. I'm happy to help with anything they need help on, but I like to focus on the horses."

"Your dad prefers that, as well. He tells everyone he's never seen anyone as good with horses as you."

"He does? I don't know about that, but I do love working with them."

"And it shows." After their talk he stood and walked her to her door. "I'm glad you're able to be up and around again, my sweet Lizzie, but be careful. Don't overdo it and end up back off your feet again."

"I'll be careful, Wyatt. I'm planning on resting it every evening with it elevated. I don't want to have to stay off of it again."

"Good. I hated seeing you hurt, and I don't want to see it again." He leaned down and gave her a sweet kiss on her lips. "Sleep well." He turned and left, and Lizzie reached up to touch her lips as she watched him mount Chestnut and head for home.

The more time they spent together the more she was sure she loved him. As happy as she was about that, she felt awful leading all of them to believe her ankle was healed enough to be on it. She reminded herself she hadn't lied to any of them. She never told any of them the doctor gave her the go ahead to be on it, but she knew in her heart that didn't matter. She'd misled them, and she felt terrible. Still, it felt good to be able to be up again and help her papa.

She put what she hoped was a convincing smile on her face and went inside. She talked to her papa and Ella a few minutes before yawning, and excusing herself and going upstairs to bed. Sleep didn't come quickly, though, as she was troubled about what she'd done. The fact her ankle was throbbing a little didn't help. She finally forced herself to shut her mind down so she could get some sleep. Tomorrow would be a busy day.

LIZZIE WOKE the next morning early, ready to get back to ranching. She stood rather tentatively, but was happy when her ankle didn't seem too bad. It hurt a little, but not bad at all. She got dressed and went downstairs slowly, leaning onto the railing for support. After greeting Ella she helped her finish up breakfast.

She and her father went over their plans for the day again as they ate. She assured him she would indeed be fine, but he reminded her of their signal on the ranch. If you need help, shoot into the sky twice, wait a few seconds and do it again. She assured him she would keep her rifle with her and remember that, but reminded him that she wouldn't be alone. Some of the hands would be with her, moving the cattle from one pasture to another.

She got to the barn, planning on saddling Shadow, but found her horse waiting for her, already saddled. Bill was in the area, saddling his horse, so she called out to him. "Bill, do you happen to know who saddled Shadow for me?"

"I did that, Miss Lizzie. We're all glad you're able to come back and help us out, but we all plan on keeping you off that ankle as much as we can for a while to be sure you don't overdo it."

"Thank you, Bill, that was very kind of you. You all don't have to do that, you know."

"Yes, ma'am, we know," he said with no hesitation, "but we all want to. You're just as capable of saddling your horse as any of us, but you're the only one doing it with an ankle and bruises that are still healing. Doing little things like that to help a little is about the only way any of us know to show you how glad we are to have you back out here working with us. We've missed you."

Lizzie had to turn toward Shadow so he wouldn't see her blinking fast, trying to hold back her tears. After swallowing hard a couple of times and taking a few deep breaths, she felt more under control and turned back toward him. "Thank you, Bill, and I mean that for all of you. I've missed being out here working with you, as well."

"We all knew you quit coming out so much when Coy started paying a lot of attention to you, and we tried to make sure one of us was in the barn if we saw him coming in when you were in working with the horses." He paused a moment before saying, "We didn't trust him and the way he looked at you. He hid it well when your papa was around, so he didn't see what we saw."

She looked at him, astonished. She had no idea they'd been doing that for her. "Thank you for that. Now, as good as it feels to be back out here, there is one thing you could do to help me, if you wouldn't mind?"

"Anything I can. What do you need?"

"Come watch and make sure I make it up on Shadow okay the first time. I'll have to put my injured ankle in the stirrup and pull myself up, and I'm not sure how that will feel. Would you mind standing over here in case I need help?"

Bill, who was a big man, a little over six feet tall and muscular, smiled as he approached her. "That might just very well be sore on that ankle. I hope Wyatt doesn't mind, but I think it'd be best if you let me help you." Without any further words he simply picked her up around her waist and before she knew what was happening she found herself sitting on Shadow. "I'll be working with you today, so when you're ready to get down, tell me so I can help you back down."

Still trying to find her voice, she nodded. A quiet, "Thank you," was the best she could get out.

CHAPTER 11

Half an hour later Lizzie, Bill, Walter and his brother Leo were approaching the pasture of cattle they planned on moving. "Okay, Lizzie, how do you want to do this?" Bill asked. "One of us will take charge of the gates so you don't have to get down off your horse, but you better go over what you want everyone to do. I've moved cattle a few times, but Walter and Leo haven't done it more than once or twice."

"Okay, I'm glad you told me that. Let me explain what we're aiming to do and how, and then we'll get started." She was impressed that Walter and Leo admitted they'd only done it once before, and listened carefully as she was explaining. They both asked a couple of questions, and when they felt ready to begin, like they knew what the plan was, she nodded.

"Okay, Leo, why don't you take charge of the gate for the new pasture. Go open the gate to the pasture we're moving them to, then wait for us by the gate. Walter, you open this gate, and once Bill and I are inside the pasture, stand close by. When we get the cattle heading for the gate stand to the side so they can go out the gate, and direct them to go toward the new pasture. The two pastures make an alley of sorts, so once you have the first of them heading the right direction they'll all follow. Then Leo, you have that gate clear open and stand next to it and head them into the new pasture. Don't let the first cows past you or they'll all follow and we'll have a mess on our hands."

"So if I wave my arms at them they'll turn and go in the pasture?" Leo asked.

"They should, yes. They'll want to avoid your waving arms and hollering, so they'll turn and go into the new pasture."

"Okay, I'll do my best," he promised.

A little over two hours later Leo closed the gate on the herd of cattle in their new pasture and climbed back onto his horse, a proud smile on his face. Lizzie, Bill and Walter rode up to him with smiles all around. "That went great! You all did such a good job," Lizzie praised. "It's almost noon," she said, looking up at the sun. "Let's go get some dinner."

They talked about their adventure on the way back to the barn. Lizzie was happy, as well. It felt great to be back in the saddle and working again, but she was glad it had all gone so smoothly. Bill lifted her off Shadow when they got back to the barn, and after they all ate a good meal he lifted her back up. They went out and moved a group of horses to a new pasture, and by the time they made it back to the barn for supper they were all four feeling good.

She was surprised to see Wyatt leaning against Shadow's stall. As she approached, he stood. "Hi, Wyatt. Is everything okay?"

"That's what I was going to ask you. I came over to make sure your day went okay and you didn't overdo it or hurt your ankle again. I was worried about you mounting and dismounting. That puts a lot of stress on your ankle and foot. Let me help you down."

Bill had overheard Wyatt's concern and slid off his horse and went to face Wyatt. "This might be a good time for me to make a confession, Wyatt."

Wyatt's eyebrows raised and he looked at Bill. "Confession?"

"Yes. Please don't get upset with me, but I was worried about the same thing. When she was ready to mount up, I lifted her up onto her horse. I give you my word that's all I did, but I didn't want to see her put so much stress on that ankle yet, either."

Wyatt nodded and reached out his hand. "Thank you, Bill. I know you, so I'm sure you didn't take any other liberties, and I appreciate you watching out for her." He chuckled and added, "But now that I'm here I'll help her down." They all laughed, but Bill felt better knowing Wyatt wasn't upset with him for putting his hands on Lizzie.

Wyatt reached up and easily lifted Lizzie to the ground. She turned to take Shadow into her stall, but Leo was right there, reaching for the reigns. "Miss Lizzie, you and Wyatt go on in, I'll take care of Shadow. I appreciate you explaining everything to me today before we started. I'm learning a lot here, and it's all thanks to you and your dad. You've both been awful good to me and Walt, and I want you to know we appreciate it."

"We appreciate that you're both good workers and willing to do what we ask, Leo. But I appreciate you taking care of Shadow for me."

Lizzie turned to go to the house and her ankle seemed to give out a bit. She stumbled and grabbed for the fence for support, but Wyatt was right there and scooped her up into his arms. He looked down into her eyes, his eyebrows raised. "That was a surprise," she said, trying to sound calm. "It must have been because I haven't been using it. It isn't sore, it just seemed to stumble a bit there. If you put me down I'll try it again and it should be fine."

"I'll put you down when we get to the house. Then we'll see if it's swollen, and then maybe try it again."

Lizzie had mixed feelings. It felt good knowing he cared about her, but she hoped her ankle wasn't swollen. If it was, knowing him and the way he worried about her, he could insist on getting Dr. Avery to look at it again. That would be horrible. She would have to admit he'd told her to stay off of it. If she didn't, he would find out when he went to get Doc, and that would be even worse. If she admitted he'd said to stay off of it he would be upset for sure, but would he allow her to stay off of it until Doc came back to check it again, or would he still want to get Doc to look at it right away?

Thinking through all this on their way to the house, it was pretty clear to her that she had to convince him it's not very swollen. Then she had to stand up on it and prove it's fine, no matter how sore it may actually be.

Unfortunately, Wyatt carrying her to the house seemed to attract attention. Ben saw it from where he was in the barn and hurried to the house to see what was wrong. Ella saw it from the house and was waiting for them with the door open. He carried her into the kitchen and set her down by a chair Ella had pulled out. Ben came hurrying in just seconds later. "What happened? Are you okay, Lizzie?"

"I'm fine," she said, but winced when she saw Wyatt's eyebrows raise and the frown on his face. "My ankle was a bit weak when I first stood on it after being in the saddle all day, and before I could try it again he whisked me into his arms, and here I am."

"Thank you for that, Wyatt," Ben said before she had a chance to say anything further.

"Yes," Ella echoed. "We don't want her aggravating her injury."

"I think my ankle was just a bit weak from not using it. I'm sure if I stand up it'll be fine."

"Whoa, stay right there on that chair until I look at it," Wyatt said, holding her shoulders down so she couldn't stand. Once he was assured she wouldn't move he turned his attention to her ankle, carefully taking her boot off first. Before her boot was off he was shaking his head. "Lizzie, I don't like the way this looks. I can tell already it's a lot bigger than your other ankle. As swollen as it is, I'm not sure you should be walking on it yet."

"What? It's swollen? Are you sure? How can that be? It isn't at all sore."

Wyatt stopped taking her boot off and turned his eyes on hers, studying her a few moments. "Lizzie, do we need to talk about honesty and how important it is to me?"

Lizzie felt her face blush, and looked down. She couldn't believe he asked her that in front of her father and Ella. "No, of course not. Honesty is very important to me, as well, but my ankle isn't sore."

His frown deepened. "I'm not a doctor, but I do know an area doesn't swell up for no reason or without a little pain. So how sore is it, Lizzie? The truth this time, please.

Lizzie was shocked, and not at all happy with the way he was treating her in front of Ella and her father. It was very embarrassing. She took a moment to consider how to answer, then tried again. "After you said that, and sitting here not moving for a couple of minutes, yes, I guess you're right. It is a little sore, but I wouldn't really say it hurts. I mean, I want so badly to be up and walking on it that maybe I did push a little discomfort to the side without realizing I'd done it. I'm sorry."

She was happy to see the smile on his face, even if it was

small, and he continued taking her boot off. "I guess I can understand that. Now that you're allowing yourself to feel it, how sore is it?"

"I feel it, but it's really not very sore. Are you sure it's swollen?"

"I'm sure," he said as he held both ankles out in front of her as he compared them. This one is quite swollen, don't you think, Ben?"

"Yes, I'm afraid I have to agree, sweetheart. It is pretty swollen."

"Does this hurt?" Wyatt asked, pressing lightly on a couple of places.

Lizzie tried to look totally relaxed as she shook her head. "Not really. I mean, I feel it, but I'm not sure I'd call it sore."

After pressing a few more places, while Lizzie made sure her face stayed neutral, he seemed satisfied. "Well, why don't you stay off of it tonight and see how it is in the morning? Maybe resting it this evening will allow the swelling to go back down."

"I think that sounds like a good idea," Ella said. "I can see how swollen it is now. I'll check it in the morning and see if it's better."

"Thank you, Ella. I would appreciate that." He turned back to Lizzie. "I know you don't want to hear this, but if it's still this swollen in the morning, I want you to stay off of it again tomorrow. I'll stop by as early as I can after breakfast, and if you're staying off of it again I'll ride in and talk to Doc about it."

"That's a good idea," Ben agreed, "but Wyatt, you shouldn't have to come over here and do that. If Ella thinks it's still swollen, I'll ride into town to get Doc, or have one of the men do it. I appreciate the offer, but she's my daughter and still living in my house, so I'll take care of it. Thank you for your offer, though." Wyatt could tell by the look Ben gave him that his offer impressed him, and he was glad. He hoped to ask Ben for permission to marry his daughter before too long, and wanted him to know he would take good care of her.

"All right. I'll come by tomorrow evening and see how she is," he said, nodding to Ben. He turned then to Lizzie, who wasn't looking very happy. "I hope I come over tomorrow evening to find out the swelling was down in the morning, you spent the day helping your father, and your ankle is looking and feeling good."

"I hope the same thing," she said as her smile returned.

"We all do," Ella said. "Now, supper's ready, so you stay right there, Lizzie, while I get everything served up so we can eat. Wyatt, why don't you turn her chair around so she's facing the table, then sit down next to her."

"Thank you, Ella. I appreciate all the meals you've been feeding me."

"We appreciate what you've done for our Lizzie. Now, enough about that, get you two up to the table."

"Let me get cleaned up and I'll help carry the food to the table," Ben said.

Ten minutes later Lizzie was trying to participate in the conversation as they ate their meal. She was extremely worried, but trying not to let it show. She had to find a way to be at the house alone when Doc came to look at her ankle again in two or three days. But now she had another concern, as well. Her ankle gave out when she tried to stand, and she had to admit to herself it was awfully sore. What if she did more damage to it by walking on it before she should? She'd never be able to hide it then, which would upset Wyatt, disappoint her father, and mean staying off of it again, maybe for longer.

. . .

THEY FINISHED their meal and Wyatt scooted her chair out for her. She told Ella she'd help her clean the kitchen, but had three upset expressions glaring at her. Before she could say anything else Wyatt scooped her up into his arms and carried her to the couch. "The only thing you're going to do this evening, my sweet Lizzie, is rest that ankle. Before I leave I'll look at it again, and hopefully the swelling will be down some. Remember what I said, though. If it's still swollen or sore in the morning, you stay in the house, off your feet. Do you hear me?"

"But Papa needs help on the ranch."

"I don't need help bad enough that it's worth risking you being hurt again," Ben said, sitting down in a chair across from the two of them on the couch. He gave her a stern look as he continued. "We'll get by okay out there for a few more days. Listen to Wyatt and take care of that ankle."

"What's on the agenda for tomorrow, Ben?" Wyatt asked. "If you need help with something I'll see if I can come over and help you some."

"Thank you for the offer, Wyatt, but we'll be okay. There isn't anything special we have to get done. I'm going to send a couple of men up to the upper pastures to watch the herds up there. I think we have a bear in the area. Something attacked a couple of small heifers, and it looked like a bear to me."

"I hope your men spot it. Sometimes you can scare it back into the woods, but you have to keep an eye on the animals for a while. If a bear gets a heifer he might start looking at them as an easy next meal."

"That's my thought, too. That's why I'll send a couple of guys up there to keep an eye out."

Wyatt shared a story about a problem bear they had that kept killing or injuring their cattle. Finally they had to shoot it to protect their animals. After they visited a bit Wyatt carried Lizzie up to her room, with Ella following close behind to help her get ready for bed. He told her good-night, gave her a quick kiss on her cheek, and told her he'd be by to see her the next day.

THE NEXT MORNING while Wyatt had breakfast with his family, his father said someone would have to go into town for supplies. Wyatt volunteered to go and asked if it would be all right if he stopped by and check on Lizzie's ankle on the way. His father thought that was a good idea, so after breakfast Wyatt got the horses hitched to the wagon and set off.

Lizzie had spent the time while they ate breakfast arguing with her father and Ella about her ankle. It was still swollen some, and it was still a little sore, although she tried to convince them otherwise. They told her she needed to stay off of it another day, but she was determined to go out and help. Ben had just told her again that he wanted her to stay in and rest her ankle, when they heard a wagon coming up their lane. She was sitting next to the window, and groaned when she saw it was Wyatt. She knew what his opinion would be.

Ben gave her one final look, then went out on the porch to greet Wyatt. "Good morning, son. I'm glad you stopped in this morning."

Wyatt was instantly on alert. "Why? Is something wrong with Lizzie?"

"Maybe you can talk some sense into her. Her ankle's still swollen, and we've been telling her she needs to stay inside and off of it today. You know our Lizzie, though; she's insisting it's fine and she's going to help me today."

Wyatt had a frown on his face when he walked into the kitchen. "Good morning, Lizzie. What's this I hear about you being stubborn?"

"Everyone's just more worried than they need to be. My ankle's hardly swollen at all and it doesn't hurt. It'll be fine."

"Let me see this hardly swollen ankle," he said, stooping down to take a look himself. It didn't take long at all for him to look back up at her with his eyebrows raised. "That hardly swollen ankle is about twice the size of your other one. It's as swollen as it was last night, sweetheart. They're right; you need to stay off of it today."

"But --"

"But nothing, Lizzie. If you don't rest that today it'll get worse, and you won't have any choice but to stay off of it because of the pain. Is that what you want?"

"No," she said quietly.

"I don't, either, so please tell me you'll stay off of it today. Hopefully after resting it today it'll be okay to try it again tomorrow."

Seeing the loving, yet stern look on his face, and looking at Ella and her father, she slumped her shoulders and nodded. "Okay."

"Thank you," he said as he kissed her cheek before standing up. "Now, do you want to stay here at the table, or would you like me to take you to the couch?"

"I'll stay here. At least then maybe I can do something to help Ella."

"Okay. I've got some things I have to do, but I'll stop back in this evening and see how the ankle's doing."

"Wyatt, Walt and Leo went out hunting yesterday and brought back several rabbits," Ella said. "We're having rabbit stew for supper, so why don't you plan on eating with us. I know you like rabbit stew as much as Lizzie."

His eyes lit up, and he smiled. "Thank you for the offer, Ella. I do love rabbit stew. If you're sure it won't be an inconvenience --"

"I've told you before, you're welcome here anytime, and it

certainly will not be an inconvenience," Ella said, wagging her finger at him. "As much as you've done for us and Lizzie, I'll hear no more about any inconvenience."

"Yes, ma'am," he said with a bit of a smile. "Thank you for the invitation, and I will certainly take you up on that."

"Good," she said, her smile returning, as well. "We'll see you then."

Ben smiled, and walked Wyatt back to his wagon. "Thank you for stopping in, son. You've always been able to get her to see reason better than I could. I'm glad you have that ability. It's why I've always felt she was safe with you."

"I care a great deal about Lizzie. I always have, but it's more than that now. Mr. Morgan, I doubt that it's much of a surprise to you, but I would really like to ask Lizzie to marry me some day. I'm not going to rush her, I know she's younger than me, only eighteen. But in my heart I know she's the one I want by my side for the rest of our lives. If she does eventually agree to be my wife, I can promise you I will do everything I can to take care of her. I will make sure she's safe, happy, and has everything she needs."

"I would love to have you as my son-in-law, Wyatt, and I don't think that's a surprise to you, either. I also have no doubt that you will take good care of her, or that she will be happy. She seems to listen to you, which means she trusts you, and I appreciate that, as well."

"I see that trust as a gift, and I won't take it for granted. I have to get into Gully Ridge to pick up some supplies. I'll take them home and be back for supper. I'll try to hurry."

"No need to hurry. Stew holds easily, so we'll wait until you get here. Have a good day and we'll see you back for supper."

Wyatt nodded and climbed up in his wagon. As he headed back out the lane Ben gave some thought to the conversation they'd had. He'd suspected Wyatt may have been thinking about marrying his Lizzie, but he was glad to know it for sure. He couldn't ask for a better man for his daughter.

Lizzie loved the ranch, and he'd always planned on leaving it to her someday. Being married to Wyatt would be perfect for both of them, with his family owning the next ranch over. He knew from seeing him working, and from speaking with his father that Wyatt was a good rancher and would be able to run the ranch and keep it going. At the same time, Wyatt knew how valuable Lizzie was working with the horses and how much she loved it, so he was sure she would be able to continue doing what she loved doing. That made him smile as he watched Wyatt heading down the road.

Wyatt made it into town and got most of his business taken care of pretty quickly. His last stop was at the general store. He walked in and greeted Tom and Claudia Lewis, the owners. "What can I get you, Wyatt?"

"I have a list for you, Tom. I haven't looked at it yet, but Pa warned me Ma had quite a few things on it this time."

Claudia moved closer so she could read the list along with her husband. "Wyatt," she said after reading it all, "some of this is going to take me a little while to get together. The last time she was in here she looked at fabric. She said she wanted to make some new curtains, and a couple of dresses for herself and a shirt for your father. She's decided which fabric she wants for all of them, but I'll have to measure and cut them for her."

"I have an idea," Tom said. "While she's doing that why don't I gather up the rest of the things on this list and load them into your wagon. Ruby's got some of the best chicken and dumplings that I've ever had, so why don't you go grab some of it before it's gone. When you're done we should have your wagon loaded and ready to go for you."

"I can help you load the wagon, Tom. I see there are quite a few things on there."

"I can get it," he assured. "It's rather slow today, so I've got plenty of time. If you don't hurry over there Ruby may be sold out of the chicken and dumplings, though."

"Well, if you're sure, maybe I will head over to Ruby's. Chicken and dumplings sound pretty good."

He walked into Ruby's a few minutes later and sat down at the only empty table. A couple of minutes later Dr. Avery came in. Wyatt watched him glance around, and knowing there were no empty tables, he motioned him over to his. "I'm here by myself today, Doc. Why don't you join me?"

"Thank you, Wyatt. Ruby's pretty busy today."

"Yes, she is. I heard she's got chicken and dumplings today. Maybe that's what brought the crowd."

"It might just be. Her chicken and dumplings are awful good." Ruby came by just then, and the two men ordered their meals.

"So, how's Lizzie's ankle doing?" Dr. Avery asked.

"Well, I'm not real sure," Wyatt answered. "It was swollen again last night and this morning, so I told her I thought instead of going out again she needed to stay inside today and stay off of it. She wasn't happy about staying inside, but reluctantly agreed."

Doc looked at him, his eyebrows furrowed together. "You said she went outside yesterday. What did she do while outside?"

Wyatt studied the doctor's expression a few moments. "She helped a couple of the men move cattle from one pasture to another," he said slowly, thinking as he talked. "I'm getting the impression you didn't tell her it was okay for her to be on her ankle again yet. Am I wrong about that?"

"Wyatt, when I looked at her ankle a couple of days ago I told her it wasn't ready for her to put weight on it yet. I told her to stay off of it for another four or five days, and I would come back out and check on it then. She was upset and tried to convince me it was fine, but I explained it wasn't healed enough yet for her to be on it. I had to leave in a hurry that day for an emergency and I'm sorry I didn't have a chance to talk to anyone else before I left, but I thought she understood she wasn't to be on it yet."

Wyatt shook his head and his shoulders slumped. "Doctor, I have a feeling she understood exactly what you were telling her. She's been insistent that she needs to help her father run the ranch now that they don't have a foreman, and she's a stubborn little thing."

"That she is," Doc said with a little smile. "I've had the impression you're pretty sweet on her, which is quite understandable. She's a very pretty lady with a heart of gold, and she's a very good cook, but she is very spirited. If you take her as your wife, she's a wonderful lady, but you'll have your hands full for sure."

Wyatt smiled and nodded in agreement. "I will at that, but I hope I get that opportunity. I've grown up with her, so I know how spirited she can be, but I do care a great deal about her."

"You two will make a good couple of, so I wish you the best of luck. In the meantime, I think maybe I need to stop out and check her ankle again."

"I would appreciate that, Doctor. Tom is loading my wagon with supplies while I eat, and I have to take them home first, but then I'm going there for supper tonight. I'd sure like to be there when you look at her foot so I can hear for myself what you have to say."

"Well, I think that will work out just fine. I was going to drop by and check on Mrs. Keller and their new son this afternoon. After I do that I'll stop in and check on her ankle. Will that work out for you?"

"That should give me time to get home and unload the supplies and get to Lizzie's. It may work out real well for you, as well. Ella invited me for supper because she's making a big pot of rabbit stew. I'll just bet they ask you to stay for supper, too."

"Oh, I do love rabbit stew, and Miss Ella and Lizzie make the best I've ever tasted," he said with a big smile. "She always tries to feed me before I leave if I'm out there. Hopefully I won't be called away so quickly this time."

CHAPTER 12

Once they finished lunch, Wyatt and Dr. Avery parted ways, with plans to meet later. Wyatt thought about Lizzie as he drove the wagon of supplies home. He hoped she hadn't done more damage to her ankle by walking on it before she should have. He knew Ben had a lot to do now without a foreman, but that didn't mean she could ignore what the doctor told her and put her health in jeopardy, and he had to make sure she knew that. The only question in his mind was how he should do that.

He had plenty of time to come to a decision as he arrived home and unloaded the supplies. After checking with his father to be sure he wasn't needed for anything more, he saddled Chestnut and headed to Lizzie's, through the fields, which would bring him in at the back of the barn instead of going up their lane. Hopefully Ben would be at the barn and he could have a private word with him before he saw Lizzie.

Luck was with him, and as he was heading for Ben's barn he saw a rider approaching him. As it got closer he recognized him as Ben, and he stopped where he was. He didn't know a better place to have a private word than out there with no one around. Ben pulled up, a questioning look on his face. Before he could ask any questions, Wyatt started the conversation. "Good evening, Ben. I came in this back way hoping I could have a word with you before I go in to see Lizzie. Do you have a few minutes?"

"Sure. What's on your mind, son?"

"While I was in town today I ran into Dr. Avery. He asked how Lizzie was doing, and I told him about the swelling last night and this morning, and that we suggested she stay in today and off of her ankle. He was shocked, since he told her he didn't think her ankle was healed enough yet to be on it. He told her to stay off of it another four or five days, and told her he'd be back then to look at it again."

He watched Ben's expression, and could tell he was disappointed, but not necessarily surprised that she'd ignored the doctor's instructions. "Ben, this morning I told you my intentions toward Lizzie, and I stand by them. I want to make her my wife, and planned on asking for your permission soon. As her husband I plan to keep her safe, but in order for me to do that she has to be honest with me."

"I understand, Wyatt, and I can assure you she is normally a very honest person."

"I know she is, and I know in this case she wants to help you run the ranch until you find a foreman. I understand why she didn't want to stay off her feet, but that doesn't change the fact that she ignored Doc's orders and she may have caused more damage to her ankle." He brushed his hand through his hair before continuing. "Ben, I have the utmost respect for you and I'm going to be completely honest with you."

"I appreciate that."

"If Lizzie agrees to marry me, as my wife I will not allow that kind of behavior to go without consequences."

Ben looked down at the ground for a few seconds, but

then met Wyatt's eyes. "I understand what you're saying, Wyatt. I also believe you will follow through with those words, and I respect you for that. It's something I should have done, but could never bring myself to do. She's my little girl and I just didn't have it in me."

"Ben, I understand that. It couldn't have been easy to raise a daughter on your own, but you did it, and you did a remarkable job. Lizzie is a beautiful young lady, on the inside as well as the outside. I don't fault you for not correcting her when she did wrong. But as her husband, I have to be able to trust her. I can't keep her safe otherwise."

"I understand what you're saying. Do you have something in mind; is that the reason you wanted to talk to me alone?"

"I do. Dr. Avery is going to stop by later this afternoon or evening to look at her ankle again, and I'm sure the truth about what he said will come out. With your permission I would like to talk to Lizzie now, before supper. With your permission, I want to ask her to marry me."

"Good luck, Wyatt. Of course you have my permission, and I believe she will say yes. I hope she does."

"Thank you. I hope she does, as well. If she doesn't, if she isn't ready yet or simply doesn't want to be my wife, I'll leave after hearing what the doctor says about her ankle. If she agrees, however, when the doctor leaves I would like to handle her lying to us and being on her feet when she knew she was told not to."

"You want to handle it," he said more to himself than Wyatt, as he digested the words. "I know I can trust you not to hurt her, Wyatt, and that's good enough for me. I don't think I want to know how you intend to handle it, but I trust you with my daughter. I know you won't hurt her, so okay. I'll talk to Ella while the doctor is looking at Lizzie's ankle, and after the doctor leaves she will retire to her private quarters above the kitchen. I will excuse myself and go to the barn to check on a new calf born this morning, and two cows which should be having their calves anytime. I'll make sure I stay out here for an hour. I trust that will give you enough time?"

"Yes, sir, that will be plenty of time. Thank you for trusting me, and for giving us the privacy."

"Certainly."

"I'm going to go on to the house and see how her ankle is doing." He paused a moment before adding, "I hope Dr. Avery hasn't arrived yet. I'm rather curious to see the expression on her face when he does."

Ben laughed out loud. "I wouldn't mind seeing that myself. She'll know she's about to be caught. Of course, she won't know she may actually be paying for it this time," he said as he sobered just a bit. "If I would have done what I should have been doing all along she may not have ignored his instructions."

"Maybe not, but then again, we don't know that. Lizzie loves you and she loves the ranch, and was worried about you trying to run it on your own. She had good intentions and you can't fault her for that."

"No, I guess not. Good luck, Wyatt."

Wyatt went on to the house and was glad that Dr. Avery hadn't arrived yet. He greeted Lizzie after Ella let him in and led him to the kitchen. "Wyatt, it's good to see you. I didn't see you come up the lane."

"I cut across the fields today, an advantage of living the next ranch over. How's your ankle doing this evening?"

"It's doing real well. I will admit a day off was probably a good thing, but the swelling is gone, so I'm sure I'll be ready to get back to work tomorrow."

"The swelling is gone, or it's better?"

"It seems to me like it's gone."

"Let me see what I think." He knelt down in front of her

and compared her ankles. The injured one was indeed looking better, the swelling was down, but he certainly wouldn't say it was gone. He hoped that meant she hadn't injured it more by being on it. That wouldn't excuse her from being on it in the first place, but he would deal with that later. First, though, he had something important he had to do. Looking back up at her, he nodded. "I agree it looks better this evening. I'm not sure the swelling is totally gone, but it's down, and that's good. Lizzie, I'd like to talk to you, but it's rather private. Can I take you into the living room so we can talk a few minutes?"

"Of course," she said with a curious look. "I can't imagine what you want to talk about, though."

"Let's go in there and you'll see," he said as he swooped her up into his arms. Once he lowered her gently onto the couch he swiveled her so she was sitting toward the end of the couch with her leg out straight on it. He got a pillow and put it under her ankle, then sat down next to her so she was leaning against him. "Are you comfortable?"

"I am, thank you. What do you want to talk about?"

He took her hand in his and met her eyes. "Lizzie, you and I have been good friends since we were small and growing up together. As we got older you became my best friend, the person I enjoyed spending my free time with, and the person I knew I could talk to about anything."

"I've felt the same way, Wyatt," she said. "That's why I talked to you about Coy. I knew you'd listen and not think I was crazy." She paused and her face flushed a bit as she added, "I also knew you would protect me, which you did. You've always watched out for me and protected me, and I appreciate it."

"You never complained about it, which I was glad of, but I wasn't sure if you liked it or if you just put up with it."

"I know that's part of you, but I always liked it."

"It's part of me?"

"Yes. You protect everyone around you that you care about, which is part of what I like so much about you. You care about people. But it always seemed to me like you do that even more so for me, and I like it. It's always made me feel kind of special." After a moment she added, "Especially lately."

"Why especially lately?"

"Because lately I've thought of you as, I don't know, more than just my best friend." Her face flushed, but she went on. "Maybe I shouldn't have said that, but I've always felt like I could talk to you about anything. I've confided things in you I haven't told anyone else."

Wyatt listened carefully to what she said, and when she'd finished, he leaned down and brushed his lips across hers. "Oh, my sweet Lizzie, hearing that makes me happier than you know." She cocked her head to one side a bit and looked at him with a puzzled look, while also reaching up to touch her lips. "Let me explain, and you'll see why I had to kiss you, too."

She looked even more confused. "You had to?"

"Yes, I did. You see, what I wanted to talk to you about today is us. Over the last several months I've been thinking of you as more than just my best friend, too. Lizzie, I'd like you to be my wife." He knelt down in front of her, still holding her hand in his. "Will you please agree to marry me, to be my wife, and the mother of my children?"

Lizzie's eyes were big, but with no hesitation she wrapped her arms around his neck. "Yes. Yes, I'll marry you, Wyatt. That's what I've been hoping for the last while."

"Thank you, my dear Lizzie. I promise I will protect you the best I can, and will cherish you always."

"And I'll be the best wife I can be," she said, but pulled

back before adding, "but I'm not real good in the kitchen because I'd rather be at the barn."

He laughed and pulled her back in against him. Rubbing her back he said, "I know, Lizzie, I know. I also know how good you are on the ranch, and I don't plan on making you give that up. Maybe we can get a lady to be a cook and housekeeper for us and you and I can run a ranch together, as soon as we save up enough money to buy our own."

"Nonsense," Ben said from the doorway, drawing their eyes. "I'm sorry, I didn't mean to eavesdrop, but I did hear --"

"No need to apologize, Mr. Morgan. So we don't have to tell you our good news?"

"No, indeed you don't, and I couldn't be happier." Lizzie started to get up, until Wyatt put his hands on her shoulders to keep her still. "Your husband-to-be is right; you stay off that ankle. I'll come to you, my dear." He hurried over and gave his daughter a big hug, which she returned wholeheartedly.

"Isn't it wonderful, Papa?"

"Indeed it is. Wyatt, now that you're to be my son-in-law I think we should have a talk. Lizzie loves this ranch and could run it just as well as I can. I also know you would be quite capable. When I die this ranch will go to my daughter, and since you'll be married, it will belong to both of you. Once you two are married maybe we can run it together. I can move to the guest house, which is plenty of room for me, and you two will have the main house. That will give you room for a family down the road. We can talk to Ella, but I hope she'll agree to stay on as is. She can take care of the house and the three of us can spend most of our days running the ranch. Does that sound like something you would be interested in doing, Wyatt? Instead of hiring a foreman, we'll run it together."

"This is rather a surprise," Wyatt said. "I'd like to give it some thought, but I will say right off the top of my head, my first thought was maybe it would work easier if I assume the role of foreman, especially at first while the men and I are getting to know each other better and I'm learning how you run the ranch."

"That is something for me to consider, and we can discuss it later. I wanted to talk to you about my thoughts now, though, before you two plan to buy a ranch. I'd rather keep you both here, close to me, and this ranch is plenty big enough to support us all and keep all of us busy."

"Thank you for this generous opportunity, Mr. Morgan, and for telling me about it now. I have been making some plans in my head, so I'm glad you said something now."

Ella stuck her head in and said, "I'm not sure what all the noise and excitement is about, but supper is about ready. First, though, a buggy is coming up the lane."

"Ella, this excitement is the best news ever," Lizzie said. "Wyatt has asked me to marry him and I've accepted."

"Oh, that's wonderful," Ella said, hurrying over to the couch to hug the young lady who had been almost like a daughter to her.

Ben looked out the window and announced, "Ella, could you put another place at the table? That's Doc coming up the lane."

Wyatt glanced over and watched Lizzie's face go pale, as Ella hurried to set another place at the table. Ben saw it, as well, and went out to meet the doctor, giving Wyatt and Lizzie some privacy. "Lizzie, look at me," Wyatt said. She hesitated momentarily, but when he repeated, "Lizzie," the stern way he said it got her attention and she looked up at him. "I ran into Dr. Avery today at the restaurant and he asked how your ankle was doing."

"Oh, no," she said quietly and looked down again.

"Lizzie," he said again, and she looked up at him again.

"I'm sorry, Wyatt."

"I'm not sure you actually are sorry right now, other than sorry you got caught in a lie. We're going to talk more about this after he leaves, and I'm willing to bet you will be sorry then. In the meantime, he said he would stop by to look at your ankle, and hopefully you haven't injured it more by getting up on it before it was healed enough. Now, I want you to remember that this isn't anyone's fault but your own, so don't pout or be hard to get along with this evening. I expect you to be quite cordial to everyone. Do you understand?"

"Yes," she said after a moment. "You're right, it's not his or anyone else's fault that you found out. Wyatt, I am sorry. I just wanted to help Papa."

"I know, Lizzie. I've thought about this a lot this afternoon, and I know you were worried about your father. We'll talk more after Doc has supper with us after checking your ankle."

They didn't have time to say anything further before they heard Dr. Avery in the kitchen, accepting Ella's invitation to stay for supper. "Let me check on Lizzie's ankle first, then I'll gladly come enjoy some of your rabbit stew. That was awfully kind of you to offer it."

He walked into the living room and looked over his glasses at Lizzie. "Now, Miss Lizzie, suppose you tell me what happened."

She hung her head, but Dr. Avery had to work to hide his smile when Wyatt reached over and used a single finger to pull her chin up so she was looking at them. "Lizzie, Dr. Avery asked you a question. Look at him when you answer."

She sighed, but she did as he said. "I'm sorry, Dr. Avery, but my ankle felt much better and I thought it would be okay to walk if I was careful. I didn't run, and I didn't walk on it any more than I had to. In fact, I was on my horse about all day. I know you told me to give it a few more days yet, but Papa was trying to run the ranch himself, without the help of a foreman, and I knew I could help. It's my fault he doesn't have a foreman now, so I wanted to help."

Before Doc could say a word, Wyatt turned her to look at him. "Lizzie, listen to me. I don't know where that idea came from, but it is not your fault that your father fired Coy. Coy is the only one to blame for that. You did absolutely nothing wrong."

"Again, listen to Wyatt, Lizzie. He's absolutely right." All three of them turned to see Ben standing in the doorway. "I was in the kitchen and didn't plan on coming in until after Doc looked at your ankle, but I couldn't help but hear what you said. Honey, Wyatt is right; you did nothing wrong. If anyone is to blame, it's me. If I would have listened to you sooner I would have fired him earlier, before he had a chance to hurt you. Then you could have helped, without a sore ankle. But it's important that you listen to the doctor now and do as he says so your ankle can heal. Then I'll welcome your help on the ranch. But until then, I can handle it. The men are stepping up and working a little harder to cover for us being a man down, so we'll be fine until your ankle is healed. Until then, though, I don't want you saying or thinking that you've done anything wrong."

"He's right," Wyatt said, "except for one thing. I won't say you haven't done anything wrong. I agree you haven't done anything wrong as it relates to Coy, but you did walk on your ankle when you shouldn't have. That was wrong, but we'll talk about that later this evening. As far as Coy is concerned, though, he's right; you've done nothing wrong."

Dr. Avery looked from Wyatt to Ben, and could tell Ben respected the younger Wyatt. He knew Wyatt had feelings for Miss Lizzie, so it was good to see Ben probably approved. It was also good to see Wyatt caring for her, but at the same time, holding her responsible. He would be good for her. He smiled at the three of them, but it was time to get back to business. He could smell some rabbit stew waiting. "Okay, let's have a look at this ankle."

Twenty minutes later they were all enjoying some rabbit stew for supper. They were glad to hear she hadn't done much additional damage to her ankle, and she agreed to stay off of it for two more days. He assured her he would be back to check on it again, but felt sure if she stayed off of it until then it would be fine. She promised to listen to him this time, and they all felt confident that this time she would. Wyatt especially felt confident that after their talk later she would follow the doctor's orders.

They had a nice visit while they ate, and Dr. Avery was happy to hear Lizzie had agreed to marry Wyatt. The five of them talked about when might be a good time for the wedding, but although there were several opinions, no specific date had been chosen by the end of the meal. Ben and Wyatt wanted time to talk and make some plans regarding the ranch, and Ella wanted time to make a nice wedding dress and plan and make decorations and a big meal afterwards. They all thought a few months or so would be an adequate amount of time. Lizzie was torn. She agreed with both thoughts, but would also be willing to marry Wyatt the next day.

When they'd finished their meal, Doc sat back in his chair and patted his belly. "Ella, that was simply delicious. I ate more than I should have, but it was too good to stop. Thank you for the wonderful food, and thank all of you for the good company. I can't remember when I've enjoyed a meal this much. Congratulations, Miss Lizzie and Wyatt, on your upcoming marriage. I can't think of a better couple of. But for now, you stay off that ankle, and I'll be back in a couple of days to check on it again."

"Thank you, Doc," Ben said. "We'll keep her off of it this time, and we'll plan on seeing you back for supper in a couple of days."

He laughed, but Ella agreed. "He's right, Doc. We appreciate you coming back out today and again in a couple of days. Is there anything special you'd like me to fix?"

"Honestly, Miss Ella, I don't think there's anything you or Miss Lizzie have made that wasn't delicious. I appreciate the invitation for supper again, and if I can make it then, I surely will. Don't wait on me if I'm not here, though. I never know when I'll be called out on an emergency."

"If you're not here when we eat we'll heat it back up when you get here."

"If you give me the okay to walk again, I'll heat it back up myself," Lizzie said, drawing smiles from everyone.

Ben walked Dr. Avery out to his buggy, while Wyatt carried Lizzie into the living room and sat her down on the couch. Ben helped Ella finish cleaning the kitchen up, then excused himself to go to the barn. "There are a couple of cows I think are going to have their calves tonight if they haven't already, so I'm going to go check on them. I'm also going to watch the little one born this morning to make sure she's walking and eating okay."

"Unless anyone needs me for anything this evening, I'm going to my rooms early. I want to write a letter to my sister before I go to bed."

CHAPTER 13

Once everyone left and Wyatt and Lizzie were alone, he turned to face her. "Sweetheart, I'm glad your ankle will be okay, but we need to have a talk about it."

"I know I should have listened to him better. I admit that now, Wyatt, and I've learned my lesson. The next time he tells me to stay off my ankle, I will."

"I'm glad to hear that, Lizzie, but there's a bigger lesson here, and unfortunately, I don't believe you've learned it yet. It's an important lesson, and as your intended husband, it's my responsibility to make sure you learn it. I intend to keep you safe, and until you learn this lesson, I'm not going to be able to do that."

Her eyes grew, and she shook her head slightly. "But we're not married yet."

"But we will be, and I think it's important to start our marriage as I intend to continue. I've talked to your father about it, and he said he trusts me and gave me permission to handle this the way I feel it should be handled. So, unless you've changed your mind about marrying me, I'm going to put you over my knee for a spanking."

Her eyes still huge, she thought quick. "But my ankle isn't completely healed yet."

He had to chuckle a bit at that attempt. "Yesterday you felt it was okay to walk on, but today it's too weak for you to lay over my lap? You know I'll be careful and make sure there's no stress on your ankle, but a spanking to your bottom won't hurt a sore ankle."

"Oh," she said as her shoulders slumped.

"So I guess I need to ask, have you changed your mind about becoming my wife?"

He was glad she didn't hesitate a bit before assuring him, "No, of course I haven't."

"Good. Then let's get this done while your father is at the barn." He carefully lifted her and moved her so she was laying across his lap, with her legs laying on the couch on one side and her upper body on the other. He reached over and placed a pillow under her ankle. "Are you comfortable?"

"As much as possible I guess, yes."

"Is your ankle sore? Is there something I can do to make you more comfortable?"

"No, my ankle's fine. I'm just – I don't want a spanking," she whispered. "Are you sure this is necessary? I said I'm sorry."

"Yes, it is necessary," he confirmed gently but sternly. "You need to listen to people when they tell you things to keep you safe. You tend to listen if it's convenient, and brush off things you don't want to hear. Your father let you get away with that for too long, but you need to know that I won't allow it. If someone, including me, tells you something to keep you safe, you need to listen to them."

With those words he started the spanking, smacking his hand down on one side of her bottom, then switching to the other. She reacted immediately, yelping and trying to squirm away from him, but he held her tight around her waist and continued. She'd just slowed her squirming, when he reached down and lifted her skirt and petticoat and draped them over her back. "Wyatt, no, you can't do that. It's not proper."

"Hush," he said with a solid swat to her backside. "You weren't feeling it enough through all those layers to learn this lesson, and it's important that you learn this. Besides, I've left your pretty pantaloons on, as well as your chemise, so it's not improper." He continued the spanking, much to her chagrin, as he continued. "Be aware, though, that once we're married any spankings you receive will be on your bare behind, unless I simply give you a few quick swats over your dress to get your attention."

"To get my attention?" She turned to look back at him and started struggling harder. "But Wyatt, you wouldn't do that in front of anyone, would you? That would be positively too embarrassing."

"Be still," he said with a few more harder smacks. Those swats, over just her drawers and thin chemise, got her attention quickly and she froze. "That's better. Now, Lizzie, I love you and will not embarrass you in front of other people. But if we're alone and you're not listening to me, giving you a few whacks on your bottom over your dress is not out of the question. I don't see that happening too often, but it's a possibility if the situation calls for it."

He continued her spanking as he continued his talk. "To be honest, I don't anticipate needing to spank you too often for anything, but you need to know I will if I feel the need. Keeping you safe, healthy and happy are things I fully intend to do when we're married, and if you do something to jeopardize any of those things, I will do what I have to do. For now what I have to do is teach you that you need to learn to listen to people when they tell you things designed to keep you safe. In this case, Dr. Avery told you to stay off your ankle for a few more days. You ignored that, and you're lucky you didn't cause further injury to your ankle. I won't allow you to ignore warnings like that, and you'll do well to learn that now to avoid a repeat of this spanking. Be aware, though, that if I need to, I'll repeat this lesson again, as many times as it takes."

"No, please stop. I understand, and I'll listen next time."

"I hope you do, Lizzie. I don't like causing you pain, but this pain is temporary. If you would have caused more injury to your ankle by walking on it too soon, that pain wouldn't have been as temporary, and could have been even more painful."

"I d-don't know ab-bout that," she said through her tears and hiccups. "This really h-hurts!"

"As it's meant to," he said casually. "The next time I or Dr. Avery or anyone else tells you to do something for your health or safety, before you decide to ignore their instructions, think back to this right here, right now. Then ask yourself if ignoring those instructions would be worth another trip over my knee for another spanking. Hopefully you'll decide it's not worth it and you'll listen to what people are trying to tell you to keep you safe."

"I p-promise I'll l-listen next t-time," she said, still struggling.

"It's easy for you to say that now, Lizzie, but I have to make sure this is a lesson you will remember in the future." With that, he tugged her a bit tighter against him and continued her spanking. He watched her closely, and after a few more whacks he asked, "What are you getting spanked for, Lizzie?"

She turned around and looked at him over her shoulder like he'd grown an extra head. "What?"

"I want to be sure your head is where it should be right now and you're concentrating on the right thing. Why are you over my knees getting a good spanking?"

"For not d-doing what Dr. Avery s-said to d-do," she said, and slumped over his lap. Her head dropped to her arms and the tears she'd been fighting poured down her cheeks. She stopped struggling. He gave her half a dozen more swats and stopped, satisfied she'd accepted the spanking now and understood the lesson he'd been trying to teach her.

He rubbed her back a few moments while she recovered a bit before lifting her again and turning her so she was sitting on his lap. She immediately leaned against his shoulder and grabbed his shirt with one hand, clenching it tightly. He checked her sore ankle, making sure it was again resting on the pillow, then wrapped her securely in his arms.

He rubbed one arm while holding her against him. "Shh, sweetheart, calm down. It's over now, and you're forgiven." He pulled his handkerchief out of his pocket and used it to gently dry her eyes and wipe the tears from her cheeks, before handing it to her.

He held her tight against him as she calmed down and used his hankie to wipe her eyes and blow her nose. "I really am sorry."

"I know you are, sweetheart, but it's over and we don't need to speak of it again, unless you want to. You made a mistake, but once you've paid the consequences for it, it's over. Hopefully you'll learn from it and we won't need to repeat it in the future. For right now, don't keep your emotions locked inside you. If you have more tears threatening, let them out while I hold you and keep you safe."

He barely got the words out before she broke down crying again. He held her, rubbing one arm as she cried. He leaned down to kiss the top of her head, and simply held her to him. When her tears started to slow he kept one arm around her while using the other to rub her back gently. "Are you feeling better?"

"Yes."

"Good. Can you tell me what all those tears were about? I know that wasn't all from the spanking I just gave you. It wasn't that harsh."

"It felt pretty harsh to me," she argued, "but you're right, it's not just about that. So much has happened today, and it's a little overwhelming."

He was quiet for several moments, but he gave her a little hug. "I'm sorry, Lizzie. I guess I hadn't thought of it quite like that."

She looked up at him, obviously confused. "Thought of what quite like that?"

"That is a lot for you to absorb in one day. I'm sorry it worked out that way, but I don't know how I could have avoided it. Let me explain. I talked to your father about my feelings for you the day Coy attacked you. It was important to me that he knew how I feel about you, and how deep those feelings run. He knew I love you and hope to marry you some day. Then today I ran into Dr. Avery at lunch. He asked how your ankle was doing, and I told him it was pretty swollen after being on it again."

"And then you found out he told me to stay off of it longer," she said resignedly, "and you were upset."

"I did, and I was," he admitted. "But as I thought about it on the way home, I realized why you did it. You were concerned about your father, and I know you were trying to help him. Lizzie, you had good intentions, and I can't fault you for that. You were trying to help, which you do often. I love that about you. But I knew if I didn't do something, your father would simply tell you not to do it again and that would be it. He and I view things a little differently when it comes to you. He says he can't correct you because he loves you. The way I see it, I correct you because I love you. I can't even think about what I would do if something happened to you, so

I love you too much not to correct you to keep you safe."

"Wyatt, you make me feel special."

"You are special, Lizzie, especially to me. So it was important to me to let you know that I won't allow you to ignore things like that once we're married. I came over and talked to your father after I unloaded the wagon at our ranch. I told him I'd like to correct you for not only ignoring his orders, but lying to all of us about it, but I didn't feel I had that right unless you had already agreed to become my wife. So I asked him if I could ask you to be my wife, and he agreed. He already knew I love you and had planned on asking you once your ankle was healed."

"You were going to ask me after my ankle healed?"

"Yes. When I went to the east coast with my parents to see my brothers I missed you so much, I couldn't wait to get back home to see you again. I had a lot of time to think on the train and decided I would ask you as soon as I got back. But then you told me about Coy, and I decided I had to make sure you were safe. I planned on talking to your father, but before I could, I heard you scream. I don't remember ever being that scared before, when I was afraid I was too late getting to you. I knew then that as soon as you were okay again I was going to ask you to marry me." He took her hand in his and kissed the back of it. "I had to. I love you too much not to."

"Just like you love me too much not to correct me for lying about something that would keep me safe," she said to herself more than him.

"Exactly," he said, leaning down to kiss her cheek.

"I love you, Wyatt. Again, I'm sorry."

"Like I said, I know you are, and we don't need to talk about it anymore. Now, there is something else I would rather talk about, if you're up to it."

"What is it?"

"Your father's generous offer. I wondered what your thoughts on it are?"

"Do you mean about us running the ranch together?"

"Yes. I take you would like to stay here, continue living on this ranch?"

"I would, yes, and I would like to continue working with the horses. But this is my home, Wyatt, and if you wouldn't feel comfortable here --"

"Lizzie, I know this has always been your home, and I want you to be happy. I could be happy living here with you as my wife. Obviously, it's next door to my parents, and I like that idea. There are a couple of things I'm not sure I feel comfortable with, though."

"What are those things? If you're willing to live here, I'm willing to work with you. I'm sure we can find a compromise."

"I don't feel comfortable with us living in this main house and your father moving to the guest house, for one thing. This is his home."

"I agree," she said, surprising him a little. "There are ways around that, as I see it. We could all live here. We would have our own bedroom, and we could take a room at the other end of the hall from his room. Or, what I think would be easiest, we could move to the guest house. I don't need a big house. I want you as my husband, and as long as I have you, I don't care where we live. The guest house has a kitchen, living room and two bedrooms. That's everything we need, at least for several years."

"I agree. I would feel better with us living there." He leaned down to give her another kiss on her cheek. "The other thing I don't feel comfortable with is us running the ranch together. It's still his ranch, and it should stay that way. I would be honored to work as the foreman, and that would give me time to learn how he's been running the ranch. He said he knows I'm a good rancher, and I appreciate that, but you can have two good ranchers that do things differently. I would rather work under him and get to know the men working here better, give them a chance to get to know and respect me, and learn how your dad runs the ranch. He's obviously been doing a good job because the ranch has been very successful, so I'd like to keep things as they are, with him running it the way he's been doing."

She looked at him a bit hesitantly, and slowly asked, "Wyatt?"

"Yes?"

"Does that mean – what do you think about --"

"Lizzie, one reason I fell in love with you and want you as my wife is because we've always been able to talk to each other about anything. I don't want that to change. What is it you want to ask me?"

"You're right, we've always talked about everything." She inhaled deeply. "After we're married can I still work with the horses? I know most wives stay inside and take care of the house, but --"

"But that's not you, Lizzie, and I know that. Like I said before, I know you love working with the horses, and I know how good you are at it. I don't think we could find another man to take your place that would be that good with them, so I'm not only okay with you continuing, but I hope you do. I want you happy."

"Thank you," she said, throwing her arms around him again. "Let's talk to Papa about our concerns. I'm sure we can work all of that out."

"You're okay with everything I said? Before we talk to your father I want to be sure we agree."

"I understand why you would feel better being the foreman for a while first. I think our hands all know you and respect you as a person, but you're probably right; you will need to work with them to gain their respect as a foreman. So yes, we can go talk to him with a united thought."

They sat on the couch, with her wrapped in his arms on his lap, and talked more about the ranch, and living next to his family, and finally about their wedding. Not surprisingly, they discovered they had similar thoughts on what they would like their wedding to be like. They were still talking about it when Ben came in the house.

They smiled at each other when they heard him making a lot of noise as he came in, giving them lots of warning. He whistled as he approached the house, then stomped his boots on the porch several times before coming inside and yelling, "Lizzie, Wyatt?"

Hiding their giggles, Lizzie responded. "In here, Papa. Come on in." She tried to slide off Wyatt's lap to sit next to him on the couch, but Wyatt held her still.

She needn't have worried about her father's reaction. He entered the living room, saw her sitting on Wyatt's lap with his arms around her and her leaning against him with a smile, and a big smile broke out on his face.

Wyatt watched him smile and knew he was relieved to see that his daughter wasn't upset. To prove to him she was fine, he motioned to the chair across from them. "If you have a few minutes, Mr. Morgan, we'd like to talk to you about your very generous offer."

"I take it you're speaking of my suggestion that we run the ranch together. What would you like to talk about?"

"First off, I appreciate your offer, but I don't feel comfortable running it together. This is your ranch and you've worked hard to build it up. I wouldn't feel right stepping in and cutting into your earnings from it."

"Son, you mentioned trying to buy a ranch for you and Lizzie, and I respect that. It's what I did when I married

Lizzie's mother. But the situation is a little different now than it was when I got married. To be honest, there's some selfishness involved on my part. Like I said, Lizzie loves the ranch, and she's very good with the horses, so I always planned on leaving her the ranch. This way, if we work the ranch together, you'll keep my daughter here, where I can still see her on a daily basis. I've watched you grow up and there's no doubt in my mind you'll be a good rancher. So if we all run the ranch together I'll not only get to continue seeing my daughter daily, but I'll know the ranch will be in good hands when I'm gone, and she'll get to work with her horses as long as she wants to. All that means a lot to me."

"Believe it or not, it means a lot to me, as well," Wyatt said. When Ben looked a little confused, he continued. "What I want more than anything is Lizzie's happiness, and to make sure she's safe and healthy. I know how much she loves working with horses, but I also know how much she loves you. Staying here and seeing you daily would make her happy. Living here would make me happy, as well, right next to my family, and I love ranching."

"Then what's your concern?" Ben asked.

"I haven't earned the right to run it next to you and share in the profits. I would feel much better if I could work as the foreman after we're married." Ben cocked his head and listened to Wyatt's feelings, and they discussed it a bit. Ultimately Ben conceded, saying he could see Wyatt's point, and it might work out better with the men, allowing Wyatt to earn their respect.

There was one thing he didn't necessarily agree with. "Wyatt, let me ask, if you would feel more comfortable being the foreman, I have no problem with that. But could you start before you two are married? I need a foreman now. Lizzie will help pick up the slack once she's on her feet again, hopefully in a couple of more days, but that will take her away from her horses, and it takes me away from the book-work that I do. The job is yours, and I'll leave it up to you as to when you start, but the sooner you're able to start, the better it will be for us."

"Thank you for the job offer. I appreciate your confidence in me. As far as when I can start, let me check with my Pa and see what he says. I've been working on our ranch, so although our foreman has been with us since I was about ten, so he's good and knows what he's doing, if I leave to be your foreman it will leave Pa a man short on his ranch. I'll talk to him and then get back with you."

"That's more than fair. Clyde may not be too happy with me for stealing one of his men."

"I think he'll like the idea of me living that close, though. He and Ma miss both of my brothers that live out east now. At least they'll know I'll still be in the area. And I know they'll be happy to hear that Lizzie and I are getting married. They've been hoping that would happen for a long time. Ma's wanted a daughter forever, and when my brothers got married they moved away, so she still doesn't have one close. They already know and love Lizzie, so she'll be real happy, I'm sure."

Lizzie blushed as she said, "I'm looking forward to it, too. I've always thought a lot of your mother. I'm glad we'll still be living here so I can see her often."

"She'll love hearing that," Wyatt said as he leaned down to kiss the top of her head. Turning back to Ben he said, "I'll talk to Pa tomorrow and let you know what he says. I'm going to try to stop by again tomorrow so I can see how her ankle's doing." He looked at her as he added, "And to make sure she's behaving herself and staying off of it."

"I will, I promise," she said, looking down, hoping her father couldn't see her red face.

If he did see it he didn't comment on it. "Well, this has

been quite a day. If you younger folks will excuse me, I'm going on to bed."

After he left Wyatt took her face in his hands and looked into her eyes. "I have to leave, too, so I can tell Ma and Pa we're going to be married, and talk to him about me coming to work here. Please stay off your ankle tomorrow, sweetheart, so I don't have to spank you again right away. I don't want to, but I will if I need to."

"I'll stay off it, I promise."

"Good. Now, let me take you up to your room and set you down on your bed, but then I'll be leaving. Would you like me to ask Ella to help you get ready for bed?"

"No, don't wake her, I'll be fine. I've learned how to lean against the wall to move around in my room."

"Okay." He leaned down, still holding her face gently in his hands, and gave her a gentle but passionate kiss, like the newly engaged man he was. He smiled at the dreamy look in her eyes as he carried her upstairs and to her bedroom, where he sat her down. She assured him again she would be fine, and he nodded. "Okay. Good-night then, darling. Sleep well."

CHAPTER 14

Wyatt went home and was glad to see the lantern on in their living room. He thanked one of their hands when he offered to take care of Chestnut for him, and hurried to the house. His parents and brother Bryce were in the living room talking. "I'm glad you're all still up," he said as he walked in the room.

All three of them turned to look at him. "Why; is something wrong?" Clyde asked, a look of concern on his face.

"No, not at all. In fact, just the opposite. I have some news to share with you."

Bryce grinned and asked, "Did you finally get around to asking Lizzie to marry you?"

Wyatt's mouth dropped open and he froze, while all three of them chuckled. "How did you know I was thinking about asking her?"

"We all assumed you two would get married from the time you were about ten, for one thing," his brother answered, laughing harder. "But beyond that, you've spent as much time over there as over here lately."

"She was hurt. I had to check on her and make sure she was okay."

"We all know that, Wyatt," Alva said softly, "because you care so much about her."

"When you love someone you do care about them and have to make sure they're okay," Clyde added. "And we've all been glad to see how much you do care for her. She's a fine young lady."

"And pretty," Bryce added with another of his grins.

Wyatt's head turned toward his brother quickly. "Yes, she is pretty, and she has now agreed to become my wife, so keep your thoughts and hands to yourself."

Bryce was laughing as he held his hands up as in surrender. "Calm down, little brother. You know I would never come between you and Lizzie. You two were meant to be together from the time she started school. I'm just saying I think you got yourself a prize there. Congratulations. When is the wedding?"

Wyatt let out the breath he hadn't realized he'd been holding and smiled. "Thanks, Bryce. We don't know yet when it will be, but probably in a few months. That's one thing I wanted to talk to all of you about."

Alva, who had been smiling and excited since he announced they were getting married, spoke up first. "I'm so glad to hear you two are getting married. I'll finally have the daughter I've always wanted, and with Lizzie it will feel like she is truly my daughter since I've watched her grow up. We'll do whatever we can to help with the plans. I'll talk to Ella in the next day or two, but I'll do whatever she wants help with."

"Thanks, Ma, I'm sure they'll appreciate that, but Pa, there's something else. I mentioned that I've been saving money and hope someday to be able to buy a ranch for us. Mr. Morgan told us that he has an idea, and asked me to consider it before I buy one. Since Lizzie loves the ranch and her horses so much, when he dies his will gives the ranch to her."

"That doesn't surprise me any," Clyde said. "Ben's told me how much she loves the ranch."

"Yes, she certainly does," Wyatt agreed. "But what he's suggesting is that when we get married he, Lizzie, and I work together on the ranch, and split the profits. He offered to move to the guest house and give us the main house. He thinks Ella would agree to stay to take care of the house, which would allow Lizzie to continue working with the horses, and he and I could run the rest of it, including enlarging the herd of cattle."

"Boy, that's a mighty generous offer," Clyde said, sitting up a little straighter. "What did you tell him?"

"I talked to Lizzie first to be sure she felt the same way I did, and once I was sure we agreed, I talked to him. I said I didn't feel comfortable doing that, at least not yet. I understand that since he had to fire Coy he doesn't have a foreman and hasn't been able to find one to hire yet. I suggested I start out doing that instead, for a wage. Lizzie and I can live in the foreman's cabin, or the guest house, whichever she prefers, and I start working in that capacity. That will give me a chance to get to know the men more, and more importantly, they'll get to know me. I want to earn their respect before I take on any other role."

"I think that's a very wise decision, Wyatt. It's important that you earn their respect, rather than have them feel you simply married the boss's daughter," Clyde said

"That was my thinking."

"There's no doubt you'd make a good foreman. You've grown up on a ranch and know the business well, but they have to see that for themselves. Now, my question is when does he want you to start? Like you said, he needs a foreman now."

"That's what I wanted to talk to you and Bryce about. I know it's going to leave you a man down and I don't want to leave you in a bad spot. How long do you think it will take you to find someone for here?"

"Ben hasn't found anyone yet to hire as a foreman, but he's looking for someone that has the experience and knows how to do everything on a ranch. I've been lucky to have you and your brother, either of whom could have easily been working as a foreman somewhere else. I'll miss you for sure, but we should be able to find someone to hire who is a greenhorn, but ready to learn. We have enough experienced men working for us that they could train up someone easily enough."

"I was hoping that would be the case."

"We'll miss having you here with us, but I've been hoping you and Bryce would settle someplace close enough we could still see you regularly. The next ranch over is about as close as you can get, and better than we could ask for." He chuckled and smiled as he looked at his wife.

"I am so happy to hear that," Alva said. "I've been hoping I don't have another son move away. Only seeing them every couple of years is very difficult."

Clyde addressed Bryce next. "What do you think, Bryce? Do you think we and the men could handle things until we can find another man to hire? I know Ben's had his hands full with no foreman, and since Lizzie's been hurt she hasn't even been able to help him. It would help him a great deal if Wyatt could start pretty soon."

Bryce thought a few moments before nodding his head. "Ben could use the help, I know. He's not only down a foreman, but Wyatt said while Lizzie's not able to work with the horses he's had to have someone else doing what she normally does, as well. I think if we put the word out that we're looking for someone willing to learn, we should be able to find someone soon enough. We don't have any major jobs coming up, like branding or culling cattle for market, so I think we can handle it."

"I do, too," Clyde said.

"I say go help your soon-to-be father-in-law before he takes back that offer. He's got an awful nice ranch over there, and knowing you'll be running it someday has to feel good."

"Oh, it does," Wyatt agreed. "I was surprised when he talked to me, though after I thought about it, it shouldn't have been as much of a shock. I mean, she is his only child and she loves it. I just never thought of being fortunate enough to think we would have that big of a ranch someday. I hoped to buy a much smaller one."

"His ranch is even a little bigger than ours, which is big enough. It'll be good that you've had experience over here when sometime in the future you're running that one on your own."

Wyatt smiled. "Oh, I don't think I'll ever be running it alone. Eventually, when her father passes, it will be ours, but I'm sure she'll always have a say in how it's run. She may even want to be out there working with the horses herself."

"That may change once you two start your family," Alva said.

"Maybe," Clyde said, "or knowing Lizzie, she may take the little ones out with her to the barn."

"She might at that," Wyatt agreed with a laugh. "But you think you'll be okay here if I tell him I can start as foreman shortly, maybe in a week?"

"I think so," Clyde said. "I'll ride into Gully Ridge tomorrow and get the word out that we're looking for someone experienced or willing to learn, and over the next few days you can train the others to do the chores you normally do. You go ahead and tell Ben you can start in a week. I'm sure he'll be happy to hear that."

"And I agree you're doing it the right way," Bryce added. "Working as foreman will not only give you time to get to know the men, but also the way Ben does things."

"I thought that, too," Wyatt admitted. "I'm not sure he does things the same way we do. He has more horses than we do and they train most of them before they sell them, so that's part of the operation I'll have to learn. I have a feeling there's a lot I'll have to learn before I feel ready to do a partnership like he's suggesting."

"I believe you're right," Clyde said. "And the sooner you get started the sooner you'll feel comfortable with it, so go ahead. And congratulations. Not only do I feel like you're marrying a good lady, but this wonderful young lady comes with a ranch. You shouldn't have to worry about how to support her and your family."

"That's true, and I am very lucky indeed," Wyatt agreed.

~

WYATT WENT to check on Lizzie the next evening, and she was sitting at the table, bubbling over with excitement. "What's got you so happy this evening?"

"I'll tell you in a minute, but it's so nice out today, would you please help me outside? Maybe we could visit out there?"

"That sounds good to me." He swooped her up into his arms and carried her out to the porch. He sat down on the swing and situated her in his lap, where she leaned against his chest.

"I like this," she said.

"As do I," he said as he used his foot to start the swing in motion. "Now, what has you so excited?"

"Ella said since I'm not supposed to be up walking around

yet, she had an idea that would keep me entertained while sitting down. We spent time today talking about our wedding and making some plans."

"I like the sounds of that. You'll have to fill me in on what plans you've made. I'm also happy to hear you stayed off your ankle."

"I told you I would. It did make it a lot easier for me when Ella suggested while I had to stay down we should use the time to make some plans."

"That was a good idea. I know you ladies said you need time to plan it all, with the decorations and meal. Now that you've had a chance to do some planning, do you have an idea as to when we might want to have the wedding?"

"We were thinking in three months might be nice. If you want it sooner we think we could be ready in two months, but we're not sure that's the best time for a wedding. It's June now and it's just starting to get hot outside. August is usually so hot here, it gets rather uncomfortable, both in the church and outside in the sun for the reception. It would also be harder to keep the flowers from wilting real fast and the food from spoiling. If we wait until September it's usually cooling off enough that it's more comfortable. Papa thought it would be nice to have a reception here at the house after the wedding, and I agree. We could put some makeshift tables and benches up in the yard, and the kids could play in the side yard."

"August can be awfully warm, you're right about that. People would probably be more comfortable visiting in September."

"And I thought it would be really nice if I could carry some of those flowers Mama planted in the side yard the year I was born. That would be like in a way she'd be with me on my wedding day."

"I think that's a wonderful idea. When are they usually prettiest?"

"The first three weeks of September is when they're usually at their peak."

"Then what do you think about planning it for the second Saturday in September?"

"I think that sounds perfect."

"Then let's talk to the preacher at church Sunday and see if he's available. If he is, I think we have a date." He leaned down to brush his lips against hers in a soft kiss.

She was sharing some of the ideas she and Ella had with Wyatt when Ben walked out of the barn, headed for the house. "You certainly seem happy about something this evening, Lizzie. Would your fiancé have something to do with that excitement?"

"He has a lot to do with it, Papa. I think we've come up with a date for our wedding, if it's okay with you and the preacher."

Ben's eyebrows raised. "When were you thinking?"

"The second Saturday in September," she answered. "That's just under three months from now. What do you think?"

"It sounds like a good time for a wedding to me. Is there something special about that day, or is that when you felt you could be ready?"

She explained her reasoning, and could tell Ben approved, especially when she told him she wanted to use some of the flowers her mother had planted. "I think that's a lovely idea. I hope Pastor Stone can do it then."

"I'd like to talk to you about being your foreman, if that offer is still good?"

"It absolutely is. I hope you're going to tell me you'll take it. Eventually I still like us all running it together, like partners, but after thinking about it, you may be right. It might be better to let the men get to know you by working with you first."

"Supper is ready," Ella said, leaning her head out the door. "Get cleaned up and you can talk more while we eat."

"Do you mind talking about this while we eat, Wyatt, or would you rather we talk in private?"

"No, this involves Lizzie, too, so we can talk while we eat."

Once everyone had a full plate Ben started the conversation. "So is this a yes, you will take the job?"

"Yes, I will, and I thank you for this opportunity. I talked to Pa last night." He turned to look at Lizzie and smiled. "Before I go on, I have to tell you, Lizzie, my mom was as excited as I've seen her in some time. She's excited to know you're going to be the daughter she's been wanting. She also said to tell you and Miss Ella she'll be up in the next couple of days to talk to you, and to assure you she'll do whatever she can to help with the preparations."

"Oh, that sounds wonderful," Lizzie said.

"Yes, it does," Ella agreed.

Wyatt turned back to Ben. "Pa agrees that's a generous offer, and said if you can give me a week to teach others to do what I've been doing on our ranch, they'll be able to handle it without me. He's going into Gully Ridge tomorrow to put the word out that he's looking for help, but he's willing to take a greenhorn that's willing to learn. So is it okay if I start in a week?"

"I would very much appreciate that, Wyatt. I'm sure your father wasn't happy about you leaving. I'll have to stop in and thank him for letting you start so soon. That brings up another question. If you're working here it would be better, easier if you're also living here. Would you --"

"I'm sorry to interrupt, but yesterday when Lizzie and I talked about your offer, we also talked about you moving to the guest house after we're married. Our thoughts on that will more than likely influence what you're about to say, so let me share that with you. We neither one like that idea. This is your ranch and your house. We would feel better with us living in the guest house, or even the foreman's house."

Ben was ready to object, when Lizzie cut him off. "He's right, Papa. We don't need a big house, and I'd feel funny if you didn't live here. I talked to Ella today and she said she would be happy to stay on and continue to run the house for us after we're married so I can work with the horses more. If she'll do that, I assume we'll still all take our meals together so we can talk about ranch business while we eat, so we can all still come here for our meals. Papa, this will always be my childhood home, family home, but I'd feel a lot better knowing it's still your home. I'm so eager to start my new life as Mrs. Wyatt Hamilton, I like the idea of starting a new life in a new place. If we live in one of those houses, it'll be a new place, but I'll still be able to come back here to eat and visit."

Ben looked from her to Wyatt, and finally to Ella. "Ella, it looks like when these two get married you and I are going to be rambling around in this big house by ourselves."

"Yes, but do you know how many people would love to have their daughter and son-in-law this close?"

"That is very true, Ella. I am a fortunate man." He turned back toward Lizzie and Wyatt. "Okay, if you would prefer it, you can choose which house you would feel more comfortable in. Lizzie, why don't you show him both houses and you two can look at them and talk about which you would prefer. Then Wyatt, you can move in as soon as you're ready. And thank you. This ranch needs a foreman. Welcome aboard."

Two days later Wyatt showed up for supper again, wanting to hear what Dr. Avery said about her ankle. Ben was in from the barn, but the doctor hadn't arrived yet. They held supper for a while, waiting for him, but eventually went ahead and ate. Lizzie was afraid he'd been called out and wouldn't make it until the next day. Finally, they heard a horse coming up the lane and Lizzie was elated. "Is it him? Is it Dr. Avery?"

Ben looked out the window and chuckled. "It is indeed. I'll go greet him."

Fifteen minutes later he gave Lizzie a clean bill of health and said she was free to walk again. She immediately stood up, gave him a quick hug, and hurried off to the kitchen. "Now, where did she go in such a hurry?" Ben wondered. He thanked Doc for coming out, even though it was later than he'd planned. Wyatt asked him a few questions about anything Lizzie should be careful of, or if there was a limit to how much she should be on her feet.

He was assuring Wyatt that as long as it didn't swell up again, she should be fine, when Lizzie stuck her head in the door. "Dr. Avery, I have your supper just about heated up, if you want to come on out and have a seat at the table. You can all talk out here, while you eat something."

The doctor laughed, remembering the last time he was here, when Lizzie told him if she could walk again she'd make sure he had a meal before he left. "Young lady, that sounds awfully nice. I was called out to the Miller residence to set a broken arm, and I stopped here on my way back to town, so I haven't had a chance to have any supper yet. I don't know what you've fixed, but there hasn't been anything fixed in this kitchen that wasn't delicious, so I'll gladly take you up on your offer. Thank you."

"The credit for this goes to Ella, since I wasn't allowed to get up and help yet. She made roast beef for supper with carrots, onions and potatoes. We had applesauce with it and a cherry pie, which was really good."

"Sounds delicious," he said as he went to the kitchen sink to wash his hands.

Half an hour later he thanked her again for his supper, and headed back to town. She did a little dance as she took his dishes to the sink to wash, happy to be walking again. Wyatt joined her at the sink and dried the dishes as she washed them. "I'm going to head home, sweetheart. I'm glad you can walk again, and enjoy your day tomorrow, but please don't overdo it. You know I'll worry about you until I see you and can assure myself you're taking it easy."

"I know you'll worry, and it's one of the reasons I love you, Wyatt, but please don't worry about me. I learned my lesson the last time, when it was so sore again. I will be out helping Papa tomorrow, but I promise I won't overdo it. If I know him and the men, they'll all be watching out for me for the next several days, so you don't have to worry."

He chuckled, but nodded. "You're probably right, and thank you for reminding me of that. They all do watch out for you, which I appreciate. When I start working with them in a few days I'll have to let them know I appreciate it."

"I'm looking forward to you working here with us, and living here. It'll be even nicer once we're married, but it will be nice getting to see you every morning and have breakfast together. When are you going to move in?"

"I'll bring my clothes and things over in a couple of days, the night before I start as foreman. Are you still thinking you'd rather live in the foreman's cabin?"

"I think so, yes, if you're okay with it. The guest house might be a little nicer, but Ella's already told me she'll help me fix the foreman's cabin up. We'll put new curtains up and I'll make some pillows and a quilt for the bed, and it'll be fine. Besides, some relatives are coming for our wedding that I haven't seen in years, and although Papa will have several extra bedrooms for quite a few to stay in the house with him, not all will fit. It makes more sense to have them stay in the guest house right behind the main house than in the foreman's cabin which is down closer to the barn."

"I'm sure they would understand, though."

"I'm sure they would, too, but it would just be easier. There's more room in the guest house, so more people could stay there. Besides, the foreman's house is closer to the barn, so if something happens there, we'll be closer to it. If a heifer has trouble calving, for instance, we'll be right here and can go help."

"Okay, if you're sure, that's fine. If you change your mind a year from now, tell me, okay? I'm sure your father would be fine with us moving to the guest house."

"I'm sure he would, too, and I promise I'll let you know if I change my mind." With that, he gave her a kiss and left. He was glad to hear she was eager for him to move in and start working with them, because he was just as eager. The idea of seeing her every morning sounded fine to him, too.

CHAPTER 15

Wyatt moved in a couple of days later, as planned. She was waiting for him at the foreman's cabin, bouncing on her heels with excitement. He laughed as he slid down off Chestnut and held his arms out for her. She hurried into them, and Ben laughed as he came up from the barn to welcome his new foreman. "I think she's happy to see you, son," he said. "Did you get everything you need, or do you want to take a wagon back to your house to get more things?"

"No, I'm fine for now, thank you. I filled up both saddlebags and the carpet bag I tied onto the saddle. I was able to fit in most of my clothes, and my personal things for shaving and showers, so I'll be fine. I can go back home and get more as I need them. The foreman's cabin has everything else I need, and I thank you for that."

"Ella helped with that. She wanted to be sure the foreman would have anything they need, so she outfitted it with a full kitchen, though the foreman generally eats with us during the week and at the bunkhouse on weekends. She put sheets and towels in the cupboard, so you should have most things you need. If she forgot anything, or Coy took things he shouldn't have when he left, let us know."

"I'm sure I have everything I'll need."

"Well, Ella probably has supper ready, so when you're ready come on up to the house and we'll eat. While we're eating I'll go over what we've been doing and what we have to do the next few days."

"That sounds good. Let me just put my things in here, and I'll be in to eat. I'll unpack before I go to bed."

"No hurry."

"I'll go help Ella finish supper so you have some time alone. See you soon," Lizzie said.

Ben offered his arm to his daughter, who gladly wrapped her arm around his and they headed to the house. "You seem happy that we hired a new foreman," he said with a snicker.

"I am," she said with a little giggle of her own. "I think he'll work out just fine."

"Well, he definitely knows ranching, and I think he'll get along fine with the other men, so I think he'll work out just fine, too." He leaned down and kissed the top of her head as they walked on to the house.

Ella was waiting for them at the door. "That's a nice sight to see, father and daughter coming into the house arm in arm for supper. Although I will have to say not too many daughters and fathers work together on the ranch."

"Not many fathers are this fortunate," Ben said.

"And a lot of daughters don't know what they're missing," Lizzie added. "Now, what can I do to help you finish up? Our new foreman will be in shortly."

Ella had to laugh, but said, "I think it's fortunate for everyone that Wyatt agreed to be your new foreman. There's no question about his being qualified."

"And it will give him experience in a supervisory role. He knows ranching for sure, but being in charge of the men will be new to him. I'm sure he'll do a good job, but it's good to have that experience under your belt. If you ladies get the food in dishes, I'll be back as soon as I wash up a little, and I'll take them to the table for you."

Twenty minutes later Ben and Lizzie were filling Wyatt in on the workings of their ranch, and Ella was watching and listening, glad things seemed to be working out so well. Wyatt and Lizzie had been such good friends for so long, it just seemed right that they would marry. Ella knew that from the time Lizzie was little Ben knew she loved the ranch, and planned on leaving it to her, but worried that she would fall in love with someone who didn't take to ranching. Now he could relax. Things couldn't have worked out better.

~

SUNDAY MORNING BEN had the buggy out and was hitching it up to go to church services while Lizzie and Ella were doing their last minute primping and adjusting their hats. Wyatt came over and helped finishing hitching the horses. "Good morning, Mr. Morgan."

"Ben. Since we're going to be working together and you're soon going to be a member of the family, call me Ben. And good morning. You're riding with us in the buggy, aren't you? It makes no sense for you to take Chestnut when we're going the same place."

"I'll take you up on that offer, Ben, thank you. I'm eager to talk to Pastor Stone after church this morning. I sure hope he's free the second Saturday in September."

"I do, too. It seems like a good time for a wedding. If he's free are you going to start telling people now, or wait until closer to then? I don't want to spill the beans before you want people to know."

"I plan to announce it to the world as soon as possible," he said with a grin. "I'm extremely proud of the fact that Lizzie has agreed to be my wife, and I want everyone to know it. I plan to have Pastor Stone announce it at church so people can keep that day open for us."

Ben laughed as he patted Wyatt on the back. "I loved Lizzie's mother a great deal, and I felt the same way. So if Pastor Stone is free, I can start telling everyone I see the next time I go to Gully Ridge?"

"You certainly can." They heard the front door open and turned to see the ladies coming out. He hurried up and took Lizzie's arm, while Ben led Ella to the buggy. Wyatt leaned down and gave her a quick peck on the cheek before helping Lizzie up into the buggy. Behind him, Ben and Ella were smiling at the two young people in love.

They all waited after church was over to speak with the preacher, and were all happy to hear Pastor Stone was free the second Saturday in September and was happy to perform the marriage ceremony. He also assured them he would announce it during church next Sunday, and several times in between now and then.

The next week went by quickly. Wyatt easily slid into the role of foreman, partially because the men all knew him already, some more than others. The ones who had known him longer treated him with respect, but yet as a friend, and the others that hadn't known him as long picked up on that. Instead of simply tell them what to do, he never hesitated working alongside them. By working together they all got to know him better, and he got to know the men working for him.

Ben was ecstatic. He had a foreman again, which eased his workload tremendously. It also allowed his daughter to get back to working with the horses, a job she did very well. He had always counted on her for heading up that part of the ranch. He had recently learned she hadn't been working with them as much as normal while Coy was here. After he fired Coy, once she was able to be on her feet again she'd been helping him manage the ranch rather than spending time working with the horses. As a result, when she started working with them again it took extra time for them simply to get to know her again.

It was a lot of work, but both Ben and Wyatt could tell she loved the work. Wyatt was impressed to see how she handled them, and with the results she got. He knew she was good with them, but he hadn't seen the results of her work before. Now he understood why Ben said she was an important part of the ranch. He agreed.

Both Wyatt and Lizzie were enjoying seeing each other at breakfast and supper. Ella was enjoying watching the two of them flirting, although she doubted they realized they were. She also liked hearing the three of them discussing ranch business during meals. It was such a nicer atmosphere than when Coy was the foreman.

Sunday morning found them all heading to church together again, eager to have Pastor Stone announce their engagement. They'd been busy at the ranch all week and none of them had made it into Gully Ridge, so they hadn't had a chance to tell anyone yet.

It became pretty clear that they weren't the only ones excited to share the news. Pastor Stone welcomed everyone and said it was a beautiful day. "Not only are we having real nice weather," he explained, "and I'm not aware of anyone who was hurt this week or has come down sick, but we also have an upcoming wedding in our Gully Ridge community. Having lived here the past twenty-three years, I am especially happy to say I've known both of these young people since they were born, and have watched them grow up. They've grown up together as neighbors and good friends, and I've seen how much they care about each other on several occasions. It warmed my heart when Wyatt Hamilton and Lizzie Morgan asked if I would officiate their wedding. They've asked that I announce it so all of you can set aside the second Saturday in September and celebrate with them."

Applause erupted around the room and people close to them congratulated them and patted them on the back. Lizzie was so overcome by the happiness, support and love she felt at that moment, it brought tears to her eyes, which she had to blink several times to keep in check. Wyatt saw her dilemma and squeezed her hand and handed her his hankie.

That simple act, and knowing he was looking out for her, was all it took for her to lose her battle. A few tears escaped her eyes, but she no longer cared. She looked over at him with a smile and eyes full of love for the man she was about to marry. Now Ben, who had seen the exchange and look in her eyes, had to blink a few times to contain his own tears. He knew his little girl would be well cared for.

~

THE NEXT FEW weeks seemed to fly by. Wyatt had been accepted quickly and easily in his new role as foreman by all the ranch hands, which made for a very good working atmosphere. He was able to take the load off of Ben and Lizzie, giving Ben time to do the administrative part of the ranch, including doing the books and looking for more good stock to introduce to his breeding herds. He was determined to grow the ranch to ensure it would easily support Wyatt and Lizzie once they were married, as well as himself and all the hands. He had more pastureland than he needed for the cattle he had, so now that Wyatt was on board to help, it made sense to add more cattle.

Lizzie had more time now to work with the horses, as

well, and she was making good headway in that regard. She had several that were now comfortable with pulling a small cart. She felt sure they were ready to be harnessed to a buggy, but Ben and Wyatt had both asked that she wait until one of them or a couple of the men were able to be there to assist the first time she did that. She didn't see the need, but knew they were still a bit concerned about her ankle, so she agreed. They promised they would have a chance to do that in the next week or two. Once they felt confident with a horse pulling a buggy they started taking it to town for supplies or church to be sure they were ready to be sold as buggy horses.

There were a few other horses she felt were ready to be saddled and ridden. She knew breaking a horse was not something to attempt alone, so she was also waiting for help with that. While she waited she kept working with them, getting them completely comfortable with the saddle being on them.

Her Papa had always done the books for the ranch, which was fine with her. She never had any interest in them, or knowing how much the ranch was or wasn't making. She knew if cash was tight he told her that, and they watched their spending until they had cattle or horses ready to sell. He had assured her there was enough money to pay for a wedding, including a special new dress, decorations and enough food to feed the community, but she knew selling a few buggy horses and riding horses would be a big help.

Things were going well for all of them. The ranch was running smoothly now and Lizzie's ankle was getting stronger every day. Meals were often laced with ranch talk, but everyone was comfortable and happy with that. Every evening after supper Wyatt would stay and visit with Lizzie a little while before heading back to his cabin.

One evening while they ate they talked about the trip Ben would be making the next day. He had made arrangements to see and hopefully buy several head of cattle to introduce a new bloodline into their stock. He planned to leave first thing in the morning and hoped to be home before it got dark. If he was successful in purchasing them, he and Wyatt and Lizzie would take two hands with them and herd them back to their ranch. That would be an overnight event, and Lizzie was looking forward to it. She had gone with her father on similar overnight operations, but not for the last few years.

It was hard work herding the animals, keeping them together and moving in the right direction, especially when they had to cross rivers or creeks, and finding a place to corral them overnight, but it was rewarding. She always felt tired but proud when they got them back safely to their ranch. Wyatt hadn't ever been on such a trip, but was looking forward to it as well, but he would admit her eagerness played a part in why he was looking forward to it.

The next morning Wyatt got Ben's horse saddled and ready for him after breakfast while he was gathering his things. He got his paperwork he needed, took the meal Ella had packed for him, filled his canteen, and finally gave Lizzie a kiss. "Be careful, Papa. I hope the cattle are good and you're able to make a deal for them."

"I do, too. But then we'll have to go bring them home in a few days."

"I'm looking forward to it. Are you sure you don't want me or one of the men to ride with you? It's a long ride."

"I'll be fine, my dear. I've ridden there enough times I know the way and I'm familiar with the area. Be careful today and don't overdo your ankle, so you're ready to go help bring them home."

"I'll be ready, Papa," she assured him. She gave him one more hug and he gave her another kiss on her cheek before turning for the door. He spoke a few words to Wyatt, and turned his horse and was off. Lizzie waved, then turned and went to the barn to work with the horses.

Wyatt gave her a quick kiss, as well, before mounting Chestnut. "Frank and I are going out to check a couple of herds of cattle at the far north edge of the ranch. After that we're going to ride the fences in the two pastures next to them so we can transfer the cattle. We'll be out all day. Leo, the bunkhouse cook, packed us some sandwiches and apples for lunch. You be careful."

"I'll be careful, but you be careful, as well. I'm eager to have you go with us so you can see what it's like on an overnight cattle drive." He nodded in agreement and met up with Frank and they headed north.

Lunch seemed quiet with just Lizzie and Ella, but it gave them time for a little girl talk. They talked about the wedding and the plans they'd made. After lunch she went back to work with the horses, spending most of her time with the youngest foals, ranging in age from one to six weeks old. She felt getting them used to her and earning their trust at a young age was a big part of her success with the horses, and in her mind they were never too young to start.

As the afternoon wore on she found herself listening and watching for her father to return. It was a rather long trip, but he planned on being home before dark. She was hoping he made it back before supper. If he had been able to make the deal, they could make their plans for the trip in the next day or two.

Wyatt and Frank made it back to the barn and asked about Ben. "I haven't seen him yet," Lizzie said.

"He should be back anytime," Wyatt said. "I'm going to brush Chestnut out, then we'll go in for supper."

"Can we wait a little while for him before we eat? I'd like to hear about his trip during our meal."

"That's fine with me, but we might want to check with Ella and see if whatever she made will hold okay."

"Knowing Ella, she probably made stew or something like that, specifically so it will hold for him, whenever he gets back."

They walked to the house together and were met at the door by Ella. "I haven't heard any horses approaching. I take it Ben's not back yet?"

"Not yet," Lizzie confirmed.

"I've got stew ready, but if you want to wait a bit, we can do that."

Wyatt and Lizzie both smiled at each other at her words. "Sounds good to us," Wyatt said.

Ella poured some iced tea while they got washed up, and they sat down to visit while they waited for Ben. Half an hour later Lizzie was starting to worry. "Shouldn't he have been home by now, Wyatt?"

"I had hoped he would be, but there are a lot of things that could have happened."

"I've been telling myself that."

"It was pretty cloudy all day, especially in that direction. Maybe it rained on him and took longer than he planned," Wyatt suggested.

"That could be," Lizzie said. "I know he's been to this ranch before and said the man and his wife are very nice people."

"Then maybe it rained, which would slow his travel down, and then their negotiations took longer than he thought they would and it got late," Wyatt suggested. "Or it may still be raining there and they convinced him to spend the night and come home tomorrow morning."

"That is a possibility," Ella said, "because you're right, he did say this was a nice couple of. If it got late he may have agreed to spend the night."

"Maybe," Lizzie said, still not totally convinced. "I think maybe we should go out looking for him. What if he had a problem, like his horse threw a shoe, or got hurt? He might be out there stranded someplace without a horse."

"Whoa, Lizzie, calm down," Wyatt said in a soothing voice. "He always takes his rifle and bedroll with him, so even if he has a problem with his horse, he'll be okay. It's getting dark out tonight, so it would be hard to see him or follow any hoof prints. If he stayed the night there he'll be home before noon tomorrow. If he isn't, we'll go out looking for him."

"That sounds like a good plan," Ella said. "Why don't we go ahead and eat. If he gets home yet tonight we can heat the stew back up."

"You guys go ahead," Lizzie said. "I'm not very hungry."

"Lizzie," Wyatt said in a rather stern voice that got her attention, "if we go out looking for him tomorrow you need to be alert. Skipping supper tonight won't help that. Eat some supper and keep your strength up so you'll be at your best if we go out. I have a general idea where this ranch is, but we'll have to both be alert to make sure we're going the right direction, and to watch for any signs of a horse having gone that way recently."

She studied his eyes a few moments before agreeing. "That makes sense. Okay. I've been to that ranch with him one time, but it's been a few years. I hope I can find it again."

Supper was rather quiet, but Ella and Wyatt both tried to reassure her he was fine and would be back the next day. After talking more that evening, they decided to go to bed early. Their plan was to get the morning chores done and eat breakfast early. They would make a trip to Gully Ridge and talk with Sheriff Williams to make sure he hadn't heard anything about anyone being hurt. Wyatt knew if someone was found hurt, if he wasn't local and no one knew him the sheriff would often send telegrams to surrounding sheriffs in case they knew of someone who was missing.

Assuming he hadn't heard of anything, they could go back to the ranch and talk to Clem and Bill. Clem knew the area better than the others, as he'd grown up in the general area and knew about where the ranch was Ben was headed to. Bill was good at tracking. If Ben wasn't back by then they would go out looking for him.

Lizzie woke early the next morning after a fitful night. Not surprisingly, Ella was already up, making breakfast. She helped finish it just as Wyatt showed up, leading both their horses. They ate breakfast, then headed to town.

Sheriff Williams was surprised to hear Ben hadn't made it home last night, but assured them he hadn't heard anything. "He'll probably be home when you get back today. If I do hear of anyone being found hurt, I'll come out and talk to you, see if Ben's back home."

"Okay, thank you, Sheriff," Wyatt said. "If he's not back when we get home we're taking some of the men and going out looking for him. Is there anything we need to be aware of?"

"No, I haven't heard of any problems right now. Good luck to you, and be careful. And congratulations on your upcoming wedding. I've heard a lot of talk about it in town."

Wyatt glanced over at Lizzie with a smile. "Thank you, Sheriff."

As the two of them were riding side by side back to the ranch, Lizzie looked a bit concerned. "Why do you suppose people are talking about us getting married?"

"I don't want to disappoint you, but it's probably not so much because it's the two of us, but more because it's a wedding. We've invited everyone, promising a reception and meal afterward. That gives everyone a day to look forward to, when people will take a day off to attend a day of fun and celebration."

She thought a few moments before a smile slowly erupted on her pretty face. "That does make sense. I hadn't thought of it that way. I hope everyone does enjoy a fun day of eating and visiting."

"I'm sure they will. Any reason to celebrate becomes a big thing. Some people get married quietly and don't tell people in advance. Sometimes they decide to get married and do it within the next few days or a week. But we're telling everyone in advance and telling them there will be lots of food afterward. That's something to celebrate."

"You're right, Wyatt. It should be fun for everyone, which would be great."

"Yes, it will be," he said as he reached over to grab her hand and squeeze it. "I'm looking forward to it."

"Me, too. But first we have to find Papa."

They were disappointed when they got home and there was still no sign of Ben.

CHAPTER 16

Wyatt sighed and turned to Lizzie. "You said he was going to the Praxton ranch near Leesburg, didn't you?"

"Yes. Do you know where that is?"

"No, but I believe Pa does. I think he bought cattle from there. Why don't I talk to Bill and Clem, see if they'll go with us to look, and you talk to Ella or Leo and ask if they can round up something for us to take with us to eat while we're out. When we're all ready, let's stop and talk to Pa first. I'm sure he'll want to know Ben's missing, and will probably want to go with us to help look, and maybe Bryce or one of Pa's hands. If he knows Mr. Paxton and where his ranch is, he can be very helpful. We'll go that direction, so we can stop there first, on our way."

"I hate to bother him, but if he knows Mr. Paxton, he could be very helpful. I'll talk to Ella and be back out here soon." She ran toward the house while Wyatt turned to go inside the barn to find Clem and Bill.

Ella had already planned to send food along if they went to looking, so it didn't take her long to have some provisions ready. Wyatt found Clem and Bill, and they both quickly agreed. Leo heard them talking, and before they had their horses saddled he returned from the bunkhouse kitchen with some food wrapped in a burlap sack, as well. "Take this with you in case you're out looking longer than we all hope. Find him and bring him back, Wyatt. He's a good man."

"Yes, he is, Leo. Thank you," Wyatt said, tucking the sack of food into a saddlebag. Bill and Clem led their horses out of the barn to join them, and Lizzie came hurrying out with her own bag of food, which she tucked into her saddlebag. Looking around at the four of them, he asked, "Does everyone have a full canteen and a bedroll? If we don't find him we'll find a place to camp for the night and go out looking again in the morning." When they all assured him they did, they started off toward the Hamilton ranch.

Wyatt's mother saw the horses coming up their lane and was waiting to greet them on the front porch. His father and brother Bryce had heard them and walked outside the barn to see what was going on. They all met between the house and barn. Wyatt and Lizzie got off their horses to greet Clyde and Alva. Before they had a chance to greet each other, Wyatt quickly explained what was going on.

Clyde didn't hesitate a moment when Wyatt said he went to the Paxton ranch near Leesburg. "I know where that ranch is and I know George Paxton. Bryce and I will come along. We can go in pairs, and that will give us three different routes to follow. Give us a minute and we'll be ready to go. Should we take some jerky along for later?"

"We've got some food Ella and Leo sent," Wyatt said as he accompanied his dad and brother to their barn.

Alva took Lizzie in her arms. "Oh, dear, I'm so sorry he's missing, but I'm sure he'll be found soon. I was so happy to hear you are going to become my daughter, but we'll talk more about that after you find Ben. Are you sure you want to go with them to look? You're more than welcome to stay here with me, and one of our hands can go along."

"Thank you, Mrs. Hamilton, but I do want to go with them. I can't stand thinking Papa could be out there stranded without a horse, or hurt. I want to be there."

"I understand. You be careful, and I hope you find him real soon."

"Thank you." She hugged the lady she'd always thought so much of, and would soon become her mother-in-law.

The men came out of the barn with canteens, and Lizzie mounted Shadow and they got started on their journey. They decided that Clyde and Bill would ride together, and would go with Wyatt and Lizzie. They would space themselves out far enough to cover as much area as possible while still being close enough to each other in case of a problem. They would take what Clyde considered to be the closest path there. It involved going over the Hamilton ranch and the Pierson ranch next to it. Both Clyde and Ben were friendly with the Piersons and they all routinely traveled over each other's ranches if it was the closest way to their destination. They were all three large ranches and covered quite a bit of ground. Beyond the Pierson ranch there was a series of roads, which weren't much more than paths, but they would follow them to the Praxton ranch.

While they did that, Bryce and Clem would follow the main roads, which would take them through three small towns on their way to the Praxton ranch. It would be a longer trip, but Ben occasionally chose to go that way. He head friends in a couple of the small towns and would stop in to say hello. If there was a problem with cattle rustlers or other outlaws in the area he felt it was safer. He may have gone the quicker way there, and if it was later when he left he may have preferred to take the safer way home.

They planned to stop at each little town and talk to the

sheriff, as well. Clem was familiar with this area, but also knew the sheriffs and some of the people in these towns. If he saw someone he knew, he could ask if they'd heard anything. They would ask the sheriff if he did hear of anything in the next few days to send a telegram to Sheriff Williams, who would relay the message on to them.

The other four spread out, with Wyatt on one end, then Lizzie, then Clyde, who would keep them all heading in the right direction, and Bill on the other side where he would watch for any tracks or other signs of someone having passed that way recently.

Clyde would also act as chaperon for Wyatt and Lizzie. He would stay close enough to Lizzie to be able to see her enough to know it was just her. That way if anyone questioned her and Wyatt going together, he would be able to assure them he was with them at all times and nothing untoward happened. Under the circumstances he doubted anyone would question it, since everyone knew how much she loved her father, but this way there would be no doubt.

At one point Wyatt fired a single shot in the air, which brought the other three to him immediately. "It looks like someone camped here," he said, pointing to an area with ashes inside a ring of small rocks. "Do you suppose it could have been him?"

Bill looked the area over carefully, but shook his head. "No, I don't think so. It looks like this was two or three days ago, maybe longer. It was probably a drifter passing through. I followed the tracks back to the other side of the creek. It looks like he caught a fish in the creek and then cooked it and slept here by these trees. Then he went on the next day, because the tracks continue on in the same direction, which unfortunately, is not the direction Ben would be going."

"Thanks for checking it out, Bill," Clyde said. "Let's keep going. We should get to the Praxton ranch in another couple of hours or so. Then we can at least find out if he was here yesterday." They separated again and continued on. Clyde called them back together when they were about at the ranch, and they rode up together.

Unfortunately, what they learned was upsetting. Ben hadn't made it to the ranch. Mr. Praxton had been wondering if something came up and Ben hadn't been able to make the trip yesterday. He was upset when he learned he'd left in the morning, headed for his ranch. "I'm sorry, Clyde, but he never made it here yesterday."

"We spread out on our trip over here, hoping to find him. When we didn't see him or any sign of a man going through that area recently we were hoping you'd tell us he spent the night here and went home via the main roads and we missed him."

"I'm sorry. If you all want to go back via the main roads, I'll send my men out and we'll scour our land. It's a large ranch and if he came the quickest way he would have gone over the majority of our ranch to get to the house. If we find him or any sign he's been here we'll send a telegram and let you know. If he became ill along the way, he may have stopped at one of the towns between here and your home to see a doctor and rest a day or two. I'd check with the doctors in the towns you pass."

"That's a good idea," Clyde said. "Thanks for your help."

Wyatt was holding Lizzie, who had now lost her brave battle to fight her fears and tears. "Sweetheart, we don't know what's going on yet, but I think we need to head on out to the first town. We'll probably meet up with Bryce and Clem on our way, and we can see if they've found anything. I know you're upset and I understand why, but I don't want you riding alone if you're not up to it. There's plenty of room in front of me on Chestnut. Would you rather do that?"

She looked up at him with a faint smile. "I love riding

with you on Chestnut, but that probably wouldn't look proper when we ride into a town. I'll be fine on Shadow. Just give me a minute to compose myself."

Clyde, who had come over to check on her as well, heard Wyatt's offer. "He's right, Lizzie. We all understand why you're upset, and I'm here and can assure everyone nothing untoward happened. It's up to you, but if you're not sure you're ready to ride Shadow alone, you'll be fine with Wyatt."

"Thank you, both of you, but I think I'll be fine. I have to find him, or find out what happened."

"Okay, we'll get started then. If you start feeling unsteady, though, you let us know so we can stop, okay?"

"I will, and thank you."

The four of them rode out his lane and onto the road leading into Danville. They were almost to the first little town when they met Bryce and Clem. Lizzie knew as soon as she saw them they had news, and it wasn't good. They all stopped, and Wyatt was at her side instantly, apparently knowing the same thing. Clyde waited until he saw that his son had Lizzie in his arms before asking, "Bryce, did you find Ben?"

"We did, Pa, and I'm sorry, Lizzie, but a man found him along the road, dead."

Lizzie leaned into Wyatt's arms and cried. He held her tight while Clem went on to explain what they'd learned. "A man found him laying along the road. His horse was in the area, as was a rattlesnake. They think the horse was spooked by the snake and reared up, throwing Ben, and he hit his head when he fell. We talked to the sheriff and the doctor. The doctor said he had a big cut and bump on the back of his head, so he thinks he hit his head when he fell off his horse, and that's what killed him."

"Lizzie, the sheriff has everything that was in his pockets. He preferred to give it to you, so we told him we would get you and take you in. He thinks it was just an accident. When someone kills a lone rider it's usually so they can steal whatever money he has on him, and they clean his pockets out. That didn't happen. A man and his son were coming into Danville for supplies and came across him. They loaded him up into the wagon and brought him in and straight to the doctor, but it was too late. They said there was a rattlesnake in the area, and it seemed agitated, kept making its presence known. The men said it seemed real aggressive and they couldn't catch Ben's horse, so they shot the snake. As soon as they did that the horse came to them and they tied him onto the wagon and brought him in."

"So that's what they think happened," Clem said, thinking out loud. "The snake spooked the horse, and reared up, catching Ben by surprise and he fell, hitting his head." Bryce and Clem both nodded.

They all gathered around Lizzie, which helped her feel surrounded by love, and ready to face the fact that her world had changed. Wyatt kept her wrapped in his arms. With his mouth close to her ear he whispered, "My dear, sweet Lizzie, we have a lot to talk about, but it can all wait. For right now, let's go talk to the sheriff. Then we can go home and when you're ready we'll talk."

"Okay," she said, trying to put a brave face on. "I have one question. I want him to have a proper burial. Has he already been buried, or can we bury him next to Mama on the ranch?"

"Of course. We'll check on that," Wyatt assured her. "Take your time, but when you're ready, I don't want you riding alone right now. I'll put you in front of me on Chestnut." They gave her a few more minutes, then rode into Danville together, with her riding in front of Wyatt, who kept his arm around her waist. Clyde rode next to them, with Shadow tied onto his saddle. The others surrounded them, offering as much support as they could.

Clem led the way to the sheriff's office, and the local doctor was there, as well. They talked to both of them, who told them pretty much what Clem and Bryce had related to them. The sheriff offered his condolences, and handed Lizzie a bag that had the things they'd taken from his pockets. He told them his horse, saddle and saddlebags were being held at the livery until they could contact his family to retrieve them.

They were told he had been brought in this morning, and hadn't been buried yet. Wyatt said they would like to take his body back so he could be buried on his ranch next to his wife. Of course they agreed.

After they asked a few questions of the doctor, the sheriff walked over to the livery with them. The owner of the livery offered to let them use one of his wagons he rents out to take his body back. He said there would be no charge for it, and he could do without it for several days, so they didn't need to be in a hurry to return it.

Wyatt thanked him and promised it would be returned within the next few days. Clem and Bryce harnessed Ben's horse and Clem's horse to the wagon, and tied Shadow on behind it. Once they had Ben's body, which had been wrapped in a blanket, in the wagon, Clem drove the wagon home, while the rest of them rode beside the wagon, with Lizzie still riding with Wyatt.

It was a quiet ride back to the ranch. They went via the road, and Wyatt and Lizzie stopped in Gully Ridge to let Sheriff Williams know what had happened. They also talked to Reverend Stone and made arrangements for a funeral the following afternoon. The preacher and Sheriff assured them they would let people know about the funeral, in case anyone wanted to attend.

Ella and the hands at the ranch kept Lizzie surrounded by caring people and made sure she knew she was loved. Wyatt stayed with her the rest of the day, and the hands did the chores that evening and the next morning so he could stay with her the next day, as well. They knew it would be a difficult day for her with the funeral. He was at the house first thing the next morning, and she opened the door and practically fell into his arms.

They were all taken back a little at the number of people that showed up for his funeral. He had been well liked, but no one expected so many people to show up, especially since it was so unexpected and sudden. The ladies in the area brought lots of food and there was a meal after the funeral. Lizzie was grateful, and a little overwhelmed, by all the people there to support her. Her heart swelled with all the good things being said about her father.

Those kind words stayed in her heart and helped her through the next week. It was difficult, but with the help of Wyatt, Ella, the ranch hands, and her neighbors and future in-laws, she gradually started getting back into her routine on the ranch.

Wyatt was concerned about Lizzie and Ella living alone in the main house, and he wasn't the only one. His parents came over to visit Lizzie several times over the next week, and during one of those visits Wyatt's father talked to him about moving the wedding up so he could move up to the house. "I'd feel better knowing there was a man in the house," he'd said. "Word will get out that two ladies live there alone. Even though you're not far away in the foreman's cabin, there's still something vulnerable about the situation."

"I know," Wyatt agreed, "and I plan on talking to Lizzie about moving up the wedding. I've been trying to give her time to accept her father's death before giving her something else big to think about, but maybe I need to go ahead and talk to her."

"When you do, let her know your mother and I will do anything we can to help with the wedding, and I would be honored to walk her down the aisle if she'd like me to. Not only will I be her father-in-law, but I've known her since she was born. If she has someone else in mind, that's fine, but I wanted to offer so she doesn't have to walk down the aisle alone."

"Thanks, Pa, I'll tell her that. Maybe I'll try to talk to her tonight after supper."

He went back to the barn to do chores, but was met by most of the hands. "Can we talk to you a minute, boss?" Clem asked.

"Of course," Wyatt said. "Is there a problem?"

"Not yet, but we hope to keep it that way," Clem said. "We're worried about Miss Lizzie and Miss Ella. A couple of the guys heard talk last Saturday night about the two ladies in that big house alone."

"We're all close by," Wyatt pointed out.

"I know, and we're all watching out for them the best we can," Frank said. "But we heard a couple of guys talking about them living in that big old house alone, and the bunkhouse and foreman's home are quite a ways away, clear down closer to the barn. They're sure Ben kept some money on hand in case they needed something for a ranch that big. They also figured he'd done good with the ranch, so he probably had some nice things in the house. They said it would be pretty easy for someone to get in the house without being seen, and gather up some money and a few nice things and get back out before anybody even knew they were there. They figure a ride's day away you could sell the stuff pretty easy since no one there would recognize any of it."

Wyatt's eyes widened. "Who was it that you heard saying these things?"

"That's the thing," Frank said. "We didn't recognize the men saying it. There were lots of people talking about Ben. He was well liked, so people are talking about him quite a bit and how hard it must be for his only daughter. If these men aren't from around here, they might see this as a good opportunity. Maybe they figure they could steal what they can get, then leave the area."

"They would make an easy target for someone like that," Wyatt agreed.

"We think you should move up your wedding day," Clem suggested. "Everyone knows you were already planning to get married, and we're probably not the only ones who think it would be better if you got married now instead of in a couple of months. Everyone around here loves Lizzie and Miss Ella like they did Ben, and no one wants to see them hurt."

"You're right," Wyatt agreed, "and if these men were to sneak into their house at night, you never know what might happen. Even if they just plan on stealing things and going on, what if one of the ladies were to hear them and go see what's going on? You never know if they'd hurt them or just run out. I'd rather not take that chance. Thanks for letting me know about what you heard. I think I'll talk to her tonight."

Hearing what the men had heard in town over the weekend told Wyatt he needed to convince Lizzie to move their wedding up. He had to keep her and Ella safe, and moving into the house with them was the best way he knew to do that.

His mind made up, as they finished supper that evening, he took Lizzie's hand in his. "Lizzie, there's something I'd like to talk to you about."

"I'll wash the dishes while you two go in the living room to talk," Ella said.

"Actually, Miss Ella, I'd like you to hear this, as well, because it involves you, too."

She had a stack of dishes and was headed to the sink, but stopped and turned to face him. "It does?"

"Yes. If you can sit down so we can all talk a few minutes, I'll help with the dishes when we're done. This is important."

Ella sat back down, looking concerned. "What's on your mind, Wyatt?"

"Lizzie, I know you've had an awful lot to deal with lately, and I hate to add to that, but what would you think about moving our wedding up? Instead of getting married in two months, I'd like to get married quicker; much quicker."

"How much quicker, and why?" Lizzie asked.

"I'd like to get married as soon as possible, and let me explain why." He relayed the information the men had heard onto them, and Lizzie and Ella looked at each other, their eyes wide. "I want to keep both of you ladies safe, and I think the best way to do that is by us getting married. I'll move into the house with you, so you'll no longer be two ladies alone in the house. I'm sure word will get around quickly, just like it did when your father died. Everyone knows we've already announced and have been planning our wedding, and I'm sure they'll all understand why we moved it up."

"The ladies looked at each other, but neither said anything for several moments. Finally, Ella nodded. "I'm sure everyone would understand. And he's right, it was announced at church several weeks ago. Lizzie, I think he's right, and it would be safer for us. I hadn't thought about it, but we are two ladies living in this house alone."

"But the bunkhouse and Wyatt's cabin are close by. If we move the wedding up, how will we get everything done?

We've already lost some time with Papa and the funeral," she said, blinking back a tear or two.

"I understand that, sweetheart," Wyatt said, "but think about it a few minutes. Ma and Pa said to tell you if we move it up they'll do anything they can to help."

"I'm sure they will, too," Ella said. "They're good people."

"I agree with you," Wyatt said with a grin. "And Lizzie, Pa said to tell you if you'd like him to, he'd be honored to walk you down the aisle."

Lizzie fought back a few tears, but held her head up and looked at Wyatt. "That was really nice of him, and I appreciate it. Papa would approve, I'm sure. He always thought so much of your parents." She was quiet, obviously thinking.

"I think we could have everything ready that needs to be done in a pretty short amount of time," Ella said. "I'm sure several of the other ladies would be happy to bring a dish with them and we could still have a big meal after the ceremony. If we can get Mabel Finley to make a couple of cakes, I can make one, too, and that should be enough so everyone gets a piece of wedding cake."

"I guess we probably could," Lizzie said. "I don't need a new dress, and that would save a lot of time."

"Oh, yes, you do," Ella argued, "but I think there's still time for us to make you one. We can check with Mrs. Fetzer first. I'm sure she's busy with orders she already has, but under the circumstances, she may be able to move your dress up and have it ready quicker, especially if we offer to help with it. If she can't do it, Alva is a beautiful seamstress. If the three of us work together on it I'm sure we can have a dress made for you in a matter of several days."

Lizzie thought about Ella's words, and nodded. "You're probably right. Wyatt, when you say as soon as possible, how soon were you thinking of? Maybe in a couple of weeks?"

"I'd like to have it sooner than that if we can, and let me

tell you why. The men told me something that is concerning." He proceeded to tell them what they'd overheard men in town saying last Saturday night. "Something else they said is very true, too, Lizzie. They said everyone in this area loves you two as much as they loved your father, and there will probably be a lot of people that will feel better if we do get married quicker and I'm living in the same house."

Ella had a heartfelt smile on her face as she turned to Lizzie. "He's right, you know. Look at how many people came to the funeral, and how many of them expressed a concern for our safety?"

Lizzie's shoulders slumped, but she agreed. "You're right, Ella. Several did mention that, but I didn't think much of it at the time. Now after what the men heard last weekend, maybe they had reason to express concern."

Ella nodded. "I agree. I hadn't thought of it at the time, either, but then, we were both thinking just of your father. They're right, it would be safer for all of us. If men were thinking of doing something like that, they may ride out to look the place over. I don't think any of us want that kind of men hanging around this ranch."

"Okay." She turned to Wyatt and actually smiled. "Wyatt, I do love you and want to become your wife. If you're okay with moving the wedding up, so am I."

"Wonderful," he said as he stood and pulled her up and into his arms. "If you'll remember, my sweet bride-to-be, when you agreed to marry me I said I would be happy to get married the next day. I still feel that way. I've wanted to make you my wife for some time now, and the sooner you can be ready, the better it will be with me."

Ella watched as the two of them shared a kiss. He pulled back and asked, "So what do you think; is tomorrow good or should we wait until the weekend?"

Both ladies laughed, but Lizzie surprised them all when

she asked, "Ella, do you think we could possibly be ready in a week? Today's Friday. Could we be ready by a week from tomorrow?"

"With Alva's help, and maybe a little from some other ladies in town, I think we can," Ella said with a smile.

Lizzie looked up at Wyatt. "Then how about a week from tomorrow? Are you busy that day?"

"Not at all. I've been wondering what I should do that day." He pulled her back in against him for another hug. He rubbed her back while she leaned her head against his chest. "Lizzie, you've made me very happy tonight. Not only by agreeing to marry me so soon, but that's the first smile I've seen in over a week. You don't know how much I've missed your beautiful smiles. As your husband, I plan on bringing that smile back more often again."

Ella couldn't help but smile at the two young people who were so very obviously in love. It looked like they had a wedding to prepare for, and quickly.

CHAPTER 17

The next week was extraordinarily busy, but once again Lizzie and Ella were a little overwhelmed with the love they felt from the community. Wyatt went to get his mother and took her to spend the morning with Lizzie and Ella so they could do some planning. Then he took them into Gully Ridge after lunch so they could get the fabric for her dress and some other things they would need for their cooking and decorations. They went to visit Mabel Finley, who agreed to make not two, but four cakes, insisting she had plenty of time and didn't want them to have to cut the cakes into tiny pieces to be sure everyone got some. Their next stop was at the dressmaker, Mrs. Fetzer's shop.

"Oh, dear, I'm so glad to hear you're moving your wedding up now," she said. "I feel much better knowing you two ladies won't be living there alone. I'd like to say I can have your dress ready for you, but I can't say for sure I can. I can work on it, but I'll probably need some help."

"I think we can help you there," Ella said. "Alva Hamilton is helping us get this wedding together quickly, and between her and Lizzie and myself, we can help."

"I'm mighty glad to hear that. I figure you ladies have your hands full already, but I do have another suggestion. Mary Alice Troyer wanted to learn how to sew and I've been working with her for almost two years now. She's become a good little seamstress and she's starting to help me out now and then when I need it. If you're okay with her helping me, I believe we can get it done on time. If we run into problems we'll let you know and see if one of you can help us, too. Will that work for you?"

"That sounds wonderful," Lizzie said. "Thank you."

"Oh, it's my pleasure. Now, my dear, let's get your measurements and see if I have any fabric and patterns you like."

Wyatt took them home an hour later, with the wagon full of supplies for the ranch, along with what looked to him to be enough food supplies to feed everyone in Gully Ridge. He heard so many plans on the way home that his head started to spin. He didn't understand everything they were telling him, but he knew his mother was planning on being at the ranch in the morning and the three ladies were going to start on the decorations first. Once they were done they would switch over to cooking the last few days before the wedding.

He was sure they would get everything done that needed to be done, and Lizzie seemed to be happy. He wasn't sure if her happiness was from the anticipation of becoming his wife, or she was enjoying what they were doing, or the company, but he sure liked seeing her smiling again on a daily basis. He could also tell his mother was enjoying the time she was spending with Lizzie, and he was happy to see that, as well.

The next week flew by, and Wyatt couldn't be happier. He was eager to make Lizzie his wife, but he was enjoying seeing Lizzie smiling and laughing again, and there was no missing the excitement she, Ella and his mother were all experiencing. His father was taking his mother most mornings to help Lizzie and Ella during the day, and he and Bryce returned in the evening, where they all had supper together before he took her home. The ladies cooked the evening meal while they were working on their decorations, so it made sense for them all to eat together.

During the first evening Clyde was there to take his wife back home, he asked Lizzie if he could speak with her a moment privately. "Of course," she said, leading him to the library.

He closed the door behind them and turned to her, picking up her hand. "Lizzie, I'd like to talk to you a minute about your wedding. I couldn't be happier that you and Wyatt are going to be married. I also know your papa was very happy about it."

"Yes, he was."

"I wish he was here to walk you down the aisle, but unless you have someone else you'd rather have, I would be honored to do that for your father. He and I have been not just neighbors, but good friends for a long time, and I think he would approve of me standing in for him."

Tears started streaming down Lizzie's face, but she looked up at him and nodded. "I know he would approve, and thank you, Mr. Hamilton. I would love it if you would do that for me. Your whole family has always been special to me, and I appreciate Mrs. Hamilton, uh, Alva, help me prepare for the wedding. Spending time with her while we do all these preparations together is making the wedding even more special. I'll feel the same about you walking me down the aisle. This wedding is not just me marrying the man I love, but it's now like your whole family is wrapping your arms around me." A few more tears escaped, but she swallowed and continued. "I feel so loved, and that's exactly what I needed. Thank you, and your whole family."

"Please call me Clyde," he said as he pulled her in against his chest for a hug. "We do love you, Lizzie, and we always have. It feels good to welcome you officially as a member of our family. We all miss your father and wish he was still here, but we want to do anything we can that he would do if he could. Please let us know if we can do anything else for you, okay?"

"Thank you," she said as a few more tears streamed down her face.

He handed her his handkerchief and waited until she dried her eyes. "When you're ready, we'll go back out."

"SUPPER'S ALMOST READY. I appreciate you and Bryce coming over here for supper so we could keep working while supper's cooking. We got a lot more done by doing that."

He laughed as he assured her, "It's our pleasure. Having a good meal with friends is certainly no hardship."

Things continued the same way, with the three ladies working together as they got everything done. Wyatt took her into town a couple of days before the wedding to try her gown on. Mrs. Fetzer, with Mary Alice's help, had it almost done. She gasped when she saw it. "Oh, my, it's beautiful," she said, reaching out to touch the fabric. Her hand then moved to the lace. "I don't remember this lace."

"Do you like it?"

"Oh, I surely do. It's beautiful, but I'm sure this was quite costly and I didn't purchase any. I didn't even see any like this at the mercantile. If someone else bought this to put on a dress for them and you mistakenly put it on my dress, they'll be upset. I don't want you to --"

"No, there's been no mistake. Miss Lizzie, years ago your papa came into my shop to pick up a dress I'd made for you. My daughter was helping me some then, and while she went to get your dress and wrap it for him, a young lady came in to ask about the cost of a simple dress. She was wearing a very thin, frayed dress, and said her other, older dress had gotten torn and she wasn't sure it could be saved. I gave her a price, and she thanked me and said she would try to mend her old one. After she'd gone your papa asked me about her. I explained that she and her new husband came here looking for work, but he got the influenza and died a week after they got here. She started taking in laundry and anything else she could do to try to make a living for herself. Your papa gave me a generous amount and asked if I would please make her a couple of dresses and see that she gets them."

"I never heard that story," Lizzie said. "Thank you for telling me about it."

"You're welcome. But when I delivered the dresses to her, she said they were beautiful, but she couldn't afford them. I told her they had already been paid for. Even though I wouldn't tell her who paid for them, she figured out that it had to be your father, since he was the only other person in the shop. She was very upset when she heard he'd passed on, and when she heard I was making your dress, she said the mercantile had just gotten in some very pretty lace and she wanted to buy enough for your dress. She insisted, in fact. I hope you like it."

"I love it. But who is she? I'd like to thank her."

"She was adamant that she donate that the same way your father donated dresses to her. I had to promise her I wouldn't tell you." Mrs. Fetzer gave her a hug. "I'll make sure she knows how much you like it, though."

When they got back home Lizzie told Ella and Alva about the beautiful lace on her dress and the story behind it. "Who do you suppose it was?"

The three ladies talked about it off and on the rest of the day, but hadn't been able to figure out who it could be.

Over the next couple of days they did all their baking and cooking, ensuring they were ready for the wedding.

LIZZIE HAD BEEN WORRIED all week that something was going to go wrong on her wedding day. She was sure they'd forgotten something, or she would suddenly gain weight and her dress wouldn't fit, or some other odd thing would happen. However, it turned out to be exactly the opposite. The weather couldn't have been nicer, and the ceremony was lovely. Her dress fit perfectly and was gorgeous.

She was nervous, but Clyde assured her Wyatt was waiting for her at the altar, and to trust him to take good care of her. That helped some, and he was right; when he led her to the church door and she looked forward and saw Wyatt's big smile when he saw her, she relaxed. As Clyde patted her hand and took the first step it felt right when her about to be father-in-law walked her down the aisle, and she saw nothing but smiles from people sitting in the pews.

The ceremony was very nice, but when Pastor Stone told Wyatt he could kiss his bride, he took her in his arms and gave her a kiss she was sure she would always remember. It was so full of love and full of passion that her knees gave out. Luckily, Clyde was right, Wyatt was there ready to take care of her, holding her up with his strong arms. When the kiss ended and she opened her eyes again, Wyatt was smiling down at her with love in his eyes, and the congregation behind them was giggling or laughing, with a bit of applause.

She knew her face was red as he steadied her, then put his arm around her waist, which was appreciated for support, and led her down the aisle. The number of people that congratulated her and wished her well, both at the church and at their house afterward for the reception, was a little daunting. Her heart was filled with the love she felt from everyone.

They spent the afternoon eating and visiting with everyone. Later that evening Wyatt whisked her off, which surprised her. They hadn't even talked about going anywhere that first night, and she assumed they would stay at the house. This had all been planned so quickly, she never considered anything else. But he had a horse and buggy waiting, and they said thank you and good-bye to all the well-wishers that were still visiting and enjoying the meal. She was concerned about Ella, but he assured her his parents had already made arrangements for Ella to stay with them while they were gone.

He took them to Silver Creek, where they had a room waiting for them. He went to the front desk of the hotel and greeted the man behind the desk. "Good evening. "We're Mr. and Mrs. Wyatt Hamilton. I believe we have a room for tonight."

"Ah, the newlyweds," the man said with a smile. "Congratulations. We have your room ready for you. I'll take you up and show it to you." A younger boy, probably the man's son, grabbed the carpetbag Wyatt had packed for them and ran up the stairs. Wyatt and Lizzie followed their host up, where he led them to the room at the end of the hall. "This is what we refer to as our newlywed room. I hope you find it to your satisfaction. There is a water closet next door. If you need anything, please let me know. The restaurant downstairs is open for two more hours, or if you'd like, we can have two meals brought up here to you. We've found a lot of honeymooners prefer that," he added with a wink.

"We would appreciate that," Wyatt said. Lizzie looked down, knowing her face was red again. "Do I need to go downstairs to order that and pay for it?"

"No, sir. I'll put your order in now and you can pay for it before you leave tomorrow. Our meals tonight are roast beef or rabbit stew, and your meal includes pie."

Wyatt smiled at Lizzie before answering, "We'll both have the rabbit stew, and any kind of pie is fine. Our favorites are apple and cherry, but any kind of pie would be fine. Thank you."

"I'll let them know. Is there anything else I can get you now?"

"No, I don't believe so, but I'd like to thank you for your hospitality." He handed a coin to the man, and another one to the small boy, who grinned ear to ear as he thanked him.

Once they were alone Wyatt turned to Lizzie and took her in his arms. "Mrs. Hamilton, I never got a chance to tell you how beautiful you were today in your wedding dress. That's a lovely dress you're wearing now, as well, and I don't believe I've seen it before. Is that another new dress, a special one for your wedding day?"

"Yes, it is," she said as she felt her face heat a bit. "Do you think it was too much? I probably shouldn't have spent the money for two new dresses."

"Nonsense. I wanted everything to be perfect for you today, so I'm glad you did. Besides, they're very pretty dresses, and you look quite lovely in both of them. They'll make nice church dresses." He leaned down for another kiss, but kept it fairly short. "They'll be here before long with our supper, so I'll keep my kiss short for now," he said with a mischievous grin and a wink, which had her blushing again.

Keeping her in his arms, he used one hand to guide her head to his chest. "While we're talking about your pretty new dresses, I'd like to talk to you about money."

She looked up at him. "I shouldn't have spent the money for the fabric for this new dress, should I? I'm sorry."

"Shh," he said, guiding her head back to his chest. "Don't be sorry, Lizzie. I'm glad you did. Like I said, it's very pretty and you look real nice in it. But what I wanted to tell you is Pa's been paying Bryce and me for working at the ranch. Since I've been living at home and haven't needed much, I've been saving most of that money, hoping to buy a ranch of our own for us some day. We don't need to worry about buying our own ranch now, but I wanted to let you know I have a fair amount of money saved. I know you and I know you won't spend it foolishly, which makes me proud, but what I'm saying is please don't feel you have to be careful and watch every penny. If you need something, a new dress or something for the house, please get it."

"Thank you, Wyatt. The ranch has been doing fairly well, so I hope we can keep it running good. I want to make Papa proud of us."

"I'm hoping the same thing," he assured her. "I'm real glad I've been working as the foreman. That gave me a chance to get to know all the men, as well as learn more about how your father has been running the ranch. Like you said, it's been successful, so I'm hoping we can keep everything the same and it will continue doing well." He kissed her again before adding, "With both of us working together on it I feel confident we can do your father proud."

"I think so, too," she said as she cuddled up against him, tightening her arms that were wrapped around him.

They were still wrapped contentedly in each other's arms when there was a knock at the door. "Ready for some rabbit stew?" He smiled, then gave her one more quick kiss before opening the door for their supper.

They enjoyed their rabbit stew, commenting on their luck that it was their special for the day. When they were done eating he put their dishes on the tray and set it outside the door. After closing and locking the door behind him, he turned to her. "Now, Mrs. Hamilton, I've waited for this moment for quite some time now." His hands cupped her face gently and he leaned down to give her a long-awaited kiss without holding back the passion he felt.

He was a little surprised, but extremely pleased when she returned his kiss with an extremely passionate kiss of her own. "Oh, Lizzie," he moaned, "I love you."

"I love you, too, Wyatt," she whispered back, her own voice as emotional as his.

"Turn around, sweetheart, and let me unbutton your dress," he said huskily.

She surprised him yet again when she replied, "Yes, please," and turned for him. Her eagerness was almost more than he could take. His hands were awfully big for those tiny buttons, but persistence paid off and he was soon laying her gently on the bed.

Almost two hours later he held his new wife in his arms as he watched her sleeping next to him. He'd been waiting to claim her as his own for what seemed like several long years, but the wait had been well worth it. She'd been even more responsive than he'd hoped, and had fallen asleep happy, cuddled against him. He watched her sleeping on his shoulder, relaxed and content. She'd been through a lot lately, and he hoped they could settle into a peaceful life on the ranch, running it together.

~

WHEN LIZZIE WOKE she was a bit confused. Then she felt Wyatt's arms around her, and she smiled, remembering the wonderful time they'd had. She'd been nervous, even a little worried about what would happen. She'd heard horrible stories about what some married ladies had referred to as the 'wifely duty', but she needn't have worried. Wyatt had been very patient with her, explaining things and answering any questions she had. She didn't have many questions, however. It had been truly amazing, and simply wonderful.

Lying next to her new husband, with his arms wrapped around her as he slept, made her feel not only very loved, but safe. She looked over at him as he slept. They'd been such good friends since they were small that she hadn't really stopped to take a good look at him lately, but now she did. He really was a handsome man, but she hadn't noticed how much he'd filled out as a man. No doubt working on their ranch accounted for the muscles he now sported in his back and shoulders, not to mention his arms.

She couldn't control the small giggle that escaped as she thought back to the time not so long ago that he'd pulled her across his lap and spanked her for being up on her ankle before the doctor approved. One thing that struck her at that time was how muscular his thighs had become. Unfortunately, it also emphasized how strong his arms had become.

Her mind was pulled back to the present when Wyatt began to stir a bit. "What's so funny, Mrs. Hamilton?"

"Oh, nothing important, Mr. Hamilton. I love hearing that name."

"I'm glad to hear that, and I hope you soon get used to it." He rolled over and gave her a kiss, then leaned back, bringing her head back to lean on his chest again. "Now, what caused you to laugh as you were looking at me?"

Her head flew off his chest and she looked up at him. "You knew I was looking at you?"

"Of course I did. I'm your husband, it's my job to keep an eye on you and know what you're doing. So back to the question, what was so funny?"

"Do you want me to be honest?" she asked with a mischievous grin.

"Always," he said absolutely. "Anything less will earn you a spanking."

She giggled again, and he frowned when he looked at her again. "I wasn't kidding, Lizzie."

"No, I know you weren't," she said, attempting to calm him. "It's just that, well, that's kind of what I was thinking about." His eyebrows raised, but he waited for her to continue. "Growing up together I hadn't really noticed how strong or handsome you've become. Looking over at you now, lying beside me with your arms around me, I saw it. I remembered realizing for the first time how strong you've gotten not long ago, when you spanked me. That day I could feel the muscles in your thighs, and most definitely in your arms."

He chuckled, as well, as he pulled her in closer to him. "Well, then I would suggest you remember that and don't earn any more spankings."

"I have remembered it, and I don't plan on earning any more. That hurt."

"As it was meant to," he said before leaning down to kiss the top of her head. "And I hope you don't earn any more, but we'll see."

"What do you mean by that? You don't sound too confident."

"I'm not," he admitted freely. "Like you said, sweetheart, we grew up together. I know you, and there were numerous times growing up when I thought you'd earned a good spanking, but your father never gave you one. In my mind, that was a mistake."

She was frowning when she looked up at him. "Are you saying I grew up to be a horrible person?"

"Of course not, or I wouldn't have married you. All I'm

saying is your father said he knew he should have spanked you growing up, but he just couldn't. Raising a little girl by himself was hard, and I understand that. He did a wonderful job with you, and you've grown up to be a very special lady."

"And you're a very special man."

"Thank you, but getting back to my point, my parents spanked us as we were growing up, and although I didn't like it at the time, I now see it as the best way I know to show someone you love them enough to be watching them and making sure they're safe."

She giggled again. "That sounded like you were saying that spanking someone is the same as telling them you love them."

"It is," he said, which ended her giggling.

"You're serious?"

"Absolutely. Lizzie, when I spanked you for walking on your ankle, I thought you understood why I was spanking you."

"I did. Because I lied about what the doctor said and was on my foot before I should have been."

"That's true, but by doing that you were putting yourself in danger. I won't allow my wife to put herself in danger." He lifted her chin so she was looking at him. "I love you too much to allow that, Lizzie. If you do something that could cause you to be hurt, or get sick, I will spank you again. Loving you means keeping you safe. Do you understand now why I spanked you, and why I'll do it again if I see you doing something dangerous?"

She paused a few moments, but eventually nodded. "Yes." A few tears slid down her cheeks as she added, "I didn't know that was why. I thought it was because I lied about what he said."

"It was in a way, but that lie could have gotten you hurt, and that's what I couldn't ignore." Convinced she understood better now, he wiped her tears away and said, "And now I think it's time I show you just how much I love you." He gave her another kiss that left no question in her mind as to his intentions, and when she moaned in appreciation, he lost himself yet again.

CHAPTER 18

Wyatt and Lizzie returned home on Monday. They both felt they needed to get back to the ranch, since it was their responsibility now, and they were trying to earn the respect of the men working for them. They knew keeping them on would be vital, and were afraid if they doubted their ability to run the ranch profitably they would move on to work on another ranch.

They had a talk with Ella, and she agreed with them, and thought it was a good idea for both of them to focus on the ranch, at least for the time being. She knew they'd been working hard to run it the way Ben had, but there was a lot to learn and figure out. She assured them she would take care of the house and have their meals ready so they could take care of the ranch. It was important to her, as well, that they succeed, as she loved both Wyatt and Lizzie. They were like her own children, having watched them grow up.

The newly married young couple of discussed everything and made their ranching decisions together, but Wyatt continued in the role of foreman, since that's what the men had been used to, while Lizzie concentrated on the horses. When they needed supplies, they generally went to town together. It gave them some time alone, and allowed them the luxury of having their dinner, or noontime meal, together at Ruby's restaurant. He generally went to the feed store and got the supplies he needed, while Lizzie went to the mercantile and gave Tom and Claudia her list of things she and Ella needed.

She enjoyed talking to Claudia and maybe browsing at things in the mercantile until Wyatt brought the wagon there and went inside to say hello to the owners, as well, before taking Lizzie to eat. When they got back he helped Tom load their wagon up. If they had any other business to take care of while they were in town they did that, then headed for home.

On one such occasion Wyatt didn't need much at the feed store, so after he finished there he went to the blacksmith, which was next to the feed store, before meeting Lizzie at the general store. "Good morning, Henry," he greeted the blacksmith.

"Wyatt, it's good to see you. How are you enjoying married life?"

"I'm enjoying it just fine," he answered with a big smile.

"I'm glad to hear that. Miss Lizzie is a special little lady. It was awful that her papa died like that. Is she starting to accept it yet, or is she still thinking someone killed him and looking for who did it?"

Wyatt's mouth dropped open. He took a moment to collect himself before asking, "What do you mean, still looking for who killed him?"

"When she was in here asking me some questions a couple of weeks ago I told her I hadn't heard anything."

"She was in here asking you questions? What kind of questions?"

Henry hesitated several seconds. "If you didn't know she was in here asking questions, I shouldn't have said anything, and I'm sorry. I assumed you knew."

"No, I didn't know, but I should have. What kind of questions was she asking, Henry?"

"I don't want to get her in trouble."

"I don't want her to get hurt," Wyatt said. "Asking the wrong question of the wrong person could be dangerous, especially for a lady. I'll talk to her about it. Did she say anything else, what kind of things she thought you may have heard?"

"No, not at all. I was surprised to hear she thought he was killed. I thought they said he was thrown from his horse and died."

"That was my understanding, too," Wyatt said, "but I knew she felt he was too good a horseman to be thrown. He was a good horseman and I was surprised when I heard what happened, as well, but I wasn't aware she didn't believe that's what happened. We'll be having a talk about it tonight. Thank you for telling me about this, Henry, and if you do happen to hear something, would you please let me know?"

"Of course I will, and good luck to you, Wyatt. Take good care of your new wife because I agree, her going around asking questions could be dangerous. Now, what can I do for you today?"

Wyatt bought some horseshoes from Henry and placed them in the wagon, thinking about what he'd just learned. Instead of going to the general store, he went across the street to talk to Mose Mullins, who made and sold furniture. After greeting him he asked, "Mose, has my wife asked if you've heard anything about her father's accident?"

"Yes, she was in a week or so after he died, and I told her I hadn't heard anything. I still haven't heard anything, but I've been listening. A lot of people have talked about him because he was so well liked. Ben was a good rider and it was surprising to hear that's how he did, but I haven't heard anything that would suggest it might not have been an accident. Have you heard something?"

"No, I haven't, but I thought I would check while I'm in town. It doesn't seem as though anyone's heard anything."

"I feel bad for Miss Lizzie, but if it was an accident, I hope she can accept that. It will be harder for her to get past it if she can't."

"I agree. I'm going to try to help her accept it. Thank you for your time, Mose."

"Of course."

Wyatt found himself getting angry as he went back to the wagon. They'd talked about Ben's accident, and he knew she was upset, obviously, and found it hard to believe since he was so good around horses and had ridden so long. On one occasion she'd questioned that he'd died from being thrown, but after they talked about it, he thought she'd accepted it. He didn't like the idea of her going around town and asking questions about it. If anything untoward had happened, hearing she's asking questions could put her in grave danger. He would definitely be talking to her about this, but would wait until they were on their way back to the ranch. He certainly didn't want anyone to overhear their conversation.

Having made that decision, he went to the general store and looked around before greeting Tom. "Good morning, Tom. Do you happen to know where my new wife is?"

"I do. My wife took your wife in the back room to show her a new sewing machine we just got in this morning. I'll tell them you're here."

He turned toward the back room, but the ladies came back out to the store. "We heard Wyatt come in," Claudia said. "I didn't want him thinking I kidnapped Lizzie. I hope we didn't hold you up, Wyatt."

"No, of course not." He met his wife and dropped a quick kiss on her head and wrapped his arm around her waist. "What did you think of the sewing machine?"

"It sure is fascinating. It would make sewing our clothes much quicker."

"We may have to get you one someday then. Are you ready to go see Ruby?"

"Yes, of course." She turned back toward Claudia. "Thank you for showing me the sewing machine."

"My pleasure. Let me know if you decide you may want one. We ordered that one to have in our store so people can see it and how it works, but we've waited for that one almost four months."

"Oh, my goodness," Lizzie said. "Thank you again for letting me see it."

Wyatt escorted his wife to Ruby's restaurant, where they enjoyed their dinner. After they ate he helped Tom load their supplies into the wagon, helped Lizzie into the wagon and they started for home. He waited until they were out of town to take her hand into his. "Lizzie, I needed some extra horseshoes, so I picked some up from Henry after I finished at the feed store." He felt her stiffen slightly before he continued. "He said to tell you he's sorry, but he still hasn't heard anything that might suggest your father's accident was no accident."

She turned to look away from him and tried to pull her hand out of his, but he held on tight. "Sweetheart, we need to talk. I know you think your dad was too good with horses to have been thrown, but is there anything else that makes you think it wasn't an accident? And most importantly, why did you go around town asking questions instead of talking to me?"

She started to answer, but was still looking away from him. He reached over and pulled her chin around and up. "Now, what were you saying?"

"I'm sorry I didn't talk to you first, Wyatt, but I didn't think you'd believe me. I was hoping someone would have heard something, and then if I told you that, along with what I've already found, you'd believe me and help me convince the sheriff."

He pulled the wagon over to the side of the road and stopped it before looking at her again. "What have you already found, and how did you find it?"

"Wyatt, you look upset."

"Answer my question, please," he said, keeping his stern expression in place.

"Okay, I will. Please don't be upset with me. Before we left Silver Creek the sheriff gave me the things he had in his pockets. It was in a burlap sack and I couldn't bear to look at them right away. When I did finally look at them, a couple of things weren't right. There was some money, which is why they felt it was simply an accident. If someone would have robbed him they would have taken his money. The little knife he always carried with him and used on the ranch was also there. But what bothered me is what wasn't there."

Some of Wyatt's anger left and he softened his expression some. "What was missing?"

"Two things. First, he left that day to buy horses. He went to town first to take money out of the bank to pay for the horses. He was on his way from Gully Ridge to Leesburg and the Praxton ranch, so he should have had enough cash on him to pay for the horses. He had a little money, but not nearly what he should have had. The other thing missing was the pocket watch that had been his father's. He always carried that with him, and it wasn't there."

He sat there staring at her several moments, not sure how

he felt about this or how to answer. He was still not happy with her, but he had to agree there was reason for concern, hearing this. Well, first things first. He would deal with her doing something dangerous without telling him later. "You're right," he agreed, "he always has that pocket watch with him. It was special to him because it had been his father's."

"Exactly. I'm disappointed because I always planned on keeping it, as well, but the fact that it wasn't there tells me something isn't right."

"I'm afraid to ask, but do you know for sure he took money out of the bank that day?"

"I do know that. When the attorney told me according to Papa's will everything would go to me, he said I had to go to the bank so they could get my signature and put the money he had there in my name. While I was there I asked him if Papa had taken out the money that morning to buy the horses. He looked at his records and said he had, and showed me where he'd signed for it. I didn't question it at all since I knew that was his plan. But that means someone did steal from him. They took most of the money he had with him, and his pocket watch."

Wyatt sighed, but nodded. "Yes, it does mean someone took some money and his watch. But we don't know anything else."

"That's why I was asking if anyone had heard anything."

"Lizzie, that's not the proper way to look into this. Asking questions like that could be very dangerous. We need to talk to Sheriff Williams and see what he suggests we do."

"I did. He won't do anything."

Wyatt's eyes flew open. "You talked to Sheriff Williams, without mentioning anything about this to me?" He got down from the wagon and walked around a bit as he took a deep breath and exhaled slowly in an attempt to calm down. When he climbed back up in the wagon he took her hand in his again. "Lizzie, you've earned a good spanking, but I'm not going to do it yet."

Her eyes wide, she looked around to be sure there was no one else on the road that could have heard him. "I would hope not here, where anyone could come by and see us."

"That's not why I'm not going to do it now. You'll soon find that I don't often like to postpone punishment. If you earn it now I will generally see that you get it now, or as soon thereafter as possible. I won't spank you in front of anyone, as my aim is not to embarrass you. However, there is usually a way to do it without having to postpone it much. In this case I would have taken you to the woods right over there and we would have taken care of it now. The reason I'm not going to do it yet is because I'm too upset. I will never spank you when I'm this angry. Other than giving you a sore bottom that will cause you to think about what you've done, I don't want to hurt you. Spanking you while I'm this angry wouldn't be safe."

She was quiet while she thought about what he'd said. "But why are you this angry? He was my papa and I loved him. I feel sure something isn't right, but no one believes me. Wyatt, I'm sorry, but I can't just forget about it. I thought you would understand that."

Tears were streaming down her cheeks as he took her in his arms. Hugging her tightly, he assured her, "I do understand that, sweetheart. I'm new at this, being a husband, and maybe I'm not doing a very good job. Let me explain why I'm upset."

"That would help. I didn't mean to upset you."

"But you had to know I wouldn't be happy with you asking people questions without talking to me first. Be honest, for yourself and for me. Why didn't you talk to me about it first, before talking to other people?"

She hesitated a moment, but when she saw the love in

Wyatt's eyes and knew he was always honest with her, she sighed. "Because we've talked about it and you always seemed to believe it was indeed an accident. I was afraid if I told you I didn't think it was you wouldn't agree with me, and if you didn't, you wouldn't approve of looking into it further."

"Thank you for your honesty. But now answer another question for me. Did I talk to you about how important it is that we communicate now that we're married, and that I want you to talk to me about everything, so we can share everything, and go through anything that comes along together?"

"Yes," she admitted.

"And that's why you'll be getting spanked later today. But we'll take care of that later, after I've had time to calm down more. I'm still upset that you didn't trust me enough to tell me about the missing money or the watch. But right now --"

"Wait. Wyatt, it's not that I didn't trust you. I do trust you."

"Then why didn't you tell me about them, so we could decide what to do about them?"

"Because I was afraid – because --"

"Because you were afraid I wouldn't believe you and tell you I didn't want you to pursue it further?"

"I guess maybe, yes."

"And that means you didn't trust me enough to tell me so we could decide what to do together."

She was quiet for some time. He could tell she was thinking it through, so he gave her the time she needed. "Wyatt, I'm sorry. I didn't think of it that way, but I guess I can't deny it. I'm used to doing what I want. If I knew Papa wouldn't approve of something I simply wouldn't tell him about it before I did it."

Now it was time for Wyatt to pause a moment before answering. "Thank you for telling me that. I don't approve, but I do believe you. I thought it was because you don't trust me, but it may not be totally that; it might be more because that's what you're used to. But either way, that has to stop. We're married now and we will do things together. We'll talk about that more later, but for right now let's talk about this missing money and watch. You said you talked to Sheriff Williams. What did he say?"

"He said we don't have anything to go on. The money could have fallen out of his shirt pocket when he fell, and blew away before someone found him. The same with the watch; it could have fallen out and rolled away. It might even still be there. When he was found, they probably didn't search the area. He thinks if someone robbed him they would have taken everything, including all his money, his knife, and his gun. They were all still there, and so was his horse. A thief would have taken that, too, according to him."

"Well, you can't really argue with that reasoning, but I tend to agree with you. Something doesn't seem quite right."

Her eyes lit up. "So you believe me? You'll help me find who killed Papa?"

"Well, slow down a little bit. Yes, I believe you, and I think we should look into it. But let me check around town and see what I can find out. It's not safe for a lady to be asking these questions. I'll go to the saloons and listen to people, see if I hear anything. If I don't, maybe I'll ask a question or two. But I don't want you out there asking any more questions. Do you understand me, Lizzie?"

"But Wyatt --"

"No, Lizzie, there are not buts about it. You let me ask the questions. If I hear you've asked one more question of one more person, you'll find yourself over my lap for a blistering spanking you'll remember for a long time. I'm not your papa, and I won't allow you to do what you want, and put yourself in danger. If you won't agree to doing this my way, we won't do it at all. I'll keep you home so you can't get yourself into trouble. Now do you understand me?"

Seeing the determined set to his jaw, she nodded. "Okay. I don't like it, but thank you for agreeing to help look into it."

"So you'll let me ask the questions?"

"Yes."

"Good." He started the wagon moving toward home again, and they talked about how they wanted to proceed. They both agreed to keep it between themselves for the time being. Wyatt wanted to see if he could unearth any relative information or facts that may help before he told anyone else they were looking into Ben's death.

They got back to the ranch and back to work. Wyatt went to check on the men, while Lizzie went to check on a horse that was due to foal any day. Neither got much done. Lizzie had a lot on her mind. She was glad Wyatt had agreed to help her look into her papa's death, but the conversation they'd had on the way home had her upset. She was not looking forward to being spanked, as she could still remember vividly the other time he'd spanked her shortly before they were married, and how much it had hurt. She had no doubt this one would be at least as bad.

That wasn't the only thing that had her upset, though. Wyatt said she didn't trust him, and although trust hadn't actually even entered her mind at the time, it was hard for her to deny what he'd insinuated. She hadn't mentioned anything to him simply out of habit. If there was any doubt in her mind that her father would approve of her doing something, she simply didn't tell him until after she'd already done it. In this case she'd simply done the same thing.

But Wyatt had been upset and immediately said she didn't

trust him enough to talk to him about it first, and although she'd denied it, the more she thought about his accusation, the harder it was to deny. She hadn't consciously thought about the possibility of him not approving before deciding not to tell him what she planned to do, but subconsciously, well, that was a different story. Although she hadn't actually stopped to think about talking to him about it first, she had to admit she would have known he may not – probably would not – approve.

Was it possible that subconsciously she knew he wouldn't approve, so she ignored him, as she had her father? She was married now, to a man she loved; a man that had talked to her about his need for her to share her thoughts and concerns with him. He wanted to take care of her, like he always had, but as her husband, he needed and deserved to know what her concerns were so he could help her. She hadn't even given him that opportunity. Was it possible she didn't trust him enough to do that?

She didn't want that to be the case. She loved Wyatt and had no reason not to trust him, since he had always been there for her and helped her out of several problem situations over the years. So why didn't she share this with him, and tell him she truly felt her father had been killed and that she intended to find his killer?

That thought bothered her the rest of the afternoon, and she couldn't get it out of her mind. When they went in for supper that night Ella could tell something had happened, that there was something between them. As much as she hated seeing them like this, she knew there was a lot of love between them, and they were both good, smart people. Every marriage had its moments, especially at the beginning, when two people were getting used to each other. She also knew they had to work things out for themselves.

With that in mind, once they finished their rather quiet

supper, she quickly cleaned up the kitchen, with help from Lizzie, and excused herself. "I'm going to retire early this evening so I can write a letter to my sister," she said. "I'll see both of you in the morning."

With that short announcement, she left, leaving the two of them alone, looking at each other. Wyatt took her hand in his. "We have some business to take care of ourselves, Lizzie. Let's go take care of that."

She nodded. "I'd like to talk a few minutes if we could before you do, before you --"

"Take care of that business?" he offered. "Certainly. We can always talk first, and afterward." He kept her hand and led her upstairs to their room, which was still her old bedroom. Neither had felt a need or desire to move into Ben's old room as yet. When they got there he closed the door behind them and sat down on the bed. He patted the bed next to him as he said, "Come sit next to me, Lizzie, and tell me what you'd like to say."

She sat down and looked down at her lap, looking for the right words. Finally she just blurted out her thoughts. "I've thought about this all afternoon."

"As have I," he said, surprising her.

"You have?"

"Yes. Why don't you go ahead and tell me your thoughts, then I'll share mine?"

"Okay." She was quiet a few more moments, then jumped right in and tried to explain her jumbled thoughts. "Wyatt, I'm sorry. I honestly didn't keep this information from you because I thought you wouldn't approve of my asking questions around town. Well, at least not consciously. I simply did what I'd always done. But when you said I didn't trust you, that upset me and made me think, a lot."

She looked up and met his eyes with hers before going on. "But we're married now and you did say we need to share everything with each other. I realize now that you were right about that, and I didn't do it. You deserve better than that, Wyatt, and I'm truly sorry. I can't promise I'll do better next time and be a better wife and never do that again, but I can promise I'll try to do better. I hope you can believe me and forgive me."

CHAPTER 19

Tears had begun streaming down Lizzie's cheeks, and Wyatt used his thumb to catch them. He could see the sincerity in her eyes, and his love and respect for her grew. "Thank you," he said as he wrapped his arms around her and pulled her in against his chest. "My dear Lizzie, I love you, and I do believe you. I'll be able to forgive you in a few minutes, but first we need to talk."

"I understand," she said, and he could tell she was resigned to the upcoming spanking. He was glad, and hoped that meant she accepted it and knew she'd earned one.

"I hope you understand why it's important to me that we share things. Because I love you, as your husband I feel responsible for keeping you safe. You asking questions around town about Ben's death could put you in a great deal of danger, and I can't allow that to happen. I know how important your papa was to you, and finding the truth is important to me, too. We're going to look into this matter, but you have to let me do it in a way that I can keep you safe. The reason I want you to share everything with me is not only to share your life, but to keep you safe. I hope you will freely talk to me in the future, and not keep things from me."

"I will, but you may have to be patient with me. I've done pretty much what I've wanted to for my whole life, and it may take a little time for me to break that habit. I promise you I will try, though, because now I understand why you're asking that. I want you to know that I love you, and I do trust you. I just have to learn to break that habit."

"You're right, Lizzie, doing what you wanted without checking with your papa or anyone else was a habit of yours, a bad habit. There were several times I thought your papa should have warmed your bottom for doing things, dangerous things on your own. You were lucky and generally didn't get hurt, but you need to understand that I'm not your papa, and I won't allow you to take those risks."

"I understand, and I will try."

"Well, I'm going to help you break that bad habit. You're about to get spanked, Lizzie, and you can expect another spanking every time you do something like this without talking to me first. I suggest you learn to talk to me – about everything." Without another word, he gave her wrist a quick pull and she found herself draped over his lap.

She gasped, more from the air leaving her lungs when she landed than from surprise. As she'd thought about this all afternoon she'd felt bad and convinced herself she was ready for this, but now that she was face down over his lap, she wasn't so sure. She tried to take a deep breath and prepare herself, but before she had a chance, he lifted her dress and underskirts, which took her by surprise.

While she'd admitted to herself that she understood why he was upset and that she deserved a spanking, she hadn't thought of the actual process. The idea of anyone, even if it was her husband, seeing her naked behind, just didn't seem proper. Instinct kicked in as he reached around to untie her pantaloons and started pulling them down, and she tried to squirm her way off his lap.

One solid swat to her bare bottom stilled her. "There will be none of that," Wyatt said. "If you remember, when I spanked you shortly before we were married I warned you that any spanking you got after we were married would be on your bare bottom. You've earned this, now settle down and accept it."

She knew he was right; she did deserve it, but accepting it was another story. It hurt. Did he really think she could just lay there and take it? She tried to, but found herself squirming and wriggling, doing anything she could to avoid his heavy hand. She had no idea a spanking could be that painful with just his hand.

Just as she was about to insist she couldn't take any more, he started talking as he spanked. He reminded her of his love for her, and explained how things could go wrong if she continued to ask questions around town. He could tell she hadn't thought of those possibilities, so he suggested a couple of more possibilities. Tears started streaming down her cheeks, and he wasn't sure if they were due to what he was saying, or from the pain of the spanking.

In his mind it didn't much matter which it was, so he continued with the spanking. She had been right when she said it was a habit of hers to do what she wanted, and he fully intended this spanking to be the first step in breaking that habit. Habits can be hard to break, so this had to make a lasting impression on her. He watched her reaction, and tightened his hold a bit as she started struggling a little more.

There was no doubt in his mind she was sore, and seeing her in pain and knowing he was the cause of that pain was harder than he thought it would be. He had to picture what could have happened to her if she'd continued asking questions in order to steel himself to continue with the spanking just a little longer. With a last reminder that he wouldn't give her this spanking if he didn't love her, he brought it to an end.

She continued to cry and struggle a minute or two before she realized the spanking had ended and he was rubbing her back. She sagged over his lap, looking limp and exhausted. He gently turned her over and brought her up to sit in his lap, and quickly had her wrapped in his arms. He held onto her, not quite sure she wouldn't try to stand and run from him. This spanking had been harder than the first one he'd given her, so he wasn't sure what her reaction would be. He relaxed and squeezed her a little tighter against him when her arms snaked around his neck and she laid her head on his shoulder.

"My sweet Lizzie, you said earlier you hope I can forgive you. The answer to that is yes, I can. I love you, my sweet wife, and I worry about you getting hurt. I'm not happy that you chose to investigate on your own without talking to me, but we've talked about that now and you know why it's important that you share things with me. You've had some consequences for that dangerous act to help you remember not to do it again, so yes, I can now forgive you. We don't need to talk about this again, unless you want to."

"Thank you," she said, hugging him tighter. They stayed just as they were, with her in his lap with her head leaning against his strong chest and his arms like a safety net around her, and talked quietly for the next ten minutes. Eventually he lifted her chin so she was looking at him. "We need to talk about your father a few minutes. I've given this a lot of thought, and I have a plan."

"What kind of plan?"

"Before I explain this, remember, you need to let me handle it. I know how much you want to know the truth, but I won't have my wife asking this kind of questions. I know you and I know how much you're going to want to be involved, and that's understandable. I'll let you help all I can, as long as I feel you'll be safe. But initially, while we search for something to go on, will you promise to let me handle it?"

She sighed, but nodded. "I've given this a lot of thought, as well, and I have to admit you're probably right. You may be more apt to hear something at the saloons, and it wouldn't be very safe for me to be going around them and asking questions. I'll let you handle that part, but please don't keep things from me. No matter what it is you find out, I want to know."

"That's fair. Now, with that assurance, I'll tell you what I'd like to do. I think our best chance of gleaning any kind of information about what may have happened to him will come not from going around town asking questions, but more from listening, especially at the saloons. I've never made it a habit to frequent them on a regular basis, but I've gone to them occasionally with the men on a Saturday night. Pa is the same; he doesn't go to them regularly, but he does go to them occasionally. Bryce goes to them more often, usually with the men on a Saturday night. I think if I start showing up at them all the time, shortly after getting married, people will wonder what's going on, and they might start talking."

"If they start talking, it's hard telling what they'll be saying and spreading around," she said, thinking out loud.

"Exactly. I don't want it going around town that you and I are having problems in our new marriage, so I came up with a plan. I'd like to talk to Pa and Bryce about Ben. They thought a lot of him, and if they knew we have reason to question that it was an accident, I know they'll offer to do whatever they can to help find the truth. I thought maybe Pa and I could go to a saloon together every now and then, and just kind of sit back and listen to what men are talking about.

People are still telling me how sorry they were about Ben, so maybe if someone mentions that we can use it to get a conversation going, see if anyone happens to mention anything."

"That makes sense, but it might take a while."

"Yes, it might, but I think it's safer since it won't look like we're poking around asking questions. If someone out there did kill and rob him, they're not going to like us poking our nose into it. If we just talk about him when someone mentions him to us, that will be safer."

"That does make sense, I guess. But you'll have to start going right away, while they're still talking about him."

"I agree. Now, Bryce is more used to going to saloons, or maybe I should say people are more used to seeing him there, especially on Saturday nights. I'm thinking I can get him to do the same thing; talk about Ben and the tragedy anytime someone mentions him. You never know what kind of conversation that can lead to or what you might find out. I figure we can do that every Saturday night for a few weeks, and the three of us will talk, or four if you want to hear it, too, and we'll see if any of us has heard anything."

"Yes, I would like to listen to what they have to say, too, please."

"I'm okay with that, as long as you let us handle it."

"I will."

"Okay. Then if we hear something that makes us think there may be more to it than a simple accident, I'll ask Pa to go with us to talk to Sheriff Williams. If we have a little more to go on then, and Pa and I are both there asking, I hope he'll look into the matter. If he still won't, I'm thinking Pa and I can go to Leesburg and talk to the sheriff there. Maybe we can even talk to Mr. Praxton and see if he'll talk to the sheriff with us. Hopefully one of them will agree to look into it further."

"Okay, that sounds like it might work. Thank you, Wyatt, for helping me."

"You're welcome, but I have to say, I'm not just doing this for you. Now that I know some money and his pocket watch are missing, I want to know what really happened, as well. If I would have known that earlier I could have been listening for information concerning this sooner. That's another reason why you need to trust me and talk to me about things."

"I see that now, and I truly am sorry. It was never that I didn't trust you; I just did things the way I've always done them."

"I understand, and we don't need to go over this again, but simply keep in mind that things are different now."

"Yes, I know," she said as her face turned red and she reached back to rub her bottom.

He chuckled as he pulled her in tighter against his chest. "Good. Now remember it."

~

WYATT TALKED to his pa and his brother, Bryce, and both were upset when they heard those things were missing from the things they gave Lizzie. They talked about his plan, and they both agreed it was a good way to approach it, and agreed to help. The following Saturday evening Wyatt and his pa went to one saloon, while Bryce went to the other, which was the one he was more used to going to. The two families ate their noon meal together after church, and they talked about the evening before. They were disappointed that they hadn't heard anything helpful, but they were encouraged by the number of people that brought up Ben. That gave them an easy way to start a conversation.

They planned to do the same thing the next Friday

evening, and have dinner together after church again next week. They all liked the idea of the two families eating together on Sunday after church, and decided they would continue doing it even after they found out what had happened to Ben. They both agreed it was a clear advantage of marrying your neighbor.

The next week went by quickly for both of them. Wyatt noticed Lizzie seemed to be happier and less moody, which he felt had something to do with the stress she must have been feeling before their talk. He decided he would watch her closely, and if she started showing signs of stress again he would sit her down and get her to talk to him, see if she was keeping something to herself again.

The next Saturday evening found the three men at the saloons again, listening for anything that may help them. Bryce said he'd heard something, but didn't want to talk about it until they were together and Lizzie could hear it as well. They hurried home from church the next day and Alva helped Lizzie and Ella fix a quick dinner so they could talk about it. "Okay, Bryce, we're eating and I can't wait any longer," Lizzie insisted. "What did you hear about Papa?"

"Well, it isn't so much that I heard anything about your father," Bryce said, "but it may be related. Didn't you say when Coy left he went straight back home, which was in Texas somewhere?"

"Yes," she said slowly. "He told Clem his father was having trouble taking care of their family farm since he hurt his back, so he was going home to take it over. Why? What does he have to do with Papa? Did he kill him?"

"I DON'T HAVE anything that says he did, but I did find out he didn't leave Gully Ridge until right around the time your papa had the accident."

Several of them dropped their forks and all eyes turned to Bryce. "He actually went back to Gully Ridge for several weeks?" Wyatt asked. "How did we not hear about it?"

"It sounded to me like he was keeping out of sight on Saturday night, when the men from your ranch or ours would be in town. No one last night seemed to know what he was doing in town, or where he went or when. He wasn't looking for a job while he was still around here because Ned Buckwalter told him he knew of a ranch over toward Silver Creek that was hiring, but he said he wasn't looking for another job quite yet. No one ever heard him say why he was still here, or where he was going. But when I asked a few questions about when anyone saw him last, it seems he disappeared just about the time Ben had his accident. Now, there's no evidence or proof of anything there, but it sure sounds suspicious to me."

"It certainly does," Clyde agreed.

"I know Ben told him if he left the Gully Ridge area he wouldn't tell the sheriff what he'd done to Lizzie. Ben told me he planned on talking to the sheriff a month or so after Coy left so if he came back the sheriff would be able to arrest him. He didn't talk to him right away, though, because he was so upset about what had happened he didn't feel he could talk about it yet. He was afraid he would break down if he told someone else, including the sheriff, what happened. He was also afraid the sheriff would say something to Lizzie or look at her differently, and he didn't want that."

"So you don't know if he ever did talk to the sheriff?" Clyde asked.

"I don't. I doubt if he did, because I know he was still pretty upset about it."

"Then it sounds to me as though we need to talk to Sheriff Williams," Clyde said, looking over at Wyatt, who was holding Lizzie's hand. "I'm sorry to bring it up, Lizzie, but if he doesn't know about what happened, he needs to be told. He also needs to know about the personal items that are missing. Then I'm sure he'll agree with us that the fact he disappeared about the same time Ben had this questionable accident needs to be looked into."

"If Coy killed him, he needs to stand trial for it," Bryce agreed.

Lizzie, who was leaning against Wyatt's chest with tears streaming down her cheeks, nodded. "I agree. Papa and I talked about talking to the sheriff. I didn't want him to say anything because I was afraid other people would find out and that news would spread. I didn't want everyone in town knowing. He said he felt he should tell him so that if he ever came back to this area, he would be arrested. I agreed with that, thinking if he came back I didn't want to have to worry about him hurting me again. We agreed he would tell the sheriff in a couple of months, after we'd both had a little more time to deal with our emotions."

"I understand," Wyatt said.

"We thought he had left this area, but were afraid he may be several towns over taking time to decide what he wants to do. We didn't want an overzealous young sheriff to find him and bring him back." She looked up at Wyatt before saying, "So this was my fault. If Papa would have talked to him right away, if Coy stayed in town, he would have been arrested."

"Maybe," Bryce said, "but there would also have been a trial, and I'm sure neither you nor your papa would have been happy about that."

"He's right," Clyde said. "He might still be alive, but there would be a pretty nasty trial going on now, so neither one would have been a good outcome. But mostly what we're trying to say, Lizzie, is don't blame yourself or your papa. I think most victims and most fathers, including myself, would have felt and done the same thing."

"He's right, Lizzie," Wyatt said, rubbing her back. "It's not your fault or your father's. It looks to me like Coy hung around town, purposely staying out of sight when men from our ranches might see him, and that wasn't by accident. I'd say he was up to no good."

"Then let's go talk to the sheriff," she said, wiping her eyes. "Surely after hearing all this he'll agree with us and go after him. Bryce is right, he needs to pay for this."

"How about if Bryce and I come over tomorrow after we do chores and have breakfast, and we'll all go in together. With all of us there to tell him the whole story, I feel sure he'll do what he needs to do. He might want to contact all the local sheriffs, and the sheriff close to his hometown in case he does go back home. Or he may want to report it to the U.S. Marshals and let them find him. Either way, I'm sure he'll agree that Coy needs to answer some serious questions."

"We'll be ready when you get here," Wyatt said. "Thank you both for going with us."

"Ben was our good friend and neighbor, too," Clyde said. "We care, too, and with all of us, we can each tell the sheriff what we know, including how important that watch was to Ben, and I'm sure he'll care, too."

AFTER EVERYONE LEFT, Wyatt wasn't surprised that Lizzie was upset. "Honey, I know this is hard. Remember, I'm here and we'll go through all this together, whatever happens. But for now, is there anything I can do to help you?"

She looked pretty ragged when she looked up at him, and he pulled her into his arms again. "Anything you think might help, sweetheart, tell me. If you just want me to keep you in my arms, we'll do that."

"Thank you." She cuddled in against him and he felt her

relax a bit, which was good. After several minutes she looked up at him again. "Could we take the horses out for a ride? I have a lot of good memories of riding with either you or Papa. Maybe that will help clear my mind."

"Of course we can, my sweet Lizzie. That's probably a good idea. Now remember, when we go to the barn, try not to let the men see you're upset or they'll wonder what's going on. I don't want them knowing the sheriff is looking into this until we're sure he is. Then once he agrees to investigate it, we'll ask all the men if they've heard or seen anything. I'm sure they've heard people talk about Ben. They may have heard something that didn't mean much at the time, but might now."

"Okay, that's a good idea. They may know something else about where he's from or if he ever mentioned any place he'd like to go some day."

They went to the barn, and when a couple of the hands offered to saddle the horses for them, Wyatt assured them they could do it themselves, as they were just going out riding. This was something they occasionally did on Sunday afternoons simply for pleasure, so no one questioned it and they went back to playing their card game.

Their afternoon away from the house turned out to be good for both of them. They stopped a couple of times to enjoy some quiet time and watch the wildlife, which helped clear their minds. By the time they went back home for supper they both felt better, and closer. A couple of the hands that were outside when they rode back to the barn smiled when they saw them holding hands. "It's good to see you two together," Frank said, and the others nodded in agreement.

Ella had supper ready for them when they got back, and she could tell they were both feeling better. Once again she was glad Wyatt was there for Lizzie as she went through this difficult time. While they ate they talked a bit about what all they wanted to remember to tell the sheriff the next morning, and wondered how this would end.

When they went to bed he could tell she was worrying about how their meeting in the morning would go. He crawled into bed next to her and pulled her close to him, with his arms wrapped protectively around her. She rolled over and kissed him. He took that opportunity to get her mind off of her father and onto him and their new marriage. She was very receptive to the kiss he returned, and an hour later he again had his arms wrapped around her. They dozed off, and woke with her still in his arms.

CHAPTER 20

The meeting with Sheriff Williams the next morning went better than she'd hoped. Wyatt held her as he told the sheriff what Coy had done and why they hadn't reported it. The sheriff was very professional about it and assured Lizzie he was extremely sorry to hear that, but assured her that information would remain private. He would put it in his records in a sealed envelope and let the deputy know Coy was to be arrested if he was in the area again, no questions asked. If he did show up again and was arrested, then the envelope would be opened.

Bryce explained what he'd learned from the saloon a couple of evenings earlier, and Lizzie explained about the missing money to buy the horses and the pocket watch. Wyatt and Clyde both told him how proud Ben had been of the watch that had been passed down to him from his father, and that he carried it with him always. Lizzie gave him a description of it and told him about the initials engraved in the back of it and where to find them.

Once they finished telling him everything they knew or had learned, they waited expectantly for his response. Sheriff

Williams took several minutes to look over his notes, asked just a few questions, then stood and leaned against his desk to address them. "First off, I'm sorry any of this happened. Coy was still here in Gully Ridge for a time, probably a few weeks after he was apparently fired. The story I heard was that he asked to court Lizzie, Ben told him no, and he quit. If I had known what actually happened I would have put him in jail, but I completely understand your waiting a while before telling me."

Wyatt squeezed Lizzie's hand, then turned back to the sheriff, who continued. "But what I've heard here definitely bothers me and deserves being looked into. Let me give this some thought this afternoon and send a couple of telegrams. I'll decide how I think would be best to handle this, and I'll come out to your ranch tomorrow, Wyatt, and I'll let you know what I plan to do. Is that okay with everyone?"

"That would be fine, Sheriff. Thank you," Wyatt said, offering his hand. "I'll let Pa and Bryce know then."

"Yes, thank you," Clyde agreed.

They headed toward the door, but before they left, Wyatt turned back to ask the sheriff one more question. "Before we go, there's one thing that's been in the back of my mind. Maybe I could get everyone's thoughts on it, especially yours, Sheriff."

"I'll give you my thought, for what it's worth, Wyatt. What's got you concerned?"

He put his arm around Lizzie's waist and pulled her close to him before responding. "Well, we know what Coy did to Lizzie, and it looks like there's a good chance he killed Ben. Do you think he took off and finally left this area, not to return, once he killed Ben, or do you think he could still be lurking around close by? Should I be concerned about Lizzie's safety?"

The room turned quiet as everyone thought about

Wyatt's words. After a couple of long minutes the sheriff spoke. "Wyatt, I have to say I hadn't even considered that angle yet, though that's why I said I'd rather get back with you tomorrow. I intend to think this whole situation through from different perspectives. Now that you brought the question up, I'll give you my initial thoughts, but I will be giving it more thought this afternoon."

"I appreciate what you're saying, Sheriff," Wyatt said, nodding his head.

"My initial thought is I believe he's gone for good, though I understand your concern. He obviously didn't leave when he told Ben he was going to, since we know he was in Gully Ridge. However, although he stayed out of sight on Saturday night when ranch hands would have seen him, he didn't make any attempt to hide from everyone. If he was waiting around to get even with Ben, he's done that now. We've been able to trace Ben's death back to him easily, so I would have to assume he would know that and want to get out of this area as soon as possible."

"I would think so, too," Clyde said. "My guess is as soon as he killed Ben and took his watch and money, he took off. He's probably far away by now."

"I hope so," Lizzie said.

"Me, too," Wyatt said, pulling her a little closer and kissing the top of her head. He looked back up at the sheriff. "If it was your wife, how worried would you be that he'll show up again at the ranch?"

"I hear you, Wyatt," the sheriff said. "It's easy for me to say I don't think he'll come back, but if it was my wife, I'll admit I would be more concerned. I will probably ask for help from the Marshals because they can send men out and telegrams out and reach a larger area than I can. Since he's from Texas I'm thinking it would be good to see if the Rangers can help, as well."

"Both good ideas," Bryce said.

"They can look into it in more places than I can, much quicker," the sheriff agreed. "In the meantime, I really don't think he'll come back for Lizzie, but it would certainly be a good idea to be extra careful until we catch him, or at least locate him. "Lizzie, I know you know how to use a gun. I've heard Ben talk about what a good shot you are. That being the case, until he's been caught, I would keep a gun with you, and if possible, I wouldn't go out on the ranch alone."

"She won't," Wyatt said, which drew a frown from Lizzie, but she didn't object or argue.

"I'll be out to talk to you tomorrow."

"Okay. Again, thank you, Sheriff."

The four of them had a discussion about the response they'd received from the sheriff as they rode back to the ranch. They were pleased that he agreed with them that it sure looked like there were some serious questions Coy needed to answer. If he did kill Ben, even though it wouldn't bring Ben back, Coy needed to answer to that horrific act.

When they reached Wyatt and Lizzie's house they thanked Clyde and Bryce for going with them to talk to the sheriff, and then went to the barn to take care of their horses. "Lizzie, I know this is hard for you, especially now that it looks like Coy killed your father. If you want to go inside and rest for the rest of the day, go ahead."

"No," she said quickly. "I need to be busy. In fact, I need to be working with my horses right now. Please don't make me stay inside again. Before Coy attacked me I had to quit working with the horses because I didn't trust him and was afraid he would try to get me alone. I felt cheated out of my time with the animals I love. Now I feel cheated out of time with my father, and again it's because of that same man. I won't let him cheat me out of anything else. Spending time with the horses is exactly what I need right now."

"Okay, sweetheart, I understand. I'm not going to try to keep you in the house again. Honest, that's not why I asked. I just thought you might want a little time to rest and deal with what all has happened. Now after hearing your thoughts, I agree with you; you should spend time with your horses now. I would like to talk to you a minute before we go our own ways, though."

"I know, you want me to keep a gun with me, and I won't argue with you on that," she surprised him by saying.

"Good. But I want to go a step further. For the next week or so at least I'm not going to need all the men out in the fields or pastures, so I'm going to have one or more staying around here to work on that list of things that need done around the barn. If you see Coy or are concerned, yell so they hear you. We all care about you, so let us all help make sure you're safe."

"Okay," she agreed.

"Also, if something happens, fire two shots in the air about three seconds apart. I'll let all the men know, and the men that work for Pa, too. If anyone hears that, we'll come on the run. I don't think he's still around here, but I want you to know there are a lot of people here for you, watching out for you."

Instead of arguing, like he was afraid she might, her eyes got rather misty. She blinked quickly several times and walked over closer to him and straight into his arms he'd opened for her. "Thank you, Wyatt. That makes me feel safer."

"Good. I hoped it would. I'm not going to try to keep you inside, but I'll still be taking some extra precautions to make sure my wife is safe. I don't want to lose you." After a quick look around the barn and a quick kiss, he looked down at her. "One more thing I want to talk to you about. Do you have any objections to telling all the men now what's going on?"

"No. I think they all should know so they can watch for Coy, too. I think you had a good idea to ask if any of them may have heard anything that might be helpful. Someone may have heard something at the saloon that may be relevant, now that we know Coy was still around."

"Okay, I'll tell them this evening before we end the day and they go to supper. Do you want to be here or would you rather not be part of the discussion?"

"Unless you think I shouldn't, I'd like to be here. If anyone heard anything, I'd like to hear it."

"Okay. When the men are all back here, we'll go in and talk to them at the bunkhouse before supper." He leaned down to kiss her cheek. "I'll walk you into the house to get your gun, then you enjoy your time with the horses. I'll go check on the men."

That night as they ate their own supper a few hours later they filled Ella in on everything they'd found out, and what they talked about with the men. "I agree with everyone else, I don't think he'll show up around here again because I think it would be too easy to link his sudden disappearance with his death. I am glad to hear you're going to take extra precautions, though," Ella said.

"I'm glad she's not fighting me, because I will always do what I can to keep my wife safe." Ella saw the look between them, and wished yet again her father would have had the opportunity to see the two of them married. He would have been extremely happy.

~

WYATT AND LIZZIE were rather surprised when they saw a rider coming up their lane while they were eating breakfast, and recognized it as Sheriff Williams. Wyatt invited him in as Lizzie got another plate and silverware for him. Once they convinced him to have breakfast with them, he filled his plate, then they talked about what he planned to do.

"I've sent telegrams to all the surrounding sheriffs to alert them I have evidence that suggests Coy Clemson killed Ben Morgan. I said a backup letter explaining it all would be posted today. Then I wrote a description of him and of Ben's watch, and explained that he was fired for attacking a lady on the ranch and was told to leave the area to avoid them reporting the crime. He stayed in the area until the same time Ben was found dead, and considerable money and the watch were missing when Ben was found. I sent that letter this morning."

"So if they see him they'll know to arrest him now, and when the letter arrives it will give them the details?" Wyatt asked.

"Yes. Then I also sent a telegram to the U.S. Marshal's office. I got a telegram back advising that they have two marshals in the area that just finished a case. They'll stop in today and will handle the case. My understanding is if they feel the Texas Rangers would be helpful, as well, they will contact them, as well. So the surrounding sheriffs know about it now and are watching for Coy. Later this afternoon the marshals will be advised and will be looking for him, as well. They will all let me know if anything happens, and if I hear anything I'll let you know."

"Thank you, Sheriff," Wyatt said sincerely.

"My pleasure. The more I thought this through after hearing what you told me, the more I'm convinced Coy is behind Ben's death, and he needs to be held responsible for it."

"I definitely agree," Lizzie said, with watery eyes.

"I'll let you two get to work, but I wanted to let you know

the wheels are turning on this, and I'll let you know as soon as I hear anything. If you hear anything or think of anything else that might help, let me know."

"We will, and thanks for letting us know."

After the sheriff left Wyatt gave Lizzie a hug. "Are you okay?"

"Yes, but I hope they find him soon."

"Me, too. Until then, though, remember to keep your gun with you."

"I will. You can go on out and get the men going for the day. I'm going to take a few minutes to absorb everything Sheriff Williams said while I help Ella clean up the kitchen. Then I'll take my gun with me and work with the horses. I plan to put a saddle on a couple of them for the first time today."

"Be careful. I'll keep a couple of the men here to work on fixing the fence on the small pasture. If you want help, get either or both of them."

"Okay, I will."

He gave her a kiss that he intended to be rather quick, but grew in length and intensity, before shaking his head as he eventually pulled back and smiled, before leaving. She was smiling as well as she turned to carry some empty plates into the kitchen. Ella was standing at the door, a big smile on her face, as well. "Sorry, I didn't mean to walk in on a personal moment, but you don't need to help me with this."

Lizzie laughed as she brushed off the apology. "It's probably us that should be apologizing to you. But if you don't mind, I'd like to help. I was hoping maybe we could talk a bit while we wash them?"

"Of course. You know we can talk anytime you want. You don't have to help me with the dishes to have a little chat."

"I know, but I enjoy talking while we work. It helps me relax, or maybe calm, and that's what I need right now."

Ella simply nodded and helped carry the rest of the dishes to the kitchen, where she had hot soapy water waiting. Placing dishes into the water she said, "Okay, we're working. Now, what would you like to talk about, or who?"

Lizzie looked over and saw a bit of a smile on Ella's face. "You know what's on my mind, don't you?"

"I might, but why don't you tell me so we can see if I'm right."

"I don't know where to start, so let me just --" She shook her head as she picked up a plate to dry. "I'm sorry, but I hate him. I just simply hate him, and I know I shouldn't hate anyone. How can I change?"

"I thought you might want to talk about Coy. To be honest with you, though, I'm not sure I'm the right person to talk to in this case. I say that because I hate him, too."

"You do?"

"Well, I'm not sure if I actually hate him, but I know I hate what he did to you, and that includes what he did to your papa."

"Do you feel guilty about that, about hating a fellow man?"

"Maybe a little, but very little. I think it's wrong to hate someone for doing something petty, or even if what they did was an accident, a one-time occurrence. But Coy has never done anything to impress me. I've never seen him go out of his way to help someone. On the other hand, he's done not one, but two horrible things that hurt you a great deal. They were major things, and they were no accident. He intentionally did them both, knowing they would cause you and your father great harm."

"But didn't Pastor Stone say not long ago during his sermon that we should forgive people and not hate anyone?"

"I think what he said is we shouldn't hate someone, but we can hate what they did. I believe a person is a complex combination of that person, along with the influences his parents and siblings had on him growing up, and the experiences he's had in his life. Therefore, I don't necessarily hate the entire person. I think that person probably started off fine, but I do hate the choices he's made and the man those choices have turned him into. Does that make any sense?"

Lizzie took a couple of minutes to think through what Ella said. "Yes," she said slowly, "I think it does. I didn't particularly like the person he was before he attacked me and Papa, but I didn't hate him. That man that Papa hired changed, and it's the man he's changed into that I hate."

"That man has hurt you badly in two ways, so I completely understand why you would hate him. Pastor Stone said we should be willing to forgive someone if they admit they were wrong and ask to be forgiven. Coy has neither shown any sign of acknowledging he was wrong, nor asked to be forgiven. It would be terribly difficult to forgive someone who has hurt you that badly without them apologizing, paying for their mistake in some way, and asking for your forgiveness."

Lizzie was quiet for a few minutes before talking softly, more thinking out loud. "Huh. I hadn't thought of that before."

"What's that?"

"That makes sense, though. It would be much easier to forgive someone if they admitted they did wrong, and asked to be forgiven, wouldn't it?"

"Yes, it is much easier," said a deep voice from behind them. They turned around to see Wyatt standing in the doorway. He made his way to Lizzie and took her in his arms. "I'm sorry, I didn't mean to eavesdrop or sneak up on you ladies, but Lizzie, I came in to tell you that Walter and Bill will be staying close to the barn today, but instead of working on the fence at the small pasture, they'll be replacing some of the boards on the corral. I wanted to let you know so if you need help you'll know where they'll be."

"Okay, thank you," she said.

He gave her a quick kiss on her cheek. "It's even easier after they've had some kind of consequences to remind them not to do it again," he whispered in her ear. He gave her a wink and a pat on her behind before going back outside. Lizzie felt her face blush and hoped Ella hadn't heard what he whispered or seen him pat her backside.

"That man does love you," Ella said. "I'll feel much better when they catch Coy, but I'm glad he's keeping a man or two at the barn in case you need help until they do."

"I'll feel better, too," Lizzie admitted. "I know he's watching out for me, and that makes me feel special."

Ella chuckled just a bit as she turned to face Lizzie. "It's quite clear you are very special to him. You're a lucky lady."

"Yes, I am," she said a bit slowly as she looked up to meet Ella's eyes. "Wyatt is a wonderful man and he does love me. After what Coy did to me and Papa I was feeling kind of sorry for myself, so thank you for reminding me how lucky I am. I needed to hear that right now."

"Sometimes it's good to talk to a friend. It can remind you of what's important. Thank you for helping me clean up the kitchen and for our talk. I miss working with you and sharing thoughts. Now, be careful out there with your horses today."

"I will be," she assured her, "and thank you for the talk. I feel much better."

As Lizzie went to the barn and began her daily care for her horses and greeting each one, she thought back to what Wyatt had whispered in her ear. As much as she hated his spankings, it was hard to argue with him on that point. When he'd said she would be forgiven after a spanking, she'd never realized there was an actual reason behind it.

CHAPTER 21

Things went fairly well over the next several days. Lizzie kept a gun with her every time she went to the barn or out for a ride. Wyatt wasn't too enthusiastic about her going riding, but he knew she often went riding when she needed to clear her head, so he allowed it. He went with her once, but when she wanted to go by herself to be alone to think, he allowed it, though he asked which way she was going.

She knew he was worried about her, so she told him the three spots she might stop at, and promised not to be gone over an hour. He thanked her and gave her a kiss before she set off. She'd been on edge, which he understood. They both hoped they caught Coy soon, but Wyatt had to wonder what would change then, other than she wouldn't need to keep a gun with her at the barn.

When they caught him he was sure there would be a trial, but there were a lot of unknowns about that trial. He hoped they held him in jail and had the trial someplace other than Gully Ridge. Leesburg, where they found his body, would be far enough away that their friends and neighbors at Gully

Ridge wouldn't travel to attend the trial. He hoped if they charged him with killing Ben and stealing his watch and money, that would be enough. If he would hang for the murder, why even mention the attack? She'd been through enough, and he wanted to do anything he could to make sure she didn't have to testify about when he attacked her, especially in Gully Ridge.

Unfortunately, as the next couple of days passed, her mood and attitude changed. Sheriff Williams had stopped by and told them the marshals were looking for Coy, as well as local sheriffs. Anywhere the marshals went they informed the sheriffs, so there were a lot of people watching for him. While Lizzie was glad to hear that, she felt they should have found him by now.

Wyatt could tell the waiting was taking a toll on her. She smiled less often, and he and Ella had to work to get her engaged in conversation. Taking her to bed at night and making love was something she'd always enjoyed, and though she was still a willing participant in it, he could tell she wasn't fully engaged in it. He tried talking to her, but she insisted she was okay, there was nothing to talk about.

As the days dragged on she had a quicker and quicker temper. Finally, after watching this for about ten days, he walked into the barn at the end of the day and overheard her. He wasn't sure who she was taking her frustration out on, but he assumed it was one of their men, and he wasn't going to allow it. They had good men working for them, and he didn't want to upset them. He listened as he quickly put Chestnut in his stall and gave him some oats so he could rescue whoever she was talking to.

"I'm perfectly capable of taking care of the horses. I've been helping Papa take care of them since I was five. I simply lost track of time this afternoon and I'm running a little late."

"Miss Lizzie, I know you're capable. You're more capable

of caring for horses than I am. I was simply offering to help, is all. I'm sorry if you thought I meant anything by it."

Wyatt thought he was hearing Walter's voice, but he wasn't positive. He was sure it was either Walter or Leo, but the brothers sounded a lot alike so he couldn't say for certain which it was for sure. Regardless, neither of them deserved the dressing down she was giving them. He headed their way, listening as he neared them.

"Well, I don't need any help. Suddenly everybody seems to think I'm helpless. Well, I'm not."

"Again, Miss Lizzie, I'm sorry. I didn't mean anything by it. None of us do. We all care a great deal about you and you've been through a lot lately. We're all just trying to help."

"And we appreciate your offer," Wyatt said, hurrying around the corner. "In fact, if your offer is still good, I need to talk to Miss Lizzie about something. Would you mind feeding them this evening for us?"

"No, of course not," Walter said, looking relieved to see Wyatt. "Have you started feeding any of them yet, Miss Lizzie?"

She was glaring at Wyatt, but turned back to Walter. "I've fed the horses in the first row of stalls at the far side, but haven't started the rest yet."

"Okay, Leo and I will be happy to get them fed and watered. You two have a nice evening."

"Thank you, Walter. I appreciate your help," Wyatt said, gently taking Lizzie's hand and leading her out of the barn.

As soon as she felt they were far enough away from the barn she tried to pull her hand free from his, but he'd anticipated that and held tight. "Why did you do that?" she asked. "I am quite capable of caring for my own horses."

"I know you are, as do all our men. Lizzie, we all care about you and know you've had a rough patch lately. All we're trying to do is show you we care. However, you repaid

Walter for his kind offer by chewing him out. Stop and think about that for a moment and be honest. Does he deserve to be treated that way for trying to do you a favor?"

"No, of course he doesn't," she admitted. "I'm sorry."

"I'm not the one you should be saying that to."

"I know," she said as she sighed and turned. "I'll tell him."

He put a hand on her arm and turned her back toward him. "Wait until morning. If you go to him now he'll know I said something to you. In the morning you can apologize before you start feeding the horses. Tell him you felt bad about it last evening, and he'll know you're sincere. Honey, they know you have a lot on your mind right now. All I'm asking is that you be polite, and let them help. They care about you, and if you let them help you a little now and then it makes them feel good, just like you feel good when you help someone who's having a bad time."

"I never thought of it like that, but you're right. I'll do better."

"Good," he whispered close to her ear, "because I don't want to have to warm your bottom right now, but if you keep letting your temper get the better of you I'll have no choice."

"You wouldn't," she said, appalled.

"You know me better than that, Lizzie. Yes, I would, if you earn it. Besides, I'm thinking maybe that's what you need right now anyway."

Her head flew up to look at him. "What I need right now? Are you serious? I absolutely do not need that right now."

"Oh, but I think you might," he countered. Again looking to be sure no one was close that might overhear their conversation, he went on to explain. "Sweetheart, I've watched you your entire life, and I know when you get all worked up about something, you lose your temper easily. I've also seen that the few times I've spanked you for something, afterward you're much calmer. I think it reminds you that I'm here for you, but I do know it settles you right down. Maybe you need a spanking now so you can settle down and feel better. I know you'd be able to handle your temper better."

She was looking at him with her mouth open, her eyes wide. "You would spank me simply because I'm upset? You don't think I have reason to be upset?"

"Of course you have reason to be upset. Lizzie, no one is doubting that. But I believe you're having a difficult time dealing with this and it's causing your temper to erupt too easily. A spanking will calm you down and help you deal with your feelings right now."

"But you can't spank me when I haven't done anything wrong."

"I disagree with you about that, but don't look so upset; I won't give you a spanking right now unless you earn one. I will warn you, though, that if you can't get your feelings under control, it won't be long before that happens. And if it does happen, I think if you're honest you'll agree that you're calmer and feel better afterward. Then maybe you'll see that when I say perhaps it's what you need now, I mean it as a way of taking care of you, knowing you'll feel better afterward. If so, we can talk then if you want to. But for now, let's go see what Ella has for us for supper. I'm hungry."

"Me, too," she said rather quietly. She was quieter than normal during supper, as well, and Wyatt could tell she was deep in thought. He knew she wouldn't believe him right now, but hopefully the first time she found herself over his knees when she was so worked up, she would see what he was saying, or trying to offer her.

WYATT HELD her in his arms as they slept that night, and the next morning she seemed to be in a better mood. After breakfast they walked to the barn together, and true to her word, the first thing she did was seek Walter out and apologize for being rude to him the evening before.

He gave her a big smile as he patted her shoulder. "You don't need to apologize, Miss Lizzie. I know that's not what you're normally like, and you've had a lot of upsetting things happen lately."

"Well, but that doesn't give me the right to be rude to you, and I want you to know that I'm sorry. I also want you to know I really do appreciate what you and Leo and the rest of them have been doing for me lately, and putting up with."

"You and your papa have done way more for us, giving us these jobs, than we've even thought of doing for you. If there's anything else we can do for you, just let us know. Now, you have a good day with the horses. I'm not sure what Wyatt's got planned for me today, but I best go find out."

He left, and Wyatt came in about ten minutes later. "Frank and Bill are going to be working in the shop today fixing some of the harnesses that need mended. They're leaving the door open to the shop, so if you need anything, go get one of them, or yell loud. With the door open they'll hear you and come running."

"Okay. I should be fine, but thank you."

He gave her a quick kiss before meeting the other men and riding out to check on the herds. She started working with her horses and it worked to get her mind off of her problems. Before she realized it Wyatt was coming to get her for the noonday meal. As they were heading to the house to eat they saw a rider coming up their lane, so they waited. They greeted Sheriff Williams and when he said he had a little news, they invited him in for some dinner with them.

Once everyone had their plates filled, Lizzie asked, "So, you have some news for us? Did they catch Coy?"

"No, they haven't caught him yet," Sheriff Williams said, "but the marshals feel they're on his trail. They've found a couple of small towns that people have said he was in, so they're hoping they catch up with him soon."

"That's all they have? They've found places he's been?"

Wyatt's eyebrows shot up and he looked at Lizzie. He reached over and took her hand, hoping she would look at him and take note of the warning look in his eyes. "Lizzie, it's only been a week. They didn't have anything to go on when they started looking for him, other than he may go to where he was raised in Texas. If they've found places where he's been, they can follow those and see which direction he's traveling, so I think they're making good progress."

"If it was your father you might not think they were moving so quick."

"I'm sorry, Miss Lizzie," the sheriff started, but Wyatt cut him off.

"We're all sorry it happened at all, Lizzie, but considering the little information they had when they started looking, I think you should be a little more appreciative of the time and work they've put in to find the direction he's heading."

His words and they way he said them got her attention and at last she looked over at him and saw the warning he was trying to portray. "You're probably right. I apologize, Sheriff. I didn't mean to imply they aren't trying."

"I understand, especially since it was your father. My thought was the same as Wyatt; since they know which direction he's headed now, unless he changes direction it shouldn't be long before they catch up with him. As soon as I hear anything else I'll be back out to let you know."

"Thank you," Lizzie said, and went back to her meal, though Wyatt and Ella both noticed she did more moving food around on her plate than actually eating it. Wyatt changed the subject and they talked about other things as they finished their meal.

When it was over Wyatt thanked the sheriff for making the trip out to keep them informed, and he walked him outside. While the men talked a bit before the sheriff left, Lizzie helped Ella clean up the dishes and kitchen. "I know you want them to find Coy, and I don't blame you," Ella said. "I want that, too, but I think we have to be patient and give them time. I'm sure they're doing all they can."

"I guess they might be. It seems like they should have had him by now, but after hearing what you and Wyatt are saying, I have to admit I don't know what's involved, or how they go about finding him. It just seems like it's taking a long time."

"I know it may seem like that, but you have to be patient and give them some time. At least the sheriff agreed with you that it wasn't an accident and they're looking into it."

"That's true," Lizzie admitted. "I guess I do need to relax and give it more time."

"I think your husband feels that way, as well," she said with a bit of a grin that had a bit of a warning mixed in.

"Yes, I think you're right. He gets upset with my lack of patience and I need to remember that."

"My Henry was like that, too," Ella said. She relayed a couple of stories about her temper and how her husband used to get so upset with her.

Later that night after Ella retired to her room Wyatt and Lizzie were enjoying the evening on the porch swing. They heard a noise from the side of the house and Wyatt was instantly up and had his gun out. It turned out to be simply one of the barn cats, and Wyatt put his gun away and sat down to swing again.

"You were afraid it was Coy, weren't you?" Lizzie asked.

"I don't trust that man. I know the sheriff said the marshals think they're right behind him, but I'll feel better once they have him locked up."

"Me, too. I hope they catch up with him soon instead of just following him around." She sighed loudly and shook her head side to side.

"What does that mean? Lizzie, are you saying you don't believe the marshals are doing their job?"

"I'm not saying they're not doing their job, but it doesn't seem like they're working very fast. You and the sheriff and Ella all seem so impressed with them, but I guess I'm not. They've followed him around for a week. How is that impressive?" Her voice kept raising as she spoke, and by the time she'd finished she was almost yelling.

"Calm down, Lizzie, and keep your voice down."

She jumped up and turned to face him, her hands on her hips. "Why do I have to keep my voice down? Wyatt, I'm upset, can't you see that? Yelling a little bit isn't going to hurt a thing. It might make me feel better, but it won't hurt a thing, so keep quiet and let me go."

"Lizzie," he said in what she should have recognized as his warning voice, "calm down and sit back down. If you yell you're going to have the men out here to see what's wrong. This is their time off, so let them relax. Some of them go to bed early so they're ready to get up before sunup."

"I'm aware of what happens on a ranch, Wyatt. I know they get up early; I do, too." Her voice was raising again as she continued. "They're probably in the bunkhouse playing cards and laughing. They certainly won't hear if I talk a little louder than normal, so don't tell me what I can and can't do."

"Okay, Lizzie, that's enough. I think it's time we go inside and up to our room." He stood and grasped her upper arm and started leading her toward the door.

"Who said I'm ready to go to bed yet?" she asked, louder

than she normally would, which told Wyatt she was losing control of her temper.

"I didn't say we were going to bed yet," he said softly, close to her ear as he again led her to the door.

They heard the bunkhouse door slam open and they both turned to see Frank coming out of the doorway, his gun in hand, with three or four men behind him. "Boss, is that you and Miss Lizzie? Is everything okay?"

"Everything's fine, Frank," Wyatt said.

"Okay. We heard what sounded like some yelling or something and thought we better come check it out, make sure it's not Coy coming back to cause more trouble."

"Thank you for checking," Wyatt said. "We heard a noise and it startled us, too, but it turned out just to be a barn cat up here by the house. I think it was chasing a little chipmunk. We're going inside now. Thanks again for checking."

"Sure thing. You two have a good night," Frank said.

He and the other men went back in the bunkhouse, while Wyatt again led Lizzie into the house and upstairs to their bedroom. Once they were inside she pulled her arm free. "Okay, so maybe I was talking a little louder than I thought," she said.

"Lizzie, it's your whole attitude. You're being rude and yelling, and it's not like you."

"It's not my whole attitude. I have something on my mind, but that doesn't mean there's anything wrong with my attitude. The only thing wrong with it is it's tired of you saying I have a problem, because I don't. Now, since we're up here, I might as well go to bed."

"Not just yet, Lizzie. This is bothering you to the point it's got you raising your voice and taking your frustration out on others."

"I am not. I talked a little louder tonight. That's it."

"How about the way you talked to Walter, or Sheriff Williams?"

"I apologized and it's fine now."

"No, it's not. That's not like you and it's not acceptable."

"Not acceptable? Wyatt, what's not acceptable is you giving me a hard time."

"That does it," Wyatt said. In one quick move he sat on the bed and had her over his lap. "If you're going to accuse me of giving you a hard time, I'll do just that."

"Wyatt, no," she said, not nearly as loud now as she was talking outside.

"Lizzie, it's obvious you need this. You're struggling and I love you too much to continue to watch that and not do anything to help you." He wasted no time getting her skirts and undergarments draped over her back. It would have been much easier to take them off first, but he knew his wife hadn't yet seen or acknowledged how much a spanking helps her in situations like this, and she would have fought his undressing her the entire way. This was much easier for now. Once they were over her back and out of his way, he made quick work of her drawers, taking them down to her knees. As he'd expected, she yelped when he did that and reached a hand back to retrieve them. "Let them right where they are. You know the rules."

"But it still doesn't seem right," she sighed.

"That's only because you know your bottom's about to become quite sore. There's nothing wrong with a husband seeing his wife's bare bottom. Or like in this case, giving her a spanking it if she needs it."

"I don't need it."

"Yes, you do. I think even you will have to admit you feel better afterward." When she turned to stare at him like he had three heads, he added, "Well, your bottom may not agree, but the rest of you will feel much better, believe me." That was enough talking, and he started the spanking, using firm but not overly harsh swats. After covering her bottom completely once, he varied the tempo and moved around on her bottom so she wouldn't know when or where the next swat would land. He'd noticed doing that while he talked to her during a spanking kept her alert and helped her listen to what he was saying.

Once he started doing that and was sure he had her attention he began reminding her why she found herself in this position. "Lizzie, I know you're upset about your papa. So am I. But you have to learn to be patient and control your temper. You've been rude to several people, and I won't allow that. These people all love you and know why you're upset, but that doesn't give you the right to treat them badly. And although I'm sure they'll forgive you this time, you can't expect them to keep forgiving you over and over."

"I know," she admitted through tears.

"You know better than to treat people badly like you have been, and it's not like you. It's your temper coming out, which is something you've never been able to fully get control of. I've seen it your whole life. I know that kind of behavior isn't like you, but I also know you can't control your temper, and this happens. You treat people badly, then feel terrible about it. Well, it's time for you to grow up and finally get control of that temper of yours, and I'm going to help you do it."

"Ow. Wyatt, this hurts," she whined. "You, you c-c-call this helping?"

"Yes, I do, and it helps because it hurts. Why are you being spanked right now?" He waited, and when there was no answer coming, he smacked her a little harder. "I'm waiting for an answer, Lizzie."

"Ow! It hurts so much."

"I know, and it will hurt more if you don't answer me. Why are you being spanked?"

"B-b-because I don't like waiting."

He gave her six swats harder than the rest had been, which got her squirming, trying to get away, then paused. "The correct answer is because you were impatient and lost your temper." He continued the spanking again, causing her to jump and start squirming again. "Let's try again. Why are you being spanked?"

"Because I lost my temper," she said as she gave up her fight and slumped across his knees.

"That's better," he said, feeling relieved himself. He gave her six more swats as he said, "And you can count on another spanking every time you lose your temper in the future." He ended the spanking and began rubbing her bottom, easing some of the pain. "You really do need to learn to control your temper, my sweet Lizzie, and I will help you do that. You'll feel better about yourself and be happier."

"I know," she admitted, which brought a smile to his face and had him lifting her up and into his lap. He quickly pulled her into his arms and kissed the top of her head when she leaned it against his chest.

"I love you, my darling wife, and I want you to be happy."

"I am happy," she said, leaning up toward him and pulling him down for a kiss.

"But you'll be happier when you learn to control your emotions and not take your frustrations out on others. That's the happy I want to see in you. You're such a wonderful lady, I hate seeing you upset with yourself after you're rude to someone."

"I know," she said with a hiccup. "I do feel bad afterwards. I just can't help it."

"Yes, you can, and you will. It may take a few more spankings, but I feel sure you'll learn to stop and think before you unleash your temper on someone you care about."

She sat straight up and looked up and met his eyes. "A few more? But that hurt. I don't want any more."

"Then remember this the next time you're struggling with your temper. Do you know what else you could do that could help?"

"What's that?"

"Come talk to me. Tell me you're having trouble and we'll talk. You don't always want to talk to me, but I think you'll admit you always feel better after we do."

"I know I do," she admitted. "But it's hard."

"Harder than taking a spanking?" She looked up at him with a shocked look. "You need to ask yourself that because I'm serious, you can expect another spanking every time you lose your temper."

"That might make it easier," she said, which caused him to chuckle.

"I hope so." He pulled her in for a hug. "Now, tell me something. Other than your sore bottom, do you feel better now?"

She was quiet for several moments before shrugging her shoulders, but nodding. "Yes, I do. I don't understand it, but I do. Thank you."

She snuggled in closer against his chest and he tightened his arms around her. "You're welcome. I'll be happy to give you a spanking anytime you want one. Or need one," he added with a smile for her, along with a sincere look of promise. She thought about that as she snuggled into his firm, hard, comforting chest.

CHAPTER 22

Lizzie felt much better the next day, which still surprised her. She was honest enough to admit to herself and Wyatt that the spanking had settled her down a great deal and she was much more able to handle waiting to hear from the sheriff. She still didn't completely understand it, but wouldn't deny the calmness that came over her. It was like the spanking had taken away all the stress she was fighting and left her feeling more content than she'd felt in some time.

Her good mood lasted, and she was still feeling good three days later when Sheriff Williams came riding up the lane as they were sitting down for supper. Ella got an extra place setting out for him as Wyatt and Lizzie greeted him and invited him in for supper. They could tell he had good news, and Lizzie had a hard time waiting to hear it.

She wasn't the only one eager, and as soon as they sat down the sheriff spoke. "I know I should wait until we pass the food and are ready to eat, but I can't wait any longer. The marshals picked Coy up last night and he's in jail."

"That's great," Wyatt said. "Did he confess to killing Ben, and did he have his watch?"

"That's a little more complicated. Let's pass the food and I'll explain what I know." As they filled their plates he continued. "One of the marshals rode out early this morning to let us know what's happened."

"I wish he would have come here with you," Lizzie said. "I would have liked to talk to him."

"I suggested that, but he wanted to get back. Apparently their work isn't quite done yet."

Wyatt set the bowl of potatoes down to look at the sheriff. "That doesn't sound good." He sighed and said, "That means there's more to this story, and I'm not sure I want to know what it is."

"I do," Lizzie said. "Did he deny killing Papa? Did he have his watch?"

"Oddly enough, the answer to both of those questions is yes," the sheriff said. He took a bit of roast beef while the others thought about that.

Wyatt shook his head. "I'm not sure I understand. He denied killing Ben, but he had his watch? Is he just stalling, not wanting to confess, or is there more to his story?"

"Well, I for one don't believe him," Lizzie said. "He was caught with the evidence. You said he had his watch, and he was upset because Papa fired him. Of course he killed him."

"Lizzie, let the sheriff tell us what he knows," Wyatt suggested. "I agree everything seems to point to him, but if the marshals are staying in the area and still working on it, there has to be some reason. Sheriff?"

"There is something else, though at this point I don't know a great deal about it. Apparently when the marshal caught up with him, before approaching him he asked the local sheriff about him. He was told he was new in town, but had indicated he liked it there and was considering staying, if he found a good job. With that information, the marshal went to talk with him, and found him sitting in a saloon. He didn't tell him he was a marshal, but sat down next to him and struck up a conversation. He asked Coy what he did for a living, and he said he was between jobs now, looking for something different. The marshal asked what he'd done in the past, and he said he'd worked on ranches most of his life, and in fact was a foreman at the last one before he quit."

"He said he quit?" Lizzie asked with an unladylike snort. After a glare from her husband, she sat back, waiting to hear the rest.

"He said he was getting older, and ranch work was hard work, so he'd like to try something else. The marshal, feeling confident this was the man he'd been looking for, asked if he knew what time it was, and Coy pulled out a watch that matched the description you'd given us. He commented on what a nice watch, and asked if he could see it. Coy handed it to him."

Wyatt's eyebrows rose. "He didn't try to hide it?"

"That's why the marshals are still on the case," the sheriff said. "Yes, he readily handed it to him. The marshal turned it over and looked at the initials you said were there, Lizzie. So with that, the marshal, with a little help from the other marshal that was sitting close by, took him outside, tied his hands behind his back and told him he was under arrest. He asked why, and they told him for killing Ben and stealing that watch and a good amount of money. The marshals said he looked truly stunned, and immediately denied it."

"Did he have an explanation for how he got the watch?" Wyatt asked.

"He did, but not enough for them to release him. He claimed he met a man in a saloon in a town he went through that was looking for a job on a ranch. He told him he'd been working on ranches, as well, and they got to talking. It turned out this other man knew who Ben Morgan was. Coy told him about a man he knew that owned a ranch not too far from there, and suggested he go talk to him about a job and tell him he sent him. He ran into him again in the next town he stopped in, and the man said the ranch owner gave him a job once he told him Coy sent him. He wanted to thank him for his help, and gave him the watch."

"He gave him Ben's watch, and Coy didn't question how he got it?" Wyatt asked.

"Coy claims he didn't know it was Ben's. He says the man told him someone that owed him some money gave him that watch in payment for what he owed him. He said it was a nice watch, but he already had one his father had given him and didn't need it. He gave it to Coy as a thank you for helping him get the job."

Wyatt nodded. "So the marshals are going to go back to that ranch and talk to the guy and see what his story is?"

"They are. Coy only has a first name for the man, but he gave them the name of the man that owns the ranch and told them where it is, so they're going to see if they hired the man within the past week."

Everyone was quiet for several moments, as they digested the new information. Finally Wyatt asked the sheriff, "What do you think?"

"I don't know. I was like you, he was found with his watch, and he certainly had a reason to be upset with Ben. But the fact that he didn't hesitate letting the marshals see the watch, I have to admit that raises some question. If the story's not true it's a pretty farfetched idea that could easily be checked out, so I wouldn't expect him to make up something like that on the spur of the moment. I think it's definitely worth talking to the man that owns the ranch."

"I have to agree," Wyatt said.

"Yes, I guess I would want that, too," Lizzie said, "but I have a question for you, Sheriff."

"I'll answer it if I can."

"If it turns out his story is true and someone else gave him Papa's watch, what happens then? Does he get to keep the watch, and is he then a free man?"

"I can answer part of that easily, but the other part is more complex. The watch will be returned to you, Miss Lizzie. No one had the authority to give that watch to anyone, so regardless how it turns out, the watch was Ben's and will be returned to you. As far as whether Coy goes free, let's talk about that. We have a report on file of what he did to you, and a warrant for his arrest. If I send a telegram to the local sheriff in Brigham, where he was arrested and is in jail, he will hold him until I deliver or send the report, and then he will be arrested for that and held for trial. What are your thoughts on that?"

Wyatt took Lizzie's hand in his and rubbed her knuckles. "Would the trial be there, or would they have to bring him back here for the trial?"

"I can see where that would make a big difference," Sheriff Williams said. "To be honest, I have to look into that. Maybe I can check with the marshals and talk to them. To tell them the whole story, I had to tell them about what he did and that he was to leave this area and never come back. They know I have a report in the files and he will be arrested if he comes back, and they understand that. I think it's going to depend on what they find out from this ranch owner."

"Yes, it will," Wyatt said. "If that whole story of the watch was given to him is false and he's tried for killing Ben, I don't think we need to even mention this. But if it looks like he was telling the truth when he said someone gave him the watch, it depends on where the trial would be held. If it could be out there, I think we would both feel better if they had a trial and he was sent away to prison. I don't want him brought back here for a trial where Lizzie will have to testify, though."

"I understand," the sheriff assured him. "Let's see what happens. If it looks like Coy didn't kill him, I'd like to ask the marshals that question. If he can be tried out there I'd like to see him pay for what he did. I wouldn't want Lizzie to have to go through a trial here, though. We'll see what happens, and I'll keep you informed. We'll worry about making that decision if we have to later."

With all of them in agreement, they finished their supper.

Over the next couple of days Wyatt and Lizzie both had to draw on their patience, waiting to hear more from Sheriff Williams. When he finally came riding up the lane four days later, in the morning as they were ready to start their day, Wyatt and Lizzie met him, eager to hear his news.

"The marshals have been busy. They followed up on the name of the ranch owner Coy gave them and indeed found the man Coy told them about."

"So Coy was telling the truth and didn't kill Papa?" Lizzie asked, looking a bit disappointed. "Then who did?"

"Well, they found the man that owned the ranch, but he hadn't hired anyone in the last week.

"So Coy lied, and he did kill him?"

"A man came to him looking for a job, and said Coy sent him."

Now both Wyatt and Lizzie looked confused. "So Coy told the truth, but the rancher didn't hire him?" Wyatt asked. "So where is the man now, and did he kill Ben and give Coy his watch?"

"The rancher didn't hire him because he'd recently hired a man and didn't need any more help. But he told the rangers he suggested the man try another ranch about an hour from there, that he heard was looking for help. He gave the marshals the man's name and where he sent him. So they went there to talk to that rancher."

"You were right, the marshals have been busy," Wyatt said. "How did they make out with the next rancher?"

"The story still doesn't end there. He hired the man, who said he would get his things and be back the next day, ready to work. After he left to get his things one of his ranch hands asked what Harold Buckner was doing at the ranch. The owner was confused because the man had told him his name was Clint Kettering. He talked to his hand about it and found out he had worked with the man on a different ranch previously, but he'd been accused of stealing and quit. When he showed up to work the next day the owner greeted him using the name Harold Buckner, and the man got back on his horse and rode off. The owner let him go, thinking if he's lying about his name, he didn't want him on his ranch."

"So do they know who he really is and where he went?" Wyatt asked.

"Wait. What did you say the two names he gave were?" Lizzie asked.

"I was going to ask you if either of those names meant anything to either of you, and I'm guessing one of them might," the sheriff said. "He gave his name as Clint Kettering, but the ranch hand said he knew him as Harold Buckner."

"The first name doesn't sound familiar, but the second one, Harold Buckner does," she said. She thought a moment before looking up at them.

Wyatt immediately stepped over closer to her and put his hand around her waist. "Are you okay, Lizzie? You're very pale. Who is this man?"

"We can ask Ella or some of the men to be sure, but I'm pretty sure he used to work for us. In fact, I think that's the man Papa said asked if he could court me a year or so ago, and he told him no. Papa said he was forty, which he felt was too old to be dating a seventeen-year-old, which is how old I was at the time. Papa said he quit shortly after he told him no. He didn't fire him."

The sheriff looked toward the barn. "Were any of the men working for you now here when he left?"

"Yes, several," she said. "I can't remember him that well or when exactly he left, but I think it was only about a year and a half ago, maybe? Clem would have known him, and Frank and Bill. Leo, the bunkhouse cook, has been here for almost twenty years. I'm not sure about Walter and Leo."

"Do you want me to grab a couple of them before they head out for the day?" Wyatt asked.

"If one or two are handy, yes, please."

Wyatt ran back to the barn and came out a couple of minutes later with Frank, Clem, and Leo. He introduced them to the sheriff. "They all worked with Harold several years and feel they knew him fairly well."

"Good," the sheriff said. He didn't mention anything about the possible connection to Ben, but quickly explained what the rancher relayed about the two names. "Can any of you shed any light on this, or have an opinion as to what may have caused him to use a different name?"

The men glanced at each other before Leo spoke first. "I can believe he was accused of stealing, because we had a few things that came up missing. No one ever found them, but it stopped after he left."

"He's right," Clem confirmed. "He went by Harold when he was here, but I never heard him talk of any family, so I can't really help you out there."

"Do you know why he left?" Sheriff Williams asked.

"He said he asked Ben if he could court Miss Lizzie, but Ben said he wouldn't allow any man that worked for him to court his daughter. Harold said it would be awkward for him to keep working here after being turned down, so he left."

"Did he seem upset about it?" the sheriff asked.

"Well, he wasn't happy," Frank said. "He'd worked here for five or six years and had watched Lizzie grow into a young lady. He'd never said anything about her, and none of us had seen him watching her or anything like that, so we were a little surprised when he asked to court her."

"A couple of us kind of figured – well, maybe you don't want to know what we figured," Clem said. "I can say, though, that he'd said something a few times about him getting a little older and he needed to find a good woman and place to settle down. I had to wonder if he was wanting Lizzie or if he saw Lizzie and the ranch she would inherit someday as his good woman and place to settle down."

Leo nodded. "I thought that, too. I was glad Ben told him no because I didn't think he was interested in her, other than as a way to get a nice ranch."

Sheriff Williams shook their hands and thanked them for the information. Once they disappeared back into the barn, he turned back to Wyatt and Lizzie. "So he knew Ben and may have been upset with him, especially if he was hoping to get his hands on the ranch. That adds to this crazy story."

"Have the marshals found him?" Wyatt asked. "It sounds like they need to talk to him."

"They're looking for him, though they may want to put a couple of more men on the search once they hear that Harold Buckner used to work for Ben and left unhappy. I'll send a telegram when I get back to town to let them know."

"What a confusing mess this is turning into," Lizzie said. "At this point I hope they find out for sure who killed Papa, and it would be nice to see both Coy and Harold go to prison or be hanged."

"I agree with you, Miss Lizzie," the sheriff said. "I'll keep you posted."

Neither of them could think of much else that day. Over

supper they shared the news with Ella, and weren't surprised when she appeared to be as confused and shocked as they were. When they'd finished their story, she shook her head. "So Coy is a big uncertainty. It appeared he did it, then he didn't, then back to he did it, and now basically we don't know again."

"That's what we thought, too," Wyatt said with a grin. Pa's been coming up every couple of days to hear if we've heard anything yet. He's going to have the same reaction when I tell him."

"Speaking of him," Lizzie said as she looked out the window, I think he's coming up the lane right now."

Wyatt looked out and agreed. "Yep, that's his horse. Let's see what his reaction is." They invited him in and explained what they'd learned to him. He sat there listening, and went from nodding his head, to shaking his head, to raising his eyebrows before drawing his eyebrows together. "Well, now that you're as confused as us, what do you think?"

"Well, that's certainly quite the story," he agreed. "Imagine what the marshals must be thinking. Every time they think they have it figured out, it changes again. Hopefully they can find Harold Buckner and get this case solved. The one thing I am very glad of is that you realized it wasn't an accident, Lizzie, and you two were able to convince the sheriff of that so they could look into it. Whoever was behind it needs to pay for killing a good man."

"Yes, I agree," she said.

"Be sure to let Ma and Bryce know what they've found out," Wyatt told his father.

"Oh, you can be sure I will. Keep me informed."

"I'll do that," Wyatt promised.

Wyatt, Lizzie and Ella talked about everything that they'd learned that evening. They were all surprised to hear Harold was involved, but Wyatt became concerned when Lizzie said, "I hadn't even thought of him until Papa said --"

Looking up at her and not liking the look he saw on her face, Wyatt pulled her in to lean against him while he put his arm around her. "Since Papa said what, my dear?"

"When Papa told me Coy had asked to court me, he told he Harold had also asked. I was shocked that someone that old would ask, especially because I hardly knew him. I mean, he was so much older than me and he never talked to me. I told Papa he was much too old. Papa laughed and said he wasn't old, he was about forty, but that was too old to date a seventeen-year-old daughter of his." She looked up at him with watery eyes. "So Papa was protecting me by telling him no, he couldn't court me, and it cost him his life?"

Wyatt picked her up and sat her on his lap and wrapped her in his arms. "Now, don't get yourself all upset, my dearest wife. We don't know yet who killed him. It looked like it was either Coy or Harold, but they don't know yet. But either way, it wasn't your fault or your father's fault. Fathers deny potential suitors the right to court their daughter all the time, and though the suitor may be disappointed, it certainly doesn't give him the right to kill the father because of it."

"No, but --"

"There are bad men out there who do bad things. When they do something terrible like this, it's no one's fault but their own, no matter how angry they were. That's why there are prisons. When someone does something like that he needs to be taken off the streets and out of society so he can't do it again."

"But if Papa wouldn't have said no --"

"Then you may have been married to Harold and you wouldn't have been happy, especially since we now know what kind of man he is. You would have been unhappy, and that would have upset your papa tremendously. He would have felt terrible for allowing him to court you."

"Yes, I guess that's true."

"I know it's true. Your papa loved you dearly, and it would have torn him apart to see you suffer. Lizzie, you can't live in the past and worry about what could have happened. Whichever of these men killed your father, it was not your fault and it was not your father's fault. He was being a good father, but these men were bad men that did something terrible, and it looks like they're about to pay for what they did. I'm very happy about that, because Pa's right, whoever killed your papa needs to pay for killing a wonderful man."

"Thank you," she said as she leaned up to kiss him. She settled back in against his chest, and said, "I feel better after we talked."

"I'm glad, but remember that," he said as he kissed the top of her head. "You always feel better after we talk. The hard part is getting you to talk."

Ella watched and listened to their conversation. Once she was sure Lizzie felt better and wasn't blaming herself any longer, she stood to leave. "He's right, Lizzie. Sometimes it's hard to open yourself up and talk, but you always do feel better if you do. My husband used to get upset with me for the same thing. It wasn't that I didn't want to talk to him; I just didn't always know how I felt or where to start."

"That's my problem a lot, too," Lizzie said. "I don't try to avoid talking to Wyatt, but I'm usually trying to sort through my feelings. I don't know exactly how I feel, and it's hard to talk about something when you're confused about it."

Wyatt hugged her a little tighter. "I didn't know that was the case, Lizzie, but thank you, both of you," he added, looking toward Ella, "for telling me. The next time I know something's on your mind maybe I can try and get you to open up a little easier with different questions. Asking what's wrong may not be the right question to ask at that moment."

"When something's on my mind and you ask what's wrong, I'm not really lying when I say nothing's wrong. There may be something on my mind, but if I don't know how I actually feel about it, it's not really wrong, it's just confusing."

"Okay, I understand what you're saying. I'll try to word my questions differently, but remember this, Lizzie; I want to know about anything that has you upset or confused. If you're thinking about it more than in passing, I want you to open up to me so we can talk about it, okay?"

"Okay, I'll try to remember that."

"And I'll try to word my questions differently. Thank you, Ella, for pointing that out for me."

"Oh, you're welcome, Wyatt. I think ladies' minds think differently than men's. I know it was a problem my husband and I had when we were first married. If I can pass a little wisdom onto you two, I surely will. Now, you two have a good night. I'm going to bed."

"Good-night, Ella, and thank you," Lizzie said as Ella left.

CHAPTER 23

It was three more days before the sheriff came back with more news. Lizzie had tried to stay calm and control her temper, but it had become more of a challenge the last day or two. She'd begun getting rather short with the men again. Wyatt was hoping they heard something soon, or he knew he was going to have to take her back over his knee to get her settled down again.

Clyde stopped in one evening after dinner to see if they'd heard anything yet, and while they were talking a few minutes they saw the sheriff riding up the lane, so they asked him to stay and hear what Sheriff Williams had to say. As it turned out, he had a great deal of news for them.

Ella and Lizzie poured glasses of iced tea for everyone and they sat down to talk. "The marshals had six men actively looking for Harold Buckner and had sent telegrams out for several more to be watching for him. They found him and took him back to Brigham, where Coy had been arrested and was in jail. With the two men together they were able to sort out what had happened."

"Did one of them kill Papa?" Lizzie asked.

"Harold Buckner did. Apparently after he left your ranch he went from job to job at different ranches, but didn't stay long at any of them. He tried to find a job other than ranching, something easier, but the only thing he knew was ranching. He'd had a plan to marry Lizzie and take over this ranch, and had been angry when Ben wouldn't allow him to court his daughter, spoiling his plan for an easy future life. That anger festered and had cost him a couple of jobs because of his constant anger and bad attitude. He'd been fired from his latest job when he ran into Ben. Ben recognized him and was friendly, asking how he'd been."

"That sounds like Ben," Clyde said.

"Yes, it does," the sheriff agreed. "Harold said it upset him to see Ben looking good, wearing nice clothes, when he was out of a job and had no money, because of him."

"So he killed him," Wyatt assumed.

"He did. He held his hand out as if to shake Ben's hand, but when he got close enough he grabbed him and pulled him off his horse."

"That explains some of it. We thought it was odd that he fell off his horse, as good a rider as he was," Wyatt said.

"Yes. He didn't fall off, he was pulled off. The men were about to scuffle, when they both heard a rattlesnake and turned to see where it was. Harold admitted he used that moment to knock Ben's feet out from underneath him. He fell and hit his head. Harold quickly realized that since he hit his head on the fall, everyone would think he simply fell off his horse. The area they were in looked like a hot bed for rattlers, and indeed he saw two of them, so someone would come along and find him on the ground. They would assume a rattler spooked the horse, and it reared up, throwing Ben off."

"Which is exactly what they thought," Lizzie said.

"That's right. He said he had a large amount of money on

him, so he took the majority of it, but left enough so it wouldn't look like a theft. He took his watch, knowing he could get a fair amount of money for it someplace back east where they didn't know Ben."

"How did Coy end up with it?" Wyatt asked.

"Harold met up with Coy later that same day, not far from where Ben was. They got to talking and Coy mentioned he'd just quit his job with Ben Morgan. They talked a few minutes about both of them having worked for Ben. He didn't say he'd been fired, but Harold suspected he might have been. Ben's ranch is known as a good place to work, so not too many hands quit working there unless there's a good reason, like they're going home to take over the family ranch, or they've been fired. When Coy told him about a ranch where he might get a job, Harold saw it as an opportunity. If Coy stayed around that area, when someone found Ben and brought him into town, he might mention Harold, since Coy now knew he'd worked for Ben, too."

"So he gave a fake name to cover his tracks," Clyde surmised.

"Yes. He got the job under the name Clint Kettering, which was someone he'd met a few years back. When the ranch owner addressed him by his real name the next morning he was afraid that meant they'd found Ben and had somehow traced the killing back to him, so he got out of there as fast as he could. Then trying to get the marshals off his trail, he went to a few small towns in the area looking for Coy. When he found him he told him he'd gotten the job and wanted to give him the watch as a thank you."

"So it was to lead the marshals to Coy and away from himself," Wyatt said.

"Indeed," the sheriff said. "It was actually pretty clever, and it almost worked. The marshals who picked up Coy said they wouldn't have taken the case any further, just assumed he killed Ben since he had the watch, except they could tell Coy was truly surprised to hear Ben was dead."

"So it was good work by the marshals," Wyatt said. "So what happens now?"

"We need to talk about that," the sheriff said. "Part of that depends on you, and whether you want to pursue the case against Coy. You'd asked before about where the trial would be held, and I talked to a couple of marshals about that. Normally they would bring him back here for the trial since this is where it happened, but in this case we can have the trial there if you'd rather. The reason they can keep it there is because there were so many things that happened that are all intertwined."

"There certainly are a lot of things intertwined," Clyde agreed.

"Brigham is where they arrested Coy, and he had Ben's watch on him. That's where he's been in jail. Since he's been there he's tried to escape twice. He actually got loose once, but they recaptured him before he got out of town. So he's going to be tried for that, and that trial will happen there. The marshals have brought in extra men to guard him and prevent another escape attempt. They talked to the judge, explained the case, and he's agreed that since he'll be tried there for trying to escape, it would be safer to have the trial for everything concerning him right there, rather than take the chance of moving him and having him try to escape again."

"That makes sense," Clyde said.

"Yes, it does. The judge wants to have Harold's trial there, as well, since the two incidents are connected, so he can talk to both men together. He said if the trials are in different towns they'll both try blaming the other, so he wants them together. Then he can hear what they both have to say, with the other in the same room. He's a good judge of men, so I think that's a good idea. So if you want to have him charged with what he did to you, Lizzie, we can have that trial in Brigham. That's a several hour ride from here, so I wouldn't think anyone from here would go to it, other than you and Wyatt. I'm sure the judge would want to hear from both of you."

"If he'll be charged with trying to escape, do we need to do anything more?" Lizzie asked. "He'll go to prison for that, won't he?"

"More than likely," the sheriff answered, "but there are a couple of other things to consider. Without any other charges, he won't get a long prison sentence because although he was trying to escape, there really wasn't anything he'd done to deserve to be in jail in the first place. That will mean the judge will have to give him a shorter sentence."

"I hadn't thought of that," she said.

"But there's something else I think you need to think about," the sheriff said. "Ben told him to leave this area and don't come back. He didn't do that. He said he would, but in reality he went back to Gully Ridge and stayed there a few weeks. When he did leave, he didn't go real far. I'm not sure why he stayed around, but he did. Was he planning on coming back here for revenge? I don't know. I do know he didn't leave like he said he would, which means you can't trust him. If he's in prison a fairly short time, what will he do when he gets out? We don't know, but I don't think you can trust that he'll leave this area."

"So we'll always have the threat of him hanging around," Wyatt said.

"That was my thought," the sheriff said. "If the judge hears what he tried to do to you, and would have if Wyatt hadn't heard you and been able to get him off, that will give him reason to give him a much longer prison sentence. The judge can also tell him he's not to be in the state of Nebraska again after he's released, and that will go out to every sheriff in the state and the marshals. They'll get notice when he's released. That would make it pretty risky for him to come back to Nebraska, knowing every sheriff and marshal will be watching for him and will arrest him if they see him. That usually keeps people away. After spending that much time in prison they don't want to go back."

"That makes sense," Wyatt said. He took his wife's hand in his before asking a couple of more questions of the sheriff. "If we do this will she have to tell everything he did to her, in front of everyone?"

"According to the marshals, this judge is a very considerate judge and in cases like this he often asks people to leave the courtroom for the testimony regarding things like that. He brings the witnesses into the courtroom after everyone leaves, so no one sees them. Then he fills the spectators in briefly when they can return to the courtroom, saying simply something like, The Defendant attempted to take advantage of a young lady, but luckily a man heard her scream and was able to fight him off. I find the testimony of the young lady and the man both credible."

Clyde and Ben were both surprised. "I didn't know a judge could do that," Clyde said.

"It's something a few judges are starting to do, to protect the victim in crimes like this. Not all judges do. Our local judge doesn't. He feels spectators watching the trial have a right to judge every witness that testifies, to determine for themselves if they believe them or not. This judge feels the Defendant has the right to be there when all witnesses testify, but not the spectators. He feels the victim is truly a victim through no fault of their own and has a right to protect their privacy."

"So we could do this without local people knowing about it?" Wyatt asked.

"Yes. It's your choice, but I think you know what I would suggest," the sheriff said.

After a fairly short conversation between Wyatt, Lizzie, Ella, Clyde and the sheriff, Wyatt and Lizzie agreed to have Coy charged. The sheriff nodded his approval and promised to send the telegram the next day. "I think one of the marshals will want to talk with the two of you before they actually charge him with it, so don't be surprised if one or two of them, possibly the main two that have been working on the case, stop by."

"Okay, we'll tell them whatever they need to know," Wyatt assured him.

"Will he be able to tell us more about what to expect at the trial, and when it might be?" Lizzie asked.

"More than likely, yes."

"Okay, we'll be waiting for them. Thank you, Sheriff," Wyatt said, reaching out his hand to shake.

"Yes, thank you for believing me and finding the man that killed Papa," Lizzie agreed.

"I'm glad you came to me with this. I took the word of the local sheriff that it was an accident, so I'm glad you questioned it and talked to me. Ben was a good man, and I'd hate to think someone killed him and got away with it."

WYATT WATCHED Lizzie closely the next several days, and made sure he took time off from work to spend a little extra time with her. He knew she would have a lot of thoughts and emotions going through her, but he wasn't sure how she would react to them. He was sure she'd be glad they caught the man that killed her papa, but would she also be angry, or nervous about the trial?

As it turned out, she was quieter than normal, but didn't appear to be too upset. She seemed to have a better control of her temper than he'd anticipated. He was proud of her. When the marshals rode in and said they'd like to talk to them, he could tell she was anxious, nervous, but at the same time relieved. She had several questions after thinking about this over the last few days, and she hoped they could answer them for her.

He held her hand, rubbing the back of it with his thumb as she explained to the marshals what Coy had done to her. When she got to the point where he had come to her rescue, he took over the story telling. He began with her talking to him earlier about not liking the way Coy had been looking at her and trying to get her alone. Then when he was riding fence on their ranch next to hers and he heard a scream, he took off on his horse. He explained what he'd found and done, and how badly her ankle had been hurt.

The marshals listened carefully, taking notes while they talked. They asked a few questions, which the two of them answered. Then they explained that the trial would be in roughly three weeks, when the judge would be in town. He verified that the judge had agreed to clear the courtroom of everyone except the two defendants and the attorneys when they testified, and would give a brief synopsis of their testimony afterward in open court. That way people would know what had taken place while they weren't permitted in the courtroom, but wouldn't know any of the details or be given their names.

The marshals said there was a hotel in Brigham they could stay at when they came to testify, but suggested there was also one in Overton, which was a little under an hour's ride from Brigham, and they may want to stay there instead.

Small towns being what they are, everyone would take note of the new people in town, staying at the hotel for a day or two during the trial, and leaving. They would probably assume they were the ones testifying when everyone was out. You never knew when someone may recognize one of them, and word would likely get around as to who it was who testified.

The marshals suggested they could stay in Overton and ride in the day they would testify. The judge would begin court at the normal time, so everyone in town would be gathered together, ready to hear and see what happened at the trial that day. He would then explain that he was going to have some testimony he would listen to, but everyone else would have to wait outside. As soon as they were finished testifying he would explain what had taken place. The marshals said that time while the judge was explaining that day would be a little different would be a good time to ride into town. They could go directly to the church, which is where they held court since it was the biggest building in town and could hold the most observers.

There was a back door to the church, and someone would be waiting for them there to let them inside. They would wait in the pastor's small office, out of sight. When the judge had the courtroom cleared they would go get Wyatt and Lizzie and take them to the front. After they testified, they would return to the pastor's office while they called everyone back inside. Everyone was always eager to hear what had taken place, so the courtroom was always packed, everyone wanting to hear for themselves what had taken place. Once everyone was back inside, Wyatt and Lizzie could slip out the back door and return to Overton, and back home.

The marshals promised they would be there helping with the trial, and would help them try to get in and out of town without being seen. They also promised that as soon as the trial was over they would ride back to their ranch and let them know if both defendants were found guilty, and if so, what their sentences were. Harold could hang if found guilty, and the marshals asked if that happened, did they want to be there. Without even having to ask Lizzie, he spoke for both of them. "No, that's not something either of us wants to see. Knowing he indeed paid for what he did will be good enough for us."

After they left, Wyatt pulled Lizzie over to sit on his lap and lean against his chest. "How are you doing, my sweet little wife? Are you going to be okay?"

"Yes," she assured him, "as long as you're there with me."

"I'll be right there beside you the whole way. If you get nervous or upset anytime during the next three weeks while we wait for this trial, or you need to talk, tell me. We'll talk about anything, any part of this that has you worried or upset, okay?"

She nodded and reached up to kiss his cheek, but he caught her chin and captured her lips in a much better kiss than simply a peck on the cheek. Afterward she cuddled in against him as he held her in his arms. They didn't talk, as they both thought of what lay ahead. Wyatt would surely be glad when the trial was over and hopefully the two men were sentenced and sent off to prison, or Harold may hang. Either way, once this trial was over, hopefully neither of them would be a threat to them any longer and she could relax and get back to taking care of her horses and helping Wyatt run their ranch. He was looking forward to that day, and he knew she was, too.

Lizzie did better than Wyatt expected over the next three weeks. He could tell she was preoccupied at times, but she hadn't lashed out at anyone more than a couple of times, and both times she caught herself and apologized. Two days before they would leave for the trial, they sat on their front porch swing and talked. He had his arm around her and she was tucked neatly in against him. "I think I know the answer to this, but let me ask anyway," he said. "Since you'll have to wear a dress to testify in court, would you rather we take a buggy instead of just riding our horses?"

"Absolutely not," she answered quickly. "Going by buggy will take so much longer, and will be much slower getting back home. I'll wear my riding skirt and ride Shadow. It will be much easier to tie them up behind the church without a buggy to worry about, and we can leave much quicker. I'll take a dress to change into once I get to the church. Then I'll change back into my riding skirt while everyone is filling back in to listen to what the judge says. It won't take long, and we'll be able to leave quickly."

"Okay. I assumed that would be your preference, but I wanted to be sure."

"You know me well, and I love you for that."

"Well, I've had our lifetime to get to know you this well."

"We have been through a lot together, haven't we?"

"We certainly have," he said, leaning down to kiss the top of her head. "Some bad, like this, but mostly good. And after this is over, I'm hoping for much more good."

"Me, too."

"I'm looking forward to having a family, and watching our children learn to ride horses and do all the things we did growing up on a ranch."

"Our children will be very fortunate. Not only will they be growing up on a ranch, but they'll be growing up close to their grandparents and Uncle Bryce. I'm sure they'll get to see them often."

"That will be special," Wyatt agreed. He chuckled and added, "It will be special for them and for their grandparents and uncle. I can see Ma and Pa spoiling them a bit."

"Do you think? If they do, I'll be okay with that, as long as it's not too much."

"I suppose a little spoiling wouldn't hurt," he agreed. "But now I think we need to get to bed. Sunrise comes early." She agreed and allowed him to take her hand and lead her inside.

The next day Lizzie was struggling with her feelings, he could tell. He found her sitting at the barn, staring straight ahead a couple of times, and pacing the floor another. On each occasion he let her go, giving her the space to work it out for herself. Hopefully if she needed help she would ask if they could talk. She'd done that a couple of times over the last few weeks, and it had helped her each time. He'd been very proud of her. If she was still struggling that evening after supper he would suggest they talk again.

She was still antsy when he took her hand and they went to the house for supper, a little earlier than normal. Once inside Ella looked up at them. "Oh, my. Supper will be ready shortly."

"It's not ready yet?" Lizzie asked in a tone not like her. "I hoped we could come in and eat and go to bed early. We have to leave in the morning, you know."

Ella stopped what she was doing to look over at her. "I'm sorry, Lizzie. You're earlier than normal and you didn't say anything about wanting to eat early. It's almost ready, though. If you want to go wash up, it should be ready by that time."

"Well, I hope so," she said as she flounced off.

"Ella, I'm sorry," Wyatt said. "She's worried about tomorrow."

"Oh, I know she is," Ella assured him, "and I don't blame her. When you get back in a couple of days she'll be back to herself again."

"I hope so," he said, "but that's no excuse for her to act like this. I'll talk to her."

"No, please don't. I'm not hurt. I know her and I know how much she loved her papa. This is hard for her."

"You're very understanding, Ella. Thank you."

Wyatt went to join Lizzie, who had gone outside, apparently deciding to wash up at the pump. As he walked up she stood to look at him. "Please don't scold me for my temper just now. I was awful, I know, and I'll apologize when I get inside." She had tears in her eyes as she added, "Do you think Ella could hold our supper for a little while? Could we go upstairs to our room and talk?"

He opened his arms and his wife practically ran into them. "Of course we can go talk. Let's tell Ella to go ahead and eat, and we'll heat it back up when we're ready to eat."

"Thank you," she said as she lost the battle with her tears. He held her, patting her back a few minutes while she got her composure back. She pulled back then and said, "I'll go talk to Ella while you wash up."

He nodded and went to the pump. When he went in the kitchen a few minutes later he found the two ladies in a hug. "Don't you worry about a thing, Lizzie. Wyatt will help you through it all."

"I know. Thank you for understanding. I don't know how long we'll be talking, so please don't wait for us. You go ahead and eat your supper, then you can go on to your rooms. I'll heat ours back up if it needs it and clean the kitchen up before we go to bed."

"I'll help her. Thank you, Ella," Wyatt added. Ella nodded as Wyatt took Lizzie's hand and they headed for the stairs.

CHAPTER 24

The two of them walked up the steps hand in hand, with Ella watching with a rather sad smile on her face. She was sure he would help her through it, but the next couple of days would be hard.

Once they were upstairs he sat them down on their bed. "Okay, what in particular would you like to talk about?"

He watched, confused, as she blushed. "Well," she said, starting slowly and talking quietly, "one time you told me if stress is getting to me I should ask you for a spanking, and it would settle me down before I earned a punishment spanking."

"That's true."

"Well, I think I'm getting real close to losing my temper, but if I do that I know you'll spank me and I'll have a difficult time sitting my saddle tomorrow."

"So you're ready for a spanking to settle you down?"

"I don't know," she said, her face red and tears escaping her eyes again. "I don't want a spanking if it's going to make it hard to ride tomorrow, but I don't know how to avoid one. Will you please help me somehow?"

Wyatt looked down at his beautiful, strong wife and his heart about broke. She was hurting so much right now, and he knew he had to do something to help her. He instinctively took her in his arms and rocked her back and forth. "Sweetheart, I can't tell you how proud I am of you right now for asking for help. You're right, one time when you'd earned a punishment spanking I told you it would be much easier on you if you would simply ask for a spanking to relieve your stress and settle you down before you earned a punishment. That's exactly what I'm going to do for you now."

"But if you spank me tonight I won't be able to ride tomorrow," she said with more tears streaming down her face.

"Yes, you will, trust me," he said. Knowing she wouldn't believe him and needed help, he lifted her and laid her gently over his knees. She gasped and whimpered a bit, but didn't try to stop him when he lifted her dress and petticoat, and finally her chemise. He untied her bloomers and pulled them apart, but didn't lower them. He patted her bare bottom gently, hoping to relax her a bit. "Trust me, sweetheart," he repeated before bringing his hand down on her bare bottom with a swat that was sharp enough to be sure she felt it, but not overly harsh.

"Oh. I do trust you, Wyatt."

"Good." He started spanking, moving the swats around in no particular pattern, and with no particular rhythm, making sure she wouldn't know when or where the next swat would land. Once he knew her skin was warming up, he began talking. "My dear Lizzie, I can't tell you exactly what is going to happen the next few days, but I can tell you I'm going to be right next to you from now until we get back home. You won't be going through this alone. The marshals assured us they would be in Overton to meet us and help us, as well. I also know worrying about something that may not happen does no one any good. It can get you so upset you're not yourself and you start taking your frustrations out on people who don't deserve it. If that happens you'll be getting a good punishment spanking, and I know that's not something you want right now, especially since you'll be riding a saddle a great deal over the next few days. So I suggest you remind yourself I'll be with you and we'll get through this together."

He watched as he spanked, and although she squirmed and wiggled and tried to avoid his hand just as much as she ever did, it didn't take nearly as long before she slumped over his knees, tears streaming down her face in a steady stream. That was his cue to end the spanking, and he gently pulled her up and onto his lap. She instantly leaned in against him, grasping his shirt in one hand and holding on tight. He pulled her in against him and held her in a cocoon, where he knew she felt safe. He rubbed her back and talked softly while she cried.

When her tears slowed he gave her a little hug and talked softly next to her ear. "I love you, my dear, more than you know. Do you feel better?"

"I do," she admitted, "though I'm not sure I'll be able to ride very well tomorrow. I may have to stop and take several breaks."

"We can do that if you want to," he assured her, "but I don't think it will be as bad as you think. You seem more relaxed now, though, and that's good to see."

"I am more relaxed, so thank you."

He couldn't help but chuckle. "Oh, my dear Lizzie, I never thought I would hear you thank me for a spanking, but let me assure you, you're quite welcome. I will always give you what you need. Speaking of what you need, you need to eat supper pretty soon so we can get some sleep before our trip tomorrow. Are you ready to go downstairs, or do you need some more time?"

"I love sitting here like this, with your arms protecting me, but you're right, we need to eat some supper and get to bed." She flushed again as she added, "And maybe you can make me forget my sore bottom."

"I'd be more than happy to try," he said with a grin. They ate their supper rather quickly, cleaned the kitchen up even quicker, and he took his time to completely make her forget about her sore bottom. They fell asleep later with his arms wrapped around her and a smile on her face.

~

THE NEXT MORNING Lizzie gladly admitted that Wyatt had been right. Although the spanking he'd given her the night before had seemed to hurt like the dickens, she could hardly feel it as they rode side by side to Overton. One of the marshals that had been to their ranch was there waiting for them, and he escorted them to Brigham the next morning.

The trial went as they had described, and by midafternoon the next day the marshals helped them slip out the back door of the church, which was at the edge of town, and they were on their way back home. They made good time and got back just before it got dark.

Ella met them at the door to welcome them back. "I wasn't sure if you'd make it home tonight or have to stay another night. I'm glad you're back, and I'm sure you are, as well."

"We certainly are," Lizzie said. "I'm glad to have that over with. Now we just have to wait for one of the marshals to tell us how the trial ended."

"Then we can put all of this behind us and focus on running the ranch," Wyatt said. "Do we have any ham we could slice and make a quick sandwich?"

"I've got better than that. I made some rabbit stew today,

hoping you would make it back. I thought if you don't I can reheat it tomorrow. I've kept it warm at the back of the stove. You two get cleaned up while I dish up a couple of bowls for you."

"Ella, that was so nice of you, making our favorite meal for us," Wyatt said.

"I thought it might be a nice welcome back home and help you relax and rest up from your trip."

~

WYATT WAS happy to see Lizzie acting much more like herself the next day. She was back to smiling at people instead of complaining. Even the horses seemed more at ease with her. As he watched her working with them from the doorway he realized she seemed more at ease with herself. She was moving more confidently, without checking over her shoulder frequently.

Five days after they got back, they had begun to settle into a more normal life on the ranch, which felt good to both of them. They had just gotten in the house and cleaned up for supper when Wyatt noticed three riders approaching. He watched out the window until they got close enough to recognize Sheriff Williams. "Lizzie, Sheriff Williams is here with two other men. Maybe it's the marshals."

Lizzie was at his side quickly and as they got closer they recognized the two marshals that had been at their ranch before the trial. Ella assured them she had plenty for all of them, and set three more places at the table as Wyatt and Lizzie went out to greet them.

Wyatt greeted them as they slid off their horses. "Gentlemen, welcome. We're anxious to hear what you have to tell us, but why don't you tell us over supper? Ella made our special again this evening, and she assures me there's plenty for all of us, plus some. We can talk while we eat."

Sheriff Williams chuckled as he looked at the other men. "I told them it seems like I often come out here right about mealtime, and you people were going to get tired of seeing me stop in."

"That won't happen, Sheriff. You're welcome here for a meal anytime, especially when you have an update for us."

"I told the marshals if they're going to be invited someplace for a meal, this would be my first choice. Miss Ella and Miss Lizzie are wonderful cooks."

One of the marshals spoke up as he nodded. "I told him the last time we were here you generously offered us supper, and it was delicious. I hate to take advantage of you, but if you're offering supper again, I certainly won't turn it down. Even if it's not more of that delicious rabbit stew, I'm sure it'll be good."

Wyatt and Lizzie both laughed as Wyatt said, "Well, I'm glad to hear you liked the rabbit stew, because that's what we're having again."

The marshals looked at each other and grinned. "We've started referring to your ranch as Rabbit Stew Ranch because we both said we've never tasted rabbit stew that good. Count me in, too. Thank you."

"I've told several people no one makes rabbit stew like I've eaten here," Sheriff Williams agreed. "It is the best I've ever tasted."

"Lizzie and I will both tell you rabbit stew is our favorite meal, and you're right, Ella's is absolutely the best around. I'm lucky because she taught my wife to cook, so hers is just as good. Come on in."

Once they had begun eating, after compliments to Ella from all, Lizzie couldn't wait any longer. "So, I hate to hurry you, but I have to know, did the judge find either of the men guilty?"

Between the two marshals they explained that the judge found both men guilty. Coy was sentenced to fifteen years in federal prison and is not allowed back in the state of Nebraska again after being released. Harold began testifying, denying killing Ben. However, as they continued questioning him, he broke down and admitted it. Since he admitted it, the judge sentenced him to fifty years in federal prison rather than hanging. More than likely that meant he will die in prison. Lizzie was satisfied with both sentences, and extremely glad it was all over.

OVER THE NEXT couple of weeks things finally settled back down on the ranch. One evening as they were swinging on the porch swing, with her tucked up against his shoulder, he rubbed her arm and asked, "Can I ask you a question?"

"Of course."

"Most ranches are named, either after the owner or something on the ranch, like the Babbling Brook ranch to the west of us. Is there a reason your father never named this ranch?"

She sat up and turned toward him. "You know, I'd forgotten about that. Papa told me he and my mother talked about a name for it, but never came up with one they liked. They didn't want something like others had, like the Morgan Ranch, they wanted something that would make people smile. He said after she died he just couldn't bring himself to name it himself. He told me some day the ranch would be mine, and my husband and I should name it."

Wyatt's eyebrows raised, and he asked, "So, what do you want to name it?"

"I don't know, but let's name it something now, since Papa wanted me to name it when it was my ranch. He was really happy that we were going to be married, and he told me he was glad the ranch would someday belong to you and me. So now that it does, let's name it as a way of honoring him."

"I like that idea. What should we name it?"

"Since we're naming it to honor him, something that will make people smile." They were both quiet for a couple of minutes while they thought, until she started laughing.

"What's so funny?"

"I might have the perfect name. You said sometimes people name it after something on the land, and Papa said he wanted something that would make people smile. I think I have one that fits both of those. Actually, the marshals came up with it."

He looked down at her and a big smile spread across his face. "The Rabbit Stew Ranch?"

"Why not? There are lots of rabbits on this land. That's the first thing Papa taught me to hunt when he taught me how to shoot. I was all for it because rabbit stew was my favorite meal, and when I'd get some rabbits Ella would make it for us. I liked it so much that it was the first thing she taught me how to cook by myself. Beyond that, what's your favorite meal?"

"Rabbit stew," he confirmed with a grin. "Especially your rabbit stew. I think we just named our ranch. What do you think your papa would think of it?"

"I think he'd love it."

"Just like I love his daughter," he said with a kiss that showed his love more than his words could. "Now we need some kids that can grow up on the Rabbit Stew Ranch."

"I hope they like rabbit stew," she said with a giggle. "When should we start on that project?"

"I say there's no time like the present."

"I agree," she said as he took her hand and led her into the house.

MISTY MALONE

Writing has been a dream of Misty's for several years. She's finally following that dream, and began writing in 2013. She enjoys writing romance stories, with a handsome man who falls in love with a lovely lady in need of a strong man who can take her in hand. Having grown up on a farm, she especially enjoys writing about strong cowboys. She lives in the Midwest with her husband and son, not far from where she grew up. Misty hopes you enjoy reading her books as much as she enjoys writing them. Reviews to her books are very much appreciated, and she would like to thank you for each one of them. She invites you to leave a message for her at authormistymalone@gmail.com.

Don't miss these exciting titles by Misty Malone and Blushing Books!

Pine Falls Series
The Town's Inheritance
Say Something
Nothing Average

Western Camping series
The Camping Cowgirl, Book 1
The Camping Cowboy, Book 2

Holiday House Series
Finding Holly

Warning Merry
Convincing Sarah

Wyoming Ranch Life series
Mail Order Surprise, Book 1
Ranch Life is Great, Book 2
Ranch Life Surprise, Book 3
Wyoming Ranch Live Collection

Life at the Ranch series
Life at the Ranch, Book 1
Christmas at the Ranch, Book 2

Last Chance Program series
Cheyenne and Jason, Book 1
Gina and Paul, Book 2
Last Chance Program set

Single Titles
Rabbit Stew Ranch
Murphy's Law
What's Good for the Cowboy
Again and Again
I Guess I Love You
The Bridge Repair
Back to the Ranch
Whoops! Wrong Ranch
How to Stir Up a Ranch
The Real Prize
That Beautiful Orange Gown
Not Just a House
I'm on a Ranch?
It's My Ranch?
My Ranch, My Way

Learning to Drive... Him Crazy
The Strange Healing
Count This Cowboy In
Cowboy Motel
A Quiet Christmas Alone...Kinda
On Probation
One Smart Cowboy
It's Just A Ranch
A Beautiful Ranch
Being Schooled
Nice to Meet You
Stealing Her Breath
Mail Order Mystery
The Best Accident Ever
She Did What?
Never Again
Not Lonely Now
Top Cop
Darn Noisy Neighbors
Listen Here, Cowboy
Can't Argue with That
Hidden Talents
It'll Work Out
Work and Play

Anthologies

Tamed By The Cowboy
12 Naughty Days of Christmas 2018
12 Naughty Days of Christmas 2021
Love of a Cowboy, Two
Sweet Town Love

Audio Books

The Real Prize

It's My Ranch?
Mail Order Surprise

Connect with Misty Malone
authormistymalone@gmail.com

BLUSHING BOOKS

Blushing Books is the oldest eBook publisher on the web. We've been running websites that publish steamy romance and erotica since 1999, and we have been selling eBooks since 2003. We have free and promotional offerings that change weekly, so please do visit us at http://www.blushing-books.com/free.

BLUSHING BOOKS NEWSLETTER

Please join the Blushing Books newsletter
to receive updates & special promotional offers.
You can also join by using your mobile phone:
Just text BLUSHING to 22828.

Every month, one new sign up via text messaging will receive a $25.00 Amazon gift card, so sign up today!

Printed in Great Britain
by Amazon

61039631R00181